MW01114112

THE
OMEGA
SCROLL

ADRIAN d'HAGÉ

THE OMEGA SCROLL

VIKING

an imprint of

PENGUIN BOOKS

VIKING

Published by the Penguin Group
Penguin Group (Australia)
250 Camberwell Road, Camberwell, Victoria 3124, Australia
(a division of Pearson Australia Group Pty Ltd)
Penguin Group (USA) Inc.
375 Hudson Street, New York, New York 10014, USA
Penguin Group (Canada)
90 Eglinton Avenue East, Suite 700, Toronto, Ontario M4P 2Y3, Canada
(a division of Pearson Penguin Canada Inc.)
Penguin Books Ltd
80 Strand, London WC2R 0RL, England
Penguin Ireland
25 St Stephen's Green, Dublin 2, Ireland
(a division of Penguin Books Ltd)
Penguin Books India Pvt Ltd
11 Community Centre, Panchsheel Park, New Delhi – 110 017, India
Penguin Group (NZ)
Cnr Airborne and Rosedale Roads, Albany, Auckland, New Zealand
(a division of Pearson New Zealand Ltd)
Penguin Books (South Africa) (Pty) Ltd
24 Sturdee Avenue, Rosebank, Johannesburg 2196, South Africa

Penguin Books Ltd, Registered Offices: 80 Strand, London, WC2R 0RL, England

First published by Penguin Group (Australia), a division of Pearson Australia Group Pty Ltd, 2005

1 3 5 7 9 10 8 6 4 2

Text copyright © Adrian d'Hagé 2005

The moral right of the author has been asserted

All rights reserved. Without limiting the rights under copyright reserved above, no part of this publication
may be reproduced, stored in or introduced into a retrieval system, or transmitted, in any form or by any
means (electronic, mechanical, photocopying, recording or otherwise), without the prior written permission
of both the copyright owner and the above publisher of this book.

Cover design by David Altheim © Penguin Group (Australia)
Text design by Janine Blackstock © Penguin Group (Australia)
Cover photograph by S Meltzer/PhotoLink/Getty Images & Digital Vision/Getty Images
Typeset in 12.5/16pt Granjon by Midland Typesetters, Maryborough, Victoria
Printed in Australia by McPherson's Printing Group, Maryborough, Victoria

National Library of Australia
Cataloguing-in-Publication data:
d'Hagé, Adrian.
The Omega Scroll.

ISBN 0 670 02896 7.

1. Dead Sea scrolls – Fiction. I. Title.

A823.4

www.penguin.com.au

For David and Mark

CONTENTS

BOOK ONE: January 2005   1

BOOK TWO: 1978 – 1979   47

BOOK THREE: 1985   143

BOOK FOUR: 1990   209

BOOK FIVE: 2004   249

BOOK SIX: 2005   357

AUTHOR'S NOTE   465

BOOK ONE

January 2005

CHAPTER ONE

Roma

The Cardinal Secretary of State to the Vatican stood at his second-floor window in the Apostolic Palace and stared out over the Piazza San Pietro. Cardinal Lorenzo Petroni had two things on his mind. Of the two, the Pope's failing health was perhaps the more urgent but the woman was now by far the more dangerous.

The most powerful cardinal in the Catholic Church was tall and thin and cut an elegant but formidable figure. His soutane, edged in scarlet, was immaculate. A pale angular face with features at once delicate and steely; eyes blue and piercing. His fine black hair streaked with distinguished grey.

Below him the early dusk of winter had already enveloped the great square of St Peter's, and although the rain had stopped the cobblestones were still wet, glistening in the soft reflected light from the Vatican buildings. A lone scrap of paper bowled across the now deserted piazza, disappearing into the surrounds of Bernini's Colonnade, the wind growling around the columns as it had for over three hundred years.

Slowly and deliberately, Lorenzo Petroni paced the spacious office afforded the Secretary of State, the deep pile of the royal blue carpet soft under the Italian leather of his shoes. At one end of the room were three crimson couches; at the opposite end, two large French-polished desks. One was almost obscured by piles of dispatches. The other, his working desk, was clear save for a black marble cross. On the wall behind, Perugino's *Saint Benedict* kept watch. As he often did, Petroni reflected on how close he was to absolute power, yet that power had become frustratingly elusive. Next month would mark his fifteenth year as Cardinal Secretary of State, a position which was second only to the Pope. Petroni had regained control of the Vatican Bank and the Church's vast international financial holdings, but for a long time the Keys to Peter had seemed unattainable. The Pope's reign seemed endless. Now the Pope's ill health provided a rare opening. A quiet, persistent buzzing on his private line interrupted the Cardinal's thoughts.

'Petroni.'

'One moment, Eminence, Father Jean-Pierre La Franci is calling.' Petroni's lips tightened. The Director of L'École Biblique in Jerusalem had been instructed never to contact him at the Vatican unless it was a matter of the utmost urgency. The phone crackled and the Director came on the line.

'*Buonasera*, Eminence.'

'*Buonasera*, Jean-Pierre. How can I help?' Long years of diplomatic training kept Petroni's irritation in check.

'I am sorry to trouble you, Eminence, but there has been a development that I think you should be aware of.'

'And that is?'

'The information has not been confirmed, but I have a contact in one of the Hebrew University laboratories here and we suspect that a substantial number of Dead Sea Scroll fragments have been subjected to DNA and carbon dating analysis.'

'Where did these fragments come from?' Petroni's voice was suddenly sharp.

'That's the puzzling part, Eminence. None of our fragments are missing. It is presumably a new find, but my sources are very good.'

'And?' Petroni demanded.

'We suspect that the DNA analysis may enable the fragments to be separated and pieced together into separate scrolls. One of them may be either the original or another copy of the Omega Scroll.'

Petroni felt the blood drain from his face.

The Omega Scroll. Petroni knew only too well that there were just three in existence; the original and two copies. In 1978 one of the copies had surfaced on the black market and for the exorbitant sum of US ten million dollars, Lorenzo Petroni, then a powerful Archbishop in the Vatican in control of the Vatican Bank, had arranged for its purchase. Pope John Paul I had seen a report on it, but he was now dead and that copy of the Omega Scroll was buried deep within the Vatican's Secret Archives.

This had to be the original, Petroni thought. The second copy had come to light only a few months ago when a Turkish dealer on the black market had offered it to Monsignor Lonergan, Petroni's man in Jerusalem. Petroni had made sure of its purchase, this time for fifty million dollars. It was also safe and secure in the Secret Archives.

'Do we know who commissioned this analysis?' Petroni already had strong suspicions but he needed positive verification.

'Dr Allegra Bassetti, Eminence.'

At the confirmation of the woman's name Lorenzo Petroni's anger was palpable and his grip tightened on the receiver.

'I want a full report in the black bag tomorrow.'

'Yes, of course, Eminence.' Father La Franci was wasting his breath. The line was dead.

The Cardinal Secretary of State stared out over the Piazza San Pietro for a long time. The Keys to Peter were dangling tantalisingly within his grasp and Petroni needed to maintain his control. Desperation was never far from the surface of his calm and powerful demeanour. At the moment two other issues were swirling around him and either one could bring him down. Cardinal Giovanni Donelli, the Patriarch of Venice, had started an investigation into the activities of the Vatican Bank in his diocese of the Veneto. Petroni knew that any investigation into the Vatican Bank would finish him and although he had been told it would be difficult, the 'Italian Solution' had been arranged. Cardinal Donelli would be meeting with an unfortunate accident. Petroni had also discovered that a journalist from CCN, Tom Schweiker, was investigating his past. If he got too close to the truth Schweiker would also be dealt with. Now there was an even more threatening issue: the woman and the Omega Scroll.

The Omega Scroll contained three coded messages that had the power to change the world. Petroni allowed himself a rare feeling of satisfaction. An American scholar had unravelled the first of them and although the coded numbers posed a critical threat to the Vatican, so far no one had taken much notice.

The second message had almost surfaced by accident. In 1973, Francis Crick, the discoverer of the molecular structure of DNA, published his extraordinary findings on where DNA had originated. In doing so, the Nobel Laureate had come perilously close to revealing the second of the crucial secrets of the scroll. It hadn't been easy to dismiss the brilliant biologist as a fruitcake, but Petroni had personally directed the campaign to discredit him and a sceptical media had done the rest. In the 1980s the threat had reappeared. Professor Antonio Rosselli at Milano's Ca' Granda University had revitalised the investigation into Crick's theory surrounding the source of DNA. Petroni had placed the Professor under surveillance.

The final message, and Petroni believed he alone knew the exact contents of the scroll, contained a crucial warning of an apocalyptic disaster that was about to befall mankind. Petroni knew that the pointers in the Middle East were already in place, but for Cardinal Petroni, the countdown to the annihilation of civilisation was secondary. He was far more concerned with the Omega Scroll's first two messages. Messages that directly threatened his own power and that of the Holy Church. Petroni had been startled when an Israeli mathematician, Professor Yossi Kaufmann, revealed that he had discovered hidden codes in the Dead Sea Scrolls. As he had done with Professor Rosselli, Petroni had immediately placed Professor Kaufmann under surveillance. Like the ill-fated discoveries of the pyramids, it seemed that the ancient scroll was cursed. Everyone who came in contact with it was in danger.

Events in the Middle East were coming together. Should the Omega Scroll ever become public there would be no doubting its authenticity and the consequences were unthinkable, but a simple purchase of the final, original, copy of the Omega Scroll might no longer be an option. Cardinal Petroni knew that Allegra Bassetti could not be bought. His mind went back to the night in Milano when she had been impertinent enough to raise her interest in the Omega Scroll over dinner. When she had gone to the Middle East, Petroni had her placed under surveillance, just in case. Now Allegra Bassetti would have to be eliminated and the Dead Sea Scroll recovered. Time was running out. The countdown had begun.

Cardinal Petroni turned his attention to the more immediate matter of the Pope's health. At the press of a button the dark panelled doors of the TV cabinet hidden in the far wall slid silently aside. The CCN six o'clock news bulletin was mandatory viewing for the Vatican hierarchy but the two lead items would surprise many of the cardinals and others in the corridors of power in Rome. Petroni was not surprised by either of them. He was irritated by the speculation about to be aired over the Omega Scroll, but not surprised. Daniel P. Kirkpatrick III, CCN's News Director in New York, was a Knight of Malta, and like the other Knights of Malta around the world, he kept the Cardinal Secretary of State informed on what might be about to affect the Vatican well before it made the news. In return, Knights of Malta had direct access to the Apostolic Palace.

'Ten seconds, Tom.' The journalist was the tall and charismatic Tom Schweiker, CCN's veteran Pulitzer Prize winning Middle East correspondent and occasional reporter on the Holy See. Dressed in a dark blue, open-necked shirt, Tom Schweiker was broad across the shoulders and his face was weathered and lined from countless hours spent in the desert sun. He had a square jaw, a long and aristocratic nose, and his well-groomed greying hair matched his inquisitive grey eyes. The cue sounding in his ear-piece came from CCN's studios in New York as Tom Schweiker composed himself for his piece to camera. Michelangelo's dome of St Peter's provided a stately backdrop.

'Speculation is mounting,' he began, in a deep, cultured voice, 'that one of the longest serving Popes of the modern age may be about to retire on the grounds of ill health.' Schweiker paused to allow his opening to have the desired effect. He had the ability to make each of the millions of CCN's viewers feel that he was talking to them personally.

'CCN has obtained the latest medical report on the Pope and it casts significant doubt on his ability to continue.'

'Does it make any recommendations, Tom?' asked CCN's New York anchor, Geraldine Rushmore.

'No, it doesn't, Geraldine, but as we all know, the Pope has been suffering from Parkinson's for many years now. This is a pro-gressively degenerative neurological disorder, and although there is some promising research being done with adult stem cells, modern medicine still doesn't have a cure. It affects the control of body movements and that, unfortunately, is all too evident in the Pope's public appearances.'

'Have other Popes resigned before this, Tom?'

'Not recently, Geraldine, although Church Law doesn't prevent it. In the entire history of the Papacy only six have done so, the last being Gregory XII way back in 1415.'

'Who will make the final decision, Tom?'

'That's the difficulty. While the Pope still has his faculties it will be up to him and he's not known as someone who readily gives up. In fact, it's his stubbornness that has been the most criticised aspect of his Papacy. Although, interestingly enough, I understand that an undated resignation document has been prepared. So perhaps the Pope is allowing for that eventuality.'

'He's still astute?'

'My sources tell me that the Pope's mind is still very sharp, but none of us can go on for ever.'

'No indeed, Tom, and on another front there is speculation that a copy of the Omega Scroll may have surfaced.

'It's only speculation. Rumours about this scroll have been around for decades, but no one has ever claimed to have seen it.'

'Do we know what's in it, Tom?'

'Not exactly, but the Israeli archaeologist and mathematician Professor Yossi Kaufmann has discovered that this particular Dead Sea Scroll contains a secret code. He's suggesting there may be a link between the Omega Scroll and the outcome of the War on Terror.'

'The "Clash of Civilisations"?'

Tom nodded. 'Kaufmann has suggested that the destruction of Western civilisation has begun, and in a reverse of the Crusades of the Middle Ages Islam will triumph over Christianity and the West. No doubt that is music to the ears of al-Qaeda and the followers of Osama bin Laden.'

Kaufmann, a respected Israeli scholar and member of the Knesset, had gone out on a limb and had been roundly criticised for his pronouncements. Hardbitten journalists had scoffed at his ideas, but now Tom Schweiker was less sceptical. The continuing US-backed Israeli attacks against the Palestinians and the US, British and Australian attack on Iraq had fanned widespread resentment in the Arab world and it was getting worse. Tom's links to the CIA were impeccable and he had seen the reports that had been kept hidden from the wider public, reports that al-Qaeda now possessed at least seven of the nuclear suitcase bombs that had gone missing when the Soviet Union collapsed.

'Thanks, Tom. We'll leave it there and I look forward to speaking to you when you return to the Middle East.'

'Pleasure, Geraldine.'

'That was Tom Schweiker reporting for CCN News from the Vatican in Rome. Difficult times for the Papacy and a sobering prediction from Israel. Now to the day in Congress . . .'

Cardinal Petroni dismissed any thought of Islam triumphing over Christianity. Tonight he was more focused on the report on the Pope's health and a gleam of satisfaction crept into his steely blue eyes. The arcane art of leaking; it was one of Petroni's many skills. He had recognised the power of the media at an early stage in his career, and had learned the rules well.

Rule 1: Establish a trust with a reputable media outlet and make sure the information you feed is accurate. Journalists hated nothing more than to get it wrong. In the dog-eat-dog world of journalism criticism from colleagues was often worse than that of irate editors.

Rule 2: Feed the media just enough to suit your purpose, but not enough to have the leak sourced back to you. Or if there was any danger of that, have the journalist disguise the source – 'Well-placed government officials, sources close to the Vatican . . .' And always refer to sources in the plural. It confused those who might be looking for the leak.

Cardinal Petroni buzzed Monsignor Servini, the Head of the Vatican Press Office.

'Yes, Eminence?'

'Why is it, Monsignor, that I have just seen that journalist from

CCN purporting to have a report on the Holy Father's medical condition?'

'I've only just viewed the broadcast myself, Eminence, but I have ordered an immediate investigation.'

'I want a report on my desk within twenty-four hours.'

'Of course, Eminence.'

Cardinal Petroni snapped off the intercom.

Rule 3: Be at the forefront of denouncing and demanding the identification of the leak.

Petroni pushed the red button on the remote and absentmindedly watched the television retreat into its panelled alcove. Well-connected Knights of Malta like Kirkpatrick had their uses, he mused. Petroni had always been attracted to the Knights' history of savaging Islam and he had often imagined himself participating in their fierce attacks on Muslim pirates in the Mediterranean, launched from the island of Malta that was granted to the Knights by Charles V in 1530 and from which they took their name. The fight against Islam, he reflected, had been going on for centuries but he had no doubt that like the earlier Knights of Malta, the one true Faith of Christianity would prevail. The item on the Omega Scroll had been annoying, but for Cardinal Petroni information meant power and Kirkpatrick's early warning had given him time to calmly consider the implications. Petroni concluded that the speculation on the Omega Scroll would die. It always had in the past and the media always moved on.

The Vatican's Cardinal Secretary of State would not have been so confident had he realised the broadcast had also been seen by Jerry Buffett, the leading televangelist in the United States.

CHAPTER TWO

Atlanta, Georgia

The Buffett Evangelical Centre for Christ could seat fifteen thousand people and tonight it was packed. The choirmaster was warming up the audience with a booming rendition of 'How Great Thou Art', while backstage Jerry Buffett was making his final preparations.

Buffett appeared younger than his sixty years. Ruggedly good looking with a tanned face, blue eyes and a square, determined jaw, his personal hairdresser had been tasked with ensuring his dark hair held no hint of grey. His no-nonsense 'all-American' approach held wide appeal across the country, especially in the southern Bible belt. September 11 had seen the rise of the religious right in America and over five million Americans, including the President, tuned in to his weekly broadcasts.

The knock on the door of the well-appointed Dressing-room One was soft and respectful.

'Five minutes, Reverend Buffett.'

'Thank you.' Jerry Buffett poured himself a bourbon. The CCN broadcast had unhinged him, momentarily. A triumph of Islam over Christianity would be a disaster for humankind and he would call the President in the morning. In the 2004 election hundreds of pastors from the Buffett Ministry had been instrumental in signing up hundreds of thousands of voters across the country, especially in the swing states of Florida, Ohio and West Virginia. That effort had kept the presidency in Christian hands and, to use the President's own words, the capital was there to be spent. If the Omega Scroll existed it would be important to quietly retrieve it before the other side used it to their advantage. Jerry Buffett drained his glass and made some hasty amendments to his opening lines.

'I have just seen a broadcast on CCN this evening,' he began, in his deep southern drawl, 'which has predicted the triumph of Islam over Christianity.' The crowd fell silent, some shifting nervously in their seats. The events of September 11 had frightened many Americans.

'You and I have kept a Christian President in the White House, and Islam will never triumph!' Jerry Buffett paused to allow his emphasis to take effect. 'Islam will never triumph over Christianity!'

The audience cheered wildly, some of them stamping their feet.

'Islam is an evil religion!' Buffett thundered. 'God only withdrew His support from our people on September 11 because we turned our backs on Him! Islamic terrorism is a message from God! It is flourishing because we no longer allow the commandments in our courthouses. Our schools no longer have prayers or Bible readings, that's why God has given up on America because we've given up on Him!' Many in the audience nodded in agreement.

'God Almighty is no longer protecting America because Americans are obsessed with wealth, sex and drugs.' Jerry Buffett began to pace up and down the huge stage. 'Homosexuality is an abomination in the sight of the Lord, yet some of us want to legalise same sex marriages,' Buffett stormed.

Back at the lectern he took his Bible in his right hand. 'The husband is in charge of his wife,' he said softly, 'just as Christ is in charge of his Church. It's right here in the book. And make no mistake,' he continued, his voice rising again as he clenched his other hand into a fist, 'just as the Almighty has sent the plague of AIDS against homosexuals, so there will be more terrorist attacks by the Muslims unless we turn back to the Lord!'

Jerry Buffett was greeted with another round of applause that rumbled loudly into the Atlanta night.

CHAPTER THREE

Roma

Petroni leaned his tall, thin frame back into his leather chair. Mission accomplished. The precedent for resignation was now out in the public domain; the softening-up process was under way. Now, as long as Cardinal Donelli, the journalist and the woman could be kept out of the equation and the Omega Scroll safely recovered, anything might be possible. After all, he reasoned with himself, it was not the first time his beloved Church had needed protection from those who might seek to question her authority. Which brought him to the reaction of the other cardinals and any possible questioning of his own authority. Seeking resignation was a risky strategy but the Holy Father might go on for quite a time yet, and with each passing year Petroni's chances of getting his hands on the Keys to St Peter were correspondingly diminished. Younger cardinals were threatening to overtake him.

Cardinal Petroni unlocked the top drawer of his desk and took out a much-thumbed black leather book. Divided into sections for cardinals, archbishops and bishops, it showed their dates of retirements, dates of promotion and ages. Chances for further promotion were assessed under Petroni's own system of stars, from a low of one to the more threatening four star rating and, in rare cases, five. Awarded according to competence, standing in the wider Church, mentors, age and a host of other factors that would have done justice to a bookmaker's form guide. By his own reckoning Petroni had three main rivals.

The first two on his list had been given five stars. Cardinal Thuku, the charismatic leader from Kenya, and Cardinal Médici, the noted Liberation theologian from Ecuador. The strategy to defeat the two Third World candidates from Kenya and Ecuador would have to be carefully managed, he mused, but he'd already developed a suitable line: 'In due course, there would certainly be a Pope chosen from one of the many Third World candidates, but perhaps not yet.' Cardinal Petroni was reinforcing this line at every opportunity. Closer to home, Cardinal Giovanni Donelli, the recently installed Patriarch of Venice and the youngest of the College of Cardinals by several years, was now a clear and present danger. Originally Petroni had countered Donelli by quietly reminding his cardinal colleagues that a long Papacy carried enormous risks if the candidate didn't turn out as expected, but Donelli's investigation into the Vatican Bank's sale of shares in a bank in the Veneto had forced a dramatic change in Petroni's approach.

He and Giovanni Donelli had worked together once. In 1978 when Petroni had been an archbishop in the Vatican and Giovanni Donelli was private secretary to Pope John Paul I. Back then the ruthlessly ambitious Archbishop Petroni had identified the brilliant young priest as a potential threat and after John Paul I mysteriously died after only thirty-three days in office, Petroni had sidelined his young rival. As a result, Cardinal Petroni reasoned that Donelli would not be well enough known by others in the College of Cardinals and he had left his name circled in his black book as 'B-list at best'. It had been a crucial mistake that would now be rectified.

Petroni took a deep breath. It was time to set the wheels of his own destiny in motion. He pushed the preset button for the Papal Physician.

'Vincenzo. *Come stai?*'

'*Bene, grazie, e tu?*'

'*Molto bene, grazie.* I am arranging for the Curial Cardinals to meet in the Borgia Chamber tomorrow night. I think it is time they were given a frank assessment of the Papal condition.' Cardinal Petroni came straight to the point. Small talk was not his long suit. 'I would be grateful if you could provide such a briefing?'

'But of course, Eminence.' Professor Vincenzo Martines politely stuck with protocol. The Papal Physician had long ago concluded he had no desire to be on anything other than professional terms with the current Secretary of State.

'*Eccellente.* I will send a car at seven. That will give us time to, shall we say, plan our approach. *Fino ad allora.* Until then.'

The Papal Physician put down the phone and stared at it. For a long time now the Pope's health had not been his only concern in the Vatican. Professor Martines was an eminent physician, but he also had an additional qualification in psychiatry. Not for the first time Professor Martines wondered whether the Cardinal Secretary of State was fit for high office. There was a long list of symptoms: egocentric and grandiose; deceitful and manipulative; a lack of remorse or guilt; shallow emotions; demanding automatic compliance with expectations; a need for excitement; and requiring excessive admiration. Martines wondered if his diagnosis was accurate, or was it something even deeper, even more sinister. Martines also wondered if there might have been problems in Petroni's childhood. Had he been privy to the Cardinal's private life, the Papal Physician's innermost fears and diagnosis would have been confirmed.

On the other side of the Tiber Cardinal Petroni buzzed to summon his private secretary, Father Thomas. Having sown the seed of resignation, his planned meeting with the Curial Cardinals could not be delayed any longer. It would be important to catch them off guard. Almost immediately there was a knock on the heavy double doors of his office.

'*Avanti.*'

Father Andrew Thomas was a quiet man in his early thirties with a reputation for ruthless efficiency. 'Yes, Eminence?' he inquired.

'How many of the Curial Cardinals are away from Rome?'

'As far as I know, Eminence, all of them are here.'

'*Eccellente*. We will not require more than one briefing. I've asked Professor Martines to come and see me tomorrow night. Give each of the cardinals my compliments and ask them if they would join us in the Borgia Chamber at eight.'

'Certainly, Eminence.'

'Apologise for the inconvenience, Father Thomas, and tell them that the Papal Physician is providing a personal assessment on the Holy Father's condition. Something that I note CCN has already done for us.' Petroni smiled thinly. 'I think you will find they will all want to be there.'

'Certainly, Eminence. Will there be anything else?'

'Just the usual, have the driver on stand-by to pick me up at nine this evening.'

'Of course, Eminence.' Father Thomas withdrew quietly and closed the double doors behind him, not questioning why such a senior member of the Curia ordered his car late every second Monday.

CHAPTER FOUR

Washington

Mike McKinnon, the CIA's expert on the missing Russian 'nuclear suitcase bombs', took one of the leather adviser's chairs along the panelled wall of the Situation Room that was located downstairs from the Oval Office in the basement of the West Wing. A veteran of thirty-five years, Mike McKinnon had spent his early career in the Middle East acquiring a background in Arabic and Islam, before moving on to Soviet East Europe. McKinnon's face was rugged and pockmarked, his dark hair closely cropped. At 5 foot 10 inches, he tipped the scales at a fit 198 pounds, unchanged from when he was on his last field assignment in Bosnia Herzegovina. Now, much to his chagrin, he was back at a desk in the Directorate of Operations at Langley.

McKinnon nodded to the new Director of Central Intelligence, who was already seated at the conference table, along with the Secretary of State, the National Security Adviser, the Secretary of

Defense, the Secretary for Homeland Security and the Chairman of the Joint Chiefs. One of the last to arrive was the Vice President and they all stood as the President entered the room.

This was not the first time Mike McKinnon had been called to the White House Situation Room. He quietly scanned his notes while the President was brought up to date with Iraq, along with the growing nuclear threats emanating from Iran and North Korea. McKinnon had heard it all before.

'Special atomic demolition munitions?' the President inquired, glancing at the next item on the agenda.

'Nuclear suitcase bombs, Mr President,' the Director of Central Intelligence responded. 'Officer McKinnon you've met,' he added, nodding towards Mike.

'Mr President,' Mike began, 'this morning's brief covers the latest intelligence reporting on the likely whereabouts of some of the nuclear suitcase bombs that were manufactured in the Soviet Union. Several years ago, Alexander Lebed, Boris Yeltsin's Security Secretary, admitted that eighty-four out of 132 nuclear suitcases produced in the nineties were missing. We have reason to believe that al-Qaeda have acquired several of these bombs and at least five of them are now in the United States. There may be two others: one in the United Kingdom and one in Australia.'

'Where the hell did they get hold of those?' the President demanded.

Mike McKinnon maintained his passive expression. 'As you are aware, Mr President, Osama bin Laden has considerable financial backing. After the break-up of the Soviet Union in 1991 several Russian officers, some of whom hadn't been paid for months, turned to the black market.'

'Several of these bombs turned up in 1994,' the Secretary of State confirmed. 'The leader of the Chechen separatists, Jokhar Dudayev, put some of them on the market when we refused to recognise Chechnya's independence.'

'So how did they get them into the United States?' the President asked.

'They may have been here already,' Mike answered.

The President looked stunned.

'We have reason to believe that Soviet agents smuggled some of them in during the Cold War and pre-positioned them. Others may have been brought in more recently, probably by sea.'

'How is this possible?' the President asked angrily, looking at the new Secretary for Homeland Security.

'As I'm sure the Secretary for Homeland Security is aware,' Mike McKinnon continued calmly, 'up until recently, less than 5 per cent of containers that came into this country were inspected.'

The Secretary for Homeland Security nodded in agreement.

'We should be able to do a lot better than that,' the President insisted.

The Secretary for Homeland Security took his cue. 'The International Shipping and Port Security Code will help, Mr President, but we have over fifteen thousand ships docking in this country every day. We are not the only Western country facing this problem. In Australia last year, nineteen out of every twenty containers moved into that country without inspection, and a similar situation has existed in the United Kingdom.'

The President grunted with exasperation. 'What sort of damage can one of these suitcase bombs do?' he asked.

'It depends on how and where they set them off, Mr President,' McKinnon answered. 'The preferred method of delivery would be an airburst from a light aircraft.'

'Why not on the ground?' the Secretary of Defense demanded.

'Buildings tend to minimise the blast and thermal effect of a nuclear explosion,' Mike explained patiently. 'Although in the case of a ground burst the long-term casualties would be higher due to a more concentrated irradiated fallout. But terrorists tend to look to the more dramatic short-term effect and for that reason I am suggesting that a nuclear suicide attack from a light plane would be their preferred option.'

'Casualties?' the Chairman of the Joint Chiefs asked.

'Even a one kiloton nuclear blast, which is the equivalent of the smallest suitcase, is no ordinary bomb. The intense heat of a nuclear fireball reaches about ten million degrees. If you want a comparison, the September 11 fireball was of the order of four to five thousand degrees.'

The President exchanged glances with his National Security Adviser.

'In New York, London or Sydney, for example, anything within 500 feet will be vaporised. Within 1500 feet from ground zero metal will melt. The blast will generate winds of over 600 miles an hour and everything out to the 1800 feet range and beyond will be destroyed. In the big cities there will be up to a quarter of a million dead on the first day, and up to a million within two weeks.'

Mike McKinnon paused to let his analysis sink in. He could sense his new Director looking at him, but he avoided glancing in his direction. The President had appointed the Congressman to head the CIA and within weeks several key Directors had resigned. A flash of bitterness crept into his thoughts. Politicians. Most of them had never seen a shot fired in anger and very few of them comprehended the Islamic mind. The Coalition's policy in the Middle East and Iraq had been an unmitigated disaster, fanning the flames of Arab and Islamic hatred around the world. Now those same 'backward Muslims' had the means to strike a mortal blow, a blow from which the United States and her allies might never recover.

'Over the ensuing days,' Mike continued, 'many hundreds of thousands more will die of radiation poisoning and burns. New York, London, Sydney or any other city that is attacked will be uninhabitable for years. Unless you have any further questions, Mr President, that concludes the brief.'

The President shook his head and leaned toward his Director of Central Intelligence. 'McKinnon's background includes the Middle East and Islam?'

The Director nodded.

'Good. I'd like to see you both in the Oval Office after the briefing.'

CHAPTER FIVE

Roma

The Swiss guard on Saint Anne's Gate snapped to attention and saluted as the Secretary of State's black Volvo slipped quietly out of the Vatican. Petroni, dressed in civilian clothes and seated in the back, waved dismissively. Rome had come to life and the traffic was heavy as the car headed into the tunnel under the Tiber and wound its way along the Lungotevere Tor di Nona on the east bank. Over on the west bank the grisly Castel Sant'Angelo maintained a silent vigil over the river, the floodlights playing eerily on the battlements that for centuries had protected her archers and ancient catapults. Within the castle's grim walls, countless atrocities had been committed in the name of Christ – Pope John X had been smothered, Benedict VI had been strangled and John XIV poisoned. Tonight the Castel Sant'Angelo looked no less forbidding, but if there was a parallel between earlier atrocities and the ones Cardinal Petroni was now contemplating, it was a thought that did not occur to the urbane Secretary of State.

The car drove on towards the ancient part of the city. Towards the Colosseum that for nearly two thousand years had stood testament to the gory history of Rome. Past the Roman Forum and the ruins of the triumphal arches and the temples to the gods where at the height of the Roman Empire the marble pavements and steps were as busy as any modern city. Past the Circus Maximus that was now a public park. And finally, up the hill to an old Roman house on the Piazza del Tempio di Diana. Apuleius, Petroni's choice of restaurant, had been deliberate. The food and wine were excellent, but more importantly it was small and relatively out of the way. Once home to an influential first-century Roman family, its décor had not changed much in the intervening millennia. Red marble pillars supported the low roof and the remains of marble tablets decorated the frescoed walls. The ancient fireplace was intact and Roman pottery had been tastefully added to the small alcoves in the two living rooms in which guests could now choose to sit.

Cardinal Petroni had reserved a table that was partly shielded from the main areas by an old leather screen. Just in case. Although Petroni was confident he was unlikely to be recognised by anyone other than Giorgio Felici, who was already seated at the table.

'*Buonasera*, Eminence.'

'No titles please,' Petroni replied, a touch of annoyance creeping into his voice.

'*Mi dispiace*. Forgive me,' Felici said, instant understanding combining with the shiftiness of his green eyes.

Giorgio Felici had been raised in the Sicilian hillside town of Corleone. At a young age he had moved to Palermo when the Felici family had taken a stake in the cattle and heroin trade. More than one member of the competing Bontate and Buscetta families had met a grisly death at the hands of the young Giorgio as the Felici family gradually took control. It was a skill he still practised with ruthless efficiency. When the business expanded the family needed a safe means of laundering the proceeds and Giorgio had moved into the banking sector. Short, fit and muscled, with smooth black hair and tanned skin, he was immaculately dressed in an expensive cream suit. Giorgio Felici had become feared around the corridors of La Borsa di Milano, but his contacts in merchant banking were not of interest to Petroni tonight. Giorgio Felici had also risen to be Grand Master of Propaganda Tre or P3, the successor to P2, the infamous secret Freemason's Lodge of the 1970s. Like its predecessor, P3 boasted among its members Italian cabinet ministers and judges, the head of Italy's financial police, several of Italy's top bankers, industrialists and media executives, as well as serving and retired armed forces chiefs and two of the secret service chiefs. P3's tentacles stretched into the most influential Mafia families in Italy and the United States, into the CIA and the FBI, and, more importantly for Petroni, into one of the terrorist groups in Israel's Occupied Territories.

'Your message sounded urgent?' Giorgio ventured, coming straight to the point. Crooked white teeth showed in what was more a quick mechanical action than a smile. Petroni waited while the young waitress delivered their first course of scallops, sautéed to perfection in the finest olive oil and garlic, with just a touch of chilli, served on a bed of steamed spinach. The Cardinal was struck by the young girl's face. Her olive skin was flawless, her hair as dark as her eyes.

'*Vi verso il vino, Signor?*' she asked, proffering a bottle of Vigna Colonnello Barolo for Petroni's approval. Petroni savoured the bouquet. A powerful wine from the Italian nebbiolo variety, it was recognised around the world as being comparable to Burgundy and to the clarets of Bordeaux. Lorenzo Petroni had long been accustomed to the perks of high office.

'*Sì. Bellissimo,*' he replied. 'I hope you don't mind the break in tradition, Giorgio?'

'*Scusi?*' Giorgio asked, somewhat puzzled.

'Red wine with seafood.'

'Oh! *Non importa*. An unnecessary restriction.'

'The contracts on Schweiker and Donelli are in place?' Petroni asked quietly.

'The journalist is under surveillance. If he gets too close to your past, he will be dealt with. The threat from the Cardinal is more difficult.' Despite not yet having a solution for the troublesome Cardinal Patriarch of Venice, Giorgio smiled. He was enjoying the stickiness of the web that Petroni had woven around himself. As long as Petroni remained useful, and he might be very useful as Pope, Felici would continue to solve his problems, for a price.

'We have another small problem, Giorgio.'

Giorgio Felici smiled once more, bemused by the powerful Cardinal's ability to give other people ownership of his problems. 'Small' invariably meant blowing someone's brains out, but he said nothing.

'There is some property that may have fallen into the wrong hands and the Church would be grateful for its recovery.'

'That does seem a small request, Lorenzo. What sort of property?'

'You have heard of the Dead Sea Scrolls, *non è vero*?'

'*Naturalmente*, but I thought they were international property?'

'They are. The Catholic Church is cooperating with L'École Biblique et Archéologique Français, the French Biblical and Archaeological School in Jerusalem, as well as the Rockefeller Museum where these scrolls are rightfully housed for translation.'

Felici looked sceptical.

'Are you a good Catholic, Giorgio?' Petroni asked. It was a time-honoured attack. No matter how unscrupulous the target, there was always that small doubt of how one might fare in the afterlife. The theology of fear. It was something the Vatican had practised for centuries.

'But of course.' The uneven teeth flashed.

'Then you would understand that anything that impinges on the Faith is properly in the domain of the Holy Father.'

'And this clearly impinges on the Faith,' Felici mused cynically. 'So who might have these wrong hands?'

Petroni unzipped his soft leather briefcase. Normally it contained crimson files with gold Papal coats of arms emblazoned on the centre of the covers, but the file he handed Giorgio Felici was dun coloured. When it suited, no matter what the target, Petroni was a master of the smallest details of indifference.

'Some further information on Dr Allegra Bassetti, the one you already have under surveillance for us in the Middle East.' Other than a photograph and the bare details of her scholarship, Petroni had avoided providing Felici with too much background information on the bothersome ex-nun. The fewer people that connected her with the Omega Scroll the better, but circumstances had now changed dramatically and the wily little Sicilian would have to be brought into the loop.

'She used to belong to one of our convents but regrettably she has now succumbed to a life outside the Church. She and her companion, the Israeli archaeologist Dr David Kaufmann, are in possession of a Dead Sea Scroll that belongs in the Rockefeller Museum. We would, of course, pay handsomely for its return.'

'What is her background?' Felici asked. Originally he had been happy to organise surveillance on the Italian woman without too many questions. It had been money for old rope, but now he was more than a little intrigued as to why a Prince of the Church might have a personal interest in eliminating an ex-nun and recovering an ancient parchment.

'Southern Italy. A little place called Tricarico. Poor farmers mostly. Decent law-abiding people, although clearly there are exceptions.' Lorenzo sniffed pointedly. 'After we accepted her into the town's convent we made the mistake of sending her to the State University in Milano to further her education, which is where she went off the rails.'

'Don't you normally send your priests and nuns to Catholic Universities?'

'Normally yes, but against my advice the Holy Father decided that the Church should better understand the youth in a secular world, and Bassetti was part of the pilot program.'

'She is a doctor?'

'Chemistry. After she resigned from her Order she took a research doctorate in applied archaeological DNA. The details are in her dossier,' he said, pointing to the file. 'Kaufmann's details are in there, too.'

'Ah yes, from the reports we are getting they seem to spend a lot of time together. Any relation to Professor Yossi Kaufmann, the Israeli mathematician?'

'His son.'

Conversation was temporarily interrupted by the arrival of the main course. Petroni had ordered his favourite dish, *bucatini all'Amatriciana*; thin hollow tubes of pasta with a sauce of tomato, garlic and ham. This time it was delivered by a young boy who could not have been more than sixteen. Had the other patrons been remotely interested it would not have escaped their attention that Petroni gave the boy more than a casual look as he topped up the wine glasses and then quietly withdrew.

'Does the fact that he is Professor Kaufmann's son matter?' Petroni probed, suddenly wary of how much P3 might know about Professor Kaufmann and the Dead Sea Scrolls.

'It might,' Giorgio responded. 'The recovery of anything in the Middle East these days is not without difficulty, Lorenzo, and this David Kaufmann is obviously very well connected. His father is not only a world-famous mathematician and archaeologist, he is a General in the Israeli Defense Force Reserves and an honorary Director of the Shrine of the Book. And you are no doubt aware that he is also running for Prime Minister.'

Cardinal Petroni reflected that Giorgio Felici was extraordinarily well briefed. He said nothing.

'It might be quite an expensive operation, Lorenzo.' Again, the quick, mechanical flash of uneven white teeth.

Petroni had expected nothing less. On previous occasions when it had been necessary for someone to meet with an accident, Giorgio Felici had never come cheaply, but he was the best in the business and the protection of the Holy Church demanded nothing less. Whatever it took, the Vatican Bank would pay.

'It is essential that we recover this scroll quickly,' Petroni replied, leaving the issue of Felici's expenses and undoubted profit unanswered. 'I want you to see to it personally.'

'As difficult as that might be, we are not without our contacts, Lorenzo, and for a price I am prepared to go to the Middle East and oversee the operation.' Giorgio Felici didn't elaborate but he knew that terrorist groups had a constant need for funds to buy expensive arms and ammunition. Even a group like Hamas could be distracted from blowing up buses for long enough if the price tag was sufficiently attractive. 'But it raises another issue.'

Petroni was immediately on guard, although he was careful not to show it. 'Oh?' he said offhandedly.

'My colleagues in P3 have been considering offering you membership. Again,' Felici said pointedly. 'We met last night and that offer is now confirmed and I'm very happy to be the one to pass on their decision. I'm sure there will be just as many benefits for you as there might be for us,' Felici opined casually.

'Membership of P3 is out of the question,' Petroni responded, a touch of irritation creeping into his voice. 'Freemasonry has long been banned by the Vatican. Have you forgotten 1978?'

'You will not be surprised to learn, Lorenzo,' Giorgio continued quietly, ignoring Petroni's protest, 'that once again we count amongst our members some of the most influential men in Italy and the United States. But perhaps you *would* be surprised to know that several of them are cardinals?'

Petroni was not surprised at all. He had a very good idea of who was on Felici's list. That sort of information could be valuable currency should a cardinal or bishop be reluctant to take a particular direction.

'That does surprise me, Giorgio,' he said. 'You must have been very persuasive.'

'We have our means, my friend. I won't divulge any names of course, but let me give you an example. One or two of our members are quite prominent in the Comùne di Roma. It is perfectly normal for a very senior cardinal to have a luxury apartment outside the Vatican. But,' Giorgio added pointedly, 'if, *come si dice* – how do you say? – the "other arrangements" were known publicly there might be some very awkward questions.' For once Giorgio Felici's mechanical smile held a touch of mirth. Like a fisherman who had just hooked a very large fish.

Petroni's lips compressed into a thin line as he felt a rush of cold, hard anger. He eyed his adversary with barely disguised contempt.

'Clearly I have been careless.'

'Not really,' Giorgio replied. 'It's just that P3 has very good intelligence. Keeping track of someone as important as you is nothing personal, Lorenzo, purely business. Besides, we're all men of the world, and look on the bright side: when it comes to dealing with rivals for the Papacy, it is much better to have P3 backing you than the other way round.'

Cardinal Petroni had chosen his apartment with the same meticulous care he had chosen the restaurant. Via del Governo Vecchio was close, but across the Tiber and far enough away from the Vatican. It was fashionable, but eclectic. On one side, the narrow twists and turns housed expensive and richly decorated apartments and exclusive jewellery salons and designer fashion stores. On the other, there was anything from Abbey's, the Irish pub, to a *servizio* for motor scooters. Anonymity, but apparently, not anonymous enough.

Lorenzo Petroni's housekeeper was petite with dark shining hair. Quiet but determined, Carmela was used to his odd hours and she was waiting for him. He would need to leave before the grey winter dawn reached the dome of St Peter's, but that thought quickly evaporated. Carmela caressed Lorenzo gently with her tongue until he was wet and hard. She had a way of using the forbidden '*il preservativo*' to heighten Lorenzo's arousal and without losing the moment she fondled him as she reached for the already prepared condom in the bedside drawer. She murmured softly and took him inside her.

Back in his own apartment Giorgio Felici punched a code into the scrambler in his study and dialled a number for Hamas in the Gaza Strip.

CHAPTER SIX

Langley, Virginia

Mike McKinnon closed the door to his office, put the file marked 'Top Secret – Special Atomic Demolition Munitions' on his desk and walked to the window of his office that overlooked the lawns and the fishpond of the New Headquarters courtyard in the CIA's complex.

'Jesus Christ,' he muttered. 'The world is going fucking mad!' Osama bin Laden and God knows how many of his mad mullahs had the means to destroy Western civilisation, and now some equally wacky Bible basher from his own side had enough pull with the White House to have the President concerned about the recovery of a mythical Dead Sea Scroll. Hans Christian Andersen had moved into 1600 Pennsylvania Avenue, he thought ruefully. Religion had a lot to answer for, and so did the politicians. At least his latest assignment would give him the opportunity to get out of Washington for a while. It had been years since he'd been to Jerusalem and apart from the constant bombings, neither the city nor his favourite hotel, the American Colony, would have changed. He made a mental note to look up his old buddy Tom Schweiker. They had got to know each other well during the years Mike had been posted to the Middle East, and Schweiker owed him one. After all, if it hadn't been for him carrying on about a Dead Sea Scroll on CCN the White House knickers would still be in reasonable order. If there was anything to this scroll, he mused, journalists were often a good source of intelligence, particularly those of Schweiker's calibre.

Mike McKinnon rubbed his eyes wearily and went back to his desk. Since the arrival of the new Director, the Central Intelligence Agency had been under siege and his own boss, the head of the power-ful and covert Operations Division, had resigned. At fifty-four, Mike had also thought about chucking it in. With the wreckage of a couple of marriages well behind him, and being ruggedly fit and healthy with no ties, perhaps it was time to enjoy life. Yet he had decided to stay on, armed with the knowledge that this time the human race seemed to be on the brink of destruction. He reached for the top file in his tray. Unusually for Langley, it was a buff-coloured folder marked 'Unclassified', containing a summary of Osama bin Laden's speeches and remarks, aired on the Arab chan-nel Al-Jazeerah as well as through major Western media outlets.

Praise be to God, who says, 'O Prophet, strive hard against the unbelievers and be firm against them. Their abode is hell – an evil refuge indeed . . .'

I tell you the American, and your hypocritical allies, we will continue to fight you . . .

You attacked us in Somalia; you supported the Russian atrocities against us in Chechnya; the Indian oppression against us in Kashmir; and the Jewish aggression against us in Lebanon . . .

It is the Muslims who are the inheritors of Moses (peace be unto him) and we are the inheritors of the real Torah that has not been changed. Muslims believe in all the prophets, including Abraham, Moses, Jesus and Muhammad (peace and blessings of Allah be upon them all) . . .

If we are attacked, we have the right to attack back . . .

It is the duty of Muslims to prepare as much force as possible to ter-
rorise the enemies of God, and I thank God for enabling me to do so.

Mike McKinnon felt a chill run down his spine. The last statement had been issued under the heading 'The Nuclear Bomb of
Islam'. McKinnon had no doubt that bin Laden had not only gone
nuclear, he planned to attack at the first opportunity. At the top of
his list were the United States of America and her two principal
allies, Britain and Australia.

CHAPTER SEVEN

Jerusalem

The taxi dropped Dr David Kaufmann on the busy corner of King George V Street and Ha Histradrut. Just over six foot, olive-skinned, with blue eyes and thick, black curly hair, he strolled casually through the Friday night crowd and into Numero Venti, which took its name from nothing more imaginative than the street number. The small, intimate restaurant had not changed since the British mandate over seventy years before.

'Good evening, Dr Kaufmann. Your table is waiting. I trust you've had a pleasant week?'

'Not bad thanks, Elie. It's been a pretty long one, so it's good to have a night off.'

The wizened old waiter with the large hooked nose smiled. His smile held genuine warmth, his old grey eyes matching the colour of his receding curly hair.

'Your colleague, Dr Bassetti. She is coming later?' Elie asked, pulling out a chair.

'At the hairdresser's,' David said, rolling his eyes.

'Something from the bar while you're waiting?'

'A beer thanks, Elie.' David stretched his long legs under the table and smiled to himself. Elie had been the head waiter for as long as David had been coming to Numero Venti and he never failed to make you feel as if you were the most important person in the restaurant. David had introduced Allegra on a very busy night and the next time they had come in Elie had greeted her as if he'd known her for years. He took the first mouthful of his favourite Maccabee lager and looked around. The restaurant was beginning to fill up. Over at the bar one or two members of the Knesset, as well as the odd prominent businessman, were in animated conversation. David glanced casually at the solidly built Arab reading at a table in one corner.

'Shalom!' The couple at the next table clinked their glasses. A toast of 'peace' in a land that had known only centuries of bloodshed and war. Always lurking behind the laughter and the camaraderie was a noise of a very different kind; the shattering sound of death and destruction at the hands of Hamas and the Palestinian Arabs.

Yusef Sartawi made it look as if he was engrossed in his book. The lone Arab at the corner table worked with Cohatek, the Israeli events company, but in reality he had a far more sinister role, of which neither Mossad nor the CIA was yet aware. He was now one of Hamas's most experienced operations planners. It had been over twenty-five years since the Israelis had murdered his family in the small village of Deir Azun. The nightmares were still with him.

Were it not for the large sum of money being offered, Dr Allegra Bassetti would not normally have interested Hamas, especially given the curious origin of the contract. It had come from somewhere high up in the Vatican, but if the Christians wanted their own killed that was their business. What had caught his attention was the target's partner, Dr David Kaufmann, the son of Professor Yossi Kaufmann. Both men were already on the Hamas target list. It was Hamas policy to become thoroughly familiar with the target of an assassination and Yusef Sartawi's planning was always meticulous. Tonight's reconnaissance was just the first step.

David Kaufmann took another sip of beer and reflected on Allegra's breakthrough. Her DNA analysis had been nothing short of outstanding, but they were still only halfway through sorting the fragments. David glanced towards the door where Elie was taking Allegra's coat. Allegra was slender with round, dark brown eyes and an oval face. In the lab Allegra normally wore her hair up, but tonight she had let it tumble to her shoulders, black and glistening in the light of the restaurant.

'You look even more stunning than usual,' David said, giving her a kiss as he pulled her chair out from the table.

'Thank you, Sir. That sort of flattery will get you a long way.'

'Beer? Gin and tonic? Champagne?'

'I think champagne,' Allegra replied, looking pleased with herself.

'Better make that a bottle, Elie,' David said, taking the menus.

'Have you heard from your folks lately?' Allegra asked.

'Both fine. Yossi's still juggling mathematics at the university with politics and Marian is quietly supportive, although sometimes I think she would rather Yossi just remain a professor.'

'An impressive woman your mother. And neither of them look much older than sixty.'

'Yes. The powers of the universe got it right when they put those two together.'

'Except they produced you,' Allegra responded quickly. 'Yesss! I love it when you leave yourself open, David Kaufmann.'

'You'll keep. Shalom!' he said with a grin. 'A good week, *non è vero*?' David said, mixing Hebrew with Allegra's native Italian.

Allegra smiled. 'A very good week. No wonder Monsignor Lonergan didn't want anyone to have access to the fragments he had in that trunk of his in the Rockefeller vault. Once the Vatican gets wind of what we've got all hell will break loose.'

'Yes,' David agreed, suddenly serious. 'It looks as if their greatest nightmare has finally surfaced, although ultimately it might not be a bad thing.'

'Meaning?'

'Meaning in the long run the Vatican may have to re-examine their dogma. You've always said that you left the Church because it was based on fear. Run by old men who refuse to shift their position no matter what the evidence.' David picked up on the shift in Allegra's body language.

'As you know, that wasn't the only reason,' she replied, the bitter memory of the Cardinal and a Church she once loved shadowing the usual softness of her eyes.

'Is there no one you can trust?'

Allegra shook her head. 'Not in the Vatican. Their response will be ferocious and whatever it takes, they will bury it. But Giovanni Donelli would help. He is one of the few people at the top who would allow debate on this scroll within the Church.'

'An impressive man, the Cardinal Patriarch of Venice,' David observed with a small touch of jealousy, aware of the special bond between Allegra and the brilliant Catholic priest. 'But even if he doesn't help, couldn't we release the information here on our own?'

'Without someone like Giovanni supporting us,' Allegra insisted, 'the Vatican will simply denounce the scroll as a fraud. They're masters of spin control, and this is arguably the most important discovery in the entire history of Christianity. This is the real message, David, a warning that civilisation has entered its final phase.'

'Do you think anyone else knows about it?'

Allegra shook her head. 'Lonergan's trunk in the vault of the Rockefeller Museum was marked "personal" so I doubt if even the Director knows what was in it. We're going to have to be careful of Lonergan when he gets back.'

'Do you think he knows what he's got, or rather had?'

Allegra looked thoughtful. 'It's hard to tell with him. He may know more than we think. Although he may not have had time to decipher any of the fragments, and without a DNA analysis to help that could have taken years.'

'You think he's on the Vatican payroll?'

'He's certainly one of Cardinal Petroni's boys.' Allegra shivered. 'The Omega Scroll is going to shake them to their foundations.'

CHAPTER EIGHT

Venezia

Father Vittorio Pignedoli watched from his position in the chancel of the huge Basilica di San Marco as Cardinal Giovanni Donelli prepared to deliver his sermon to the packed congregation. This cardinal, he reflected, was like no other he had ever known and at fifty-two, one of the youngest. Thick black hair, deep blue eyes and a warm, infectious laugh, slim and fit – he even worked out in the gym. There was no hint of high office, and he was relaxed and accessible. Cardinal Donelli had only been in Venice for a short while and already everybody, both in the Church and outside it, was talking about him. There had been quite a few snide remarks from wealthy and powerful Venetians about Giovanni's 'lowly' southern origins, the little town of Maratea on the west coast of Basilicata. Venetian society relished the pomp and circumstance of their ancient fiefdom and their patrician noses were put decidedly out of joint when Giovanni resisted invitations to the glittering and expensive events he was expected to attend. Giovanni's distaste for excessive ceremony had Vittorio fielding indignant calls of complaint. The first was from an exasperated Chief of Police who had stumbled on the newly installed Patriarch of Venice out for a walk, dressed in the black soutane of a simple priest. The Polizia had found him in a trattoria near the Canal Grande happily chatting to some gondoliers and eating pizza *al taglio*.

'What if something happens to him!' il Capo di Polizia had complained. 'The very least he could have done was accepted the ride home.'

Giovanni had politely refused the offer of a police escort and had unwittingly added insult to injury by accepting a lift from the gondoliers. The gondoliers, he reasoned, were a more than adequate and less pretentious substitute. The priest with the big winning smile – it was the first thing people noticed about him. The gondoliers, the fishermen and the rest of the working class of Venice loved him.

Vittorio glanced nervously around the congregation. His cardinal's choice of a subject that questioned the very beginnings of life on the planet had attracted wide publicity, not all of it confined to the narrow streets and covered alleys of Venice. 'Science and Religion' reflected Giovanni's educational background – a doctorate in theology and an honours degree in science majoring in biology and chemistry. Giovanni's choice of subject had been prompted by an article in the *Corriere della Sera* – the respected Italian paper *Courier of the Evening*. Vittorio knew it was dangerous territory and that the Vatican would denounce any departure from the Church doctrine of Adam and Eve. As Giovanni climbed the marble stairs to his pulpit, a shadowy figure took a seat in the back row of the seats reserved for the clergy.

Giovanni had insisted on using the smaller of the two ornate pulpits. He rested his hands on the marble railing and smiled warmly.

'*Buongiorno. È molto buono vi vedere!* Good morning. It is very good to see you! Some of you may have seen an article on bacteria last week in the *Corriere della Sera*. For those of you who may have missed it, don't worry, it's not a sin to have no interest in bacteria.' The laughter reverberated off the gold tiled walls of San Marco and Giovanni's fulsome smile permeated even the coldest and most sceptical of hearts.

'This particular article was about a different type of bacteria known as archaebacteria, which thrive in boiling water. What, you may ask, has this to do with the Church and theology?' Giovanni paused and looked around his congregation, drawing them to him.

'I want to take you deep below the surface of the ocean. Imagine we are all inside the research submarine *Alvin* several kilometres below the surface. It is pitch black and the waters are very, very cold. Suddenly, the powerful lights on our submarine pick up molten lava spewing out of volcanic vents, and we watch as it comes in contact with the icy water. Deep beneath the seabed the lava and fluids cascading from the vents have been heated to temperatures well in excess of 300°C, but the crushing pressures at this depth prevent these fluids from boiling. Instead, they form tall, lava-encrusted chimneys known as "black smokers". Imagine our surprise to find that the edge of this inferno is teeming with life. Worms and other forms of life that thrive in temperatures well above that of boiling water. Now, I've been wondering whether or not such a discovery is a problem for our theology.'

Giovanni realised he now had everyone's attention. 'Here on the surface of our planet we all know that the energy source of life is sunlight. Without it the plants would die, and without plants the animals, including our species, would die too. But at these depths there *is* no sunlight. In this part of the ocean these forms of life don't need the sun; they feed on sulphur and hydrogen. There is now a growing body of scientific evidence that points to these oceanic bacteria being the very first forms of cellular life on Earth, from which all other forms of life, including humans, have evolved. It also means that there might be similar forms of life deep beneath the surface of planets like Mars and the moons of Jupiter and further away into the icy wastes of any one of the billions of galaxies like our own.'

It was as far as Giovanni was prepared to go. Already he sensed the unease that his challenge to the accepted biblical story of creation had created amongst the faithful and he dared not raise the issue of the origin of DNA. This was not the time to raise the possibility of a powerful spiritual force that he felt sure was driving the cosmos; one that encompassed the inadequacy of all of humanity's attempts at religion.

'So where does that leave the Bible and Adam and Eve?' he asked. 'Where does it leave us as Christians?' Not a shoe shuffled. 'As both your Patriarch and a scientist I see only positives in this. For me, this is just another revelation of "how" it was done. And such is the brilliance of the Creative Spirit I am certain that we have only scratched the surface.'

Vittorio listened, deep in thought. He had always believed in the creation doctrine that was laid out in the Catholic catechism: *The Lord God caused man to fall into a deep sleep; and while he was sleeping, He took one of the man's ribs and closed up the place with flesh. Then the Lord God made a woman from the rib*. Genesis was a beautiful story with no hint of bacteria, yet Vittorio felt a growing sense of trust for this intectually gifted man who was so willing to share his knowledge. It was as if the great cathedral had been opened up to an *aggiornamento*. A wind of modernisation was blowing hard through the portals of San Marco. In time it would become a gale.

Unseen by either Giovanni or Vittorio, the shadowy figure in the back row was quietly taking notes.

Night had descended on the Piazza di San Marco and the nearby stone alleys and narrow streets of Venice. The ever present gondolieri were competing for 'sea room' on the Grande along with a myriad of lesser *canali*, expertly guiding their seemingly flimsy craft amongst the *vaporetti* and the barges that waged a ceaseless battle to supply the water city's needs.

Oblivious to Venice's elegant pulse, Giovanni sat in his study overlooking the Piazza and reflected on his sermon. Francis Crick's theory on the origin of DNA had threatened many in the Vatican's corridors of power and the brilliant scientist had been success-fully discredited. In the 1980s Università Ca' Granda's Professor Antonio Rosselli had revived Crick's investigation with strong support from the Israeli mathematician Professor Kaufmann. But Kaufmann's analysis of the codes in the Dead Sea Scrolls had gone a lot further than DNA. Had the final countdown begun? Rosselli had been convinced it had.

Giovanni's thoughts went back to the time when he had stud-ied under the great mind, a time when he and Allegra Bassetti, the stunning young nun from southern Italy, had been students together. A time when Rosselli's theories had prompted passionate arguments over pasta and cheap red wine in La Pizzeria Milano. It had been over twenty-five years since they had been assigned to Milano's Università but it seemed like only yesterday. If it hadn't been for the extraordinary series of events in 1978, they might never have met and the proposal for them both to study at a secular university would have remained buried in the Vatican's archives.

BOOK TWO

1978 – 1979

CHAPTER NINE

Roma

Archbishop Lorenzo Petroni, Sostituto for General Affairs in the Secretariat of State, was the most influential archbishop in the Vatican. Following the death of Pope Paul VI and the election of Cardinal Albino Luciani of Venice as Pope John Paul I, Petroni had continued in the appointment as the new Pope's Chief of Staff, retaining control of the vast finances of the Vatican Bank. Nothing went in or out of the Pope's office without Petroni seeing it, or so he had thought, but today, less than a month after the new Pope's election, Lorenzo Petroni was a very worried man. Cardinal Luciani had been elected as someone the Curial Cardinals thought they could control but the quiet cardinal from Venice had turned out to be quite the opposite. The very careers of both Archbishop Petroni and the French Cardinal Secretary of State, Cardinal Jean Villot, were now seriously threatened.

Archbishop Petroni frowned as he read the memo from Father Giovanni Donelli, private secretary to His Holiness.

His Holiness has expressed a wish that a small number of priests and nuns be given the opportunity to study at a secular university. The aim is to promote an exchange of experiences to enable the Holy Catholic Church to better respond to changes in the wider world and to become acquainted with the thinking of the next generation.

His Holiness would be grateful for advice.

'Exchange of experiences!' Angry at having to even consider such a proposal when other events were spiralling beyond his control, Petroni screwed the memo up and threw it into the bin, wondering who or what might have prompted the Holy Father to even contemplate such a move. A move fraught with danger, even if the right people could be found. His thoughts were interrupted by the quiet buzzing of the intercom.

'Petroni!'

'His Holiness would like to see you, Excellency.'

'Subject!'

'I think it might be about the university proposal,' Father Donelli replied calmly. He was getting used to the Chief of Staff's irascibility.

'It would make life easier if we were sure,' Petroni snapped, switching off the intercom, relieved that the summons had not been the one he was dreading. He quickly composed himself and focused his thoughts on how he might best head the university proposal off at the pass.

'*S'accomodi!*'

'You wished to see me, Holiness?'

'Have a seat, Lorenzo.' Luciani's demeanour was polite but uncharacteristically cool, something that was not lost on Petroni.

'This university proposal. You've had a chance to look at it?'

'Not in much detail, Holiness, but I will.'

'It has some merit, *non è vero*?'

'Certainly, Holiness. Although I think there are some pitfalls that should be examined before we go ahead.'

'Oh?'

'It will be important to select the right people, and of course the right university. The course content will also be crucial. With all that in mind I think it would be prudent to establish an inter-departmental committee that should be asked to report on these and some of the other issues.' Lorenzo Petroni had learned early the value of an inter-departmental committee. With the right man at the helm, in this case himself, a proposal like this could be buried before it even got off the ground. If someone did remember to ask, an interim report could be relied upon to cause further delay until whoever had made the proposal in the first place had moved on.

'Inter-departmental committees can be useful things. Sometimes,' the Pope added meaningfully. It was not the first time the young Petroni's arrogance had led him to misjudge an adversary, and it would not be the last.

'I have already had a very favourable response from the Chancellor of Ca' Granda, the Università Statale in Milano.'

'There is an excellent Università Cattolica in Milano,' Petroni countered.

'We know that, but our mind is made up.' The Holy Father's rare use of the Papal plural carried a note of finality. 'I would like the Cardinal Prefect for the Congregation for the Clergy to examine it and get his people to provide four nominations.' Luciani's smile lacked its customary warmth.

Furious at being outmanoeuvred, Petroni stormed back to his office. Exposing young Catholic priests and nuns to the perils of an uncontrolled secular world risked corruption of their minds, but the university proposal could wait. Right now Petroni's biggest problem was the Pope's rumoured investigation of the Vatican Bank.

A week later Lorenzo Petroni, more worried than ever, was summoned to see the Cardinal Secretary of State.

'Of course, Eminence, I'll come down straight away.'

Cardinal Jean Villot was slumped, ashen-faced, on one of the crimson couches in his office. A large ashtray overflowing with cigarette butts sat next to a copy of *L'Osservatore Politico* on the coffee table. The headline could not have been worse – 'The Great Vatican Lodge'.

Membership of a Masonic Lodge, especially one as well connected as P2, had significant benefits but the Catholic Church had always been very clear on the 'sons of evil'. Any Catholic found to be a Mason would be excommunicated, and the editor of *L'Osservatore Politico*, a disgruntled former member of P2, had published a list of a hundred and twenty-one prominent Catholics who were members of Masonic Lodges. The Cardinal Secretary of State's name was at the top of the list, along with several other cardinals. Petroni's gut clenched. He had been accepted for membership just the week before.

'I have just been sacked,' the Secretary of State said simply.

'The list?' Petroni asked, glancing towards the paper. 'May I?'

'You're not on it.'

'I don't understand, Eminence,' Petroni replied, struggling to keep the relief from his voice.

'Your membership was agreed but it hasn't been processed yet.'

'I'm sorry about your name being published, Eminence,' Petroni offered belatedly. 'I guess I've been lucky this time,' he added, seeking confirmation that he had indeed escaped.

'Not really. The Pope intends to relieve you of all your duties tomorrow. Yesterday he received a preliminary report on your activities in the Vatican Bank and he intends to hold a thorough investigation into all Vatican finances. If that goes ahead I don't have to tell you that it will result in criminal charges that will have some of us behind bars for a very long time.'

Lorenzo Petroni returned to his office, his face the same colour as the Secretary of State's, his mind in turmoil. The investigation could not be allowed to go ahead. He would need to confer with Giorgio Felici, the young Sicilian from P2.

Giovanni Donelli made his way to the Papal dining room on the third floor of the Vatican's Apostolic Palace. It had been thirty-two days since Luciani's election and tonight, Pope John Paul I had asked Giovanni to dine with him alone.

At Luciani's request the sisters of the Papal household had prepared a simple meal of clear soup, veal, fresh beans and salad.

'You look troubled, Holiness,' Giovanni ventured.

'Some of what I have to tell you tonight, Giovanni, will become common knowledge tomorrow, but some of it will not. You've seen *L'Osservatore Politico*?'

'I was shocked, Holiness,' Giovanni said. Freemasonry was an anathema to him, let alone Lodges that were linked to the Mafia.

Albino Luciani nodded. 'This afternoon I relieved the Cardinal Secretary of State of all duties. He will be sent back to France to a retirement home where hopefully he will find some peace. The other cardinals and bishops on that list will be found dioceses where they can reflect and are unlikely to have any contact with a Masonic Lodge.' It was a measure of the man; bitterly disappointed and shaken, he still found time to consider those who had betrayed the Church.

'The preliminary report on the Vatican Bank that I gave you for safekeeping, did you read it?'

'No, Holiness, I wasn't sure if I should. I put it in the safe.'

Luciani smiled. Had the positions been reversed he would have done the same. 'We need to apply the same rules here as we did in Venice, Giovanni. Neither of us is used to Vatican politics but you need to be across all the issues. When you have time I'd like you to read the investigation. I'm not sure how to proceed yet, but tomorrow I will be relieving Archbishop Petroni of all his duties.

'Your Chief of Staff?' Giovanni was no great fan of the arrogant and aggressive Petroni, but he was still stunned at the levels to which corruption and deceit had reached within the Vatican.

As Pope John Paul I and Giovanni continued their conversation, and the nuns of the Papal household relaxed in the kitchen, a figure dressed in a priest's black soutane left the Pope's bedroom as quietly as he had entered.

'The Vatican Bank has been involved in serious criminal activities for at least as long as Petroni has been at the helm.'

Giovanni listened intently.

'Over the past few years we have criminally abused our position as a Papal State and our immunity from investigation by the Italian authorities. The Vatican Bank has been laundering billions of lire for the Mafia and we are heavily involved in a fake invoicing scheme that is defrauding the Italian people of billions more. We have shares in companies that make tanks and munitions, and I'm told that of the more than ten thousand accounts in our Bank, fewer than 10 per cent have a legitimate purpose. Most of them are slush funds for Petroni's cronies in the Mafia.'

'We should make a clean breast of this, Holiness,' Giovanni observed astutely.

'I intend to, including the fact that at one stage, Istituto Farmacologico Sereno was owned by the Vatican.'

'The big pharmaceutical?'

Pope John Paul I nodded. 'One of their biggest selling products is Luteolas, the oral contraceptive pill. You know my views on our doctrine on contraception, Giovanni, but to be condemning birth control while at the same time manufacturing millions of contraceptive pills because it makes us money plunges us to a new depth of hypocrisy. There is, however, an even more sensitive issue. The investigation has revealed that earlier this year we purchased a Dead Sea Scroll for ten million dollars. Have you ever heard of the Omega Scroll?'

'I've heard of it, Holiness, but I had no idea it actually existed, much less that the Vatican might have bought it.'

'We have known each other for a long time, Giovanni, and when I'm long gone it will be up to you and others like you to carry the Church forward. If what I'm told is true, the Omega Scroll will force us to rethink much of our doctrine and that will upset a great many people, but we must never shy away from the truth. At my request, an old retired Professor of Middle East Antiquities from Università Ca' Granda, Professor Salvatore Fiorini, has been here for the last week secretly translating it. I have a brief that I will read tonight. My initial impression is that amongst other revelations, the Omega Scroll contains a terrible warning for us all.'

Giovanni woke to the urgent ringing of the Holy Father's bell. He looked at the alarm clock on his bedside table. It was just after five in the morning. Giovanni struggled into his robe and hurried down the corridor that connected his own small apartment to that of the Pope's.

'Sister Vincenza. You look ill!' Giovanni said as he reached the end of the hallway. 'What on earth's happened?'

'Something terrible, Father. His Holiness . . . He's . . .' Sister Vincenza choked on the words.

Giovanni recoiled in shock when he entered the Pope's bedroom. His Holiness was upright in bed, his face twisted in agony, eyes bulging. His glasses had slipped to the end of his nose. Giovanni felt a strange and overwhelming need to remain calm as he glanced at the Pope's slippers that had been kicked off in disarray beside the bed, the toes covered in vomit. He picked up the phone beside the Pope's bedside and rang the Cardinal Secretary of State in his Lateran Palace Apartment. The Cardinal answered almost immediately.

'*Mon dieu, c'est vrais tous ça?* My God, is that true?'

The Cardinal, Giovanni would reflect later, sounded awake and alert.

'When did you find him, Sister?' Giovanni asked.

'Just before I woke you, Father,' Sister Vincenza replied, tears streaming down her kindly old face. 'I left the Holy Father's coffee outside his room at four-thirty as I always do and when I checked just before five it hadn't been touched, so I knocked and then . . .' Her voice trailed off as she started to sob.

'You did all you could,' Giovanni said, comforting the old nun. 'Make yourself a cup of tea,' he said, giving her something to do.

'Would you like one, Father?' Sister Vincenza asked, ever concerned about the welfare of those in her care.

'Only if you feel up to it.'

When the old nun had left Giovanni looked more closely at the dead Pope. In the short time he had held the Keys of Peter, Albino Luciani had come to be loved by most and feared by some. He was a man of unassuming charm and softness, with a searing intellect. Giovanni glanced at the small bottle of medicine the Pope kept on his bedside table for low blood pressure, then at the crimson folder clutched in the dead Pope's hand. The papers that had spilled from it onto the bed were part of Professor Fiorini's brief on the Omega Scroll. Giovanni felt a cold fear in the pit of his stomach as he scanned the scattered pages.

And in the beginning, the third will triumph over the first and second . . . all mankind will be annihilated.

'Don't touch anything, Father.' Lorenzo Petroni's voice was steely, his lack of emotion sinister. 'Does anyone else know that the Pope is dead?' He was clean-shaven and fully dressed in the formal robes of an archbishop. Only minutes had passed since Giovanni had alerted the Cardinal Secretary of State. It was not yet five-fifteen.

'Only Sister Vincenza and the Cardinal Secretary of State.'

'You should have rung me as well, Father Donelli. To protect Sister Vincenza from the media she is to be returned to her convent in Venice. Immediately.'

'Eminence, a terrible thing,' Petroni said smoothly. The Cardinal Secretary of State, also fully dressed and clean-shaven, hurried into the room. He was followed a little later by the Papal Physician, Dr Renato Buzzonetti. While Dr Buzzonetti examined the body, Archbishop Petroni systematically removed the papers and the file from the bed, as well as the dead Pope's glasses, his slippers and his medicine. He crossed to the Pope's desk and removed the file on the impending sackings and transfers, as well as the Holy Father's appointment book.

Later in the morning Giovanni, still trying to come to terms with both his and the Church's loss, was stunned to hear the official announcement of the Pope's death on Vatican Radio:

> This morning, 29 September 1978, at about five-thirty, the private secretary of the Pope, not having found the Holy Father in the chapel of his private apartment, looked for him in his room and found him dead in bed with the light on, like one who was intent on reading. The physician, Dr Renato Buzzonetti, who hastened to the Pope's room, verified the death, which took place presumably around eleven o'clock yesterday evening, as 'sudden death' that could be related to acute myocardial infarction.

'The Vatican Radio has got it wrong, Excellency,' Giovanni remonstrated with Petroni.

'The Vatican Radio has got it absolutely correct, Father Donelli. Their statements are in accordance with the official press release, which is going on the wire as we speak. All press inquiries are to be handled by the Vatican Press Office and should anyone else ask, the Holy Father was found reading a copy of the devotional *The Imitation of Christ*. Do I make myself clear?'

'Excellency,' was Giovanni's only response, a touch of steel in his own voice.

Petroni watched the young priest leave his office and wondered how much of the brief on the Omega Scroll he had seen. Time enough to deal with him after the conclave elected the next Pope. Hopefully this time, the Curial Cardinals would get it right and the Church could return to the right path.

Tom Schweiker prepared to go to air, adding to the growing calls for the truth about the death of John Paul I. Up until now the CCN network had not had a reporter dedicated to 'religious affairs' and although Tom Schweiker was CCN's correspondent across the Mediterranean in the largely Muslim Middle East, given the relative proximity to Rome, management had not objected to Tom's request to cover the Holy See. Management had no idea the request was part of Tom's search for his own haunting truth, something that had driven him since his youth.

'And this evening we cross live to Tom Schweiker reporting from outside the Vatican. Tom, there are growing calls for an investigation into Pope John Paul's death.' The anchor in New York was the grey-haired, avuncular Walter Casey, a household name in the United States.

Tom nodded as the satellite cross from Washington reached his earpiece. 'That's right, Walter. The respected Italian newspaper *Corriere della Sera* has been just one of those in the forefront of calls for the Vatican to come clean.'

'Do you think the Vatican is hiding something?'

'That's very clear. The Vatican has lied about this from the outset, Walter, and the web of fiction has been almost childish. Pope John Paul I was not found by his private secretary, as claimed in the Vatican's initial press release. We now know that the body was found by a member of the Papal household, Sister Vincenza, who has been spirited away, and the Vatican is refusing to say where she is.'

'And there is a question about the documents the Pope was reading when he died?'

'Initially the Vatican claimed he was reading a devotional book, *The Imitation of Christ,* but that claim fell apart when the book couldn't be found in the Pope's apartments in the Vatican but turned up in his old apartments in Venice. The Vatican has now claimed the Pope was studying a list of new appointments but there are claims that this is also not true, and that he may have been reading a brief on the legendary Omega Scroll.'

'Will there be an autopsy do you think, Tom?'

'There is enormous pressure for that, Walter, but the Vatican are resisting it on the basis that Canon Law forbids it. The problem with that argument is that several theologians have confirmed that Canon Law doesn't say anything about autopsies. As far as Italian law goes the injection of embalming fluids is not allowed within twenty-four hours of death without the express permission of a magistrate, yet Pope John Paul's body was injected immediately. There is now a very strong sense that Pope John Paul I was murdered, possibly by the addition of digitalis to a regular medicine he took for low blood pressure.'

'Do we know if he was in good health?'

'He was examined by Dr Giuseppe Da Ros only a few days before his death and Dr Da Ros said, "*Non sta bene ma benone* – he is not well but very well," and his personal doctor in Venice says Albino Luciani was a very good mountain climber with absolutely no history of heart problems.'

'Tom, thank you for joining us tonight. That was Tom Schweiker reporting from the Vatican on the suspected murder of Pope John Paul I. In news just to hand the Vatican has announced that the conclave for the election of his successor will be held on 14 October, the earliest possible date that such an election can be called. Now to the news from the White House. President Carter today expressed confidence for peace in the Middle East after the signing last week of the Camp David Accords between Egypt's President Anwar Sadat and the Prime Minister of Israel . . .'

Later that night in his hotel room Tom Schweiker tossed in his sleep, haunted by the day's coverage of the Vatican. The nightmares had been with him ever since his boyhood days, spent on a dirt-poor potato farm in Idaho; nightmares that continually motivated Tom's search for peace, taking him back to 1960 when he was twelve, missing a father who had died six years earlier. A time when a new priest, Father Rory Courtney, had arrived in their little parish out on Snake River Plain.

The big car pulled up outside the house, scattering the chickens. There was a knock on the old wooden fly-screen door.

'I'll get it,' Tom called to his mother, taking the wooden stairs two at a time.

'Father! Please come in,' Tom said, getting used to seeing their priest at the door. Rory Courtney was a big man in his midtwenties but his reddish hair had started to thin and he was putting on weight. A deep scar ran almost the length of his left cheek, the result of a whisky-induced brawl in his earlier days as a young mining geologist.

'Thank you, Tom. Is your mother at home?'

'Who is it, Tom?' his mother called from the kitchen.

'It's Father Courtney, Mom.'

Tom's mother came hurrying into the front room, wiping flour from her hands as she untied her apron.

'Oh Father, excuse the mess. Please, have a seat.' Eleanor Schweiker hastily cleared her sewing from the old couch, somewhat dismayed that their priest should find her in anything but her one good dress that she kept for Sundays.

'Not at all, Eleanor, not at all. I won't stay long. I'm just doing my rounds, checking on my flock.' Rory Courtney had an easy manner and Tom had begun to look forward to his visits. Father Courtney always managed to find time to throw a football around the back paddock with him. It went some way to easing the pain of missing his dad.

'Would you like coffee, Father?'

'Perhaps next time, Eleanor. I was wondering, if Tom is not doing anything next Sunday afternoon we could take a drive down to the river. I've found a great little place where we can pan for gold.'

'I don't know how to, Father,' Tom said awkwardly.

'Ah, but I do and I'll teach you. Just bring your rubber boots and I'll bring the rest of the things we'll need.'

'Oh, Father, that would be so kind,' Eleanor Schweiker responded gratefully. Tom had lacked a father figure for too long. 'I'll pack you both a picnic lunch.'

'Thank you, Eleanor. I'll call by after Mass in the morning,' he said, getting up to leave.

'Bye, Father.' Tom and his mother waved from the front porch. Father Courtney's big old Buick left a trail of dust as he headed down the hill.

The winter sun had reached the zenith of a low arc above the thickly wooded mountains. The Buick rocked gently as Father Courtney drove across the clearing bringing the car to a halt near the bank of the swiftly flowing river. The cold clear mountain waters, swollen by the early rains, gurgled over the rocks.

'Is there really gold in this river, Father?' Tom asked excitedly, munching on a bread roll his mother had baked earlier that morning.

'Bound to be.'

Tom helped Father Courtney unpack a shovel, a pick and two buckets to collect the gravel, a bright blue plastic dish fitted with a small screen and a strange ribbed oblong box about 5 feet long made out of lightweight aluminium.

'What's this, Father?'

'A sluice. Give me a hand and we'll set it up.'

Tom followed Father Courtney through the tumbling waters of the river to the opposite bank. This new priest, Tom thought, was really nice.

'The gold is heavier than the gravel so it sinks to the bottom while the gravel runs over each of the riffles and back into the river.' Father Courtney propped two large rocks on either side of the sluice to steady it, picked up the shovel and gave Tom the pick. Tom grinned and swung on the pick with gusto. They took it in turns to shovel and pick, and after ten minutes of hard digging both large buckets were full of gravel.

'The most important thing is not to dump too much gravel into the top of the sieve, otherwise it will run out the other end taking the gold with it. You've always got to be able to see the tops of the riffles,' Father Courtney explained, feeding the gravel slowly into the top end of the sluice. Tom watched as the gravel washed over the riffles, leaving the concentrate behind.

'OK, Tom, now we get to see if we're rich,' Father Courtney said with a big smile, filling a pan with the black concentrate. Holding the pan just under the water, he shook it gently to get the lighter dirt to the surface and then swirled it over the lip. Suddenly a small flash of yellow appeared in the bottom of the pan.

'Father! Look!' Tom pointed. Father Courtney picked the small nugget out of the black sand. It was about the size of a pea, but as far as Tom was concerned it could have been the mother lode.

'There you are, Tom. I told you we'd find gold here.'

It was the only 'nugget' of the day. After two more hours the pan yielded about half an ounce of gold flakes, which Father Courtney put into a small plastic cylinder. Tom couldn't have been happier.

'Can you drive, Tom?' Father Courtney asked as he finished loading the car. Tom shook his head.

'Well, get in this side and you can steer some of the way back.' Father Courtney held the driver's door open and Tom stepped onto the running board and slid under the white bakelite steering wheel with its shining chrome horn.

'Nice car, Father.'

'It is, isn't it. Grab the wheel,' he said, putting his arm around Tom. For about a mile they drove up from the riverbank, Tom grinning as he piloted the big car around the potholes and puddles.

'If you like I'll teach you to drive. I'm generally free after Mass on a Sunday.'

'Thanks, Father. That would be terrific,' Tom said, his eyes shining as Father Courtney took the wheel. His excitement turned to confusion when Father Courtney took one hand off the wheel and rubbed the inside of Tom's thigh.

'It's a good thing to be close to your priest, Tom. God meant it to be this way.'

Father Courtney pulled Tom's hand across and put it down the front of his trousers. It hadn't occurred to Tom that Father Courtney might have loosened his black priest's belt, or the fly on his black priestly trousers. Black. Priestly black. Sinister, evil black. Father Rory Courtney had planned the whole outing meticulously, right down to the loosening of his belt. A simple manoeuvre as Tom had turned his back and clambered excitedly into the car. Father Courtney's timing was the result of years of practice. Each time there had been complaints and each time the Vatican had hushed them up and moved their priest to prey on another unsuspecting group of children. This was Father Courtney's third parish in three years.

Tom tried to pull his hand away but Father Courtney held it on his erection. With an expert flick of the wheel he pulled the big car over onto the side track he had reconnoitred earlier in the week and they drove back towards the river. When the track finally petered out in thick brush he turned off the engine and with both hands free he started to fondle Tom. To Tom's horror he found himself getting an erection as well.

'There see. Isn't that good?' In one movement Father Courtney slipped his own trousers down, grabbed Tom's hand again and masturbated with it until he came with a high-pitched cry.

Stunned, Tom sat pressed up against the passenger door, putting as much of the big bench seat as possible between himself and the priest.

'It won't do any good to tell your mother, Tom. She would never believe you, but we can still do the driving lessons, eh?'

'No thanks,' Tom said sullenly. Angry. Ashamed. Confused. Betrayed. A whole mix of emotions that even his weekly bath that night could never remove.

When Tom refused Father Courtney's invitations to pan for more gold from the river, his mother had been puzzled.

'It will do you good, Tom. Besides he's our priest, you should be grateful he wants to spend time with you.'

'No thanks.'

'But why?'

Tom wouldn't answer. His response had been to run upstairs, slam his bedroom door shut and refuse to come out for hours. His mother had become angry, very angry. For weeks there had been a cold distance between them. Then the rumours started. Big Mitch Coburn, a fourth-generation potato farmer and elder of the Church, his complexion more florid than usual, outlined the complaints to the little gathering in his front parlour. Eleanor Schweiker listened with a growing sense of horror as realisation dawned on her.

'Bobby Shanahan, Hughie Taylor and little Jimmy Osborne. All of them. Not eatin', wettin' the bed, sullen, just not themselves. The first one to suspect anything was Grandma Taylor. She came to me and to my undyin' shame . . . to my undyin' shame I told her I would have none a' that sorta talk in ma parish.'

Mitch Coburn was normally a big jovial gentle giant. Today he looked as if he'd been run over by a Massey-Harris tractor.

'Ahm afraid to say ah was wrong. Ah've been in touch with the Bishop and he's told me on the quiet that it's not the first time it's happened. He's removed Father Courtney and the Cardinal is coming down next week from Chicago to make amends.'

'What do you mean it's not the first time it's happened, Mitch?' Eleanor asked, a steely edge to her voice. 'What sort of "amends" does this Cardinal think he can make?' Her stomach was churning like a washing machine. 'My Tom has never been the same since he went out with that priest and now he refuses to discuss it.'

Eleanor's face was white, matching an anger that was directed at the only target she could find. 'I stood up for the priest and now you're saying this might have happened before! My son has had heaven only knows what done to him and all I can do is stick up for a Church that protects its priests and ignores my child and every other child they allow Rory Courtney and others like him to be with. Well, you and your precious Church and that priest can all burn in hell!'

Mitch Coburn blinked at the ferocity of a mother's anger.

'I know, Eleanor, I know. It's the most terrible thing. Terrible,' was all he could say.

Tom Schweiker groaned wretchedly in his sleep at the memory of a Church offering each family fifty thousand dollars provided that everyone agreed to secrecy. The searing memory of a mother refusing to sign unless the priest was struck off and a cardinal who insisted that was the Church's business, not hers.

He woke sweating at the memory of a little town that had been destroyed by the suicides of Bobby Shanahan and Hughie Taylor. An anger at a Church that couldn't care less, callously protecting its image and leaving the Rory Courtneys of the world free to go to the next parish and destroy more lives, all in the name of Christ.

Lorenzo Petroni had good reason to feel satisfied. Karol Wojtyla of Poland had been elected as Pope, taking the name John Paul II. Cardinal Villot had been reappointed as Cardinal Secretary of State and Petroni had been retained as the new Pope's Chief of Staff with control of the Vatican Bank. But there were still two loose ends. Petroni drummed his elegant fingers on his desk as he wrestled with the available solutions. The Omega Scroll had been removed to a little known part of the Secret Archives and the brief destroyed, which left the old professor from Ca' Granda and Father Giovanni Donelli. Professor Fiorini would have to be dealt with quickly. The 'Italian Solution' would need to be applied. Lorenzo Petroni resolved to speak with Giorgio Felici at the earliest opportunity. Which left Donelli.

The new Pope had brought his own private secretary and Petroni had assured Pope John Paul II that Donelli would be looked after. Angered by Donelli's calmness in a crisis and his resistance to the Vatican's press line on the death of John Paul I, Petroni had immediately found him a mind-numbing filing job in the Vatican library in the hope he would resign. Young priests, he reflected angrily, were usually much easier to control. So far there had been no sign of resignation and Petroni had resolved to get Donelli out of the Vatican and the corridors of power at the earliest opportunity. Still considering his options, Petroni began to scan the files that were marked for the new Pope's attention, only allowing those he was happy with to pass to the Pope – an investigation into a Sainthood . . . a delegation from Opus Dei . . . a request from the US Ambassador to Italy for an audience with His Holiness . . .

The next file irritated him immediately – the university proposal. Petroni had forgotten about it, but now the doddering old cardinal in charge of the Congregation for the Clergy had dutifully provided the four names that the dead Pope John Paul I had insisted on. Petroni was about to consign it to archives when he had a second thought. He glanced at the four names – two priests and two nuns. At least they got the number right. There was less chance of a priest getting close to a nun if there were two others watching. None of the names were familiar which meant that there was less control over the program but, he mused, if Donelli were put on the program it would get him out of the Vatican.

Again he wondered how much of the brief the young priest had absorbed in the minutes he had been alone in the dead Pope's bedroom, and he fleetingly reconsidered the 'Italian Solution'. Donelli was too close to the dead Pope; it would be too risky. The speculation on the death of John Paul I had wound down and eliminating Donelli might open up a full-scale inquiry. Donelli had worried Petroni from the moment he'd met him. The athletic young priest appeared to have a razor-sharp intellect and an astute ability to effortlessly grasp the most complex of issues. Unable to feel a genuine liking for anyone but himself, Petroni had reverted to his standard jealous response to any rival. He had done his customary detailed research into Giovanni's personal history which had revealed a very close family background. No doubt a major reason for Donelli's ability to mix easily in all walks of life. An image of his own violent father flashed into his thoughts and Petroni subconsciously redirected a burning hatred towards the unsuspecting Giovanni. While this emotion ran hot he marked the young priest with a single star in his little black book. True to form, Petroni calmed his anger and realised the university proposal could work to his own benefit. Sending Giovanni back to university would give Petroni a double advantage – it would get Giovanni out of the corridors of power and

stall his growing reputation. More importantly, it would give
Petroni a channel of communication and a measure of control
over this unwanted secular program. Petroni smiled thinly as he
put a line through one of the priest's names and substituted that
of Father Giovanni Donelli.

In answer to Archbishop Petroni's summons Giovanni paused
before knocking on the door to the inner office. He collected
his thoughts and went over the issues that he thought might be
exercising Petroni's mind. This week the Curial Cardinals and
the Archbishop would again be discussing Vatican II and contraception. He knocked and entered the office.

'Have a seat, Father Donelli.' Archbishop Petroni waved his
right hand towards the high-backed chair that had a permanent
position in front of his desk. Petroni had arranged for his desk
and his own chair to be raised several centimetres so he could look
down on whoever was sitting in the chair opposite.

'The Curial Cardinals will be meeting tomorrow to receive a
progress report on Vatican II.' As he spoke, Archbishop Petroni
absentmindedly examined his fine bony fingers. Giovanni recognised the ploy – one of feigned indifference – and he was instantly
on guard.

'You've served in a small parish, where was it again?' Petroni
asked.

'Maratea, Excellency. It's a small village south of Naples on the
Tyrrhenian Sea.'

'Ah yes, I remember. Tell me, how did the parishioners react
to Vatican II?' It was a fearfully loaded question. In 1962 when
Pope John XXIII was asked why the second Vatican Council was
needed, His Holiness had got up with a twinkle in his eye, opened
a window and said, 'I want to throw open the windows of the
Church so that we can see out and the people can see in'. Faced
with that sort of logic the Curial Cardinals had been careful to
support Vatican II in public, but in private their opposition had

been scathing. Concepts such as the possibility of ordinary people gaining salvation outside the Catholic Church seriously threatened the power of the priesthood.

'When Vatican II was introduced I had only just been made an altar boy, Excellency.' Giovanni's mind flashed back to the little fishing village of Maratea where he had grown up in the Faith. His first day as an altar boy was not only a defining moment for himself; it had been a cause for celebration for his whole family.

High above the fishing port of Maratea, the parish church of the Addolorata nestled amongst the terracotta roofs of the houses on one of the Apennine ridgelines that tumbled into the Golfo di Policastro and the emeralds and blues of the Tyrrhenian Sea.

Giovanni Donelli was robed in the white cassock his mother had stayed up sewing the night before. He glanced at his family who had arrived half an hour before the service to make sure to get the front pew. Papà was beaming, Mamma quietly proud, and his younger brothers Giuseppi and Giorgio were trying to look uninterested. The old wooden pews protested as the congregation settled back and Father Vincenzo Abostini prepared to address them all. The beautifully kept little church didn't have a pulpit, but Christ and his Mother Mary would have certainly approved. The altar was covered in the finest white lace, which *le donne* of the village laundered every week. High on the wall behind the altar between two marble pillars was a life-size statue of Mary, standing watch over the little congregation, six gold candlesticks at her feet. Giovanni could still remember sitting on the marble steps that led up to the chancel, listening to Father Abostini, a quiet gentle man with an ample waistline, thinning hair and flushed, pudgy cheeks.

'I have a message from the Holy Father himself,' Father Abostini began, grasping the sides of the lectern. On Sunday 14 October 1962, the same message was being read in tens of thousands of

Catholic parishes around the world but Father Abostini had the ability to make it seem as if it was a personal message to the villagers of Maratea.

'Il Papa sends his blessings to each of you and he asks for your prayers. Under the auspices of the Virgin Mother of God, the Second Vatican Council is being opened in Rome beside St Peter's tomb. I want to add my own message to that of Il Papa. I know that many of you have great hopes for Vatican II, but, *i miei amici*, please understand that reaching a conclusion will take time.'

Like a true priest of the people, Vincenzo Abostini was warning them against expecting too much. He had spent time in the Vatican and knew well the formidable power of the Curial Cardinals massing against any change.

'Many of you, I know, have deep concerns over issues such as birth control, but I would caution that change will not happen overnight.' The Vatican's dogged ban on contraception had caused millions of Catholics enormous pain. He glanced at Giovanni's mother sitting in the front pew. He had shared the guilt of her confession as they'd sat either side of the grill in the church's little white wooden confessional the previous day. Like so many of his flock, tormented by the Church's teaching. A dogma that had very little to do with the Bible and a lot more to do with the Vatican using sex to maintain its power over the masses.

'In convening such a Council our much loved Holy Father has shown great leadership,' Father Abostini continued. 'In his own words, he has flung open the windows of the Holy Church to what he has called *aggiornamento*, a process of renewal and modernisation of the Faith. He has reached out to the Jewish faith with a concern for the Church's anti-Semitism of the past. Instead of denouncing other religions he has rejoiced in their common spirituality. Il Papa is truly a man of the people. He is one of us. I am reminded of the story of him catching a reflection of himself in a mirror and remarking *'Sono fa brutto* – I am so ugly!'

The laughter of the villagers of Maratea was full of affection for a Pope who was truly 'one of them'. A Pope who held the view that the Church should be less hierarchical and more open. More responsive to her grass roots congregations and the world outside the walls of the Vatican. In the tradition of Christ himself, Pope John XXIII held that the villagers were the most important part of the Church. Rather than a tree with the Pontiff and his bishops at the top, Pope John saw the Church more like a field, each blade of grass making up the People of God.

It was this view of the Church that made an indelible impression on Giovanni and it had become stronger as his career progressed. It was a philosophy that resonated deeply within him and formed the foundations for his interpretation of his faith and its teachings. This philosophy was a guiding light in times of doubt and darkness. It gave him an inner strength that would be sorely tested in the not too distant future. Archbishop Petroni and his supporters were quietly massing against any departure from the dogma and were preparing to silence the echoes of Vatican II. But across the Mediterranean, as the heat haze shimmered off the Dead Sea and a few grains of sand trickled from the roof of a cave, a much greater threat to the dogma was yet to be discovered.

'And what did Father Abostini have to say about Vatican II?' Archbishop Petroni demanded, frustrated with Giovanni's non-committal answer.

Giovanni was jolted back to the present with the realisation that, on the one hand, Archbishop Petroni seemed to need reminding as to which parish Giovanni had belonged but on the other, he knew precisely which priest was in charge.

'He was supportive of the Holy Father's message, Excellency.'

'Of course. And what were the peoples' views on *Humanae Vitae*?'

'Maratea is only a small village, Excellency, but the news of the world does not go unnoticed and many villagers follow *The Catholic*

Weekly. When it reported that the Canadian bishops had allowed informed conscience on birth control, it was also reported that this had provided a great many Canadians with relief from the burden of guilt. Many of the villagers in Maratea expressed their disappointment, Excellency, that they did not receive the same relief.

'The disobedience of the Canadian bishops has not gone unnoticed, Father.'

'The people of Maratea are fishermen, Excellency. They have a strong faith that is a great comfort when times are hard.'

Archbishop Petroni got up from behind his desk, turned his back and walked over to the windows overlooking La Piazza San Pietro. Giovanni remained seated.

'The Holy Father has decided to introduce a pilot scheme whereby selected men and women of the Faith are to attend a state university. It is something I have opposed, Father Donelli, but the Holy Father is adamant.' Pertroni returned to his desk but remained standing, looking down on Giovanni, his blue eyes cold and steely. Petroni did not enjoy being overruled, even by the Holy Father.

'You, Father Donelli, have been chosen to lead the program and to provide periodic reports on its effectiveness or otherwise,' Petroni said, with a chilling emphasis on the 'otherwise'. 'You are also to ensure that the more junior members of this program do not go off the rails.'

'I already have two degrees, Excellency, in theology and chemistry,' Giovanni said, more than a little puzzled.

Petroni's eyes narrowed and Giovanni instantly regretted his response. 'I am aware of that, Father,' Petroni said slowly. 'I have at least persuaded the Holy Father that theology continue to be taught where it should be, within the correctness of a Catholic university. You and three others have been enrolled in a new degree, the Philosophy of Religion. The details including the reporting requirements are in this folder. I require only one copy of each report and there are to be no duplicates. They are to be submitted for my personal attention and the reports are to include a general summary on the approach of each lecturer, highlighting where there are departures from the teachings of the Church.'

In years to come Giovanni would have cause to remember Archbishop Petroni's paranoia.

'You leave for the Università Statale in Milano at the end of the year.'

With that Giovanni was dismissed, but it would not be the last time the ambitious Archbishop would impact on Giovanni's career. As Giovanni would discover, the Holy Spirit worked in strange ways. Two weeks later Petroni was summoned to see the new Pope.

'Lorenzo. *Avanti. Avanti.*' The Holy Father waved Archbishop Petroni to a comfortable chair. 'Now that I am settled in I have been going over the list of suggested new appointments and I think it is time we got you out of these dusty corridors in the Vatican.'

Petroni's heart sank. His power base was firmly rooted here in the Vatican and the Vatican Bank. Immediately his disappointment swung to anger as he wondered who might have engineered the move to sideline him. Petroni struggled for control, but the Holy Father was smiling.

'I need a good man in Milano, Lorenzo. You are a very good archbishop, but I think you would make a better cardinal, *non è vero?*'

Not one given to any outward show of emotion, Petroni simply nodded in acquiescence, while inwardly he congratulated himself. 'Thank you, Holy Father. Wherever I can be of service.'

Petroni left the Pope's office with a feeling of satisfaction. If he had to serve outside the Curia, Cardinal Archbishop of Milano was a powerful post and he was on track to acquire the Keys of Peter. His satisfaction didn't last long. It rarely did and back in his own office he slowly and meticulously worked his way through the personnel files of the other university candidates. So far nothing unusual – proven attachment to the Church, all living in regional areas of Italy. One candidate, Allegra Bassetti from Tricarico, did stand out academically – prizes for academic achievement, outstanding grades in all her subjects – a bright young thing. Petroni knew her education would come to nothing, she was a woman after all. He buzzed the outer office.

'Put me through to the Bishop of Tricarico,' he demanded, annoyed at having to waste his time organising a university scholarship for some poor nun in a village backwater. Petroni would soon find out that the power of a woman should never be underestimated.

CHAPTER TEN

Tricarico

In southern Italy on the 'instep of the boot', the little town of Tricarico had stood for centuries, battered but unbowed, perched high on the side of a hill off the ancient Appian Way. The mountains had once been covered with huge oak forests but the progress of man had ensured the forests would never be seen again. Roman engineers had carved their roads through the thickly wooded countryside, and before them the Greeks had settled in the surrounding hills. The higher peaks of craggy granite were dusted with a light covering of early snow, the patchwork of fields seamed by deep ravines of limestone rising from the stony bed of the river that twisted and turned on itself through the valley.

The thirteenth-century Convent of San Domenico stood alone on a hill across from the town. The only connection between the convent and the town was an old wooden bridge at the bottom of a ravine that had been etched and scarred by the rains of countless millennia.

Allegra Bassetti crossed herself at the end of another hour of silent devotion and moved to the window of her small and sparsely furnished room, her dark hair hidden under her novice's veil, her trim figure similarly hidden under her habit. The battered once-white buildings of Tricarico seemed less dirty in the cool autumn light. The jagged and broken terracotta roofs were tinged with orange as the sunset signalled the end of another day. Under the terracotta, the people of Tricarico lived as they had lived for centuries. Cheek by jowl. Nearly eight hundred families crammed into a maze of one- and two-room houses connected by alleys, stair-streets and tunnels filled with shopkeepers, shoemakers, blacksmiths, builders, peasants and *padroni*. At the top of the hill an old Norman tower stood sentinel over the town and just below it the Bishop's faded and terraced palace formed the high side of the top piazza. Il Comùne, a dirty grey building housing the Mayor and what passed for administration, stood on the left of the Bishop's piazza. L'Ufficio Postale was on the right. The bottom piazza lay a hundred metres away at the other end of the town's main and only street. On either side of it, shops in various states of disrepair leaned drunkenly against one another.

As the shadows grew longer Allegra's thoughts turned to her family and she pictured her father, her mother and her three older brothers, Antonio, Salvatore and Enrico, hoes over their shoulders, all wending their way home after another backbreaking day in the fields. Her father, Martino Bassetti, as befitted his status as head of the household, would be riding the family donkey, precariously balancing a thatch of twigs for the evening fire on its neck. Her two younger brothers, Umberto and Giuseppe, would already be home from school and Nonna would probably be scolding five-year-old Giuseppe, the youngest of the six Bassetti children, who always seemed to be in trouble. Allegra said a silent prayer for her family and thanked God for each and every one of them, adding an additional 'thank you' that tonight she would be allowed to see them. On the last day of every second month, except when it fell on a Sunday or on a holy day of obligation, nuns who had family in the village were allowed to cross the rickety little bridge and go home for dinner. Normally Allegra looked forward to these days more than she would like to admit, but tonight she was troubled. An hour earlier she had received a message that the Mother Superior wanted to see her in her office at nine tomorrow morning, which made her wonder what sin she had committed that might have brought her to the attention of Mother Alberta.

By the time she set out for the town, Allegra was less troubled and she made her way down the clay and limestone path, on steps cut into the rock. Some of the early snows had melted and the cool clear mountain stream gurgled under the bridge as Allegra picked her way across the gaps where the weathered wood had rotted away. The climb through the gullies to the village was steep but at the top it merged into the cobblestones of an alley where a cacophony of sound echoed off the dirty walls of the houses. A dozen radios were tuned, or more likely untuned, to the only station that reached these parts and the crackling blare from the old speakers mixed with the cackling of chickens being shooed by Nonnas in black. Discordance was given an entirely new meaning as donkeys and the family pigs were herded to the back of the house towards a small bale of hay and a bowl of scraps. An argument had broken out in a house a little further up and the screams of abuse from a wife of thirty years and allegations of her husband's lust for the much younger wife next door rose above the cries of the children, animals and the rattling of pots and pans. Southern Italy at dusk. Allegra paid the chaos no attention. The sounds were no different from the ones she had grown up with in the house that had been home to generations of Bassettis and she headed for the concrete steps that formed a 'V' over the opening to the stables and walked up to the entrance of the house.

She poked her head around the open door.

'*Buonasera!*' she called.

Giuseppe was the first to spot her. Fat legs propelled him forward and he launched himself at his sister, grabbing hold of her habit.

'*Mamma! Papà! È Allegra!!*'

'*Bambino!*' Allegra swung Giueseppe into the air. His dark brown eyes shone with delight. Then she gave her Mamma, Nonna and her brothers a hug. Papà was still shaving, but when he finished preening himself in preparation for his evening in the top piazza, he welcomed her with a hug.

The big rough wooden table was already set for *la cena* with one huge bowl, *forchette* and a thick wooden *pane di tavola* – the family breadboard. *La cena* was a simple affair.

'You're just in time, Allegra,' her mother said, forking great strands of steaming linguine out of a big old pot that dwarfed the tiny two-ring burner that passed for a stove. She carried the large, chipped pottery bowl that had been around for as long as Allegra could remember and placed it in the middle of the table. Papà sliced the big loaf that Nonna had baked earlier in the day and Giuseppe reached towards it.

'Giuseppe! Not until Allegra has said grace and Papà has been served,' his mother scolded. Giuseppe withdrew his little paw and gave his sister a sheepish grin, his brown eyes sparkling mischievously.

'Bless us, O Lord, and these Your gifts which we are about to receive from Your bounty. Through Christ our Lord. Amen.'

'Amen,' the family murmured and they all waited for Papà to pour some hot olive oil and garlic over the pasta and for Mamma to grate the cheese. Papà twirled a generous serving of linguine around his fork and then the rest of the family was able to attack the big bowl all at once.

'So how are things at the convent?'

'Fine, Papà,' Allegra replied, quietly asking for forgiveness in the event that they were not. 'And here?'

Her father shrugged. He was a tall, thin man but the years had brought a hunch to his shoulders. '*Non troppo bene*. We need rain for the potatoes,' was his simple reply.

'I shall ask Mother Superior to include rain on our list of supplications,' Allegra offered, ever the optimist.

'It's the same everywhere,' said her mother. Caterina Bassetti was as short and plump as her husband was tall and thin. 'La Signora Bagarella says it is El Niño.'

'La Signora Bagarella,' Martino snorted. 'What would she know! It's just a drought. Nothing more, nothing less.'

'But we are getting them more often now, Papà. There was an article in *La Gazetta* only last week,' Allegra declared, frustrated with her father's legendary stubbornness. 'The global warming is being linked to El Niño and the forest clearing. In the Amazon they're destroying over six million acres a year. That's seven football fields a minute!'

'You read too much, *la mia sorella piccola*,' Antonio, her eldest brother admonished, quietly proud of his clever 'little sister'. He was often bemused by her passionate defence of the environment and a dozen other causes that, in his view, were equally wacky.

'And you boys don't read enough,' their mother scolded. 'The frogs are disappearing and that's a sure sign that the forests aren't well.' She too had read the article in *La Gazzetta del Mezzogiorno*. Mamma Bassetti might have left school when she was fourteen, but like her daughter her inquiring mind never stopped exploring.

The meal finished and Martino Bassetti got up from the table, adjusting his old and battered felt hat on his grey, brushed-down hair.

'It's just a drought and La Signora Bagarella would do well to stick to her knitting,' he grumbled stubbornly as he disappeared out the door towards the top piazza.

'*Buonasera*, Papà,' Allegra called after the retreating form of her father. Martino Bassetti waved without turning around, already focused on the night's activities. Ever since she could remember, every night after dinner Papà would trudge the short distance to either the wine bar or, on the first Monday of the month, to *il cinema*. The monthly western was for 'Men Only' and Martino Bassetti and the rest of the town's menfolk would sit either side of the flickering projector, its beam of light probing a pall of cigarette smoke before landing uncertainly on a chipped plaster wall.

'I don't see why the western should only be for men,' Allegra remarked defiantly.

'Because the Bishop said it is,' Enrico said smugly. Enrico was only one year older than Allegra and there had always been a constant tussle between the two 'middle' siblings. The previous week the Bishop of Tricarico had reminded them in his sermon that 'westerns were full of temptation' and that no self-respecting Tricarican woman should ever be seen in one of the torn canvas seats that littered the cinema's dusty wooden floor.

'The Bishop isn't right about everything,' Allegra retorted, getting up to help her mother clear the table. It was an early sign of rebellion against the restrictions of the Church and a male-dominated society. Coming home always made Allegra miss the normal life of the little village. She felt removed from the daily activities that her family took for granted – the evening promenade from the bottom piazza to the top piazza, gossip at the markets, chats with neighbours and friends – experiencing everything that life outside the convent had to offer. Occasionally she wondered what it might be like to have a boyfriend like some of the girls she had known at school, what it would be like to be totally comfortable with another person to voice her real thoughts and fears. Then her Catholic training would kick in and she would quickly admonish herself for such selfish and ungrateful thoughts and would later ask forgiveness in her prayers before bed. It was part of a constant tension between her faith and her own view that a woman should have a greater role in the world. An inner battle between *accettazione* and *testarda* – acceptance and rebellion.

'Do you miss living in the village?' her mother asked, as if reading her mind.

'Sometimes, Mamma,' Allegra replied carefully, as they finished the dishes. 'But then it seems such a small sacrifice,' she added quickly.

Her mother smiled, the laughter lines on her old but gentle face creasing even further. 'We are all very proud of you, *la mia figlia – molto orgogliosa*.' To have a daughter accepted for the local Order was almost as great an honour as having a son accepted into the seminary.

'*Grazie,* Mamma,' Allegra said, picking up her wooden stool and following her mother out to join two of the next-door neighbours. La Signora Farini and the champion of El Niño, La Signora Bagarella, had already set themselves up at the bottom of the concrete stairs in the old cobbled street that doubled as a 'lounge room'. The latter was repeating her assertion that the mysterious El Niño was responsible for the country's woes.

'*È El Niño non è vero?*'

La Signora Farini was having none of it. 'No. *È testamento di Dio!* It is the will of God!' she retorted passionately. La Signora Farini was President of the Bishop's Ladies' Guild and a leader of the 'Will of God Brigade'. Last week, when La Signora Marinetti's son was injured in a fall at school, it was clear and incontrovertible evidence of what befalls a family if they should miss a Sunday Mass. For many of the good citizens of Tricarico everything that happened in their lives was God's will. To the believers God was all seeing and all knowing. Every thought, every transgression was recorded. If a child died or a building collapsed, it was God's punishment on the sinful residents of Tricarico. It was retribution for failing to meet God's standards.

'Isn't it, Allegra?' Signora Farini demanded, invoking Allegra's greater knowledge of all matters theological.

'You may both be right,' Allegra said diplomatically. She had been part of this evening ritual many times and had no wish to take sides.

It was after nine when she picked her way back across the rickety bridge by the feeble light of her pocket torch. Restless, Allegra tossed and turned during the night, worrying about Mother Alberta and why she had been summoned, while her mind rebelled against the strictures of the Church. *Accettazione* and *testarda*.

Despite her nervousness, Allegra knocked firmly on the open office door.

'You wished to see me, Reverend Mother?'

'Come in, my child, and sit down.' Mother Alberta did not look up, but went on writing. She was a thin, severe-looking woman. Even when she was seated the knife-edges in her habit remained uncreased, and not a single grey hair protruded from underneath her perfectly pressed veil. The Reverend Mother's tone was not unfriendly and Allegra sat a little less nervously on the wooden chair. While she waited in the sparsely furnished office Allegra gazed at the simple wooden crucifix on the whitewashed wall behind the older nun.

When she had finished writing Mother Alberta placed her steel-framed glasses on the paperwork in front of her and clasped her hands on the desk. She looked at Allegra for some seconds before finally speaking.

'Some time ago I received a letter from our Bishop. It seems the Holy Father is concerned as to how our Mother Church can better reach out to the youth in our community, particularly in our universities. Some of the Church's younger priests and nuns are to be granted scholarships for study.' Mother Alberta swallowed, her eyes hardening. If it had been left up to her she would have simply replied that she had no one suitable, but the Bishop had insisted, pointing out that one member of her Order had achieved the highest grade in the region for science and mathematics. Allegra's nomination had been the cause of considerable friction between the strong-willed Mother Superior and her equally strong-willed Bishop, but in the end she had no choice but to give way.

'You have been enrolled to study at Ca' Granda, the Università Statale in Milano. You will take a major in the Philosophy of Religion and your options include archaeology and chemistry, although to what use you might put the latter is certainly not clear to me. You will spend the next six years studying.' Mother Alberta sniffed loudly.

'Oh Reverend Mother, me? In Milano!' Allegra gasped.

'I would have much preferred that you attended one of our fine Catholic universities,' Mother Alberta said quietly, 'but I am assured that the dangers of the state universities have been fully appreciated.' She fixed Allegra with her stern gaze. 'Nevertheless, my child, those dangers must not be underestimated.' It was as close as Mother Alberta would ever come to disloyalty to Rome. 'You have been chosen not only for your academic grades, but for your ability to resist the temptations of a dangerous world.'

'Reverend Mother, I won't let you down, I promise!'

'I'm sure you won't, my child. You will leave in the new year and our prayers will go with you. We will miss you,' she added, in a rare moment of warmth. Mother Alberta replaced her glasses, signalling that the interview was at an end.

For all of her nineteen years Allegra had lived in Tricarico. Now her Church had made a decision that would have a profound impact on her life. Despite her sadness at leaving all that she had ever known, Allegra could feel butterflies of excitement and she knew it was God's will that she be allowed to go out and explore the world beyond her Convent and her village. For once, she did not question the decision.

In a world that Allegra was yet to discover, the idea of God's will was being used in a different way. In Israel it was being used for political purposes, as an explanation to champion the interests of secular politicians. The pointers in the Middle East were coming together.

CHAPTER ELEVEN

Jerusalem

Each year it seemed that the tiny State of Israel faced an ever increasing threat.

Professor Yossi Kaufmann had exchanged his trademark open-necked shirt and slacks for the uniform of a Major General in the Israeli Defense Force. At a time of crisis all Israelis had obligations to the defence of the country and being a Professor of Mathematics and Honorary Director of the Shrine of the Book didn't excuse him from those responsibilities. The Head of Israeli Intelligence was ill and Professor Kaufmann, a previous Head of that office, was the ideal choice to step into the breach. The distinguished, square-jawed Israeli was tall with sandy-coloured hair and a face that bore the creases of the years. Yossi Kaufmann was widely respected, but today even his standing might not be enough to avert disaster. He looked around the Cabinet Room with increasing concern.

The Prime Minister sat at the centre of one side of the big table. In front of each minister was a salmon-coloured folder marked 'Top Secret – Cabinet Eyes Only'. Some of them, Yossi knew, would not have read his report so he had backed it up with a detailed verbal brief, but to no avail. It was the detail they were all ignoring.

'And so, Prime Minister,' Yossi concluded, 'notwithstanding the strategic importance of the Palestinian village of Deir Azun and its close proximity to Jewish settlements in the West Bank, we have no firm intelligence that the attacks on our settlements originated from that particular village.'

'But given its location it seems logical?' The question came from the Defense Minister, Reze Zweiman. A big walrus of a man and a veteran of both the 1967 Six Day War and the 1973 Yom Kippur War, he was a staunch member of the hard right faction of the Likud Party and no friend of the Arabs. Zweiman had seen too many of Israel's sons die on the battlefield.

'We have an open mind, Minister,' Yossi replied, 'but you can be assured that we are doing everything that is humanly possible to pinpoint the source of these attacks.'

'That may well be, Prime Minister.' The Defense Minister shifted his gaze from Yossi to the small man sitting in the imposing brown leather chair, the back of which was just slightly higher than the others. Prime Minister Chenamem Gebin looked very grim; his broad, tanned forehead creased and worried.

'But these Arabs,' the Defense Minister went on, 'need to be taught a lesson they will not forget. It's not only the future of the government, it's the very future of Israel that is at stake here. There have been no fewer than three attacks on the settlements in the past week; fifteen Israeli citizens, including six children, are dead and three members of the Armed Forces have also been killed. This village is a seething mass of terrorism and we should force the occupants out. Permanently.'

'No one is condoning these attacks, Reze, but we need to tread carefully.' It was the Foreign Minister, Shome Yadan. Yossi Kaufmann silently thanked the voice of reason coming from the elder statesman of the Likud Party. 'Right now,' the Foreign

Minister continued, 'the United States and international opinion are firmly on our side but if we go in hard against a Palestinian village without proof, and there are civilian casualties, that support can change very quickly, particularly outside the United States. We'll be seen as the bad guys, especially if we force the Palestinians out and replace the village with an Israeli settlement. Worse still, it will fuel Muslim resentment against the West.'

Reze Zweiman sniffed arrogantly, making no attempt to disguise his contempt for anyone he labelled a 'dove'. 'You seem to forget one thing, Minister. At the end of the day, Israeli flesh and blood is the responsibility of this Cabinet and this government. Not some shiny-arsed bunch of international bureaucrats in the State Department in Washington or anywhere else. The only way we will ever make Israel secure is to occupy the West Bank to the extent that it is firmly under our control. Over time the strategy should be to incorporate it into Israel and force the Palestinians out.'

'Where would they go?' asked the Minister for Agriculture.

'Who cares,' the Defense Minister shot back. 'Jordan. Lebanon. Baluchistan. As long as they're out of Israel.'

'The Palestinian people are a reality and our policy should reflect that.' The Foreign Minister's voice was quiet but insistent. 'If we push them over our borders and take over their land it will turn international opinion against us and I predict the rest of the Arab world will be more inclined to provide support and bases for terrorist operations. I would urge a more restrained approach.'

'I am being restrained!' the Defense Minister exploded. His nostrils flared and he spat the words across the table. 'The Arabs are a creeping black cancer that needs to be excised!'

The Prime Minister was used to outbursts from his Defense Minister and without responding he turned to his media adviser and asked, 'What are the public opinion polls saying?'

'Three to one in favour of direct action against the Palestinians, Prime Minister.'

The Defense Minister sniffed again and leaned back in his chair with a self-satisfied look on his face.

Silence settled over the Cabinet table until finally the Prime Minister broke it.

'I think there are arguments on both sides,' Gebin said, trying to keep the fractious Cabinet together. 'If we move against the village of Deir Azun it is clear there are dangers, especially if there are heavy casualties. It is equally clear that we can't just sit back and allow these attacks to continue.' He turned to Yossi. 'You say there are three houses that are possibly suspect in this village?'

'Yes, Prime Minister, but they are only suspect. Our source is unreliable.'

'It seems to me that if these houses are suspect they should be destroyed. And if that is not enough the whole village should be destroyed,' said the Minister for Defense.

'Taking that into account . . .' Again the Prime Minister refrained from responding to the roaring walrus opposite him and this time he looked to the Israeli Defense Force Chief of Staff, Lieutenant General Halevy, a smaller version of the Defense Minister. 'I propose an operation of limited scope,' the Prime Minister ordered. 'The village is to be surrounded and occupied, but not permanently. The occupants of the houses that are suspect are to be brought in for questioning and the soldiers are to be instructed to use minimum force.' He turned to his media adviser again. 'And those directions should be spelled out to the international media, but only after the operation has commenced.' Prime Minister Chenamem Gebin surveyed the faces at the table. No one spoke. 'If there is nothing further we will meet at the same time tomorrow.'

Yossi felt distinctly uneasy. As the Prime Minister issued his orders of restraint, the unmistakable gleam of hatred in the Defense Minister's eyes intensified.

Deir Azun

The earth in the Samarian hills of the West Bank was red and parched. As the sun began to set behind the mountains that cradled the little Palestinian village of Deir Azun, Yusef Sartawi scooped up the last of the bitter black olives from the nets spread at the bottom of the gnarled and twisted tree he'd been working on. Rivulets of sweat ran down his bare chest and back, soaking the top of his faded baggy shorts. He stretched to his full height of 186 centimetres and pulled his shoulders back, pressing against the dull ache in his muscles and momentarily resting his forehead against the rough wood of the ancient tree. As four generations of his family before him had done, and as the Greeks and Romans had done centuries before that, Yusef shouldered his battered wicker basket of fruit. His cracked leather boots kicked up puffs of red dust as he marched purposefully down the side of his father's hill between the rows of trees.

'Muhammad!'

Three rows over Yusef's ten-year-old brother sat up, startled. Guilt was plastered all over his young face.

'They won't pick themselves, you know.'

Muhammad got to his feet sheepishly.

'I was just having a minute's rest,' he said, doing his best to sound indignant.

'I suppose that's why you were asleep,' Yusef retorted, but he said it without malice. At twenty-one Yusef was the second of five children and as a Palestinian he was one of the lucky ones. His parents had worked long and hard to ensure that all their children would receive an education, and now Yusef was enrolled at college in Nazareth, training to become a sound engineer. During semester breaks he came home to help with the harvest. Yusef and his younger brother Muhammad were separated by two sisters, Liana, who had just turned fifteen, and seventeen-year-old Raya. Their eldest brother, Ahmed, was studying to become a cleric and was in his last year at Al-Quds University in Ramallah. Today Ahmed was coming home on two days' leave to celebrate Liana's birthday. It would be good to see him, Yusef thought. And to have the family together again.

As he approached the old wooden pressing shed Yusef could hear the unmistakable rumble of the big granite wheel, the *Hajar al-Bad*. The family donkey was plodding a well-worn circular path, laboriously grinding the fruit into a paste, the leather straps and wooden harness creaking in protest at the weight of the wheel. Yusef's father, Abdullah Sartawi, was hard at work bearing down on the paste in the old lever press. He was not as tall as his sons, but he was lean and fit, his shoulders broad and muscled from years of working in the groves. His dark, closely cropped hair was peppered with grey and the years of Palestinian sun could be seen in his face. Abdullah Sartawi was a man of strong ethics and had passed on his rock-solid faith in Allah and Islam to his family which, despite the Israeli occupation of Palestinian land and the constant threat of war and uprising, gave the Sartawi family a sense of purpose, dignity and hope.

The first-pressing virgin olive oil was trickling into the vat where it would settle. Yusef sniffed at it appreciatively. Sartawi oil was among the finest in Palestine and the subtle aroma had seeped into every crevice of the shed.

'It is a good crop this year, eh Yusef?'

'The best, Father, the best.'

'I will tell your mother tonight, this year I think we might be able to afford a water pump for the house.'

'She would like that, Father.' Ever since Yusef could remember, water for the household had to be hauled in buckets. The mud-brick house with its dirt floors was at the end of one of the red dusty tracks that led from the village square. Every day his mother Rafiqa or, now that they were old enough, one of his sisters would trudge down the hill and queue at the rusting, squeaky water pump.

Up at the house in the old kitchen preparations for Liana's birthday were well under way at the rough wooden bench.

'Tonight we have an appetiser,' Rafiqa announced, delegating the slicing of the sweet green peppers to Raya and the tomatoes to Liana. '*Shakshoukeh*.' A dish of sweet green peppers and tomatoes fried in olive oil with thick slices of garlic, pepper and salt.

Despite the years of village life and five children, there was a certain elegance about Rafiqa. She was slightly built, with burnished olive skin, an oval face and dark hair parted severely. Over the years her serenity had calmed the energy of a house full of children. Raya was like her father. With his heavy eyebrows, she was quiet and reflective. Liana, as much as she was allowed to be, was energetic and rebellious.

'Your father has brought in a chicken.'

Liana's dark eyes danced. 'Chicken *fatteh!*'

'Just for you, my child, with your favourite seasoning – cardamom and nutmeg.' Rafiqa stoked the cantankerous old wooden stove with an expertise born of long years of practice. Water for the rice simmered in a well-used blackened pot.

Judging the temperature of the oven to be about right, Rafiqa placed the chicken and some onions in a battered baking pan, poured some of the precious water over the top and placed it in the oven. She reached for the pita bread she had baked earlier in the day and sliced it ready for frying.

'What time will Ahmed be home, Mother?' Liana asked excitedly.

'Any time now, I expect,' Rafiqa replied, her dark eyes softening at the thought of seeing her eldest son again.

The old bus from Ramallah wound up the hill towards the dusty square. Ahmed was surprised to find the driver having to slow down to negotiate his way past lines of Israeli tanks and armoured vehicles on either side of the road. The command vehicle was at the head of the tank column. Four thin aerials flexed in the light breeze and a group of officers in kevlar helmets were clustered around a senior officer spreading a map out on the desert camouflage of the jeep's bonnet. Towards the top of the hill two Israeli helicopter gunships circled menacingly overhead. Above them, even more menacingly still, two F-16 fighters supplied by the United States were turning, their wings flashing briefly in a sun that on the ground had already been obscured by the mountains.

The bus juddered as the driver crashed the gears; it took him three attempts to get it into low, the gearbox clanging more loudly each time. Ahmed held onto the rusty iron of the seat in front as the bus lurched forward. A great cloud of black smoke belched from the various orifices of what passed for an exhaust system and a little more grime was caked onto the cracked and rusted blue and white paint. Ahmed knew he was almost home.

'Ahmed! Welcome home!' His father embraced his son warmly as he walked through the door. 'The sun is almost set. You are just in time to lead us in prayer,' he said, stepping back and holding his son out at arm's length so he could look at him. Ahmed embraced his mother, brothers and sisters and after they had all washed, Abdullah led them out to the veranda where seven old but clean sheepskin mats faced, in accordance with the Sartawi's *qibla,* towards Mecca. Each day, regardless of where they were or what they were doing, every member of the Sartawi family would observe the second of the Five Pillars of Islam – Prayer or *Salat.* In any one day there were five prayers that were regulated by the position of the sun. At dawn, *Fajr;* after midday, *Zuhr*; late afternoon, *Asr.* Immediately after sunset, *Maghrib*; and before midnight, *Isha.* Together they stood saying the intention or *Niyya* to say four *rakas* of a prayer for God.

Allah Akbar – God is Great
Bismillah ir-rahman ir-rahim – In the name of God, the Most Gracious, Most Merciful . . .

Finally, with the whole family still sitting, Ahmed intoned first to the right and then to the left.

Assalamu 'alikum wa – Peace and Mercy of God be on you.

And with that, the Sartawis rose and gathered for Liana's dinner celebration.

'There were Israeli tanks on the road as the bus pulled in, Father,' Ahmed said as they sat on the mats around a low table.

His father shrugged. 'It's just show,' he said philosophically. 'They're only soldiers doing the politicians' bidding.' Not even a whole regiment of Israeli tanks could disturb Abdullah's quiet optimism or diminish his thanks to Allah for his daughter Liana. Abdullah Sartawi could not have been more wrong.

Jerusalem

The Israeli Chief of Staff, General Halevy, strode into the Command Centre and planted himself in front of one of two big operations maps that showed the West Bank and the Gaza Strip in great detail, along with the rest of Israel and the Golan Heights. General Halevy stared at the borders of the West Bank. How he detested the Palestinians.

The border with Jordan was a straight line formed by the west bank of the Jordan River and the Dead Sea. From there it was as if a big kidney had been cut from Eretz Israel, a cut from the land. This Arab scum fouled the surrounding landscape. To the south of Jerusalem were the Palestinian cities of Bethlehem and Hebron. To the north, Ramallah, Nablus and Jenin, and not far from Jenin was the festering little pustule of Deir Azun. The slightest excuse and he would erase it from history.

'Get me the Commander of the 45th Brigade.'

The Director of Operations nodded to his communications officer.

'Eight Nine Zulu this is Zero Alpha, fetch Falcon, over.'

The speakers in the Command Centre crackled and the voice of Brigadier General Ehrlich boomed in loud and clear.

'Zero Alpha, this is Eight Nine Zulu, Falcon speaking over.'

Halevy took the handset and depressed the transmit button.

'Eight Nine Zulu, this is Eagle. Confirm H-hour, over.'

'In ten minutes, over.'

'Roger. Minimum force might apply but should there be any resistance, the lives of your soldiers are not to be put at risk and you are to respond accordingly, over.'

'Understood, over.'

'Be prepared to stay as long as is necessary,' Halevy said, adding yet another layer of interpretation to the Prime Minister's original direction. 'Out.'

Brigadier General Eliezer Ehrlich towered over his commanders with an understated presence. His demeanour was quiet and self-contained. Highly respected by superiors and subordinates alike, the tank general was a soldier's soldier. He always made sure he was never far from the front. General Ehrlich passed the handset back to his signaller. Privately he didn't have much time for politicians and even less for generals who followed them like an arselick. Whatever had happened in Panic Palace today, he thought, had caused old rubber dick Halevy to get his knickers in a right royal twist. Something was not making sense. Fleetingly he recalled the conversation he'd had with his wife Marilyn as he'd left his house the previous morning.

'I wish you didn't have to go. I have a bad feeling about this, Elly. When will they see this is not the answer?'

'I know. One day they will try for peace,' he'd answered, giving her a hug, telling her not to worry. Marilyn and his two sons, Yoram and Igael, waved until his staff car was out of sight.

As dusk approached Brigadier General Ehrlich kept his troubling thoughts to himself. It was not his place to complain, especially in front of his men. His task was to minimise the danger.

For both sides. Ehrlich knew better than anyone the difficulties of the operation they were about to conduct. It was a filthy war and the expectations of those who judged from the comfort of their leather armchairs in the Cabinet Room were well nigh impossible to meet. Expectations that men who were trained to kill could, in the heat of a fire fight, somehow determine the difference between an innocent civilian and a terrorist. It was an advantage that terrorists and insurgents had been putting to devastating use ever since Nebuchadnezzar had patrolled the banks of the Euphrates.

'There are three suspect houses,' he said, 'Here, here, and here.' General Ehrlich tapped his finger on the map. 'The one at the end of this track is highest on the list. Regardless of resistance we should remember that the majority of these people are innocent civilians. Only use as much force as is necessary. Any questions?'

His commanders shook their heads in unison. Eliezer Ehrlich looked at his watch.

'Synchronise watches. Ten, nine, eight . . .

Deir Azun

Salim a'Shami was only nineteen but was already a veteran of more than twenty hit-and-run attacks against the Israelis. The Israelis had killed his two brothers, and Salim's hatred was etched on his soul.

Hamas had trained him well, and the wiry young Salim had been a good pupil. His dark eyes were clear and his face devoid of emotion as he showed his two fifteen-year-old accomplices where to set up the mortar base plate behind some rocks in the hills overlooking Deir Azun. To the south, the outline of the Mar'oth minaret could be seen clearly against an orange skyline; to the east, he picked out Mount Malkishua in the Gilboa range. Taking a battered compass from his pocket he took a back bearing on each. Working deftly, Salim converted the magnetic bearings to grid and marked the exact position of their mortar base plate on his precious 1:100000 map. Taking an equally battered and treasured pair of binoculars, he scanned the road leading in to the village below. He stopped scanning and adjusted the binoculars to get the clearest possible focus. The tall figure of Brigadier General Ehrlich was unmistakable. This man had been pointed out to him on more than one occasion. The general and some of his officers were looking at a map that was spread out on the bonnet of a jeep. Salim knew they would not get a better chance than this. The two boys had finished setting up the mortar and were eagerly waiting for orders. Motioning to them with a slow hand movement signalling they should remain calm, Salim took a bearing on the jeep and made a rough alignment of the mortar bipod. More deliberately he calculated the range and direction to the target and adjusted the direction and elevation on the mortar sights. There would be no time for any corrections as this would allow the Israelis to take cover. The four high explosive rounds had all their charge bags attached and he gave the thumbs up to fire.

Chooonk. Chooonk. Chooonk. Choonk. One after another the rounds were dropped down the tube. Looking up Salim could see the small black shapes of death arcing silently towards their target. With all four rounds gone and without waiting to be told, the two younger boys quickly dismantled the tube and sight from its base plate. Salim didn't move as he observed his target through the binoculars. All four rounds exploded either side of the road and a slow smile spread across his young face.

Death to the Israelis.

'Let's get out of here! The next hill. And stay low!' he hissed. The hunters were now the hunted.

Death to the Arabs.

'Watches synchronised at 17:52.' These were the last words General Ehrlich uttered. With a thumping roar the first mortar round landed barely 20 metres away. Red earth shot skywards and a lump of hot, jagged shrapnel ripped a great chunk out of General Ehrlich's skull, spattering the jeep and his officers in blood and flesh, killing him instantly. Another piece of shrapnel tore his wallet from his shirt pocket and it lay open 10 metres away. A photograph of Marilyn and the two boys covered in dirt. Three more explosions peppered the Israeli position but the soldiers of the 45th Armoured Brigade were already hugging the red earth in the ditch at the side of the road and the rest of the casualties were light.

'Medic!' David Levin, General Ehrlich's young Brigade Major, knew that it was a futile gesture and with a murderous look in his eyes he reached for his compass and took a bearing on the muffled thumps he had recognised as coming from a Palestinian mortar. Crouching in the ditch he called up the lead Cobra gunship.

'Hawkeye One Five, this is Eight Nine Zulu. Bearing Three Eight Five Zero. Enemy mortar base plate in the hills south-west of here, approximately one two hundred metres over!'

'Hawkeye One Five, copied out.' Captain Raanan Weizman hauled on the collective and banked the aircraft into a tight turn. The Cobra AH-1G gunship, made famous in the Vietnam War, was barely a metre wide with the gunner's seat in the nose and the pilot on a raised seat behind. Captain Weizman had only been flying this particular machine for ten months, but it felt like an extension of his flying gloves. The 1800 horsepower Lycoming T53-L-703 turbo shaft engine whined effortlessly as the rotors swatted the air.

'Did you copy that, Dan?' Two quick bursts of squelch on the intercom between pilot and gunner indicated that he had and Raanan checked his heading while his gunner readied the Cobra's rockets and three-barrelled 20mm cannon.

Like an angry wasp with a blue Star of David in a white circle tattooed on its body, the sandy-coloured Cobra's nose tilted forward as it touched on 130 knots. Captain Weizman put the aircraft into a dive and he and his gunner scanned the hills in the distance, while on the road below the men of the 45th Armoured Brigade prepared to avenge the death of their Commander.

'Got 'em! Eleven o'clock, bottom of the second ridge.'

'Roger.' Captain Weizman calmly adjusted his heading.

Thirty seconds later the aircraft recoiled slightly as two rockets snaked towards the ground. Before they exploded below the three fleeing figures, the 20mm cannon smoked like a chainsaw and Raanan's young gunner held the crosshairs on the targets as the deadly rounds followed the trajectory of the rockets. The young Muslims were torn into shattered fragments of flesh and bone as the Cobra's rockets and 20mm cannon found their mark.

Death to the Arabs.

Death to the Jews.

'So how are your studies going, Yusef?' Ahmed asked.

'Radio circuitry this semester. I got an A,' Yusef announced proudly, his dark eyes flashing. 'And there might be a chance for an opening with Cohatek.'

'The events people?'

Yusef nodded. 'Although there is only one position and there are ten of us going for it from our university.'

Cohatek was the biggest promoter of concerts and other events in Israel. Despite the violence the government had encouraged as much 'normalcy' as possible and big events were still staged in both Jerusalem and Tel-Aviv. Competition to join the company was fierce, and only the best were chosen. Even Palestinians were not ruled out if they were cleared and at the top of their field.

Suddenly four explosions echoed around the hills. Abdullah Sartawi frowned and conversation stopped. Everyone looked at the ceiling as if expecting something to fall on the house.

'Peace be upon us,' Abdullah said finally, getting up to stoke the fire. 'We are out of wood. I meant to split some before dinner.'

'Sit down, Father. We'll fix that. Come on, Yusef, move it,' Ahmed said, cuffing his brother good-naturedly on the shoulder.

'What about Muhammad,' Yusef grumbled, giving their youngest brother a questioning look. 'He's spent the day sleeping in the olive grove.'

Muhammad looked sheepish but shot Yusef a triumphant look as his mother intervened.

'Two is enough to split the wood, Yusef. Muhammad can help Raya and Liana clean up in the kitchen.' Muhammad rolled his eyes, his look of triumph disappearing as Yusef wrinkled his nose at him from the back door before joining Ahmed, heading towards the trees at the bottom of the yard where the logs were kept ready for splitting.

'I have some good news, Yusef,' Ahmed said, putting his arm around his brother. 'I am to be assigned to Mar'Oth.'

'That's only twenty minutes walk away. You can help with the harvest,' Yusef said with a huge grin, secretly pleased that he would see more of his brother.

'It's good to see him again, Abdullah. He is such a good boy.' Rafiqa's eyes glistened with the hint of a tear. 'I wish he wasn't so far away.'

Suddenly the roar of centurion tanks and armoured personnel carriers shook the whole house. Moments later, in a simultaneous assault from the front and rear of the house, both doors were kicked off their hinges and ten helmeted Israeli soldiers burst into the room, Uzi machine guns cocked and ready. Raya and Liana screamed but as their mother moved to comfort them she was knocked to the ground by a soldier.

'Stay where you are, you Palestinian scum!' Sergeant Emil Shahak had been Eliezer Erhlich's centurion tank driver twenty years before, when Ehrlich had joined the 45th as a troop commander. For Sergeant Shahak the long war against the Arabs had suddenly got personal. Brigadier General Ehrlich was one of the finest generals in the long and proud history of the regiment, but now he was dead, killed by the people from this shitbag village. Emil Shahak's blood was up and he and his soldiers were itching for any excuse to exact revenge.

Rafiqa was racked with pain as she lay on the dirt floor quietly sobbing. The Israeli soldier had rifle-butted her with such force that two of her ribs were broken. Muhammad rushed towards his mother, brandishing a saucepan at the nearest Israeli. The young soldier, a reservist on his first operation, fired instinctively. The burst caught the Sartawi's youngest son in the chest and he was dead before he slumped to the kitchen floor, a bright red stain seeping across the cotton of the white shirt he'd worn specially for his sister's birthday. Raya and Liana screamed again, cowering in the corner of the kitchen. Abdullah Sartawi was pale with shock, and as he tried to make a move towards his son he was struck with a rifle and thrown to the floor.

'Nobody move!' Flecks of saliva had appeared at the corners of Sergeant Shahak's mouth. 'Watch those two!' he yelled. The young reservist jerked his Uzi uncertainly, first at Raya and then at Liana, his bottom lip quivering as the enormity of what he had done began to sink in. 'Search the other rooms!' Emil Shahak was bellowing now.

Yusef started towards the house, but Ahmed pulled him back and down into the cover of the trees. 'No, Yusef!' he hissed. 'Think. They have guns, we don't.'

'There is firing, Ahmed!' Yusef's eyes filled with tears.

'And there will be more if you burst into the house,' Ahmed urged him quietly. 'Allah is with us but we can't help if we're dead!' Ahmed kept his arm wrapped tightly around his brother as they lay on the ground, staring at their house.

'Empty, Emil.' The look on the corporal's face was one of resentful disappointment as he reported to his sergeant.

'*Ben zsona*! Son of a bitch!' Sergeant Shahak walked over to Liana and Raya. With a burning frustration he kicked their dead brother as he stepped over him. Pistol in one hand, his other clenched, he stood contemptuously over the terrified girls. Emil Shahak was furious that he and his men had not found what they were looking for.

He grabbed Liana by the chin and wrenched her face up, forcing her to look at him. Her face was pale and beautiful, but her eyes blazed with a resentment that only fuelled Sergeant Shahak's sense of impotence. He turned to his corporal, drawing his lips back into a snarl.

'You can have the ugly one,' he sneered, pointing his pistol at Raya. He grabbed Liana's hair and pulled her to her feet, pinning her slender arms together with his huge, hairy hand.

'I get first crack at her crack,' he rasped. 'Privilege of rank.'

'No! Please!' Abdullah Sartawi was on his knees, pleading, his weathered face streaked with tears.

'Palestinian scum!' Sergeant Shahak kicked at him but despite the pain Abdullah grabbed the Israeli's boot and clung to it in desperation.

'No! No! No!' he cried.

Sergeant Shahak had crossed the point of no return and he struggled to free his boot. He pointed his Jericho pistol at Abdullah and fired. Twice.

Rafiqa screamed and fell on the body of her husband. Shahak moved the sight of his pistol to the back of Rafiqa's neck and fired twice more. Rafiqa convulsed and her body slid down beside Abdullah's.

'Palestinian shit!' Sergeant Shahak shoved Liana into her parents' bedroom, banging the flimsy door behind him.

Numb with shock and dimly aware of what was going on, Liana began to struggle to free herself. Sergeant Shahak's grip was unbreakable.

'*Zsona! Inahl rabak ars ya choosharmuta!* Bitch! Go to hell with your fucking father!' he yelled in Liana's ear, his fetid breath hot against the side of her face. He cracked her on the back of the skull with his pistol and threw her on the bed. In a frenzy he tore the clothes off her slender body, and ripped his trousers down to his boots. Liana froze at the sight of Shahak's ugly erection, acutely and terrifyingly aware of what was about to happen.

With a guttural growl Shahak climbed on top of her, pinning her hands above her head. Liana shrieked as he forced himself inside her, grunting like an animal, his body giving off a stench of stale sweat and the diesel of the armoured personnel carrier that was his home.

'You're next, Yigal.' Shahak came out of the bedroom hitching up his camouflage pants as he eyeballed the young reservist.

'Me?' Yigal croaked, shaking his head.

'There's a first time for everything, son, and you're never going to get an easier one than this. Get in and give it to the bitch.'

'Come on, Yigal!' one of the regulars yelled. 'Are you a man or what?'

Feeling more miserable and confused than ever, Yigal allowed himself to be pushed into the room. Liana was curled up on her parents' bed, her head against the wall, her body shaking with uncontrollable sobs.

Yigal thought he was going to be sick. He wanted to comfort the girl but he was upset over killing her brother and was too afraid to touch her. He waited until he thought enough time had elapsed for him to claim he had done what they had sent him to do, then dropping his trousers, he opened the door and emerged, pulling them up and doing up his fly.

'Next!' he called, his voice dry and uncertain.

'Ehhhhhh!' A roar of approval echoed around the Sartawis' house.

The flimsy doors to the two rooms opened and shut until the last of the Israeli soldiers had finished with both sisters. After releasing his rage, Shahak became officious as he considered the implications of what he and his men had done.

'Get the two Kalashnikovs from the carrier,' he barked at a soldier. The soldiers all knew where their sergeant kept two Palestinian weapons hidden. They were a legacy of a previous engagement and Sergeant Shahak had decided against handing them in, keeping them as insurance against any investigation or allegations that might be made against his troops.

'Listen up. Tonight didn't happen.' Each of his soldiers looked at the dirt floor. Sergeant Shahak took one of the weapons and wiped it clean with his sweat-stained scarf. He grabbed Abdullah's lifeless hand, made prints on the rifle and left it beside the body. He did the same with the body of Muhammad. Raya and Liana's despair could be heard from the bedrooms as Shahak's Corporal took the Army-issue camera from its case, the flash illuminating Abdullah and Muhammad.

'Tonight our general was killed by Palestinian terrorists and the reports of this scum giving them shelter are true. Get the two bitches out here.'

Raya and Liana could hardly stand.

'I'm giving you five seconds to get out of here!' He shoved them out the back door and watched the girls stumble into the night. Shahak emptied his magazine into Raya's back and then into Liana's.

'No fucking witnesses!' he snarled at his troops. 'And remember, it didn't happen. Let's go!'

Ahmed and Yusef, deep in shock, waited amongst the trees until they were sure the soldiers were gone. In a daze they stared at the carnage of what had once been their home, their family gone.

The Defense Minister, Reze Zweiman, and General Halevy fronted the cameras together.

'Brigadier General Ehrlich was one of the nation's finest soldiers and our deepest condolences go to his wife and sons,' Zweiman intoned, opening the media conference to the 'when, where, and why' of what might have happened at Deir Azun.

One of the final questions came from Tom Schweiker from CCN.

'The Palestinians are claiming there was a massacre at Deir Azun, General. Is the Israeli Government going to investigate these claims?'

'I can assure all of you,' Halevy replied, barely keeping his anger in check, 'that the only massacre at Deir Azun was the death of an Israeli commander tasked with keeping Israelis and peace-loving citizens free from terrorism. You've seen the photographs. These people were armed and have been responsible for countless attacks against innocent civilians.' Israel's Chief of Staff closed his folder, ending the tightly controlled conference.

Tom Schweiker watched the men and their minders leave, and wondered.

Back in the Minister's office General Halevy nodded in agreement as Reze Zweiman vented his spleen on the Palestinians. The loss of one of their commanders had serious implications for the public image of the government and Reze knew his political enemies would use it to turn up the heat.

'Keep the fucking media away, especially that Schweiker shit from CCN. Occupy the village for as long as it takes and get rid of the scum that live there. If need be, carry out armoured manoeuvres in their olive groves.'

'Leave it to me, Reze. By the time I've finished with them they'll want to live anywhere but on the West Bank.'

On the dusty red hillside on the edge of the Sartawi olive grove Israeli soldiers looked on sullenly as the villagers buried Abdullah and Rafiqa Sartawi, their two daughters Raya and Liana and their youngest son, Muhammad. After the last of the mourners had left Ahmed and Yusef stood alone at the gravesides.

'You should have let me try, Ahmed,' Yusef said angrily through his tears.

'And have you dead, too?'

'You don't know that.' Yusef spat the words at his brother. 'Even poor little Muhammad tried to protect them!'

'What will you do now?' Ahmed asked, realising that it was not the time to argue the point.

'What does it matter!' Yusef stormed away, tears streaming down his cheeks, a hatred for the Israelis and a new hatred for his brother's cowardice blazing in his heart.

With great sadness Ahmed watched him go. He sat beside his buried family trying to make sense of it all. He would not see his brother again for many, many years, and then only fleetingly in circumstances that no one could have predicted.

CHAPTER TWELVE

Tricarico and Milano

'*Buona fortuna,* Allegra!'
Tricarico's top piazza was crammed with well-wishers and a huge banner had been hung from the old stone balcony of Bishop Aldo Marietti's palace. News travelled fast through the hill towns and there was not a single villager for miles around who was not aware that the Vatican had selected Allegra for this singular honour.

'The Holy Father has approved it, personally,' La Signora Farini, leader of the 'Will of God Brigade', said to anyone who could hear her over the more than slightly out of tune town band that was playing with gusto. The music reached a crescendo as Tricarico's only car driven by the portly Bishop Marietti inched its way through the crowd. Allegra's father had taken the front seat and Allegra, her mother and her two oldest brothers were crammed into the back of the little Flavia. Nonna wiped away a tear while Giuseppe clung to Nonna's faded black dress, waving vigorously, his curly black hair shining in the morning sun that bathed the craggy granite of the mountains surrounding Tricarico.

It took over an hour to travel the 20 kilometres to the valley below the village. Bishop Marietti was not renowned for his driving skill and he struggled to keep the little car on the rough mountain track that led to the train station on the single rail line that served hill towns such as Tricarico and Grissano.

'We are all very proud of you, Allegra,' Bishop Marietti said, as they climbed onto the small deserted platform. 'You will be a wonderful ambassador for the Church.'

'I won't let you down, Bishop Marietti. I promise.'

Mamma wiped at her tears as Papà beamed. The mournful whistle of the Taranto–Napoli Express could be heard in the distance as the old locomotive struggled through the mountains further down the line. The ramshackle train arrived in a cloud of steam and the driver waited patiently during the seemingly endless ritual of hugs and kisses. The whistle echoed across the valley again and the train lurched forward.

'*Arrivederci! Scriva presto!*'

As the train rounded a bend and the little group frantically waving on the siding disappeared from view, Allegra settled back into her empty compartment with its cracked leather seats and wire luggage racks, her mind in turmoil. A short while later the train slowed for a herd of goats on the track, nibbling at the weeds and in no hurry to get off. Allegra was oblivious to the heated exchange between the driver and the gesticulating, wizened goatherd that could be heard above the noise of the engine. She reflected on how hard it had been to leave home to join the convent across the ravine. Milano seemed like the other side of the world. The train lurched and she gazed out the window at the granite foothills and beyond them to the mountains of Basilicata, rebellion and excitement competing with sadness and acceptance. *Accettazione* and *testarda*.

With so many thoughts buzzing around her head, Allegra could not settle down and she spent the twenty-four-hour trip dozing fitfully. When Trenitalia's overnight service from Napoli via Roma arrived at Milano's Stazione Centrale adrenaline took over. She clambered down the carriage's absurdly high steps and looked around for a Father Giovanni Donelli, the senior postgraduate student charged by the Vatican to meet her. It was seven in the morning and as Allegra stood on the platform she was faced with what seemed like thousands of people rushing to work. She wanted to take in everything at once – the people, the fashions, the warm glow of the cafes, the smells, the noise. She knew she was ready to take on the biggest challenge of her life and she scanned the crowd eagerly.

As if on cue, a ruggedly handsome priest materialised out of the mêlée. He was dark-haired and at 175 centimetres, just a little taller than Allegra.

'*Buongiorno, Signora!*' Allegra was immediately captivated by the warmth of the brilliant smile that lit up Giovanni's tanned face, and his blue eyes held an irreverent sparkle that was infectious.

'Sister Allegra Bassetti?' he asked, extending his hand. '*Mi chiamo* Giovanni Donelli. *Benvenuta a Milano!*'

'*Grazie,* Father. You are very kind to have met me at such an early hour,' Allegra replied shyly.

'I know habits die hard, no pun intended, but you must get used to calling me Giovanni,' he said, taking Allegra's battered suitcase and guiding her through the crowd. The Piazza Duca D'Aosta was even more frenetic than the train station but it didn't faze the taxi driver at all. The car horn had been installed to overcome that problem and they charged across Via Vitruvio towards Ca' Granda, a short distance away in the historic centre of the city. Allegra's eyes widened; from the single-car mountain town of Tricarico to Milano was a thrilling culture shock.

'I'll call by later tonight to see you're OK,' Giovanni said after he made sure Allegra was officially admitted to the university. '*E benvenuta di nuovo a Milano!*'

It did not take Allegra long to unpack her meagre belongings. With a mixture of trepidation and excitement, Allegra headed out to explore the busy grounds of the old university. Built in 1456 it had once been a hospital but now the Renaissance archways and lawn courtyards were home to the liberal arts faculties of Milano's Università Statale. Orientation week was in full swing and everywhere she looked there seemed to be students handing out brochures and pamphlets. Candidates for the Student Union, invitations to join anything from the Ca' Granda Debating Society and book clubs to UNICEF. There was even a University Film Club and from the look of the upcoming attractions, Allegra decided that the Bishop of Tricarico could be more relaxed about the 'men only westerns'. An hour later and overwhelmed by information Allegra headed through Ca' Granda's main stone archway towards Milano's cathedral.

Il Duomo was only a short distance away and when she arrived Allegra stood for a time in the piazza, staring up at the vast cathedral in awe. Three and a half thousand statues adorned the roof and the stone walls, dominated by a 45-metre gold statue of the Madonna. Inside, the five aisles were separated by massive stone pillars and high above the space reserved for the choir, Allegra could see the small red light that marked the vault where, since 1841, a nail from the Cross had been secured. The world's third largest church, after St Peter's and the cathedral in Seville, it had taken over four hundred years to build.

Allegra had promised Nonna she would say prayers for the family, as Nonna had insisted that in Milano they would carry greater weight, and she sank to her knees in one of the pews, not far from the altar where Napoleon had been crowned King of Italy. Silently she mouthed the words, 'Hail Mary, full of grace, the Lord is with you. Blessed are you among women, and blessed is the fruit of your womb Jesus . . .' Allegra asked her God to protect her family and to see her through the coming years of study. 'Holy Mary, Mother of God, pray for us sinners . . .'

The security of the Catholic Church she loved so much could not be put into words. From deep within Allegra felt that she was destined to serve the Church and she thanked God for the opportunity to study so that she might help others. In her naivety Allegra was unaware that her quest for knowledge and deep spirituality would also lead her down a path filled with pain and confusion. Her quest would take her into an unknown world of deceit, discovery and the brutal reality of life and death.

As the sun set behind the Alps to the north of Milano, Allegra waited in her room for Giovanni. The thought of a man visiting her seemed strangely exciting, although she knew Mother Alberta would have been horrified, even though Giovanni was a priest. In the Mother Superior's world men were not to be trusted in other than a crowded room, and even then caution was advisable. Allegra's guilt about men was deep seated and she constantly fought against it. One particular incident often crept into her thoughts, causing her to pray for forgiveness.

Allegra had just turned sixteen in the early spring of her last year of school and one Sunday afternoon she had gone walking on the banks of the river. She turned off the old Roman Appian Way and made her way down to the river through one of several farms outside Tricarico. The winter snows still capped the highest parts of the mountains, but the lower snows had melted and the river tumbled over dark boulders worn smooth over the ages. She wandered along the bank until she came to her favourite place at the base of a large rock. It stood like a sentinel at a sharp bend in the river and was hidden from the fields by a small grove of oak trees. Allegra stretched out on the grass and as the warm afternoon sunshine filtered through her light cotton dress, she drifted off into a peaceful sleep.

Sometime later she woke, startled by a movement a little further downstream. Sitting up she instinctively clasped her jacket to her as she heard someone approaching.

'Carlo! You startled me!'

Carlo grinned. His swarthy young face was tanned and his long black fringe swung over his forehead.

'Sorry. I didn't mean to,' he said, sitting down beside her.

'How did you know I was here?' Allegra demanded, sounding more accusatory than she meant to.

About two months before, Carlo Valenti had suddenly arrived in Tricarico with his family. The Valentis were Sicilians from Marsala, and their purchase of a large farm had created more than a ripple of conversation among the town's traditional inhabitants. Dark rumours of drug money and Mafia connections and contracts on Carlo's father had ebbed and flowed down the alleys and laneways of the little mountain village; but drug money and the Mafia were not the only topics of conversation, especially among Allegra's class-mates.

'He's not *that* good looking,' Allegra's best friend, Anna, had said.

'Probably arrogant,' Rosa, another of their group, decided.

'Full of himself. All Sicilians are,' agreed another. Among the young women of Tricarico Carlo had become an instant celebrity.

'I saw you walking down the road,' Carlo replied truthfully, not adding that he had seen her walking on the two previous Sundays and today he had deliberately waited for her to appear.

'Carlo Valenti! You followed me here.' Allegra was mildly offended by the invasion of her favourite place but strangely pleased that she should find herself alone with someone like Carlo.

'It wasn't like that,' he said. 'Sometimes I think things are just meant to happen. It's God's will,' he added, using a line that had generated more than a little success with the young women of Marsala, particularly when he thought religion might be a barrier to conquest. 'When I saw this figure walking from the top of the farm I hoped it would be you, and it was.'

Allegra felt a warm flush and her mind raced. Despite his suspicious background, she found the young Sicilian exciting. She knew her family wouldn't approve, especially Papà, but deep down there was a small, insistent voice. It was one thing to be dux of her class but quite another to realise any of her potential. If she was ever to spread her wings and explore the world outside the mountains of Tricarico, the small voice seemed to be saying, she would need someone who was a little more worldly than the awkward young men of her area.

'How are you finding Tricarico?' she asked. 'I suppose it's a little dull after Sicilia?'

Carlo shrugged. 'It's different and the farm needs some work. It's what you make of it, I suppose.'

She nodded and they fell into silence. The breeze was gentle and the sound of the river was soothing. Allegra began to relax and unselfconsciously she leaned back against her sentinel rock.

'Why did you leave Sicilia?' she asked, breaking the silence.

Carlo grinned disarmingly. 'No doubt my father had his reasons. There are some things I don't ask, but I wouldn't believe everything you hear. We used to work my uncle's farm in Marsala, and when this one came up, my father thought we should make the move to buy one of our own,' he said. He leaned over and kissed her on the cheek. Startled, Allegra turned to face him and he kissed her on the lips.

At first Allegra didn't know what to do, then feeling slightly heady from the warm sunshine, she responded. Slowly at first, then she let Carlo take her in his arms and they slid onto the grass. She could feel him hard against her and suddenly one part of her mind was arguing with another. Carlo kissed her again and started to unbutton her dress.

'No . . .' she said weakly, her voice strangely hoarse. Before she knew what was happening, Carlo had undone her bra and when he kissed her nipples she found herself responding again, pressing against him. Carlo's hand slid inside her pants and Allegra felt as if she was being lifted on a wave. 'No . . .' she whispered again. She gasped as Carlo guided her own hand to his trousers, which were undone. He was wet and hard.

'No! You mustn't!' she said, struggling against him now. Fear had taken over, extinguishing her own desires. The harder she struggled the stronger he held her. He bit her nipples roughly as he continued rubbing her hand against him. Tears fell onto Allegra's cheeks as Carlo arched back and let out a low growl. She could feel him on her hands, first warm, then sticky, until finally he released his grip.

Allegra half ran, half stumbled along the river back towards the village. Tears ran hotly down her cheeks as she struggled to breathe. When she was sure he was not following her she sat down on a rock to calm herself, her tears slowly subsiding.

It was late afternoon by the time she managed to wash the stains from her dress and, with her eyes still filled with tears, Allegra knelt by the river.

'Blessed Mother, I have sinned before you and all of heaven and I am not worthy to gather up the crumbs under your table.' She asked the Blessed Virgin to pray for her and intercede on her behalf, for she knew that she would surely burn in hell. She recalled the Gospel of Mark very clearly and any sense of *testarda* had, for the time being, vanished. The nuns had quoted Mark often enough. Her Lord had said that 'if your eye causes you to stumble, tear it out; it is better for you to enter the kingdom of God with one eye than to have two eyes and be thrown into hell, where the worm never dies and the fire is never quenched'.

Later that night Allegra lay awake in the family bedroom, her sobs hidden by the snores of her parents and brothers. How could she possibly be forgiven for such a momentous sin. She recalled the words of her Lord and Saviour and the truth began to dawn on her; this was a message. A reminder of the evils of sex that had so often been emphasised by the Bishop. The Lord Jesus would never ever have allowed himself to get in such a dreadful position. He had been perfect. Matthew was very clear. He had been celibate for the sake of heaven. 'Let anyone accept this who can,' her Lord had commanded.

What had happened between her and Carlo was a mortal sin because she had allowed it to start of her own free will, and she realised what she must do. She would join the local Dominican Order and devote the rest of her miserable life to making amends. Already the pain and the guilt seemed to be easing as she recalled the vision of St Catherine of Siena where the Blessed Virgin Mary had held Catherine's hand while Christ put a ring on it. It would mean sacrificing all her dreams of exploring a world outside Tricarico, but it seemed a trivial price to pay for the ultimate marriage. She would become a Bride of Christ. The Mother Superior at the Convent of San Domenico had described it as the most mystical union, a gift that came directly from God.

Allegra was brought back to the present with a start by a quiet knock on the door. She opened it to find Father Giovanni balancing a basket of biscuits, coffee, some sweet cakes and chocolate.

'Essentials for students!'

'Father,' she replied awkwardly. 'Do come in. Forgive the sparseness,' she said, offering him the only chair.

'Please! Don't apologise. Mine is exactly the same. And remember, it's Giovanni. Have you settled in?'

'More or less. It all seems a bit daunting.'

'It always is for the first week or so until you find out where everything is. This is your first time at a university?'

Allegra nodded. 'It was a real surprise, Father . . .'

Giovanni raised his eyebrows with a questioning grin.

'Forgive me, I'm not used to calling priests by their first name.'

'It's all part of the program. Did they give you a briefing at your convent?'

'Not really Fath—Giovanni,' Allegra said, still struggling with the familiarity. 'In fact, Mother Superior seemed a little cross about it.'

Giovanni laughed. 'Sometimes change does not come easily,' he said, 'but I think there is method in John Paul I's idea.' A dark cloud shadowed Giovanni's thoughts at the memory of the man he had so admired and respected. 'We will have to write a brief report for the Vatican at the end of each semester,' he continued. 'Our impressions, how we relate to other students, their reactions, that kind of thing, but I dare say if we can open up the dusty corridors of the Curia to what is happening in the real world that will be no bad thing.'

Allegra started to relax, warming to the company of a man who seemed to know so much about everything, yet seemed so down to earth.

'Have the others arrived?' she asked.

'Oh. You haven't heard? Father O'Connell's diocese is so desperately short of priests his Bishop won a last minute reprieve and I'm not sure who the other Sister was, but she resigned from her Order last week, so it's just you and me, I'm afraid. If there's anything I can do to help you settle in, let me know. I'm in Room 415 down the corridor,' he said. 'If you feel like getting out of here at the end of the week, there's a great little pizzeria that's within walking distance. On a Friday night they do a terrific wood-fired pizza and wonderful pasta especially for impoverished students like us.' Giovanni bade her *buonanotte* and Allegra felt a little less alone.

That had been at the start of the academic year. As the year went on, although she was still troubled by some of the faculty teaching at Ca' Granda, Allegra was more at ease with her new environment. With each passing week, she found herself looking forward to Friday night discussions with Giovanni over pasta.

Allegra hurried back from the little bookshop she'd found in one of the backstreets of Milano, a second-hand copy of John Allegro's

The Dead Sea Scrolls Revealed in her bag. She checked her watch and realised she had just enough time to get to Professor Rosselli's introductory class on the Dead Sea Scrolls without actually running. Still wary of the traffic, she checked it twice and crossed the Corso di Porta Romana that led back to the university. Allegra slipped into the lecture theatre, just as the lecture was beginning.

'*Buongiorno. Mi chiamo* Professor Antonio Rosselli.' A small man in his fifties with a weathered and lined face, the Professor wore a coat that was frayed and round black-rimmed glasses that were perched halfway down his large Roman nose. His white hair flopped in disarray, covering his large ears, and his dark eyebrows were bushy and as untidy as his hair.

'Not one to spend much time with a comb,' Allegra thought, intrigued by his mischievous smile.

'Over the next few weeks we will be looking at the Dead Sea Scrolls,' he began. 'Over two thousand years ago, a mysterious sect of the Essenes lived in an isolated settlement known as Qumran on the northern shores of the Dead Sea. They were not, as the Vatican and others have suggested, a reclusive, pacifist and celibate bunch of monks, but rather one of the most advanced and enlightened communities of ancient civilisation. Their lifestyle followed that which Pythagoras had ordained for the ancient Greeks. Dressed in Pythagorean white, they rose before dawn to pray, and like Pythagoras, the Essenes were very advanced astronomers, mathematicians and well versed in philosophy.' Professor Rosselli paused to tamp his pipe. 'In this balanced society where women were considered the equal of men, work would cease at midday and they would bathe naked together in a ritual cleansing in one of several deep pools they had built in Qumran, before eating a simple communal meal,' he continued. The Professor's enthusiasm for the ancient community was obvious. 'The Essenes meticulously recorded every aspect of their lifestyle in an extensive library of scrolls. Part of their philosophy was to make their knowledge accessible to future generations. When the Roman armies advanced on Jerusalem in 68 AD the Essenes hid their scrolls in the caves above Qumran.' Professor Rosselli surveyed his class over the top of his glasses. 'But ever since the discovery of the Dead Sea Scrolls, there have been rumours of one particular scroll that reveals far more than the life-style of the mysterious sect of first-century Judaism,' he said, his voice holding more than a hint of conspiracy. 'Does anyone know what scroll that might be?' Professor Rosselli asked.

Giovanni felt a sudden chill. 'The Omega Scroll,' he answered.

'Yes, the Omega Scroll,' Professor Rosselli said, his eyes gleam-ing. 'The modern day equivalent of the Mummy's Curse. As soon as people find it, mysterious things happen. It is also said to contain a revelation for humanity, a terrifying warning for civilisation. A secret so great that many seem to have been silenced in their search for this elusive archaelogical treasure.'

A revelation for humanity. Giovanni thought back to what he had witnessed in the Pope's apartments, and he wondered whether there was any connection between Professor Rosselli and Professor Fiorini who had provided the brief for Pope John Paul I. Giovanni had tried to track the retired Fiorini down without success, and he resolved to speak to Professor Rosselli after the lecture.

'So how did these scrolls come to light?' Professor Rosselli, one of the world's experts on the Middle East had a rare ability to trans-port his students back through time and space, and Allegra was not the only one to see the heat distorting the hills surrounding the Dead Sea. It was 1947.

The morning sun beat mercilessly on the Bedouin tents clustered in camps on either side of the long dusty road that since before the time of Christ had led from Jerusalem, east towards Jericho and down to where the River Jordan flowed into the Dead Sea. Centuries before, Christian pilgrims had been astounded at the sheer lifelessness of the water, and had given the sea its name.

About 30 kilometres from Jerusalem the road forked. Straight ahead the river formed the border with Jordan, and the road led on to Amman. To the right, the road turned and led south towards Qumran where the cliffs stood like sentinels, watching over the ruins. The orange flintstone was caught by the sun, and the heat haze rose from the shimmering surface of the sea. On the other side lay Jordan and the wadis and canyons of the biblical mountains of Moab and Edom.

The young Muhammad Ahmad el-Hamed, nicknamed edh-Dhib or Muhammad the Wolf, cursed his errant goat and scrambled up the side of a cliff. By the time he reached the dusty ledge where he had last spotted his charge, the nimble-footed goat was nowhere to be seen. Edh-Dhib rubbed the back of his hand across his sweaty forehead and wiped it on his dust-encrusted robe. It was more than his life was worth to lose a sizeable chunk of his family's livelihood and he stayed very still, listening and scanning the desolate cliffs for any sign of life. Then he saw it. From the ground below it would have looked like an indentation in the rock, but up here edh-Dhib could see it was the entrance to a cave.

'So, my little goat, that's where you've got to. We shall have to get you to come out,' he murmured to himself. Edh-Dhib picked up a small stone and silently picked his way over the boulders. Stopping, he took careful aim. Even without a slingshot edh-Dhib was deadly accurate, and the stone flew straight through the centre of the entrance. Instead of startling a goat, he heard the sound of shattering pottery echoing out of the cave. Edh-Dhib moved forward, clawing his way up the cliff until he reached the narrow entrance. Squeezing himself through he dropped to the floor to find that he was in a narrow, high-ceilinged cave that was no more than 20 metres at its widest and about 65 metres long. Finding that he could stand up edh-Dibh looked around. There was no goat and no footprints in the fine dust, and no other sign that anyone had been around for a very long time. In fact, it had been nearly two thousand years since anyone had set foot inside the cave. In the gloom at the far end, nestled in the sands of centuries, stood several earthenware jars. The silence was eerie. Like the Egyptian farmer who had found manuscripts in a jar at Nag Hammadi two years before, edh-Dhib wondered what spirits of the past lurked within the cool dark cave and he backed slowly out towards the entrance. Two hours later he finally retrieved the goat.

Later that night he confided in his friend Abu Dabu. His friend was wiser by two whole years and he scoffed at any suggestion of spirits.

'What if there is gold inside the jars?' Abu Dabu suggested greedily, his dark eyes reflecting the light of the glowing embers of the fire.

'Who would it belong to?' edh-Dhib asked, uncertain as to what they should do.

Abu Dabu didn't hesitate. 'Whoever finds it, owns it,' he said emphatically. 'There is a Turkish trader in Bethlehem, Ali Ercan. My uncle has dealt with him before and he will know who will give us a good price with no questions asked.'

Early next morning, emboldened by his friend's wise counsel, edh-Dhib led the way up the treacherous cliffs. He paused just below the entrance to the cave and cupped his hand to his ear, motioning for his friend to listen. The only noise was the wind growling across the face of the cliffs. Abu Dabu pushed past him impatiently, scrambling over the broken rocks and disappearing into the crevice. By the time edh-Dhib had dropped onto the soft, sandy floor, Abu Dabu was already at the far end of the cave.

'Give me a hand,' he urged, his voice rising with excitement. Together they wrestled the largest of the jars into the feeble light of the entrance. Abu wrenched off the large earthenware lid and reeled back as a putrid odour filled the cave. Covering his face with his robes he peered into the jar, reached in and took out a long oblong package.

THE OMEGA SCROLL **119**

'It doesn't look like gold,' edh-Dhib ventured, not hiding his disappointment.

'No,' Abu Dabu muttered, fingering the ancient linen cloth. He tore impatiently at the end until what looked like a roll of old leather appeared. The rest of the jars yielded more rolls that were intact, as well as thousands of fragments that had succumbed to the ravages of time.

'Whatever they are, edh-Dhib, someone thought it was necessary to hide these scrolls where they would not be found,' he said, his Bedouin cunning coming to the fore. 'We'll hide them in my tent. Tomorrow we'll take them to Bethlehem.'

Edh-Dhib had been told that sometimes an ancient scroll could be worth a lot of money and he tightened his grip on the hessian bag.

'What time did you say the trader opened his shop?' he asked Abu Dabu for the third time.

'Don't worry,' the older boy assured him. 'He will be here soon.'

As was his habit for the past thirty years, Ali Ercan walked down King David Road towards his antiques shop near Manger Square in Bethlehem. The snows of Christmas had long since receded and Bethlehem, perched on a hill about 8 kilometres south of Jerusalem, was in for another scorching day. The tower of the Church of the Nativity dominated the town and the surrounding Judaean desert as it had done since the days of the Crusaders, but neither the ancient surroundings nor their religious significance to the faithful concerned Ali. As long as the faithful had money to spend, he would be happy. Money for any of the hundreds of olive wood statues of Christ, the Virgin Mary or the Saints, or perhaps copper plates and goblets or brightly coloured Bedouin rugs and cushions. For the more discerning customer, an old and battered safe held some very fine filigreed silver. Ali catered for the discerning but less scrupulous customer as well, especially the ones interested in black market antiquities.

As he approached his shop, instead of tourists, Ali could see that two Bedouin boys were waiting for him and one of them was carrying a tattered hessian sack.

'What do you want?' Ali muttered. He fumbled for the large bunch of keys he kept suspended from a belt beneath his robes and wrestled open the rusting security grate.

'My uncle sent us,' edh-Dhib answered hesitantly. 'We have some leather scrolls he thought you might be interested in.'

Beckoning the boys inside the shop that smelled of spices and olive wood, he checked the street and quickly closed the door behind them. Ali cleared a space on a bench at the rear of the shop and with the aid of an old silver magnifying glass he peered at the strange looking characters on one of the scrolls. Finally he put the glass to one side and picked his large nose thoughtfully, not immediately able to decipher the ancient script.

'Where did you get these?' he demanded.

'In a cave near Yam Hamelah,' Abu Dabu answered quickly, not wanting edh-Dhib to be any more specific than the Dead Sea.

'They might be of interest but you will have to leave them with me while I make some inquiries. I will send you word in a few weeks. In the meantime, don't tell anyone that you have found them, or of our meeting.' With that he ushered them back out to the street.

Ali Ercan spent the next two nights examining the boys' find. He still could not decipher the script but three scrolls appeared to be more carefully protected than the others, although one of them was in pieces. He separated them from the rest, put them in olive wood boxes and hid them in a cavity under the floorboards. The Ministry of Antiquities had visited the previous week and inspected his safe, but they were not likely to rip up the floor. Covering the floorboards with a rug, Ali resolved to get some advice from the Syrian Metropolitan at the Monastery of Saint Mark in the Old City of Jerusalem.

'So what might be in these scrolls that seems to so worry the Vatican?' Professor Rosselli concluded, abruptly bringing Allegra away from the Old City of Jerusalem and back to the lecture room at Ca' Granda.

'There seems little doubt that in the past the Vatican has vigorously opposed their publication,' he said, his eyes twinkling again. As Allegra would come to know well, Professor Rosselli loved a good mystery. 'Ever since their discovery the Vatican has prevented any access to the scrolls, other than by a team of a few privileged and, for the most part, Catholic academics from Europe and the United States. A group that has become known as the International Team. Curiously, the Vatican has gone to great lengths to assert that Christ had nothing to do with the Essene Community at Qumran, a stone's throw from where John the Baptist baptised him in the Jordan.'

The *accettazione* side of Allegra was becoming more and more troubled as the discussion went on, but when she glanced at Giovanni he seemed very relaxed, encouraging Allegra's *testarda*, her rebellious side, to inquire more deeply into the inflexible dogma of her faith.

'Which has prompted some to suggest there is something in the scrolls, and the Omega Scroll in particular, that the Vatican will not allow into the public domain,' Rosselli continued. 'The American scholar Margaret Starbird has pointed out that the authors of the New Testament used gematria. This is a literary device where numbers are assigned to the letters in the words. Certain phrases add up to equal significant sacred numbers which in turn convey hidden meanings. I suspect that part of the answer lies in what has become known as the Magdalene Numbers.'

Professor Rosselli took a piece of chalk and turned to the blackboard.

'Neither Hebrew nor Greek have separate symbols for numbers, instead individual letters stand for different numbers. If we take Greek,' he said, writing on the board:

Alpha   α = 1
Beta   β = 2
Gamma   γ = 3

'And so on,' Professor Rosselli explained, exposing the entire alphabet, down to omega, Ω.

'Which means that each word in Greek or Hebrew has a numerical value that is obtained by adding up the sum of the letters. Margaret Starbird draws our attention to Christ comparing the Kingdom of God to a grain of mustard seed. The Greek for mustard seed, κοκκος σιναττεως, totals 1746. At first glance, Christ's description of the Kingdom of God as a grain of mustard seed seems very peculiar, but it is deceptively simple.' Professor Rosselli's eyes danced as he warmed to the mystery.

'The number 1746 is made up of the union or sum of 666 and 1080, and as a Jewish rabbi, Christ would have been well aware of the significance of the numbers 666 and 1080. For the Essenes, 666 represented the solar energy of the male. Many interpretations of the parable of the mustard seed are bizarre,' he continued, 'but when we understand that the other part of the union – the number 1080 – represents the lunar creativity of the feminine, the meaning becomes very clear. Not only does this parable link Christ with the Essenes, but the numerical code of the mustard seed is a simple and clear statement from Christ that the Kingdom of God, the Spirit, is not exclusively male but a combination of male and female, a balance of yin and yang. Christ's 1746 of the mustard seed contains the lost feminine of Christianity.' Professor Rosselli paused, a slightly sad look on his face. 'The early Church Fathers brutally suppressed this message. Can anyone give me an example?'

Again it was Giovanni who answered.

'All copies of the Gospels of Thomas, Mary Magdalene and Philip, the Gnostic Gospels, were destroyed on the orders of

Iraneaeus, the Bishop of Lyons in 180 AD because they threatened the power of the male priesthood.'

Rosselli looked at his pupil with a growing respect. It was unusual, he reflected, to strike such a visible, intelligent candour in a Catholic priest.

'Or so the early Church Fathers thought,' Giovanni continued, 'but someone took the trouble to spirit copies of the Gnostic Gospels down the Nile and bury them in an earthenware jar at Nag Hammadi, where they remained for nearly two thousand years. The Gnostic Gospels were carefully wrapped,' he said, 'and a Bedouin Arab discovered them digging for *sabakh*, the under soil that *fellaheen* use to fertilise their crops on the banks of the Nile. Many scholars are now of the view they should be included in the Bible to provide the feminine balance that was suppressed by the early Church Fathers.'

'Not unlike the Dead Sea Scrolls and found just two years apart,' Professor Rosselli added. 'It's almost as if the cosmos has coordinated the time of their respective discoveries, linking them together, and Father Donelli raises a critical point. The religions of the ancients had a balance of gods and goddesses and it is only in relatively recent times that religion has been hijacked by the male of the species. I am one of those who think that male-dominated religions are dangerously out of balance and as a result, they have done untold damage in the world. With the advent of weapons of mass destruction, male-dominated religions are a threat to humanity.'

It was a chilling prophecy and Giovanni wondered once again how much Rosselli knew about the contents of the Omega Scroll. It was as if Rosselli had read his thoughts.

'It would be interesting to see if Starbird's theories on the hidden numbers of the New Testament are borne out by the Omega Scroll.' Rosselli's eyes darkened momentarily. 'Although I suspect the Omega Scroll contains a great deal more than the Magdalene Numbers. After the mid-semester break we will examine the significance of the number I think the Vatican fears most: 153. I have always been an optimist and some of you may wish to do some research on that over the break. It may have something to do with fish and cities falling out of the sky,' he added mischievously. 'And when we come back it would be useful to hear from someone other than Father Donelli.'

La Pizzeria Milano was crowded with students but even 'out of uniform' Allegra spotted Giovanni at one of the small corner booths.

'*Buonasera*, Allegra!' Giovanni got to his feet to allow Allegra to squeeze into the small booth. He poured her chianti from the carafe he had ordered. 'Pasta is coming,' he said. '*Salute!*'

'*Salute*,' she responded and immediately relaxed in his company, as usual.

'So what did you think of old Rosselli today?' Giovanni asked, leaning forward to make himself heard over the normal student excesses of a Friday night.

'He's provocative, isn't he! I enjoy that, although I'm still on a pretty steep learning curve. Until I got to Milano I hadn't even heard of the Essenes and their Dead Sea Scrolls, much less that the Vatican might be blocking access to them, but what really got me thinking was the Omega Scroll. Do you think it exists?'

Giovanni was saved from answering immediately by the arrival of the pasta, two steaming plates of *puttanesca*, spaghetti with olives, tomatoes, anchovies, chillies, garlic and basil. He knew he had to tell someone about his concerns over the connection of the death of Pope John Paul I and the Omega Scroll, as a way of trying to guarantee that a search for the truth would continue. Everybody connected with research on the Scroll had disappeared without a trace, academic papers had gone missing and prominent scientists had been ruthlessly discredited. Giovanni was wary of dragging anyone else into the dangerous maelstrom that clearly surrounded the Scroll, but he needed a confidante. Allegra was the only person he could implicitly trust. She had one of the finest minds he had encountered in a long time.

'You think he was murdered,' Allegra said solemnly after Giovanni had recounted the events at the Vatican.

Giovanni nodded. 'Albino Luciani posed a threat to too many people, not least to our Cardinal Petroni here in Milano. The Vatican Bank's criminal activities bothered him greatly, but that was not the only thing threatening the Curia. Petroni and the Curial Cardinals vigorously deny it but I know from the papers that Luciani wrote when he was in Venice, papers that have now mysteriously disappeared, that Luciani was strongly in favour of artificial birth control.'

A few short months earlier Allegra might have been taken aback. It had been a steep intellectual climb from the little backwater of Tricarico but the *testarda* in Allegra was rapidly taking hold.

'I'm sorry I didn't meet him,' she said. 'I used to accept the teaching against contraceptives but I'm coming round to his point of view. If I remember it correctly, the basis for prohibiting birth control in the twentieth century is a three-thousand-year-old text in Genesis where God puts Onan to death because he spills his semen on the ground, rather than perform a duty for his dead brother's wife, right?'

Giovanni nodded, smiling. He had come to enjoy their Friday night intellectual joustings.

'A text that was passed on by word of mouth for thousands of years before it was even written down,' Allegra added. 'That sounds more like an excuse for the male hierarchy to use sex as a means of control, and a pretty powerful one.'

'It has always had far more to do with maintaining the power of the priesthood than any logical theological basis and Luciani would have agreed with you,' Giovanni responded, a touch of sadness in his voice. 'He was a great loss, not only to the Church but to the world. We were talking about birth control in Venice one day and he told me he had just read a report that over a thousand children die every hour from malnutrition. He saw effective birth control as part of the solution and after he was elected he told me that at last he was in a position to do something about it. In the end I think his views on contraception, his decision to investigate the Vatican Bank and his discovery that the Vatican had bought the Omega Scroll all combined to sign his death warrant.'

'You didn't get more than a glance at the brief?'

Giovanni shook his head. 'Knowing what I know now I should have gathered up the entire file. Petroni arrived very quickly.'

'Very odd that he was fully dressed at that hour,' Allegra agreed. 'Why didn't you try to recover the Omega Scroll? Why not go to the Press?'

'As soon as I could I searched the Secret Archives but someone had clearly been there before me. I seriously thought about going public, but I think there is more chance of finding the Omega Scroll if I stay low for the moment. Without the Scroll the Vatican would simply deny it as a figment of my imagination and put it about that poor old Donelli's become unhinged as a result of Luciani's unfortunate heart attack.'

'From what you've told me that's the least they would do. What about Professor Fiorini, can't you go to him?'

'This is where it gets very murky. I went to see Rosselli after the lecture today. I only gave him the bare bones of what I've told you, that I thought the Omega Scroll existed, and he seemed quite upset. He wouldn't say much, but he told me Professor Fiorini disappeared the day after he returned from Rome.'

'Murdered?'

'It's the classic "Italian Solution" and if these people in the Vatican are as closely linked to the Mafia as I think they are, it's quite possible. It won't stop Rosselli speculating in his lectures, but I'm guessing he's been warned not to take his investigation too far and deep down he's more than a little frightened. He told me to be very careful.'

'So what do we do?'

'For the moment, nothing. Play our cards close to our chests. Eventually something will give, the truth always outs.'

Giovanni reached over and refilled Allegra's glass.

As they walked back towards the university Giovanni linked his arm through Allegra's. A little voice told Giovanni that this was wrong, but the chianti seemed to blur the insistent voice and he rationalised that he had met his soulmate. Had he been more honest he might have admitted that the feelings he had for this intelligent and beautiful nun had thrown him into turmoil.

'What are you doing over the semester break? Will you go home?'

Allegra shook her head. 'I can't afford it. I guess I'll stay here and wrestle with Mary Magdalene, 153 and what was it? Fish and cities falling out of the sky,' she said, laughing.

It was Giovanni's turn to shake his head. '*Quello non va!* That won't do at all. I am going home to see my folks – I've even been invited to say Mass. You must come too. My family said they would love to meet you.'

'I couldn't,' Allegra said quickly, without quite knowing why.

'Why not?' Giovanni demanded.

'Well, there is Professor Rosselli's research,' she responded lamely.

'My, my! He has got you worried. I'll tell you what. While we're at home we'll spend some time on the pros and cons of Christ and Mary Magdalene and we'll write it up when we get back.'

'That would be nice,' she said, giving in to his logic. Allegra felt the warmth of Giovanni's body and nearly put her head on his shoulder. *Accettazione* and *testarda*. Deep within, strange feelings were stirring. The voice of Catholicism was telling her that it was wrong to be this close to a man. Like Giovanni, she put it down to feelings of friendship for someone whose intellect, warmth and compassion she had come to admire deeply.

'Do you know, I don't think I've even asked you where you live.'

'Used to live,' he corrected her, 'but I still call it home. It's a little fishing town on the Gulf of Policastro. Maratea. Have you heard of it?'

'No, but now I'm looking forward to visiting it very much.'

'You will love it. Everyone is very friendly and the mountains look like they fall into the sea. It is the perfect escape for students.'

'Mmmm,' murmured Allegra dreamily, and without a thought to what she was doing, she rested her head on his shoulder.

Giovanni knew he had to change the subject before the voice in his head completely disappeared. 'One day I would like to go to the Holy Land and see all of those places that are in the Bible and visit Qumran.'

Allegra lifted her head from his shoulder.

'And we could find the Omega Scroll – and put an end to all of Rosselli's assignments,' she said and her eyes sparkled.

Without realising it, the quest for the missing Omega Scroll had begun and their lives would change for ever.

CHAPTER THIRTEEN

Maratea

Giovanni stopped his battered Fiat on Mount St Blaise over-looking Maratea. He and Allegra got out and walked up the stone steps to the very top of the mountain where a wealthy Maratean resident had erected a 22-metre-high statue of Christ, arms spread, watching over the little town of Maratea nestling on the side of the mountain below. They stood looking at the stunning view, a light breeze blowing Allegra's hair.

'Oh Giovanni, *è bellissimo!*'

The Apennines tumbled into the Tyrrhenian Sea, forming a rocky coastline that stretched north and south as far as Allegra could see, the sharp jagged peaks finally fading into the clouds. Carob trees competed for space with pines, smaller oaks and olive trees. Nestled in each of the promontories were little inlets of emer-ald lapping at the rocks and sand, the water turning a deeper blue further out into the Gulf of Policastro. Below them, the road coiled down the mountain like a piece of curling spaghetti until it reached Maratea itself, and further down, the port of Maratea Marina. The bright blues, reds and oranges of the wooden fishing boats drawn up on the beach and moored behind the rocky breakwater added to the charm of the little port. This place was seemingly untouched by tourism and the pace of a more urgent world.

Allegra, conscious that once again she and Giovanni were standing very close together, closed her eyes. The sun felt warm on her face. Fleetingly she thought of her family back in the cold, misty hills of Tricarico. She missed them dreadfully and wrote regularly, but in her heart she knew that she could never go back. Allegra had come to realise that the Church and the little convent of San Domenico had put her in an intellectual and experiential straitjacket. Her faith was as strong as ever but she was starting to spread her wings. The Vatican's control over Allegra was being eroded.

'*È molto bellissimo*, Giovanni. Really lovely.'

Giovanni smiled and let his arm rest around her shoulders. 'I thought you'd like it,' he whispered. 'While we're here we'll borrow a boat and have a picnic on one of those little beaches down the coast.'

Allegra leaned in against him. She wanted to stand there for ever.

'Sure beats doing assignments,' she murmured.

The road down to the town contoured around the steep side of the mountain and Giovanni had to coax the ageing gearbox into second to supplement the Fiat's equally ageing brakes. When they reached the little port Giovanni parked in one of the several empty spaces on the piazza beside the marina.

'See that house with the orange shutters?' Giovanni was pointing to a group of whitewashed concrete houses at the southern end of the beach overlooking the port. It was as if the little village had been carved into the side of the mountain. In front of the houses a small limestone cliff dropped vertically down to the water and the brightly painted wooden boats rocked gently under its protection. Behind the houses the dense brush of the foothills rose sharply to meet the majesty of the Apennines. 'That's home.'

'It's lovely, the view must be wonderful.'

'It is, but don't be deceived by the view. That part is expensive but we Donellis are simple folk. The house was owned by my great-great-grandfather and it's been in the family ever since.'

'It looks lovely just the same, although I'm feeling a little nervous about meeting your family.'

'You shouldn't be. It's not as if I'm bringing home a fiancée.'

Allegra's embarrassment was obvious, her blush rising through her tanned skin, and Giovanni instantly regretted the comment.

'Sorry, I didn't mean that the way it sounded.' For a moment there was an awkward silence between them as they each wrestled with thoughts they dared not put into words, then just as quickly the moment passed.

'Giovanni!' Giovanni's sister Maria had spotted the car, and run like a young schoolgirl through the alleys and laneways to meet her favourite brother. 'Giovanni!' She flung herself at him, kissing him enthusiastically on each cheek.

'Maria! You are taller than me now.'

'That wouldn't be hard, would it,' she said, raising her eyebrows. Her dark eyes twinkled with the same mischief that Allegra had come to love in Giovanni. Maria's black hair was cut short around her oval face. At just fifteen Maria Donelli was already a beautiful young woman. Without waiting to be introduced, Maria turned to Allegra.

'You must be Allegra,' she said. *'Benvenuta a Maratea!'*

'Grazie, Maria. You are very kind.'

'And look!' Maria said. Giovanni winked at Allegra. He was used to his sister's boundless enthusiasm for life. Maria was pointing across to the arm of rocks that formed the protective breakwater for the little port. 'There's Papà and the boys!'

Signor Donelli, like his father and his father before him, had been a fisherman all his life and, like Giovanni, he was short and wiry. Giuseppi and Giorgio, however, were both tall and broad across the shoulders, the former a legacy of distant genes and the latter a result of leaving school as soon as they were able for a life hauling fishing nets. Papà and Giovanni's brothers had just finished repairing the nets and had folded them back onboard the *Aquila del Mare*, the *Eagle of the Sea*, in preparation for the next day's fishing. But that would not be tomorrow. Tomorrow was Domenica and the whole family and the rest of the little village would be in church. Giovanni had been invited to celebrate Mass with Monsignor Vincenzo Abostini, the long-serving priest who had inspired Giovanni to follow his heart and his faith.

'*Vi vedremo a casa!* See you at the house!' Giorgio yelled, waving and grinning beside Papà and Giuseppi.

'*Fate presto!* Don't be long!' Maria picked up Allegra's bag. 'Come on you two. Mamma is waiting. She has been cooking all morning.'

'You could put jumper leads on her and she'd power the whole village,' Giovanni said to Allegra.

'I heard that,' Maria flung over her shoulder as she headed across the piazza.

Giovanni slung his bag over his shoulder and they followed Maria out of the piazza into a labyrinth of narrow flagstone alleys that were covered by concrete archways. Here and there, the damp had seeped down from above and the once white arches were covered in a dark green mould. At intervals a bare light bulb was suspended from an ancient blackened chain. The alleys were made narrower still by the storekeepers' habit of hanging their wares from hooks in the concrete – copper pots and pans, wicker baskets and bags, and coffee mugs suspended in wrought-iron racks. Everywhere there were steps coming down from houses or up into shops and bars. Some freshly whitewashed, others worn and cracked, the steps twisted impossibly, pot plants lining one side or the other. Doorways were overhung with terracotta tiles and occasionally a faded canvas shade. Finally they reached what seemed to Allegra just another part of the maze when Maria bounded up a whitewashed staircase lined with the inevitable pot plants.

'Mamma! Mamma! Giovanni! *È a casa!* He is home!'

Giovanni had always spoken of his mother with great affection and the matronly La Signora Sophia Donelli was as Allegra had imagined. A ready smile in a round face that was creased with the lines of wisdom. She came out from the kitchen, arms outspread, and embraced her son in the hallway.

'I have missed you,' his mother said, stepping back and pinching his cheeks. She turned to Allegra. 'Sister Bassetti. Welcome to Maratea and while you are here, *si metta a suo agio* – you must make yourself at home. Maria will put your bag in your room.

'*Avanti! Avanti!* The bread is almost ready.'

The kitchen was the focal point of the family. A big wood-fired oven sat at the back of the room and a long, heavy wooden bench stood in the centre. The two big windows with the orange shutters that Giovanni had pointed out overlooked the port. Home-made pasta – *menate* – lay on a board, coiled like rope. Nearby was a cracked pottery jar marked *olio*. It was full of Lucanian olive oil that had been made from olives cultivated in Basilicata since the time of the Greeks. The region's volcanic soil gave the oil a unique aroma and it gave Basilicatan cuisine its flavour. Sophia Donelli never used anything else. Another bowl was filled with *lampascioni* – a type of wild onion; another held *peperoncino* – the red peppers found throughout Basilicata. Goat's cheese and *lucanega* – Lucanian sausage – were on the table and the smell of freshly baked bread filled the house. *Ragu di carne*, a sauce made from lamb, pork and kid, was simmering on the stove.

'Giovanni!'

'Papà! Giuseppi! Giorgio!' Embraces and kisses on both cheeks, unabashed affection between an Italian father, sons and brothers.

Many would argue that God got it right when she made the Italians – a sense of family, of community, a passion for life.

'Allegra, meet the rest of the family!' More embraces, more kisses.

Signora Donelli served the steaming *ragu di carne* into terracotta bowls while Papà carved the freshly baked bread.

'Bless us, O Lord, and these Your gifts, which we are about to receive from Your bounty. Through Christ our Lord. Amen.'

'How was the catch, Papà?' Maria asked.

Signor Donelli smiled.

They all had that same warmth in their eyes, Allegra thought.

'The Orata were running today. Tomorrow after church, Mamma will be able to serve you the specialty of the house,' he said, beaming at their guest. 'And if the weather is good next week, Giovanni, you should take the dinghy and show Allegra some of our beaches.'

Allegra felt as if she was a part of the family and this feeling was only strengthened when she accompanied the Donellis to Mass the next day.

Nicola Farini, the village bell-puller, toiled on the frayed rope underneath the bell of the parish church of the Addolorata. He was in his eighties, and his white moustache was neatly trimmed and he was wearing his felt hat and his Sunday best. Nicola had been the parish's only bell-puller for as long as anyone could remember and today he bent to his task with the will of a man half his age. It was not every day that the Mass was celebrated by one of the village's favourite sons and the joyful toll of the old iron bell reverberated around the Apennine ridgelines.

Giovanni reflected that the small robing room with its worn wooden floor hadn't changed since he'd been an altar boy. With a sense of pride he followed his old mentor into the chancel and was instantly embarrassed. In a rare departure from the form of the Mass the congregation stood and applauded. Giovanni waved, smiling, while Monsignor Vincenzo Abostini winked at his protégé conspiratorially. He had let it be known beforehand that he did not think the good Lord would mind. In another rare event, the bell-puller's wife, Signora Farini, had been pressed into rehearsing on the small pedal organ.

'And now that we have welcomed Father Donelli, let's all sing the Lord's praises with Hymn number 803, "All glory, laud and honour, To thee redeemer King".'

La Signora Farini, her plump face flushed with pride, pumped the wooden bellow pedals for all she was worth and the organ stool creaked alarmingly under her weight. The Vienna Boys' Choir would not have felt threatened, but what the little congregation of the parish church of Addolorata might have lacked in choral training, they made up for with enthusiasm.

Thou art the King of Israel, Thou David's royal Son . . .

Israel was nearly 3000 kilometres away, but as the words of the old hymn echoed through the little Italian village, it was clear that Christ's impact on the shores of the Tyrrhenian had been no less than on the shores of Galilee – love, tolerance and a sense of community. When it was not distorted by the power and corruption of the Vatican and other Christian hierarchies, Christ's message had a surprising resonance with that of Abraham and Muhammad.

'I could get used to this life,' Allegra murmured, leaning back in the stern of the dinghy and closing her eyes, soaking up the rays of the morning sun. 'Do we have to go back tomorrow?'

Giovanni pulled on the oars with a powerful and steady rhythm and with each stroke the little dinghy surged forward, the emerald and turquoise of the Tyrrhenian Sea glistening behind the wooden keel.

'I thought you said you would rather be working on Professor Rosselli's assignment?'

'It's a toss up, but this probably wins,' Allegra said, half opening one eye. 'Where are you taking me, Giovanni Donelli?' she asked, feeling strangely mischievous. 'Because I'm not sure Cardinal Petroni would approve.'

'Well, I wasn't planning on telling him, but there's a little cove around the next point. Papà used to take us there for picnics when we were kids. You can only get to it from the sea so the whole family would get in the fishing boat and he would anchor it off the rocks and row us ashore.'

'*Sei fortunato!* You're very lucky to have grown up here. Do you know this is the first time I've ever been in a boat?'

'Really?' For a moment Giovanni was surprised, then he laughed. 'I don't suppose they have many dinghies in Tricarico. We've been spoilt here. I miss the sea.'

The two fell into an easy silence, punctuated only by the rhythmic thud of the oars in the rowlocks. Allegra let her hand dangle over the side, watching the sandy bottom through the crystal water. At first she had been apprehensive and had thought about telling Giovanni her secret but the day had dawned so beautifully and the breeze was so light that the Gulf of Policastro held only the gentlest of swells, and fears. The Apennine promontory was covered in small pine trees and as they rounded the point and the little beach came into view, Allegra felt completely at peace with the world.

The keel grated gently on the grey stony sand and Giovanni shipped the oars and helped Allegra out of the dinghy. Together they carried the rug and the picnic basket up the beach onto a small tongue of grass under some pines.

'Swim before lunch?'

Allegra's peace was suddenly shattered. 'Giovanni . . .' She hung her head. 'I've been meaning to tell you. I can't . . .'

Giovanni was suddenly concerned and he took her gently by the shoulders. 'Can't what? Is something wrong?'

'I can't—' she stammered. 'I can't swim,' she blurted out and coloured with embarrassment.

Giovanni gently lifted her chin with his finger so their eyes met.

'My fault. And I could kick myself. I should have realised that when you said this was your first time in a boat. Were you really saying this is your first time on the coast?'

Allegra nodded.

'Hey,' he said quietly. 'Think of it as another one of life's little adventures. If you feel up to it we'll just wade in up to here.' Giovanni measured his hand against Allegra's slender waist. 'And I'll give you your first lesson, deal?'

Allegra nodded again, still miserable.

'Only if you smile.'

'Thank you,' she said gratefully.

He took her hand and guided her down to the water's edge. 'It's pretty natural to feel nervous but trust me, if you need to you can reach the bottom. The first thing I will show you is how to float. Watch this.'

Allegra followed him into the warm water and with Giovanni's hands supporting her, she allowed herself to be coaxed onto her back. Then she panicked and flung her arms around him, coughing and spluttering.

'I've got you. I've got you. *Rilarssasi*. Relax,' he said softly, holding her.

'You must think I'm such an idiot,' she said, her head down, arms still around his neck.

'You should have seen me on the end of a rope off the breakwater with Papà holding the other end. I was terrified.'

His voice was steady and reassuring but as Allegra raised her head her thoughts were thrown into confusion. Carlo had been a terrible transgression but somehow this was different. This seemed like a natural force that was overwhelmingly strong.

How could something that felt this right be so wrong in the eyes of the Church.

'Want to try again?' Giovanni's voice sounded strangely hoarse as Allegra laid back in his arms. At first he supported her and then he slowly let her sink until the only thing holding her up was the Tyrrhenian, and a trust in this man who seemed even more pleased than she was at her achievement.

Back on the beach the sun was warm on Allegra's shoulders as she opened the picnic basket Giovanni's mother had packed.

'Olives, smoked fish, fresh bread, pickled onions – your mother must have thought we were coming for a week!'

'Now that would start people talking,' he said, handing her a plastic cup. Little rivulets of condensation dribbled down the sides of the bottle of Bianco Malvasia as Giovanni filled their glasses.

'*Salute!*'

'*Salute!* And thank you for the swimming lesson,' she said, conscious again of how close they were sitting.

'You were a natural. Well, almost,' he said, his blue eyes dancing as Allegra grinned sceptically. 'Another couple of lessons and you'll be swimming the bay from point to point.'

'Can we come back here again one day?' Allegra asked, handing Giovanni a roll with a little of everything from his mother's hamper.

'Probably, although it is hard on both of us, *non è vero?*' Giovanni mused, for the first time putting his own inner struggle into words.

Allegra nodded, acknowledging her own feelings. 'Why did you become a priest, Giovanni?'

'That part wasn't hard. A deep love for the Church. A need to give my best to those around me, and the fact that I would follow Christ wherever he sent me,' he said, smiling warmly.

'Do you know where he is going to send you?'

'No. And I think that is only revealed bit by bit. Who knows where we will end up after university?'

'It would be nice if we could finish up somewhere together,' she responded, the wine dissolving her inhibitions.

Giovanni took Allegra's cup and put it next to his on the sand. His lips were salty as she moulded herself against his body. Giovanni held her more tightly and she found herself responding, willingly. Allegra found herself searching out Giovanni's tongue with her own.

'Oh, Giovanni.'

Giovanni was torn.

'Allegra,' Giovanni whispered. He fumbled with the clip on her swimsuit and she reached around to help him. Her small breasts were wet with beads of saltwater, her nipples hard and erect. Allegra groaned as he licked them softly and gently took them in his mouth.

That night both had knelt for a long time asking forgiveness. *Accettazione*. Now they lay awake. Confused and uncertain. Allegra stared out of her window at the night sky. Her room was upstairs, next to Giovanni's at the front of the house. The lights from the marina were subdued and a light breeze feathered the Tyrrhenian below.

Why? she asked her God for the hundredth time. Why was this so wrong? She knew the episode with Carlo had been wrong, but this was so different. *Testarda*. Brilliant, gentle Giovanni, and so much fun to be around. He was someone she felt she could spend the rest of her life with, helping him achieve whatever it was that God wished him to achieve. Someone from whom she had learned so much. Someone with whom she was now deeply in love. Yet the Church forbade it. Why? Allegra began to sob, silently. Sobs born of desperation and frustration, and an increasing questioning of her faith.

In his room Giovanni was on his knees again praying for forgiveness to a God who, tonight, seemed very, very distant, silent, immoveable. He had asked for forgiveness, but he felt alienated because his feelings for Allegra were stronger than ever. Alienation from his God was new territory for Giovanni. He tried to distance his heart from his head, but that didn't help. As a young seminarian he had accepted celibacy without too much thought. It had not seemed an extreme price to pay to serve Christ, until now. Giovanni opened his eyes and stared up into the night sky and the galaxies that stretched for billions of light years. Years of study, as both a theologian and as a scientist, had caused him to think more deeply, and never more deeply than tonight, struggling with the Church's hypocrisy on sex. A Church that taught one thing, yet often secretly practised another. Giovanni knew that many Catholics were unaware that for a thousand years after Christ, Catholic priests had been happily married and were more effective because of it. Then in 1074 Pope Gregory VII, while keeping a mistress himself, had decreed that priests could only owe allegiance to the Church. Thousands of married priests 'were to be freed from the influence of their wives' and divorced. Giovanni also knew there was a more sinister reasoning behind the damaging policy of celibacy; the early Church had moved to protect her vast holdings of property because there had been a danger at law that the children of priests might inherit that property and deprive the Church of an accumulation of wealth.

Christ had absolutely nothing to say about celibacy. Never even thought it worthy of a mention, other than that he had chosen not to marry – or had he? The Church always downplayed Christ's enjoyment of the company of women. Giovanni reflected on Luke's description of Jesus travelling through the towns and cities of the Holy Land with several women among his disciples. 'Joanna, the wife of Herod's steward Chuza, and Susanna, and many others – who provided for him out of their resources.' All this in a culture where it was forbidden to speak to a woman in public, let alone travel with them. Jesus was charismatic, spiritual and a gifted speaker, and he treated women as equals. No wonder they were attracted to him. Perhaps Mary Magdalene's relationship with Jesus was much deeper than the Church allowed. Perhaps the hypocrisy of the Church on sex and the role of women in religion covered up something that was more spiritually balanced. A sense of harmony between male and female that was a crucial element to the patterns of creation, as Professor Rosselli had hinted at in his lectures.

When sleep came, it was fitful. Giovanni drifted in and out of a drowsy wakefulness, deeply troubled. Somewhere along the line the Faith had become perverted by a male hierarchy intent on increasing their power. The Church had somehow corrupted Christ's message, of which celibacy was but one element. It didn't have to be that way.

Giovanni changed gears three times from fourth down to second before he had to stop the Fiat on one of Maratea's notorious hairpin bends. The gearbox grated and protested as he searched for low gear. An awkward silence had settled over Allegra and Giovanni, broken only by the protests of the little car as they ground up the valley between the mountains in the still of the early morning, the port town of Maratea and the Tyrrhenian slowly receding behind them. The crunching of the gears reflected the cranking up of Allegra's anger at the restrictions of her Church and she was equally angry at herself for dreaming about a partnership with Giovanni. Why did the Church try to overrule human emotion, and had it always been that way? Perhaps the Omega Scroll did give some insight into a more human Church, a Church that recognised human nature and what people felt in their lives.

'I'm sorry about yesterday,' Giovanni said, interrupting her thoughts.

'Are you?' she snapped, angry that Giovanni should be sorry for what they both felt for each other, something that was so natural between them. Rebellion had surfaced again, but this time even stronger than before. *Molta testarda*.

Giovanni was taken aback by Allegra's response. It wasn't like her. He felt a shift in Allegra, a strength and determination starting to surface within her.

'I'm sorry too,' Allegra said, finally controlling her anger. 'For the way I sounded. It's just that I'm not sorry for how I feel and how we responded to each other.'

Giovanni didn't reply immediately. 'Me neither,' he said. 'But it can't happen again. We both know that.'

'I know, but that doesn't mean we can't see each other,' she said defiantly.

Giovanni took one hand off the wheel and reached out for hers. 'Of course not. There's no rule against pasta on a Friday night. But . . . there's nothing I want more than to be back on that beach with you, but that is too difficult for both of us.' Giovanni hesitated. 'I love you, Allegra.'

Allegra turned to face him, her brown eyes gentle.

'I love you too, Giovanni.'

BOOK THREE

1985

CHAPTER FOURTEEN

Milano

It was winter. The snow during the night had been unusually heavy. In the Piazza della Scala, the stone coats of Leonardo da Vinci and other statues in the old historic centre of Milano were dusted in white. The cold snap matched the mood of the Cardinal Archbishop of Milano, Lorenzo Petroni. In a concise hand he wrote just one word on one of two documents in the morning dispatches, *Accetti*, directing his private secretary to accept the invitation to attend the graduation ceremony at the Università Statale. The second document did nothing to improve his temper. It was a letter from the Chancellor.

> *Eminence,*
>
> *I am writing this letter because Signor Donelli and Signora Bassetti have achieved marvellous results in Philosophy, Archaeology and Chemistry . . .*

The reference to Catholic students as *Signor* and *Signora* irritated Petroni, but it was the Chancellor's description of the pilot program as a brilliant success that annoyed him intensely. It didn't surprise Petroni that Father Donelli had achieved the University Medal for Philosophy, but at least the problem of what to do with him next had been solved. There had been some initial surprise when Petroni had suggested posting Father Donelli to the Middle East, but there were more pressing issues in Rome than the posting of a young priest to Israel. An ageing Cardinal Secretary of State had acquiesced with a shrug of his shoulders.

But how to deal with the nun from Tricarico? She could not so easily be dispatched to some far-flung corner of Catholicism without some eyebrows being raised. Sister Bassetti was to be awarded the University Medal for Archaeology and the University Medal for Chemistry. How could a woman achieve this? This signalled a danger for the Holy Church. Trying to control his frustration Cardinal Petroni reflected on Genesis. In the Garden of Eden Woman had been responsible for the Fall of Man and all women needed to realise that like the snail that carries its house on its back, a woman had been put into the realm of Man to manage his household and to provide sex for the procreation of mankind. In his next report to the Pope, Petroni had already decided to describe the education program as 'an interesting experiment'. This would be accompanied with a strong recommendation for a return to the normal Catholic channels of education that had appropriate controls in place.

As he studied Allegra's photograph that had now found its place on the inside cover of her file, Petroni grew thoughtful. Dark brown eyes and black hair, a tanned oval face; a very beautiful young nun who was obviously academically gifted was an interesting combination. Perhaps it was time to get better acquainted with Sister Bassetti. Madonna, whore – Petroni could always see advantages in any situation. The religious conundrum would be a perfect one to explore. Petroni's eyes narrowed as he chanted the words of the apostle Paul to the Ephesians: 'Wives, be subject to your husbands as you are to the Lord. For the husband is the head of the wife just as Christ is head of the Church.' The hum of the wise words of Paul soothed him. It was time to put Sister Allegra Bassetti in her place.

Allegra pulled her coat tightly around her as snow was still falling lightly on the thickly covered grounds of the university. The summons to dinner had been delivered that morning by Cardinal Petroni's driver and, try as she might, Allegra had not been able to come up with an excuse to refuse the invitation from the powerful Cardinal. She made her way through the now familiar cloisters surrounding the quadrangles of the main square towards Ca' Granda's main entrance. Giovanni had only been gone two days and she missed him more than she thought possible. It had been hard, but they had honoured the pact they'd made on the way back from their fateful visit to Maratea. For her part, Allegra had thrown herself into her studies and the increasing number of High Distinctions and Distinctions were impressive. Delving into the intricacies of biochemistry, the exquisite phosphodiester bonding and nucleotides of DNA, and the development of life on Earth from a single primordial cell line intrigued her. The more she learned, the more she realised that the creation story of Adam and Eve didn't gel.

Giovanni and Allegra had agreed to try to not be alone together, or if they found themselves in one or the other's room, they would leave the door open. Friday nights were always a big danger. Discussions over pasta and a few glasses of wine on anything from the origins of humankind to Christ's relationship with Mary Magdalene had nearly brought them undone on more than one occasion. Somehow they had managed to transcend the love they had for each other, and that love had grown into something even more powerful. They became closer than ever. Now he was gone, of all places to somewhere in the West Bank of the Occupied

Territories of Israel. It was a posting that made absolutely no sense at all, and he'd been sent there the moment he completed his last exam. Giovanni had asked for a week's leave but the Cardinal Archbishop of Milano had been adamant he was needed there immediately. Beyond Ca' Granda's stone archways she could see the shiny black Volvo and Cardinal Petroni's driver.

CHAPTER FIFTEEN

Jerusalem

By the time Giovanni paid the cab fare the sun was setting over the Old City's ramparts. Saint Joseph's, the convent of the Sisters of Charity and home of the Catholic Bishop in Jerusalem, Bishop Patrick O'Hara, was in the Christian Quarter Road, not far from the Church of the Holy Sepulchre, which had been built over the site of Christ's crucifixion. The narrow two-storey building was crammed between two shops and the flagstone street was still jammed with tourists looking for souvenirs. The rusty gate creaked in protest as Giovanni pushed it open. The white steps leading up to the front door were chipped and the windows were shuttered with broken wooden slats, paint peeling from the iron security bars. One of the Sisters opened the old door in answer to Giovanni's pull on a weathered piece of rope.

'Welcome, Father, I'm Sister Katherine.' Sister Katherine was short with a cheerful, plump face, grey hair caught up in a bun and a habit that looked as if it had seen better days.

'Thank you, Sister. Giovanni Donelli,' he replied, shaking her outstretched hand.

'Let me take your bag, Father,' she said, reaching for his suitcase. Giovanni resisted unsuccessfully and followed her up another narrow flight of stairs.

'Make yourself comfortable,' she said, showing him into a large room overlooking the street. 'I'll put your bag in your room and let Bishop O'Hara know you've arrived.'

Giovanni sat down in one of the big overstuffed chairs and looked around him. The walls were lined with bookcases that stretched to the ceiling. Works of Augustine juxtaposed with those of the later theologians: Barth, Bultmann, Niebuhr, Schleiermacher and Rahner. Surprisingly, there was also considerable space devoted to the three men condemned by the Vatican for their awkward questioning of accepted Church doctrine: Pierre Teilhard de Chardin, Schillebeeckx and, perhaps the greatest living theologian of all, Hans Küng. There also seemed to be a copy of every book that had ever been written on the famed Dead Sea Scrolls: Hershel Shanks, Geza Vermes, Edmund Wilson – all the great scholars of the Scrolls. Even the controversial Australian author Barbara Thiering. Giovanni's thoughts were interrupted by a booming voice from the doorway.

'I hope it was a pleasant trip you've been having, Father?' Nearly twelve years in the Middle East and six years before that spent in Washington had not diminished Bishop O'Hara's lyrical Irish brogue. He was a big man with thinning hair, bushy grey eyebrows, a round, ruddy face and gentle green eyes. Patrick O'Hara's sizeable stomach reflected a passion for good food and wine, and his greeting was full of warmth.

'Yes thank you, Excellency, although security at Tel-Aviv seemed a little excessive,' Giovanni replied honestly.

'Welcome to the Promised Land. And please, it's Patrick. You can call me Excellency when the Vatican's coming to visit, which thankfully is not very often.'

'I'll try and get used to that,' Giovanni replied, warming to his larger than life superior.

'And I think you'd better be reserving judgement on being here until you see where I'm sending you,' the Bishop replied. 'A little town called Mar'Oth, about 25 kilometres from here, but it might as well be a thousand. The town is Palestinian, divided by both a road and a religion. On one side of the road the village folk are Palestinian Christians, our lot, and they've not had a priest there for many years. On the other side of the road they're Palestinian Muslims. There's only one school and the children from both sides of the road attend it. Diplomacy is in far greater demand here than theology, Giovanni.' He shuffled over to a well-stocked sideboard. 'Part of the sanity routine here.' His green eyes danced as he passed Giovanni a large glass of Irish whiskey. 'Shalom!'

'Shalom.' Giovanni raised his glass. He did not often drink whiskey but he had a feeling that whenever Bishop O'Hara was around he would get used to it, regardless of the time of day.

'Strange, isn't it.' Patrick settled his vast bulk into one of the other overstuffed chairs. 'A toast of peace in a country that is continually at war.'

'Do you think there will ever be peace in this country?'

'Not until they come to their senses and reach an agreement with the Palestinians.'

'Is that likely?'

'There are many on both sides who are longing for just that, and an end to the cycle of violence. Sometimes there's a glimmer of hope and then just as quickly the hope is dashed. Usually on the egos of inept, incompetent and corrupt politicians, aided and abetted by a culture of fanaticism that is as misguided as it is intense.'

'I suppose the clash of religions doesn't help,' Giovanni mused, a newcomer to Middle East politics and intrigue.

'A lot of people see Islam as a violent religion, when in fact it's just the opposite. Islam means "surrender" and a Muslim is one who surrenders completely to Allah and observes Allah's requirement that people behave towards one another with justice and compassion. The fundamentalist Muslims don't represent the true Islam, any more than the Jerry Buffetts of this world represent the true Christianity.'

'Unfortunately a lot of people believe the fundamentalists' view that there should only be one religion – theirs,' Giovanni observed ruefully.

'It is an interesting question, isn't it. What sort of perverse God would create human beings whose search for meaning in religion generates so much intolerance towards one another?'

Giovanni was a little taken aback. It was unusual for a bishop to refer to God as perverse.

'You're looking surprised, Giovanni.'

'I am a little,' Giovanni admitted.

'Don't be. When you get to my age you tend to question a great deal.'

'Your faith?'

'Especially my faith. Have you been reading any of Teilhard de Chardin?'

'I thought the Vatican had banned his work, although I couldn't help noticing you have several of his books.'

'Cardinal Petroni and his ilk wouldn't be amused,' Patrick replied darkly. 'But as there's as much likelihood of him coming to Jerusalem as there is an agreement on peace, I think I'm pretty safe,' he chuckled, his humour returning as he got out of his chair and moved to fossick through the shelves, returning with a much-thumbed book and an equally dog-eared *Journal of Mathematics*.

'*Comment Je Crois – How I Believe*,' he said, handing Giovanni the book. 'It's in French but I gather you speak that language fluently, along with English, German, Spanish and Latin?'

'Someone has kept you informed,' Giovanni said with a grin.

'Oddly enough it was the Vatican. They're not renowned for

including us peasants in their debates but they did send me your biographical notes.' Patrick poured himself another whiskey. 'Chardin was a very interesting man. After he was ordained as a Jesuit priest, he served in WWI as a stretcher bearer. Among other things he won the Military Medal and the Legion of Honour. Like you, he was also a scientist.'

'It is sometimes difficult being a priest and a scientist. There are times when I wish I was one or the other, not both.'

'Chardin would agree with you, but he also had the courage to disagree with the Vatican, which got right up their Eminences' nostrils and they did what they always do.'

Giovanni nodded. 'Excommunication.'

'It is their standard response to anyone with the intellect and temerity to question their power base. Anyway, you may have both of these,' he said. 'The second one is a paper by the Israeli archae-ologist and mathematician Yossi Kaufmann. He's convinced there are codes in the Dead Sea Scrolls that contain a warning. Have you heard of the Omega Scroll?'

Giovanni felt a chill and nodded, measuring his response. His instinct was to trust this bishop of the people, but it was too soon to divulge what he knew. 'It's had quite a bit of press from time to time but I thought it was mostly speculation,' he replied carefully.

Bishop O'Hara shook his head. 'Yossi Kaufmann doesn't think so. Yossi's a man of many contacts, quite a few of whom reside in the back alleys of this Holy City. Not only is he convinced it exists, he thinks the Vatican bought a copy of it in 1978, and he's equally certain the original is still out there, but you can ask him yourself. You'll need to come back here once a month or so, more frequently if I have the need of company,' Patrick added. 'I'll arrange for you to meet him over dinner. Sister Katherine is an excellent cook.'

It was after ten before Giovanni managed to escape to his room. He propped himself up in bed and turned to Yossi Kaufmann's paper published in *The Journal of Mathematics.* As another distinguished Israeli, Dr Eliyahu Rips, was doing with the Torah, Professor Kaufmann had applied a computerised analysis to the Hebrew and Aramaic of the Dead Sea Scrolls, and he had discovered a similar problem to Rips. Words like 'terror' and 'end of days' were found by the program, but Kaufmann had been unable to determine what the hidden warning was. Professor Kaufmann's paper had been written for a professional audience but Giovanni grasped the underlying permutations and progression theorems with ease. He blinked at Kaufmann's conclusion. The codes that were in the Dead Sea Scrolls all pointed to the message being found in a particular scroll, the Omega Scroll. The words 'revelation' and 'end of mankind' kept coming up.

Overtired, Giovanni couldn't sleep so he flicked the bedside lamp back on and reached for Teilhard de Chardin's banned *Comment Je Crois.* Chardin had a gift for writing and the French came easily, and when Giovanni next checked his watch it was two in the morning. Reluctantly he closed the book and turned out the light. No wonder the Vatican had banned Teilhard de Chardin. The great French theologian and scientist had dared to suggest that God was not some all-powerful and vengeful Being, but a spiritual force within creation itself; in the rivers, mountains, mists, elephants, microbes and within every human being. For Chardin, God was not the God of Wrath of the Church but rather the 'spirit within', and he was daring to challenge the Cardinals' powerful claim that God could only be reached through the priests of the Church.

Giovanni finally fell into an uneasy sleep. Chardin had left an indelible mark on Giovanni, colouring his approach to his faith and helping him in his never-ending search for true meaning.

The Spirit smiled as revelation dawned.

CHAPTER SIXTEEN

Milano

The trip took less than five minutes and the door to Cardinal Petroni's apartments was promptly opened by a petite, attractive Sister on the Cardinal's personal staff.

'You may hang your coat on that hook, Sister Bassetti,' Sister Carmela said icily.

'*Grazie. È molto gentile*,' Allegra responded with a gracious smile. Perhaps the dark-haired nun had had a bad day, she thought.

'His Eminence is waiting for you in the drawing room, Sister Bassetti, if you will follow me.'

Allegra trailed behind as Sister Carmela set a brisk pace down the sumptuously carpeted hallway, where priceless artworks on loan from the Vatican hung from high picture railings on either side. The heavy gold frames were beautifully set against the deep blue wallpaper. There were paintings by Margaritone d'Arezzo and Vitale da Bologna, Lorenzo Monaco and Guido Reni, and at the entrance to the drawing room, a fresco by none other than Raphael, the master himself.

'Sister Bassetti, Eminence.' Sister Carmela announced Allegra and then withdrew.

'Sister Bassetti. How good of you to come.'

The first thing Allegra noticed was the voice, perfectly modulated with a cultured resonance that reinforced the charm of the Cardinal.

She took his outstretched hand and felt him almost caress her palm. 'It's a pleasure to be here, Eminence,' she replied diplomatically.

'Quite the contrary, the pleasure is all mine,' he said, directing her to a lounge chair with a sweep of his hand. 'It is not often that we cardinals get the opportunity to dine with the people who really matter. Usually it's politicians and industrialists. Very boring.' He smiled urbanely. 'I have taken the liberty of opening a bottle of Krug.' Petroni did not have to ask whether or not his guest drank wine; he already had a report on Allegra and Giovanni's Friday night activities from his secretary. 'Nineteen sixty-four, I think you will find it was a very good year.'

Allegra would have given anything to trade the fine crystal flute for the heavy glasses and carafe of equally rough wine La Pizzeria Milano reserved for impoverished students, and she wished Giovanni were here. He would have handled these irritating formalities with ease.

'*Salute!*'

'*Salute*, Eminence,' Allegra responded.

'Have you been given your results yet?'

'Not yet, Eminence. I expect we will know in the next day or so.'

'Well, I'm probably not supposed to tell you, but I have an advance copy. You have done very well, Allegra.' He used her first name easily, as if they had known each other for a very long time. 'But I will keep you in suspense until after dinner.'

Allegra followed him into the sumptuous dining room. The wallpaper here was crimson. A large gold and crystal chandelier hung from a ceiling covered in frescos of various scenes of the historic centre of Milano. Just two places were set on either side of the huge mahogany dining table. The other chairs that Allegra assumed often seated politicians and captains of industry lined the walls, all of them richly embroidered in gold and red with the Cardinal's coat of arms. Petroni graciously held her chair out so she could sit.

Petroni's chef, who appeared to Allegra to be rather more agreeable than the nun who had greeted her, appeared with the entrée. *Baccalà con i ceci* – salt cod with chickpeas.

'I hope you don't mind but I've kept the meal simple. Sister Maria is preparing one of her oldest recipes. *Cotolette alla Pontremolese* – veal cutlets with garlic and capers.'

Allegra found herself wondering what the Cardinal might eat when the menu wasn't simple.

'And to go with it, a 1966 Château Margaux. I think one of the more elegant of the Appellation Médoc,' he said, pouring from the crystal decanter in which the rare vintage had been allowed to breathe.

'I'm not used to such fine wine, Eminence. We students in Milano tend to appreciate the cheap and cheerful,' Allegra said, her remarks designed to needle Petroni's arrogance, although she knew she would have to be careful. He was a dangerous man.

'Consolations of office, and please, it's Lorenzo. When we are alone there is no need for titles.' Giovanni had said a similar thing but Petroni's nuance was very different. He was smiling but his eyes remained cold, dark and expressionless. Allegra felt chilled, as if she was looking into the eyes of a snake. Even the warming alcohol could not help her shake the ice in the pit of her stomach. Allegra's senses were in overdrive, warning her to stay on guard.

Petroni continued smiling and his tongue briefly licked his lips.

'*Salute*,' he offered again and moved to clink glasses with her. 'Have you enjoyed your time at university?'

'Very much,' Allegra said, determined to match Petroni in the conversation. She knew her remark would put Petroni off balance. Something was instinctively telling her that he wouldn't be prepared for honesty.

Apart from the almost imperceptible narrowing of his eyes, Petroni gave nothing away.

'Of course. So what aspects of your degree have you found most rewarding?' His anger at this nun's defiance and lack of subservience was rising, as was his excitement for the game ahead. He probed for the slightest weakness in Allegra's armour. He was strangely aggravated by both her beauty and her intellect. He knew now that he wanted to crush her, totally.

'That's a difficult question,' Allegra replied with a disarming smile. 'I suppose my time in the laboratory and the promise that the study of archaeological DNA holds for the future would be one of the highlights.' Allegra sensed the mention of DNA had found its target.

'Are there any aspects that you have found disturbing?' Petroni asked, his frustration rising.

'Not so much disturbing, more profoundly interesting,' Allegra replied, almost insolently. Petroni remained expressionless but Allegra sensed his discomfort and was determined to enjoy it. 'Professor Rosselli has a theory about the origin of DNA, that it might be too intricate – exquisite is the word he uses – too complex in its design to have evolved in the relatively short time between our planet becoming habitable and life appearing. He is convinced that DNA arrived from a higher civilisation, and I think he has a point. Given that scientists have confirmed there are billions of galaxies like our own, it seems virtually impossible that some of them would not contain life, and that at least one or two of those civilisations might be considerably more advanced than our own.' Allegra paused, raising her eyebrows ever so slightly.

'Please. Go on. This is very interesting,' Petroni prompted, suppressing an inner fury.

'His theory seems to be somewhat at odds with the Vatican's teaching but it seems that Francis Crick, who discovered DNA's structure, held a similar view.'

'That old nonsense again.' Petroni's laugh was strangely hollow. 'Don't even worry about it, Allegra. That's the trouble with some of these old professors in secular universities. They have no training in the Canon but keep peddling all sorts of conspiracy theories.'

'Professor Rosselli seems to think there is a connection with Crick's theory and the Omega Scroll.' Let's see what your response is to that one, she thought, allowing herself a moment of satisfaction.

Petroni's eyes hardened perceptibly. 'What did your professor have to say about that?' It took a supreme effort, but Petroni kept a smooth modulation in his voice.

'Just that if it could be found, the Omega Scroll might confirm the theory.'

Cardinal Petroni's laugh now sounded slightly hysterical.

'That mythology has been around for years, Allegra,' he said, coldness entering his voice. 'The Omega Scroll and the Loch Ness Monster have a lot in common – total fantasy. I see that as well as your degree in Theology you have also achieved Honours in Chemistry,' he said, adroitly turning the conversation back to Allegra and away from any further mention of the Omega Scroll. 'An impressive achievement by any standards. Science is one of the great seats of learning, but some might be intrigued by your choice.'

Petroni had recovered his charm and it masked both the nature of his question and his anger at discovering the Vatican had not exercised more care in preventing study in areas that threatened established doctrine. It seemed that his usually impeccable intelligence network had failed. It was bad enough that normal priests should study science but for a nun to be allowed near a laboratory was something he would not allow to be repeated.

'I found science interesting at school, I suppose,' Allegra answered carefully.

Allegra's response was interrupted by the Cardinal's chef bringing in the main course.

'Thank you, Sister Maria, and please, you needn't bother to stay tonight. The entrée was superb and the main looks equally so.'

'Coffee, Eminence?' Sister Maria protested but Petroni was not to be dissuaded.

'I haven't totally lost my skills in that area,' he said, smiling. 'I insist, you work far too hard.'

'You are most kind, Eminence.' Sister Maria withdrew, grateful for an early night.

'The problem is, Allegra,' Petroni continued, 'as I shall explain to you shortly, you have done so well that I now need to find a way to put your new-found knowledge to the best effect. Do you have any suggestions?'

Allegra paused before deciding to follow the freedom she had found at Ca' Granda.

'If I were given a choice, I think there is considerable scope for research into the Dead Sea Scrolls.'

Lorenzo Petroni smiled. A cold, hard, humourless smile. His eyes glittered and he could hear a drumming of blood in his ears. Inwardly he thought, How dare she. Outwardly he replied, 'We shall have to take that into account. Shall we?'

Petroni served coffee and a late-picked dessert wine in his private lounge off to one side of his study. Allegra admired the fine art and delicate sculptures scattered around the room although she was surprised and a little concerned when Petroni chose to sit next to her, very closely, on one of three plush crimson lounges that were arranged in an open square around the fire. Allegra was very aware that she was feeling a little light-headed. It seemed that during dinner her glass had never been allowed to get below half-full. She sipped on the dessert wine sparingly.

'I have here a letter from the Vice Chancellor of Ca' Granda,' Petroni said, opening a red folder that had been pre-positioned on the coffee table. 'You are to be awarded not one university medal but two. The first for Biblical Archaeology and the second for Chemistry.'

Allegra was stunned. She thought she had done well, but never imagined she'd won two university medals. Petroni put his arm around her and kissed her on the cheek. 'My congratulations.' When he didn't remove his arm, Allegra's delight at her results changed to concern.

'How would you feel if I offered you a position on my personal staff?' he asked.

Allegra turned her head towards him. His face was only centimetres from hers and his smooth, urbane voice gave way to a quiet whisper, unnerving her.

'Oh, Eminence . . .' she stammered, suddenly very uncertain of what was happening. 'I don't know what to say.'

'Please, it's Lorenzo,' he responded, taking her hand in his. 'We need the brightest and best around here and your appointment will not be without its compensations.'

Allegra's heart began to beat faster as the Cardinal placed her hand between his legs. She could feel his erection through his soutane.

'Relax, Allegra. *Rilarssasi*. It is God's will.' For a bizarre moment Allegra thought of Giovanni urging her to relax in the water. Petroni was closer now, whispering in her ear. So close she could smell the wine on his breath. Now Allegra felt pure fear and she tried to work out a way to escape from this man, this room.

'Our Lord has always had a very high regard for the women around him. Even those like the adulteress. It was always his wish that his disciples provide one another with love and affection,' Petroni whispered, using Allegra's hand to stroke his erection. 'There is a secret codex in the vault of the Vatican, Allegra, to which only the Curia have access. It outlines a sacred communion between a cardinal and his chosen nun.'

Allegra lost her power of speech as Petroni undid the middle buttons on his soutane. He moved his arm from around her shoulders and massaged her neck roughly. Allegra tried to move away but Petroni held her neck with a steel-like grip. She fought and kicked at his legs but the deadly mixture of physical strength and the dark power of the Church played on her fear, draining her and causing a mind-numbing paralysis. Just as Allegra was about to scream, Petroni forced her head into his lap and she gagged as a burst of warm liquid hit the back of her throat.

'A secret communion and a sharing of affection with a cardinal must never be disclosed,' he warned, buttoning himself perfunctorily and assuming a tone of formality. 'God's will is sometimes hard to understand, but think about my suggestion for an appointment here. I'm sure you will find it worthwhile.'

Shocked and betrayed, Allegra angrily refused Petroni's offer of the car and she stumbled back to the college, stopping more than once to vomit in the gutter. As she closed the door to her room she leaned back against it, weak and shaking, her faith shattered and spent. This time there was no prayer for forgiveness, only numbness as she looked out of her small window at the stars and thought about an unseeing, unhearing, unfeeling God. Mechanically she made her way to the bathroom and scrubbed herself until her skin was red and raw, but it wasn't enough to bring any feeling back. She climbed into her narrow single bed. For a long while she stared at the ceiling until emotional and physical exhaustion took over and she finally fell asleep. Before dawn she awoke to find herself crying uncontrollably. Her numbness had been replaced by anger, a deep anger that pulsed through her very being. She realised that it was not God and His Cardinal she had let down but the reverse, and the Cardinal and God could go to hell.

Later that morning there were four items of mail. Two incoming, two outgoing. Allegra opened the first letter feeling nothing but a strange emptiness as she scanned the result slips and a string of High Distinctions. The second was from the Vice Chancellor, Professor Gamberini, warm and encouraging with a suggestion for study for a Masters in applied archaeological DNA and the offer of a scholarship. She wrote a short letter of thanks and a grateful acceptance for the offer of the scholarship, then she penned an even shorter resignation from her Order.

CHAPTER SEVENTEEN

Mar'Oth

Giovanni gripped the chipped bakelite steering wheel of the dilapidated Volkswagen he had been provided with, and headed towards the village of Mar'Oth near the northern border of the West Bank. A hot wind blew through the open window and the distinctive metallic whirring of the air-cooled engine rang in his ears. Eventually Giovanni found the black and white signpost at the turnoff Bishop O'Hara had told him to watch for; Mar'Oth, it announced, was 3 kilometres away in the mountains to the east, but it was the second sign that caught his attention – Nazareth.

Pulling up in a cloud of dust at the side of the road Giovanni felt a surge of exhilaration. Barely 9 kilometres to the north, across the border of the occupied Palestinian West Bank, lay what was now the city of Nazareth. Christ himself had walked the streets of this old hillside town as a boy. To the east he could see Mount Tabor, the mountain that Christ had climbed with Peter, James and John, where he had been transfigured before them in robes of dazzling white, reappearing with Moses and the prophet Elijah. Giovanni looked at his watch. It was already after two and he felt a pang of disappointment. So near, yet so far. He smiled to himself. Nazareth had been there for well over two thousand years. It could wait another day but he resolved to go there at the first opportunity.

Reluctantly he grasped the worn stubby gear lever, changed to first with a grinding crunch and turned towards Mar'Oth. The Volkswagen lurched drunkenly as Giovanni picked his way up the steep, dusty road. Olive groves proliferated on either side, leathery leaves flashing green and silver. The hardy trees seemed impervious to the scorching sun.

Like many villages in Israel Mar'Oth was built on a hill. More accurately on two hills that were like the dusty humps of a camel with a saddle in between. Giovanni slowed as he reached the top of the first rise. The dirt road divided the town down the middle, finishing halfway up the second rise. He drove down past a small mosque and mudbrick homes. A group of children with black soulful eyes stopped kicking a cardboard box to watch him pass. Giovanni waved but they didn't return his greeting. A mangy brown dog scratched incessantly in the doorway of one of the houses. At the bottom of the saddle there were two stores, one on either side of the road, but unlike Jerusalem there were no tubs of olives or spices spilling out of the doors. A small whirlpool of dust eddied in front of him, gathering strength, only to die moments later. What few people there were on the hot dusty track averted their eyes, sullen and unfriendly. A single track ran down to a knoll where an old stone building stood. Giovanni guessed it was the school. He reached for the worn stubby gear stick and again the Volkswagen protested as it climbed up the second rise until he brought it to a stop outside a small and very old red mudbrick church.

One of the two half doors was hanging lopsidedly, the top hinge rusted away from the wall. The cross directly above the doors drooped in sympathy. Giovanni eased open the door that still had two hinges and he stepped into one of Christ's many houses. The corners of the small church were dim but a ray of bright sunlight shone through an opening high up in one of the walls. Dust particles danced thickly in front of a rickety table that served as an altar. Four plank benches completed the collection of furniture. Giovanni kicked at the dirt floor, holding down his disappointment. A cloud of thick, dirty red dust rose in response. He walked towards the only other door, opened it and stepped back hurriedly as the smell of stale urine assailed his nostrils from a single windowless room. On the floor in one corner was a chipped enamel bowl and a dented bucket. In another corner was an old stove covered in black grease. A yellow-stained mattress sagged in the middle of an iron-framed bed. Giovanni looked underneath it to find the wire supports had rusted away and in among the broken springs were several large empty whisky bottles. An old school desk and a chair filled the rest of the room. A candle had almost burned down to the rough lump of wood that served as a base and a rusty iron nail protruded through wax that had dribbled off the table, solidifying into a greasy brown stalactite.

Giovanni walked back into the church, leaving the door to the room open. He sat down on the nearest bench and stared at the wall behind the table. There was a patchwork of jagged brown mud where the whitewash had fallen and scattered in big flakes on the dirt floor. Fighting back another surge of disappointment, Giovanni put his head in his hands, closed his eyes and prayed to a God that he was no longer sure of.

'Heavenly Father, I have sinned against you and against your Holy Catholic Church. I am not worthy to pick up the crumbs from beneath your table. Forgive me my disappointment at being sent here and help me to understand that there is a reason. Help me to reach out to these people and bring them to you. And,' he added, with a pang of guilt, 'help me to make sense of Pierre Teilhard de

Chardin. Amen.' Giovanni crossed himself and made his way back out onto the dusty track. The steering wheel was almost too hot to touch and he made a mental note to try and find some sort of cover for it. As he headed back towards the other end of the village he noticed a crowd gathering outside the little mosque on the other hill. Even at a distance the people seemed agitated; some of them were bending over something on the track.

When he pulled up, Giovanni could see that the crowd were mainly older men, their black robes faded to grey. Their heads were covered with what were once white kafiyehs and as he got out of the car he could see there was a man lying near the front steps of the mosque. Giovanni found age amongst Arabs hard to fathom, but he judged the man on the ground to be about the same age as he was, somewhere in his late twenties to early thirties. He looked fit, but he wasn't moving. Giovanni thought he might be dead, and mechanically wondered if he should offer the last rites. Just as quickly he realised his naivety. As he reached the crowd, a small man with a face like a blackened walnut gesticulated at him and started yelling in Arabic.

'Can I help?' Giovanni asked. He was met with sullen stares and was immediately conscious of the need to have a grasp of the local language. The walnut started yelling at him again, spitting invective through the gaps in his tobacco-stained teeth.

Giovanni held up his hands submissively.

'Does anyone speak English?' he asked, raising his voice to be heard. The men glared at him.

'I do.'

Giovanni thought the boy could not have been more than about nine or ten. Like many Palestinian children he had dark olive skin with the same soulful eyes as the children Giovanni had seen earlier. Like most of the village children he wore shorts and had no shoes.

'What happened?'

'Imam Sartawi fell off the roof.'

Giovanni refrained from asking why his opposite number might have needed to be on the roof of the mosque. Probably a case of do-it-yourself, as it clearly would be for Giovanni. He moved towards the crumpled form and the men reluctantly drew aside to let him through. Once again the walnut protested.

'Tell them I have first aid.'

The boy looked puzzled.

'*Tebeeb*, doctor,' Giovanni said, stretching both the truth and his elementary Arabic in an attempt to communicate.

The boy nodded, recognition in his eyes.

'*Tebeeb*.'

The murmur was almost respectful now and the gap widened to allow Giovanni to kneel in the dust. He recalled the only first aid he had ever done, from way back in his football days, and took hold of the Imam's wrist; the pulse was not strong but at least it was there and he was breathing. Giovanni checked around the man's neck, and as he checked to see if his pupils were of equal size, the Imam groaned.

'What is his name?' he asked, beckoning to the boy. 'Translate for me please.'

'His name is Ahmed Sartawi, but you can talk to him.'

For a moment Giovanni was puzzled. 'He speaks English?'

The boy nodded.

Ahmed groaned and tried to sit up but Giovanni motioned for him to lie still.

'What is your name?' Giovanni asked again, not noticing the quizzical look on the boy's face.

The Imam squinted. 'Ahmed. Ahmed Sartawi,' he replied hoarsely.

'And do you know where you are?'

'Yes, in my village.' It was Ahmed's turn to look puzzled.

'And do you know what day it is?'

'Why are you asking me all these questions? I was fixing the roof when I fell,' the Imam replied, agitation creeping into his voice.

Giovanni smiled at him. 'It's all right. You've been unconscious. Can you see clearly? Your vision is not blurred?'

'A little, but it's my ankle that really hurts.'

The blurred vision was not a good sign, Giovanni thought, more worried about that than Ahmed's ankle. 'Which one, left or right?'

'Right.'

Giovanni checked for any sign of a break, but apart from the swelling there was no puncture or discoloration of the skin. 'Can you move it?'

Ahmed slowly raised his leg and gingerly moved his foot from side to side.

'I don't suppose you have any ice around here?' Giovanni asked the young boy who was watching intently. The boy laughed.

'No. I didn't think so. Can you get me some newspaper, lots of it, and some cord?' Giovanni turned back to Ahmed. 'I don't think it is broken, but just to make sure I will drive you to Nazareth.'

Giovanni made two rolls out of the papers. The murmuring among those craning to see grew louder as he bound the makeshift splints together.

'Now,' Giovanni said, supporting Ahmed from behind, 'let's get you to the car.' Their path was suddenly blocked by the walnut, waving his arms. A torrent of Arabic directed at Giovanni in particular and everyone else in general.

Not a happy nut, Giovanni thought wryly, stifling a smile as Ahmed intervened with a few sharp words and the walnut fell silent.

By the time they reached Nazareth the last of the sun's rays were sliding from the dome of the Basilica of the Annunciation, the top of which looked like a massive lantern. It was the largest church in the Middle East, constructed on the site where legend had it that the angel Gabriel told Mary that she would bear the Christ child. Nazareth Hospital was perched on a prominent hill overlooking the basilica and the town.

'I hope the hospital has a doctor on duty,' Giovanni said dubiously as he drove as fast as he dared up the winding Wadi el-Juwani.

'There will be. Nazareth may not be the most picturesque town on the map, but there are sixty thousand Arabs, not to mention another fifty thousand Jews in the new part of the town.' Ahmed winced as Giovanni swerved, not entirely missing a large pothole.

'Sorry,' Giovanni offered. Ahmed looked relieved when they finally parked and Giovanni helped him to Casualty. The hospital staff seemed harassed and it took over an hour before Ahmed Sartawi's name was called and he was taken through two plastic doors.

Giovanni looked up from his seat in the crowded waiting room to find a young Arab nurse standing in front of him.

'We are going to keep him in for observation overnight.' Her voice was strangely aggressive.

'Is he all right?'

'We're not sure yet.'

'How long before you will know?' Giovanni asked, wondering why after nearly another hour they had not reached any decision.

'There are other patients in this hospital,' she replied curtly. 'The Israelis have been shelling a village to the south of here and some of the casualties are not expected to live.' As if to emphasise her point, sirens could be heard in the distance.

'Why don't you come back in the morning,' she said, a little more gently. 'By then the specialist will have had time to examine the X-rays and we will be able to tell you a little more.'

Giovanni nodded and the nurse quickly disappeared through the two plastic doors.

As Giovanni reached the main entrance the first of the ambulances roared past heading towards Casualty, the siren dying as it came to a halt. Orderlies in blood-spattered white raced to open the doors, and a young Arab boy, one leg missing, the other wrapped in blood-soaked bandages, was wheeled inside. Giovanni took a deep breath. He couldn't have been more than eight or nine years old.

CHAPTER EIGHTEEN

Nablus

The Hamas training centre looked like any other house in an ordinary street on the outskirts of Nablus. It was eight o'clock in the evening and curfew. The narrow and twisted laneways were deserted, save for the intermittent Israeli patrols. Since 1967 the Israelis had gradually imposed more and more restrictions on the Palestinian people and now they were forbidden to travel from one village or town to the next. Palestinians were imprisoned in what had once been their own country.

At just twenty-eight years of age, Yusef Sartawi was now the deputy chief sound engineer for Cohatek Events. It hadn't been easy. Most nights he would wake up screaming, the images of his sisters being cut down by the Israeli sergeant burned into his memory. The only thing that kept him going was his hatred for the enemy and his dual role with his more sinister and shadowy employer, Hamas. His instinctive thirst for knowledge was being put to good use devising ways of destroying the Israelis, and he wouldn't rest until every last one of them had been pushed into the Mediterranean. It was a hatred that was also directed at Ahmed, his cowardly peace-loving brother who had forced him to watch the massacre. Yusef had promised himself that Ahmed would pay and had marked out his house in Mar'Oth as a potential target. Normally Yusef would not be attending a lecture on pipe bombs, but too many of Hamas' young suicide bombers were being detected before they could reach their target and Yusef was here to ensure they took the right precautions.

Mahmoud Aqel was short and rugged. He was the same age as Yusef and had originally trained to be a chemistry teacher. When he had lost his entire family in an Israeli helicopter gunship attack on Jenin, he had enlisted with Hamas. Now he taught young suicide bombers the rudiments of making explosives and pipe bombs.

'Tonight we commence instruction on how to make explosives from simple rock salt,' Mahmoud began. The four Palestinian boys sitting around the table were listening intently.

'Some of you might argue that the ammonium nitrate in fertiliser might be more suitable. It is and the Israelis know it, so buying large quantities will draw attention. Rock salt is in abundant supply and is used extensively for cooking so it will not arouse any suspicion.'

Mahmoud spread a large sheet of paper out on the table.

'Tonight we are making a chlorate-based explosive that starts with the production of sodium chlorate from sodium chloride, commonly known as salt. A word of caution,' he added, seeing the eagerness on the faces of the teenagers. 'Explosives are dangerous. Contamination can make them unstable, and friction and heat can cause them to detonate. You need to exercise the utmost care in handling them so they remain in the position of the servant, not the master.'

Mahmoud took them through the process of electrolysis, explaining how the hydrogen produced in the reaction had to be vented through the roof to avoid an explosion, how the saltwater had to be circulated to avoid excessive temperatures developing, how to calculate the sizes of the cathode and the anode to achieve the right current densities, how to collect the crystals of sodium chlorate, how to carefully crush them and mix them with Vaseline, and finally, how to calculate the critical loading density for a pipe bomb.

'The process might seem time-consuming,' he said, 'but the explosive we produce is quite powerful, and it is cheap to make.'

Mahmoud withdrew a short length of piping from a canvas satchel and placed it on the bench. 'You can see that this pipe is an ordinary piece of medium-sized water pipe, threaded at both ends with two caps. One cap has a small hole drilled into it to take the fuse. The drilling must be done before any explosive is placed in the pipe,' Mahmoud warned.

Mahmoud then weighed out the explosive on the set of kitchen scales and carefully filled the pipe. 'Wherever possible use equipment that has a household use,' he said. 'Then if you are raided, there are no awkward questions.' He tamped the explosive into the pipe carefully and packed it with wadding before threading the protruding fuse through the remaining cap and screwing it on.

'Be careful there is no explosive in the threads of the pipe because the friction can detonate it. Safety is paramount and this is not a job to be rushed. If there are no questions, my friend Yusef has a few words to say on tactics.'

Yusef nodded to Mahmoud, picked up his training manual and moved in front of the group.

'My friend Mahmoud has given you some excellent instruction tonight, but all that will be to no avail if you fail to reach your target,' Yusef began, the confidence of many successfully planned attacks evident in his voice.

'The best means of getting to your target is by public transport, unless it is the transportation itself and the people on it that are the target. Private vehicles are far more likely to be searched. There are a few simple rules outlined in the training manual that you must be familiar with.' Yusef tapped the cover with his finger for emphasis.

'Firstly, always try and select a bus or a train that is crowded. Crowded buses and trains are less likely to be checked, and when you are travelling don't get involved in any discussions. If you are travelling by taxi don't get involved in a discussion with the driver; some of them are not what they seem. Secondly, get on and off at minor stops and walk part of the way if you have to. Major terminals are more likely to be the subject of surveillance so always assume you are on camera. Make sure your appearance matches the transport. There may be occasions when you will target a first-class compartment. When this is the case you will be given the means to dress accordingly. The same goes for a five-star hotel. If you are carrying important documents, risk putting them in with the normal passengers' luggage, that way they can't be found on you if the bus or train is searched. If you are on a train, put your luggage in another carriage. Finally, your documents must be a precise match for whatever cover you are using and you must be thoroughly familiar with them and have rehearsed your answers to any questions. Are there any from you?'

'What about the selection of targets?' one of the Palestinian boys asked.

'That is worked out according to the overall strategy. Obviously your targets will be carefully chosen to inflict maximum damage on the infidels but there are other factors which will also be taken into account. Things like whether or not the target is heavily guarded or under surveillance and whether there is ease of access. And while we're on surveillance, it is one of our principles that wherever possible you should become completely familiar with a target. If it's a restaurant you will be given the money to eat there. The exact placement of a pipe bomb can be critical.'

That night Yusef lay awake imagining the bombing of the Hebrew University or the American Colony Hotel in Jerusalem, while not very far away in Mar'Oth, his brother Ahmed was deep in conversation with Giovanni Donelli.

One brother thinking of revenge, the other talking of peace.

CHAPTER NINETEEN

Mar'Oth

'You must give me the recipe for that, Ahmed, I have never tasted anything quite like it.' Giovanni leaned back against the cushions that littered the floor of Ahmed Sartawi's modest mudbrick house.

'Welcome to Middle Eastern cuisine, although you will have to ask the women of the village for the recipe. It's a very famous Palestinian dish, *Msaqa'a*, eggplants baked with onions, tomatoes and spices. Simple, but the secret is in the cooking.'

'And the pancakes?'

'*Qateyef*. Filled with crushed walnuts, coconut, cinnamon and a touch of lemon juice, another famous recipe they will also give you. It is the least we can do after all your kindness.'

'I'm sure you would have done the same for me.'

'Perhaps. Although unfortunately there are many who might not. It was not always so but the fighting between the Israelis and the Palestinians has poisoned our people. It has not helped that the West has been so one-sided in its support for the Jews.'

Giovanni studied his host. Ahmed was just in his thirties but his brown face was etched with lines. He had thick black hair, a prominent nose and his dark brown eyes were gentle.

'Are there problems in this village?'

'Between the Muslims and the Christians, you mean?'

Giovanni nodded.

'There were. You had a predecessor. Quite a few years ago but we all still remember him. Father Lonergan was, how do you say it, somewhat rigid. For him Christianity was the only path. That sort of teaching creates a lot of difficulty, especially in a small village like Mar'Oth. You will forgive me for saying so, but if we are to live in harmony together we should be honest with one another. Your predecessor seemed preoccupied. Troubled by something personal, I think, and fond of a drink.'

That explained the empty whisky bottles, Giovanni thought. 'Your English is exceptional, Ahmed. I hope to pick up some Arabic.'

'I would be more than happy to help you with that. The villagers are very receptive to anyone who makes the attempt, the mistakes don't matter to them.'

'Well, there will be plenty of those!' Giovanni said. 'What is your view of Christians, Ahmed?'

'As a Muslim or as Ahmed Sartawi?'

'Both, I guess.'

'The Qur'an recognises Jesus as a prophet, but for me the answer lies not in a discussion on the Christian Christ versus the Muslim Christ, nor does it lie in an argument over Christ's ascension from the Mount of Olives versus Muhammad's ascension from the Dome of the Rock. For me the answer goes much further back.'

'Meaning?'

'Meaning that whether we like it or not, Judaism, Christianity and Islam all have a common ancestor, one we all claim as our own.'

'Abraham,' Giovanni said quietly. He too had reflected on the undisputed patriarch of the three great monotheistic faiths that all had their genesis in the Middle East. Perhaps there was an unseen hand that had posted him to this little village far away from the corridors of power at the Vatican. The ruins of a tiny church with its foul-smelling room was but a symbol of man's decay, a decay and corruption that had infiltrated the very top layers of the Holy Catholic Church.

'Abraham,' Ahmed agreed reverently. 'The Qur'an explains that Abraham is one of the four great prophets and the one to whom Allah said, "I have appointed thee to be a leader for mankind." In the Torah, to the Jew, he is the one to whom God said, "Lech Lecha . . . Go forth from thy father's house and I will make of you a great nation." In the New Testament, for the Christian, Paul mentions Abraham more than any other figure, bar Christ.'

'Yet we fight over ownership of Abraham,' Giovanni observed.

Ahmed smiled, recognising that he was in the presence of a fellow thinker. 'Many believers, especially the young, have no idea of our common ancestry through Abraham, but it is the fighting over religion that will eventually bring us all undone, Giovanni. I have a feeling that the countdown for civilisation has begun.'

Giovanni instantly thought of the warning in the Omega Scroll. Again he decided against bringing it up, but he had the same feeling about Ahmed as he had about Patrick O'Hara. Here was a man who was to be trusted.

The Spirit smiled.

'Does the Qur'an warn of that?'

'The signs are there if you want to heed them. Surah 20 tells us that the hour is surely coming. Some of the signs are already with us. The 54th Surah of the Qur'an refers to man digging and furrowing the moon, which happened in 1969. Many Islamic scholars point to signs of increasing warfare, the destruction of cities like Hiroshima and Nagasaki, and increased earthquakes and poverty.'

'Those same warnings are in the Bible, Ahmed,' Giovanni replied, not for the first time wondering if there had been revelation through the Prophet Muhammad as well as Christ. 'The increase in earthquakes is predicted in Matthew and I saw some figures before I left Italy that confirmed that the number of earthquakes around the world is rising dramatically. The prophet Daniel made four predictions. Three of them have already passed.'

'It was the empires, wasn't it? With one still to go?'

'You have studied the Bible?'

'You sound surprised, Giovanni. To the Muslim, Jesus is to be revered as a prophet, peace be upon him. Am I right about Daniel's prophecy?'

'I wish I had as good a grasp of the Qur'an, but yes, you're right. So far Daniel has been chillingly accurate. As I recall his interpretation of Nebuchadnezzar's dream he said, "You were looking, O King and there before you stood a large statue. The head of the statue was made of pure gold. Its chest and arms of silver, its belly and thighs of bronze, its legs of iron." Nebuchadnezzar's dream was a prophecy for the four empires, each of which would fall. Gold for the mighty Babylonians, silver for Medo-Persia which began with Cyrus the Great when he conquered Babylon in 539 BC, bronze for the Greek Empire and Alexander the Great, and the Iron Empire still to go.'

Ahmed nodded. 'Iron being the extension of the Roman Empire which is now embodied in the European Union.'

'Where do you see the United States in that?'

'I don't think the United States has the finesse in foreign policy to ever become an empire. If people like my brother Yusef have their way, many cities in America and those of her allies will be totally destroyed before the fanatical elements of Islam finally turn their attention to greater Europe.'

'Yusef is intolerant of other religions?'

'Our family was killed by the Israelis and we are the only ones left. A story I will tell you another time, but Yusef has sworn to take his revenge and he can't understand why I won't do the same. I understand his hatred but I can't condone it because hatred breeds more hatred. On our side, Arafat has had many chances for peace but he is incapable of delivering.'

'Have you ever thought of running for politics, Ahmed?'

'Not while Arafat is around. He is totally corrupt and it would be a waste of effort even running, always assuming that we get to have elections, but if he ever moved on, I would think about it very seriously. Someone has to do something about this ever-increasing cycle of violence, Giovanni. There is a whole generation of kids who are being brought up to hate the West, something that the US politicians seem to ignore. Once this hatred starts to spiral out of control, the warning on the countdown to the destruction of humanity becomes very clear.'

CHAPTER TWENTY

Jerusalem

In the days that followed, the parishioners of Mar'Oth banded together to help their new, unassuming priest settle in, and some of the Muslims joined their Christian brothers to help as well. Giovanni's kindness to their Imam had not gone unnoticed and within a remarkably short time the little Christian church and Giovanni's quarters were clean and functional. Patrick O'Hara kept his word too, and less than two weeks after Giovanni had settled into Mar'Oth, he was summoned back to Jerusalem to meet Yossi Kaufmann, his wife Marian and their son David. Giovanni arrived early and Patrick, ever sensitive to the people around him, briefed Giovanni on the Kaufmann family background.

'Over the years the Kaufmanns have had more than their fair share of family tragedy. Yossi and Marian both lost their parents in the Holocaust and their eldest son, Michael, was killed in the 1967 Six Day War. David fought in that as a young platoon commander and took part in the assault and liberation of the Old City.

In fact he was responsible for capturing the Rockefeller Museum from the Jordanians and with it the vaults that held the Dead Sea Scrolls. David hates telling the story but I'll be prevailing upon him to tell you how he did it. It makes fascinating listening.'

After dinner, Patrick, Giovanni, Yossi, Marian and David settled into the big comfortable armchairs in Patrick's rambling study.

'*Basta*, *basta!* Patrick. An excellent dinner as usual but *domani!* Tomorrow! I have to work tomorrow.' Professor Kaufmann was used to his host and he protested as Patrick filled his glass. Yossi Kaufmann was tall and square-shouldered, his face fair-skinned and sculpted with laughter lines. His sense of humour was also reflected in his gentle blue eyes.

'You speak Italian, Yossi?' Giovanni asked.

'*Soltanto un poco*,' he replied, putting his thumb and forefinger close together to indicate a little.

'Yossi's too modest,' Marian protested. Marian Kaufmann was tall and elegant. Her long dark hair shone in the soft light, framing her unlined face and her soft but alert brown eyes. They were, Giovanni thought, a very striking couple. 'As well as English and Hebrew, Yossi is quite fluent in Italian and he also has some quite passable Arabic and French.'

'What about you, David?' Giovanni asked.

'I get by, I guess,' David replied with a boyish grin. 'My pursuits have been a little less glamorous than Italian and French. Not much call for ordering a beer in Koiné or Aramaic!' David's playful demeanour made him look much younger than his thirty-nine years.

'I've been trying to converse with the villagers of Mar'Oth in Arabic. All I can say is that they are very tolerant,' Giovanni said. 'You were a platoon commander in the Six Day War?'

'A very good one,' Yossi replied, always ready to give his son credit.

'Have you ever wondered if the Omega Scroll was amongst those you liberated from the Rockefeller Museum, David?' Patrick loved a good conspiracy.

'The Professor and I,' David replied, using his father's title as a term of endearment, 'have often wondered about that. It was pretty chaotic and we had enough trouble securing the building without counting and checking what was in the vault.'

The Professor's face was inscrutable. Yossi Kaufmann had seen some recent Mossad reports indicating that the original and one copy of the Omega Scroll had indeed been in the vaults.

'You should tell Giovanni the story, David,' Patrick prompted.

'Oh, I'm sure Giovanni doesn't want to hear about the war,' David replied reluctantly.

'I'm sorry,' Giovanni replied, mindful of the loss of David's brother. 'I don't want to raise any painful memories.'

'Don't be sorry,' Marian said gently. 'We miss Michael but we've come to terms with his loss. It just makes us all the more determined for peace.'

'But it can't be peace at the expense of one side,' Yossi warned. 'There will never be peace until we reach a solution with the Palestinians that is equitable for both sides. The Palestinians must be given their own State. On the other hand, those who criticise the Jewish nation for warmongering have very little understanding of how reluctant we have been to fight, how divided the Cabinet was in 1967 and that the Palestinians are not the only ones to have suffered terrible losses. In the end we were given little choice. Even today there are still some who want to push us into the sea and if nothing else, the 1967 war serves as a reminder of how futile that approach is. Wars are not the answer,' Yossi said sadly. 'But when the Jewish nation is pushed into a corner we will fight with every means at our disposal.'

'Yes, but David is such a reluctant hero,' Marian added with a warm smile. 'Perhaps I should start, Patrick?'

'Let me refill your glass,' Patrick replied, reaching for the red wine.

Acre

From the day Yossi and Marian had arrived in Acre as teenagers on a fishing trawler after their escape from Vienna in 1938, they had both been captivated by the old city with its Crusader walls, minarets, mosques, souks and the great Khans, where the merchants of Italy and Provence had plied their trade. By 1967 they had found a modest holiday house that was close to the ancient harbour. It was on a narrow, twisting street and one of a row of houses that dated back to the Turkish Ottoman Empire of the eighteenth century.

Marian Kaufmann had set the table simply. Two candles representing God's commandments: *zachor*, to remember, and *shamor*, to observe the Sabbath; a glass of wine and two loaves of *challah* that would remain covered with a white cloth until after the blessings. Marian had long ago lost her own Jewish faith behind the forbidding bluestone walls and wire of the Nazi charnel house at Mauthausen, the concentration camp in Austria where both Yossi's and her own parents had been brutally murdered. Despite this, Marian had a deep respect for Yossi's beliefs and she was happy to observe the Jewish ritual. Yossi and Marian had agreed that both of their sons would receive instruction in the Torah, but the matter of faith had been left to the boys to decide for themselves. David, Marian knew, would never have time for religion. Michael, blond, tall and three years older than David, had the same strong faith as his father. Given the boys' natures it could have been expected to be the other way round – Michael was brash and aggressive; David, mischievous but thoughtful.

Yossi removed the white cloth from the bread and holding one loaf in each hand, he blessed it:

Barukh atah Adonai Elohaynu melekh ha-olam – Blessed are You, Lord, our God, King of the Universe.

Ha-motzi lechem min ha-aretz. Amein – Who brings forth bread from the earth. Amen.

Like the Christians and the Muslims, it was a 'thank you' to the God of Abraham, the same God for all the faiths. The same God and the same hope for peace, yet once again the war clouds were gathering over the cities of the Jews, Christians and Arabs.

'How is the flying going, Michael?' Yossi asked.

'Very well,' Michael responded enthusiastically. 'By the end of next week I will have two hundred hours on the Mirage,' he added proudly.

'Do you think there will be a war, Yossi?' Marian asked, dreading the thought.

'I hope not. Going to war with the Arabs will not solve anything. I think it's time both sides pulled back from this madness. It's time we both tried to walk a mile in the other man's shoes. Palestinians simply want the opportunity to work in peace and make a contribution, but a man without a country is a man without dignity and until we reach agreement on the Palestinian State, the killing will continue.'

'I don't agree,' Michael said. 'I think it's about time we taught these lying Arab bastards a lesson, one they won't forget in a hurry!'

'Michael Kaufmann! I will have none of that language in this house.' Marian had some clear rules when it came to swearing. Yossi suppressed a smile. The language in the officers' mess would no doubt be a lot worse. Yossi was proud of his sons but he, like Marian, had often reflected on how very different their sons were. It was almost as if there was an old soul and a young soul.

Michael was the young soul; full of the enthusiasm and invincibility of youth, a zest for war and adventure without the wisdom to consider the consequences. All he ever wanted to do was fly, and after graduating at the top of his pilot's course he had been assigned to a conversion course for the Dassault Mirage III, dubbed by the Israeli pilots as the Shahak, the 'skyblazer'. After achieving another graduation first, Michael had been posted to the Israeli Defense Force's premier fighter squadron, the 101st, at the huge Hatzhor Air Base. Yossi knew that if it came to war the 101st would be the first into combat. David was the old soul. Partway through an archaeology degree at the Hebrew University at Mount Scopus, he too was in the Reserves as an infantry platoon commander. Yossi also knew from bitter experience that all wars were vicious, but for the infantry they were particularly so, especially if it came to hand-to-hand fighting.

'I shouldn't be telling you this,' Michael continued, unabashed by his mother's rebuke, 'but the Arab scramble time is at least twice that of ours. We'll have 'em on toast!'

'What about you, David? Are you looking forward to teaching the Arabs a lesson?' Marian asked.

David shrugged. 'If we have to fight, we have to fight. But I don't agree with Mikey. The Palestinians have lost their homes and their livelihood and I guess you're right,' he said, looking at his father. 'They're just as much a family people as we are. At the end of the day we took their land. They need a country, too.'

'I always knew there was a reason I didn't go to university,' Michael retorted. 'They're Arabs, for hell's sake.'

Marian sighed. Always it was war – race against race, white against black, Arab against Jew, Christian against Muslim, faith against faith, hatred over tolerance – a vicious and unbroken cycle of escalating violence. It was in man's power to break it, but he had chosen not to.

Jerusalem

Lieutenant David Kaufmann knocked before entering Brigadier General Menachem Kovner's office.

'You sent for me, Menachem?' David asked. Brigadier General Kovner looked up from a desk cluttered with intelligence reports filed in different coloured folders. The green ones were marked 'Confidential' and the red ones 'Secret'; the one open on Kovner's desk was crimson, marking it as a 'Top Secret'.

'Come in, David, and have a seat.' Kovner, a wiry, fit-looking professional soldier, picked up the file and joined his much taller lieutenant at the small conference table that was jammed in one corner of his office.

'What I'm about to tell you must not go out of this room. You are not to discuss it with anyone, except your battalion commander, who is aware of the task I'm about to give you. There is now a strong possibility that we will go to war with Egypt. If we do, the General Staff hope to restrict the war to the one southern front but that will depend on what the Syrians do in the north and what the Jordanians do in the east. It is the Jordanians that I want to talk to you about.'

'Me?' David was at a complete loss as to why a platoon commander could have any influence on the eastern front.

'The Old City and the Dead Sea Scrolls are now in the hands of the Jordanians. The scrolls are being held in the Palestine Museum. When we went to war with Egypt in 1956 the Jordanians stayed out of it. The view in the Cabinet is that they will do so again, but I'm not so sure.'

'You think the Jordanians will attack?' David asked.

'To put it bluntly, yes. Unlike November 1956, the Jordanians know that this time Israel stands alone. Neither the British nor the French will be there and the United States and the Soviets will try to stay out of it. The Jordanians have had your university and our small enclave on Mount Scopus under siege for nearly twenty years. They would dearly love to get it back. The most important of the Dead Sea Scrolls are housed in the Rockefeller Museum.' Brigadier General Kovner got up from the table and pulled down one of several maps that were held in a rollerblind cabinet on the wall. It was a map of

Jerusalem and its environs showing the locations of Jordanian units. He opened the crimson file on the table and placed some aerial photographs and the floor plans of the museum in front of David.

'The Rockefeller Museum is located on Sultan Suleiman Street.' Menachem Kovner pointed to Kerem el-Sheik, a hill just outside the north-eastern corner of the Old City walls where the museum had been built. 'Three months ago the Jordanians nationalised the museum.'

'So it's now Jordanian property?'

'Correct. And whilst I'm not sure the Rockefeller family are overjoyed, in a way the Jordanian Government has played into our hands. If they attack us and enter the war, and if – and this is a big "if" – we drive the Jordanians out of Jerusalem, the museum and more importantly its contents will fall into Israeli hands.'

David realised very clearly what he was being asked to do.

'You want me to capture the Dead Sea Scrolls.' It was a statement rather than a question.

His Brigade Commander smiled. 'Not single-handedly. From time to time your battalion commander and I will be taking an interest in your progress. Given your background and your knowledge of the Scrolls' importance, it will fall to you to ensure these priceless antiquities are not lost to the scholarship of the world. To help you I have arranged for Private Joseph Silberman to join your platoon, but Silberman is a rather unusual recruit.'

'Unusual?'

'Up until a couple of weeks ago he was an inmate of Ramle, and other than teaching him how to shoot to protect himself, we haven't had time to give him the normal military training.'

'Ramle! What's he done?' David asked, intrigued as to why his platoon would need the services of someone confined to one of the harshest prisons in Israel. 'Why is he coming to me?'

Brigadier General Kovner reached for a slim green file marked 'Silberman'. 'His service record, such as it is, and a short biography.

He's not dangerous and very intelligent. He is being assigned to you because he is a master safecracker, one of the best.'

'You want him to crack the Rockefeller's vault?' David ventured quietly.

'Precisely. The vaults in the Rockefeller are big and heavy and they would take a considerable amount of explosive to gain access. Unfortunately, despite our best efforts, Mossad have not been able to get hold of the combination. I don't need to tell you that the Dead Sea Scrolls are irreplaceable, and the world would be less than amused if they were damaged in the process of our blowing up the doors.'

'A locksmith?'

Brigadier General Kovner shook his head. 'There is no way of knowing how much time you will have. You might capture the museum, only to have the Jordanians put in a heavy counter-attack once they tumble to what we're after. Silberman is used to working quickly under pressure. Besides, it's in his interest to get the vault open.'

'A pardon?' David asked insightfully.

Kovner nodded. 'A job working in Mossad for the good guys.' Defining Mossad as the good guys was equal to assigning a degree of benevolence to the CIA, David thought, but he didn't comment.

'You never know, Silberman might be able to teach you a few things.'

'I can't imagine when I might next need to break into a safe, but I shall watch him with interest. Is the museum heavily guarded?' David asked.

'Heavily enough. Last night Jordanian infantry were deployed around the museum itself and there are more infantry and tanks deployed around the Dome of the Rock and the Western Wall.' Kovner traced his finger around the remains of the temple the Romans had destroyed in 70 AD.

'Think of it, David! We might just get it back. For the first time in two thousand years Jerusalem might again be our capital, and for the first time in nearly two decades Jews will be able to pray at Judaism's holiest site.'

'It's been a long time,' David agreed, aware of his superior's strong Jewish faith.

'Of course it all depends on whether Jordan attacks first, but between you and I, I hope they do!'

Menachem Kovner would not have long to wait.

In the Knesset in West Jerusalem, Israel's Military Intelligence Chief, Brigadier General Yossi Kaufmann, was winding up his briefing to a divided War Cabinet. 'Nasser will go to war to shore up his own position in the Arab League,' Yossi concluded.

'We have no choice, Prime Minister.' It was the Defense Minister, Moshe Dayan. 'If we wait for them to strike first we face the very real possibility of defeat. We are outnumbered by overwhelming Arab strength on the ground, in the air and on the water.' Moshe paused and eyed each of his colleagues. 'If we strike first, we will have the advantage of surprise, and that is a critical principle of war,' he concluded, quoting the great war strategist Von Clausewitz.

The Cabinet fell silent. All eyes turned to the Prime Minister.

Prime Minister Eshkol looked at the faces of his Cabinet ministers sitting around the table.

'I am reminded of our ancient forefathers and Psalm 27,' the Prime Minister said. '"Though an army encamp against me, my heart shall not fear; though war rise up against me, yet I will be confident." We go,' he said sadly, 'and may God go with us.'

Once again the trumpets of the *shofars*, the ram's horns, were sounded as they had been sounded so many times before. As they had done under Joshua and King David, the twelve tribes of Israel were once again going to war. This time, instead of the sound of swords being unsheathed, the chilling sounds of war would be those of 105mm Howitzer rounds being slammed into steel breeches.

Opposite the Gaza, in the Negev, and in the Sinai the big guns exploded with a roar of flame and smoke, jumping with the recoil. Before the shock absorbers could fully retract, young Israeli warriors, sweat already beading, sprang at the gun levers. Steel breeches clanged open and smoking brass casings bounced to the ground, to be replaced immediately with another deadly round. Like mini express trains, thousands of rounds roared into the night, each with an Arab life etched on the high explosive casing.

A father, a mother, a son, a daughter.

Death to the Arabs.

A taxi driver, a sales representative, a bank teller. Death to them all. It was time to teach them all a lesson.

Underneath the roar of the big shells the huge twelve-cylinder Merlin engines of the centurion tanks snarled into life, forming three separate spearheads. Before the sun rose on yet another bloody Middle East battle, the Israeli armoured divisions roared into the Gaza and across the ancient desert of the Sinai, battalions of young Israeli infantry soldiers lurching crazily in their wake.

Hatzor Air Base, south of Tel-Aviv

Like every other pilot on the giant Hatzor Air Base, Lieutenant Michael Kaufmann had been woken at four in the morning. The waiting was over; the squadron safes had been opened and the sealed orders for the high-risk Operation Moked broken out.

In the past, air superiority had been achieved by operating the Mirages in large numbers to attack the Egyptian air bases. At the same time as the runways were bombed, base installations were attacked with rockets and the anti-aircraft defences were suppressed. Now, the Soviet-supplied Egyptian Air Force was much bigger and the Israelis had been forced into a strategy of operating small groups of three and four aircraft against a greater number of targets. The Egyptian air defences would be ignored, as would the base installations, and more importantly for the pilots, there were no Israeli fighters assigned to provide protection from Egyptian interceptors. The Israeli pilots would have to watch their own backs.

Hatzor Air Base was still shrouded in pre-dawn darkness as Michael found a space and perched himself on a table at the back of the crowded briefing room. The room was noisy, but the laughter was nervous. No one knew what the Soviet-supplied surface-to-air missiles were really capable of and that was every Israeli pilot's greatest fear. Suddenly the room hushed as their Commanding Officer, one of the Israeli Defense Force's most experienced pilots, made his way to the front of the room.

'What we've all been waiting for,' he said confidently. 'As you can see from the board behind me, H-Hour is in just under three hours at 0745. The strategy is to hit hard and destroy the Arabs on the ground, and given that their reaction is on a par with a wet week, that shouldn't be too hard.'

More nervous laughter echoed around the room.

'A total of seventeen air bases will be hit simultaneously. Our task is to destroy the enemy aircraft at Bir Tmada and Cairo West. The first strikes will take out the runways to prevent the Egyptians getting their aircraft into the air. The next waves will target the aircraft on the ground. I will lead the first wave into Bir Tmada with Captain Linowitz on my wing and Major Shapirah will lead the first wave into Cairo West with Lieutenant Kaufmann on his.'

Michael nodded, his face set with determination.

'Benny and Michael,' he said, looking first at Major Shapirah and then at Michael, 'when you have released you are to refuel and return to the navigation turning point here.' The Commanding Officer turned to the operations map and indicated a point off Bardavil and Port Said.

Michael listened with rising excitement as their Commanding Officer flicked on an overhead showing the enemy deployments and the tasking detail. The Egyptian line-up was impressive: one hundred and fifty MiG-15 and -17s; eighty MiG-19s; one hundred and thirty of the latest Russian MiG-21s; twelve SU-7s; and thirty of the massive TU-16 strategic bombers.

'We will take off in complete radio silence with our radio sets switched off. Our strategy depends heavily on surprise.'

'What happens if we have a problem after take-off?' one of the younger pilots asked. 'The base will be busy with aircraft behind us and we'll be on radio silence.'

'You set course for the coast and eject.'

Several of the pilots exchanged glances. Even under normal conditions the chances of being found in the sea after ejecting were by no means certain. The chances of being found when no one knew where or when you had ejected were almost nonexistent.

Michael had no such fears. Instead he felt a surge of exhilaration. He was in the first wave and a short time later he and the other superbly trained young Israelis strode from the 101 Squadron crew room at Hatzor Air Base into the crisp early morning air. It was still an hour before dawn, and darkness cloaked the quietly humming air base. The bus to take them out to their aircraft was ready, its engine running. Unlike their fellow airmen across the Suez Canal, the Israelis had been careful to disperse all of their precious aircraft in blast shelters and one by one the bus dropped each pilot at his allotted bay.

Michael's ground crew were waiting. With the exception of the sergeant, every one of them was a civilian and like much of the Israeli Defense Force, they were a ragtag-looking outfit with not a matching windcheater in sight, but appearances could be deceptive. They might have seemed a far cry from the immaculate pit crews of the world's Formula One racing teams, but Michael's crew and the other Israeli ground crews would have been employed by any Formula One pit boss on the circuit. They could re-fuel, re-arm and turn an aircraft around in under eight minutes. It was one of the factors that would decide the war in the air. For the first two days of the war, the Israelis would manage to have their jets in the air for 80 per cent of the day. It was a feat that no other air force in the world could match, and certainly not the Arabs.

Michael greeted his crew with his customary smile and sprang up the aluminium ladder propped against the fuselage of his aircraft. He eased himself into the narrow cockpit and gave the ground crew the thumbs-up.

The Mirage IIIC was coiled in its nest like a giant three-legged bee with sand and brown coloured camouflage and a touch of green that on low-level runs made the Shahaks very hard to pick up from above. The Star of David was emblazoned on the starboard and port air intakes of the fuselage; some things were not meant to be hidden. The trademark delta wings were swept back at sixty degrees and external fuel tanks were suspended under each wing like two giant cigars. Under the fuselage were 150-kilogram runway-piercing bombs along with two 30mm cannon on either side that could fire over a thousand rounds a minute. In Michael's case, his aircraft's wing racks were also fitted with Matra 'Diamond' air-to-air missiles.

Michael flipped open his pre-flight checklist and commenced his pre-start checks. He could have done it blindfolded:

Ignition/Ventilation switch – ignition
Pre-heat switch – off
Low-pressure fuel pumps – off
Afterburner cock – on
Speed brake switch . . .

Halfway through his pre-start he pressed the rudder trim light to test it. He grinned as he glanced at the next check. Radio sets – on. Skip that one, he thought wryly. One after another he tested the armament master light, the speed brake light, the incident warning lights and the undercarriage flasher. Satisfied, he looked to his flight crew sergeant and gave him the thumbs-up for an engine start. Checking that the fuel cock and pumps were both on, Michael depressed the starter button and confirmed the ignition light. When the engine reached 700 rpm he moved the throttle to idle. Automatically his eyes flicked across the instrument panel, monitoring the fire warning lights, and the oil and hydraulic lights. With the rpm stabilised at 2800, he gave the thumbs-up again to his crew chief and when the wheel chocks were away he moved slowly out of the blast shelter to join the first wave of aircraft, sashaying down the taxiway to the far end of the runway – navigation and anti-collision lights extinguished, dark menacing shapes, engines with wings. The faint glow of the instrument panels reflected on the visors of the young Israeli pilots.

Death to the Arabs.

The Jordanians started shelling the Jewish sector of the Old City a few hours after the Israelis launched their attacks in the south against the Egyptian forces in the Sinai. At first the Israeli Cabinet was unperturbed. The High Command had expected that King Hussein would show a measure of loyalty to the Arab cause, but when the shelling got heavier and spread along the whole of the eastern front, the Cabinet began to realise that war with Jordan was inevitable.

As a lieutenant, David was not accustomed to attending even battalion orders, much less brigade, but these were not ordinary times and he took his place alongside his Commanding Officer and waited for Brigadier General Menachem Kovner to begin.

'Last night the Jordanians machine-gunned innocent civilians on the Jaffa Road. This morning they captured the United Nations Headquarters at Government House and they have started shelling the city. Over six hundred buildings have been damaged including the Prime Minister's residence, the King David Hotel and many of the holy sites, including the dome of the Church of the Dormiton.' The Church of the Dormiton was just south of the Old City, close to King David's tomb, and reputedly the place where Christ had presided over the Last Supper.

'Mount Scopus has also been captured by the Arabs.' Menachem strode over to the operations map. 'The Jordanian presence south of the Old City threatens to outflank the entire city, including the Knesset. As a result, the 19th Armoured Brigade is now moving from its positions east of Tel-Aviv and has orders to re-take Mount Scopus and the Hebrew University to the north of the Old City. The 6th Brigade has orders to advance in the south and re-take the Mount of Evil Counsel. From there they will turn north towards the Garden of Gethsemane and the Mount of Olives. We have possibly the most difficult task of all. The American Sector and the Rockefeller Museum.' Kovner paused and looked at his commanders. 'It has taken nearly two thousand years, but a little over an hour ago, Cabinet approved plans to re-take the Old City of Jerusalem.'

His announcement was greeted with a loud cheer. As in the time of King David, the Israelites were preparing once again to take back their ancient capital. The modern equivalent of King David's warriors were the crack paratroopers of the 9th Airborne Brigade, all of them Reservists.

When the applause had died down Brigadier General Kovner outlined his plan. If successful, the results of the battle would be broadcast in minutes, not only to Israelis, but to Jews in every corner of the world. If they failed, they would not be forgiven lightly.

'Because of the holy sites, not only Jewish, but Christian and Muslim as well, there will be no artillery or air cover over the Old City itself. It will come down to hand-to-hand fighting,' Menachem Kovner said, 'but we have one advantage. We are experts at night-fighting, and for that reason we go tonight.'

Crump. Crump. Crump. The night sky over Jerusalem lit up as the Jordanians pounded it with artillery and mortar shells.

Death to the Jews.

David and the rest of his platoon took shelter in doorways and around corners as a sudden burst of machine gun fire crackled across the deserted road. When viewed from behind, the lines of green and red tracer seemed surreally graceful as they ricocheted off the old stone walls and climbed into the night sky, but on his platoon's side of the road it looked decidedly ugly and David ducked as the bullets cracked and thumped around him.

'Above the Gate! On the ramparts!'

'I see him!' One of his section commanders raised an M79 and took cool and deliberate aim.

'Grenade!' The shoulder-fired grenade snaked across the road and exploded on top of the Damascus Gate. The machine gun fell silent.

Death to the Arabs.

'Cover me!' David dashed forward another 45 metres to the next alleyway. Centimetre by centimetre, metre by metre, grenade by grenade, the platoon fought their way up Sultan Suleiman Street towards the Rockefeller Museum. The small-arms fire was sporadic now but again David asked for cover as he ran towards the corner of Haroun al-Rashid and Suleiman. Suddenly the world exploded and he was thrown to the ground. Dazed, he shook his head and crawled into the nearest alleyway.

'Shit!' he muttered to himself. 'Fucking tanks!' He felt his right cheek. Blood. And a lot of it. Another flash appeared from the bottom of the Mount of Olives and David hugged the cobblestones as the round exploded 45 metres in front of his position. Obviously the 6th Brigade had been unable to dislodge the Arabs.

Lieutenant Michael Kaufmann forced himself to relax as he waited to roll. The radio silence was eerie. They had done it before in practice but this time it was for real. He scanned his instruments again, looking for the slightest sign of a mechanical problem but all the warning lights were out, and the Mirage had an advantage over normal aircraft. Even if rotation and the point of no return was reached, Michael could still deploy his braking chute and bring the aircraft to a stop in the wire barrier at the far end of the runway. Once the nose wheel was up and he had lift-off, however, any engine failure could be catastrophic. Despite his thirst for battle Michael had no desire to join the select few who had survived an ejection during take-off.

Trims neutral. Booster pumps on. Afterburner cock on. Hydraulics normal, switch down. Canopy locked. Like a well-oiled machine, he routinely ticked off each taxiing check. Again he tested the controls for freedom of movement. A tongue of flame exploded from the rear of the first Mirage on the runway. His Commanding Officer was rolling. Michael was fourth in line and when his turn came he followed the other aircraft onto the 'piano keys' and checked his gyro against the runway heading. At the same time he applied the foot brake and quickly ran the engine up to 'full dry'. The rpm needle spun around rapidly and when it reached 8500 he released the brakes and lit the after-burner. Checking for ignition, Michael pushed the throttle forward and was almost immediately pushed back in his seat as 6200 kilograms of thrust from the Snecma Atar 9C turbojet blasted out of the exhaust and the fully laden Mirage accelerated down the long runway. At the rotation point Michael eased the stick back and launched after the three glowing orange flames that were already well above him. Afterburners. They increased the aircraft's climb rate to over 1500 metres a minute. The undercarriage lights went out abruptly and Michael checked his rudder trim. He quickly levelled out and closed on the three points of orange light in front of him. Out over the inky blackness of the Mediterranean towards the navigation turn-ing point, selected to give the Israeli pilots an attack vector from the north from which the Egyptians would least expect them.

The launch of the fighters and the rest of Israel's precious one hundred and sixty combat aircraft had been timed so that each would arrive over the seventeen Egyptian air bases at 0745, when the Egyptians would be at their mandatory breakfasts. To avoid the Egyptian radars the run in to the target would not be above 20 metres. It called for some very precise navigation and flying from the Israeli pilots.

Across the Suez Canal the Egyptian pilots and their ground crews slept peacefully. At the big Abu Suweir Air Base the main radar was turned off for repairs, the unconnected cables and technicians' tools still strewn around the building. As Lieutenant Michael Kaufmann and the rest of his squadron streaked low across the Mediterranean towards the Nile and Cairo West, many of the Egyptian aircraft still had their protective covers on and were parked wing tip to wing tip.

At 0743 Michael followed Benny Shapirah as they climbed and turned on their final bombing run, bracing himself for the Egyptian anti-aircraft fire he felt sure would come soon. He watched as Benny dropped the specially designed 150-kilogram runway-piercing bombs right over the runway in front of him and then Michael held them in his bomb sight as the parachutes deployed, slowing the bombs down. The retro-rockets fired, burying the bombs deep in the runway concrete. As the runway erupted in front of him, Michael calmly screamed towards it and added two more bombs to the destruction of the strip.

In an instant they were past the airfield and climbing. Back to their base to refuel and then out over the Mediterranean where they would provide the combat air patrol high above the turning point, just in case the Egyptians woke up to the Israeli navigation plan.

That didn't seem likely, Michael thought, grinning behind his visor as he watched the Mirages behind him streak in to strafe the Egyptian planes lined up like ducks in a shooting gallery.

Lieutenant Michael Kaufmann couldn't have been more wrong.

Two more flashes from the Mount of Olives and seconds later the road in front of Lieutenant David Kaufmann erupted with a deafening roar. Red hot pieces of flying metal tore great chunks of stone from the ancient walls of the Old City while David and his platoon hugged the ground. When the shrapnel had shrieked past, David held his hand up, thumb towards his ear and little finger towards his mouth, the sign to summon his radio operator from further down the alley. Ignoring the blood streaming from the wound to his cheek, David focused his binoculars on the general area of the flashes. Slowly and deliberately he scanned the foothills of the Mount of Olives on the other side of the Valley of Kidron. Desert camouflage did not blend well with the greenery in an olive grove and it was not long before he picked out the first of the Jordanian tanks. Tanks usually operated in troops of three and David scoured the hillside until he had found the other two. Sliding his compass from the side pocket of his trousers he took a bearing and did a quick mental calculation to convert the magnetic bearing to a grid bearing on the map.

'Two this is two two, over.'

'Two, over.'

'Two two, fire mission battery. Grid 950619, direction 285, three tanks dug in, over.'

'Two, roger. Wait, out.'

Thank God there were no restrictions against artillery targets on the Mount of Olives, David thought, not fancying his chances of getting into the museum with the cross-hairs of three 105mm guns watching him from a little more than 1300 metres away. More importantly, his superiors would not be too pleased if the priceless scrolls were blown into any more fragments than they were already in.

'Shot, over.'

'Shot, out.'

The Israeli guns supporting David's brigade were about 6 kilometres back in the Rose Park, not far from the Knesset. A muffled and distant crump was followed by the hollow roar of an express train as the 105mm armour-piercing round whistled overhead, but it missed its target, exploding further up the hill from the tanks and to the right. David remained unperturbed. Close he thought, but not close enough. In any case it was rare to score a direct hit with the first round.

'Left 100, drop 100, fire for effect, over.'

'Left 100, drop 100, fire for effect, out.'

David watched the Mount of Olives explode in brilliant flashes of orange. A bigger explosion and the unmistakable shape of a tank barrel rose briefly through the smoke. One down, two to go, but then first one and then the other tank broke cover, throwing large clumps of dirt and broken olive trees behind their tracks as they withdrew at high speed towards the safety of the next hill.

David turned his attention to his own target. He positioned a machine gun so that it had a good view of the foyer of the museum and he broke cover.

'Let's go!'

The first section followed their young leader towards the entrance. With just 45 metres to go a burst of fire from the gardens around the museum tore into his signaller running beside him. Once again, a grenade arced towards the Arab position and the score was settled.

'Grab the radio!' David yelled. He checked for a pulse. There was nothing that could be done other than to press on with the attack. His signaller had been married a week. Angry, David doubled forward to the wall beside the museum entrance where he paused. He then leapt into the foyer and sprayed the courtyard with a sustained burst of fire. Two goldfish in the pool were added to the casualty list. The Arabs had fled.

Wall by wall, corridor by corridor, room by room, Lieutenant Kaufmann and his men cleared the museum. When David was satisfied that no Palestinian or Jordanian forces remained, he posted sentries on the roof, then headed unerringly towards the vaults in the basement, taking three men and Joseph Silberman with him.

If Private Silberman had been shaken by being in the thick of a fire-fight with only a few days military training behind him, there was no sign.

'This is it. Think you can crack it?'

Silberman smiled. 'It's 1930s technology. Fifteen minutes. Twenty at the outside.'

David watched, fascinated, as Joseph took a stethoscope from the little black bag he had over his shoulder, plugged in the earpieces and placed the diaphragm against the combination dial. First, he spun the big dial to the left to clear the tumblers and then he turned it one revolution to the right.

'Twenty-five,' he announced as his stethoscope picked up the distinct click of the cam and lever mechanism engaging. 'Last number.'

David wrote it down in his notebook. In the short time Joseph Silberman had been part of his platoon he had actually come to like the little Israeli from 'the other side of the tracks'. Silberman had offered to show David how to break into a safe and pick a lock with the special tools he kept for just that purpose. Out of curiosity, David had found time to understand and practise Joseph Silberman's illegal craft on a wall safe and a padlock. Now he was watching the master in action.

Silberman continued to turn the big silver dial with its hundred black gradations. When he was satisfied that the old vault had only three tumblers, Silberman started to rock the dial back and forth, advancing one or two gradations each time. Suddenly he stopped.

'Eighteen,' he said as the soft 'nikt' of another tumbler slot being lined up sounded in his stethoscope. Silberman was better than his word. Ten minutes later he turned the big wheel on the vault door and the huge retaining bolts slid noiselessly from their recesses.

'After you, Lieutenant,' he said, stepping back with a satisfied grin on his face. The challenge of breaking in. Nothing gave Joseph Silberman greater pleasure.

'I'm glad you're on our side,' David said as he stepped past Silberman and into the vault. The Mossad agent had not been mistaken. Rows of small black trunks were coded and stacked in racks that reached to the ceiling. Two were stored separately from the others and David opened one of them and stepped back in awe.

The Isaiah Scroll. Up until now, the oldest known text of the complete Book of Isaiah had been the Ben Asher codex from Cairo which had been dated to 895 AD. David knew he was looking at leather from Qumran that had been inscribed at least a thousand years earlier. Had he had time to open the trunk next to it the world might have been a different place. The Omega Scroll held the clues for civilisation to avert the final countdown. David was jolted from his thoughts by the sound of running footsteps. One of his section commanders burst into the vault.

'David! They have reached the Wall!'

For twenty years the Old City of Jerusalem had been part of the border between the Arabs and the Jews. No Jew had lived in the city's Jewish Quarter since the Israelis, mostly elderly rabbis and their students, had been forced out when the Arab Legion stormed through the narrow streets in May of 1948. The most holy of Jewish cities had been turned into a tangle of blocked alleyways and barbed wire. Today the concrete barricades, twisted wire and rusted tin had been stormed by a different legion. The 9th Airborne Brigade could now add 'street fighting' to their list of skills. House by house, alley by alley down the Via Dolorosa where Christ had laboured with his cross on the way to Calvary, past the Mosque of Omar where Muhammad had ascended to heaven. With grenade after grenade, sniper bullet after sniper bullet, the Israeli paratroopers had fought their way to the Wall. As the sun rose above the Old City, battle-hardened veterans leaned against the ancient stones erected by King Solomon and wept. The chaplain to the Israeli Defense Forces, Rabbi Shlomo Goren, raised the *shofar* to his lips and the discordant blare of the ram's horn rose above the intermittent sniper fire and the heavier sound of distant artillery. Rabbi Goren opened his old Torah.

'Praise the name of the Lord!' His voice echoed around the Temple Mount. 'Trust in the Lord Israel, for He is thy strength and thy shield. He has heard thy supplication. He has become thy salvation. Give thanks to the Lord for He is good and His steadfast love endures for ever.'

The Israelis were back.

Brigadier General Kaufmann was in the Command Centre when the news was received. He had never witnessed anything like it. Loud cheers echoed around the room and generals and sergeants had tears streaming down their cheeks. It was a memorable day amongst the many in the long battle-scarred history of the Jewish nation.

Elsewhere the war was going better than any Israeli could ever have dreamed it would. Nearly half the Egyptian Air Force had been annihilated in the first few minutes of the war. The surprise had been complete and absolute. The news came in that David had captured the Scrolls and Yossi silently thanked his God for his son's safety, adding a prayer for Michael.

En route to the navigation turning point the two Mirages were just passing through 3000 metres when Michael's earphones crackled.

'Ilyushin-14, 900 metres. Cover me!' Benny yelled. The need for radio silence had long since disappeared. Without waiting for a reply, Major Benny Shapirah rolled into the attack and dived on the unsuspecting Russian Ilyushin-14 transport.

Michael scanned the skies and then he saw him, coming out of the sun at about 6000 metres.

'MiG-21 on your tail,' he reported quickly.

'Got 'im. Let him come,' Benny replied.

Michael watched, almost mesmerised as Major Shapirah broke off the attack on the Ilyushin and allowed the MiG-21 to close on his tail. Benny slowed his aircraft, forcing the Egyptian pilot to overshoot, a manoeuvre that would not be found in any text-book on dogfighting. It required nerves of steel and Benny, one of Israel's aces, had spent many hours perfecting it. As the hapless Egyptian shot past Benny's Mirage, Benny loosed off three short bursts of cannon fire. Seconds later the MiG-21 disintegrated in a ball of flame as the 30mm cannon found its mark.

Michael recovered his vigilance just in time to sight the second Russian-built MiG-21 'Fishbed' coming in below him and lining up for an attack on Benny's Mirage.

'Second Fishbed on your tail, am engaging,' he reported non-chalantly as he rolled into the attack behind the second Egyptian. The Egyptian had made the mistake of allowing his focus to remain on his target to the exclusion of everything else. By the time the Egyptian pilot realised he wasn't 'clean' it was too late. Michael held his sights on the now twisting and turning MiG until he had closed to less than 200 metres. He depressed the trigger on the joystick repeatedly, slowly and deliberately, and short bursts of cannon ripped into the fleeing Egyptian. It exploded in front of him as the cannon found the high-octane starter fuel tank that the Russian aeronautical engineers had inexplicably posi-tioned beside the pilot's oxygen bottle. For a moment Michael was blinded as he flew straight through the black pall of smoke.

'Michael! On your tail!' A third MiG had joined the fight.

Instinctively Michael broke hard right, then left, but his aircraft was already shuddering as the Egyptian's cannon found its mark. Michael rolled, broke left again and pulled up hard in a desperate bid to shake off his pursuer. Another burst of cannon shattered the canopy, shrapnel hitting Michael in the neck. As the Mirage spun out of control, throttle still fully forward, Michael tried to reach for the ejection handle, his arm strangely heavy and unresponsive.

'Eject, Michael! You're hit! Eject! Eject!'

Lieutenant Michael Kaufmann never heard the message. At close to the speed of sound the Mediterranean was like a concrete wall. One of Israel's finest young pilots had flown his last sortie.

'General Kaufmann, could I have a word?' The young Israeli captain's eyes were misty. Instinctively, Yossi knew what she was about to tell him.

Jerusalem

'I'm very sorry about Michael. Such a senseless loss,' Giovanni sympathised. 'It must have been very hard to deal with.'

'Yes, even though it was nearly twenty years ago, we still miss him every day,' Yossi said with a sad look in his eyes. 'It has made me very determined that his life and the lives of others will not be wasted, although we don't seem to learn much from history,' he added ruefully. 'Unless we stop building settlements on Palestinian land and start genuine negotiations we're all going to be on a very slippery slope,' Yossi said. 'Today it's hijacking airliners, tomorrow it might be something far more sinister.'

'What makes you say that?' Giovanni asked.

'I spent a long time in military intelligence, Giovanni. It's common knowledge that several of Israel's enemies are keen on acquiring nuclear technology, but there is something else. Have you ever seen any of the work I've done on the codes in the Dead Sea Scrolls?'

'Patrick was kind enough to give me one of your papers. I found it fascinating.'

'Then you will have seen my analysis on the horrifying warning that is in the Omega Scroll.'

Giovanni was tempted to lay his cards on the table. He felt sure he could trust Patrick and Yossi but he held back. The Vatican would deny it all emphatically.

'The Essenes were a very advanced and thoughtful scientific community,' Yossi said, 'and I believe if they saw fit to record this warning, we should take notice.'

Long after Patrick's guests had left, Giovanni lay awake in his room overlooking the Old City's Christian Quarter Road. Could it be that when the Romans destroyed the Essenes at Qumran, an ancient seat of scientific learning had been lost? Giovanni knew that many people would be sceptical, but he also knew many ancient civilisations were far more advanced than at first thought. The dry cell battery, he recalled, had been invented over two thousand years before it had appeared in Western civilisation. The ancient versions had been made out of a copper cylinder set in pitch with an iron rod inside and there was an example of one in the Baghdad museum, but when the Greeks and Romans developed a preference for oil, the technology had been lost. Was it possible there was a lot more to the Essenes than modern scholarship had allowed? The answer lay hidden in the Judaean desert.

BOOK FOUR

1990

Ω

CHAPTER TWENTY-ONE

Milano

Allegra was quietly confident. She had gained her Masters with Distinction and enjoyed some notable successes assisting Professor Rosselli researching archaeological DNA. The Professor had persuaded her to take her doctorate and the moment of truth had arrived. It was now two months since she'd handed in her doctoral thesis and it seemed that a little piece of her had gone with it. Three long years of painstaking research. She had been confident during the two hour grilling by the Examination Board, although Professor Rosselli had not looked at her when she left, so she was in a bit of a quandary as to how the oral exam might have gone. When she went over her responses, she realised that perhaps a different emphasis might have been given to the mitochondrial DNA, or to the links to dendrochronology, but it was too late for that and she knocked on Professor Rosselli's door.

'*Avanti! S'accomodi.*'

Allegra had grown used to the smell of the Professor's pipe and it no longer bothered her, which was just as well. Somewhere in amongst the smoke and the piles of books on philosophy and science there was a desk and a person. Her mentor had his back to her, busy at the smaller computer at his side desk, trademark white hair as untidy as ever, smoke spiralling above it. He swivelled back behind his main desk to face her, a look of puzzlement in his normally mischievous eyes.

'Sit down, Allegra,' he said, offering her the old 'Captain's Chair' that leaned lopsidedly in front of the academic chaos on his desk.

'So, how do you think your doctoral thesis might have been received by the Board?' Rosselli was frowning now.

Allegra felt a small twinge of doubt. 'I gave it my best shot, Antonio,' she said.

'Hmm,' he responded with uncharacteristic haughtiness, and Allegra's doubts gained ground.

Professor Rosselli rummaged in what passed for an in-tray, retrieving a letter from the pile, his quizzical look more evident now. 'In your case the Board have reached an interesting conclusion, Dr Bassetti.'

Allegra braced herself for bad news.

'You seem nervous?'

'I am a bit.'

'Not happy with the title?'

'Of my thesis?' she asked, puzzled now.

'Doctor?'

Allegra looked at him uncomprehendingly and then realised what he'd called her. Her hand went to her mouth.

'Oh. You mean I've been accepted?'

'If you have a fault that needs correction, young lady,' Professor Rosselli said, his frown replaced by a broad smile, his old eyes dancing with delight at the success of his subterfuge, 'it is that you underestimate your abilities. You are confident enough on the outside, but I would like to see more from within.' Professor Rosselli glanced at the letter.

'The Board was unanimous. We thought it was one of the most outstanding doctoral theses on DNA that we have seen for a very long time. The Vatican will turn itself inside out to discredit your work, but we particularly liked your linkages to carbon dating and the Dead Sea Scrolls. Your theory that some of these scrolls date from around the time of Christ will no doubt stir up a hornet's nest. My congratulations. An amazing piece of work, Dr Bassetti. I think the title suits you.'

'I'll try and get used to it,' Allegra replied, her feelings a mixture of relief and exhilaration.

'We intend to publish it widely, if that's all right with you.'

'I would take it as a compliment, Antonio.'

'Good, because I am under some pressure from church groups to justify my views on the usefulness of scientific techniques in dating archaeological artefacts such as the Dead Sea Scrolls. I would like you to give a lecture on carbon dating, primarily for our students, but one that will also be open to the public. We've already put out some feelers and a lot of people want to come, including one group from the Buffett Evangelical Centre for Christ. As you might gather, they're fundamentalist Christian and they want equal time to present proof from the Bible that the Earth is only a few thousand years old and that carbon dating is fatally flawed.'

Allegra rolled her eyes.

'Don't worry, I'm not about to let a scientific discussion be taken over by a bunch of fruit loops. I've given them a polite no to equal time, although of course they're entitled to their wacky views and I've told them they are welcome to come.'

'And are they?' Allegra asked, suddenly concerned that she was being dragged back into a world of dogma from which she had long freed herself.

'Welcome? On a par with your mother-in-law announcing she's coming to live with you. Will they come? On a par with the sun rising tomorrow. They're talking about sending one or two of their heavies over from their Atlanta headquarters, but you needn't worry. I'll be there to chair so they won't be able to hijack question time.'

Allegra breathed a sigh of relief. 'Are you sure you shouldn't be giving this lecture, Antonio?'

The old maestro could have given the lecture with practised ease but he knew that the beautiful young woman on his staff possessed a very fine mind, and he was determined she should be given the opportunity to stretch her wings. Outside the University of Milano Dr Allegra Bassetti was still unknown but Rosselli knew that would change.

'I could,' he said, 'but I won't be here for ever. Sooner or later someone has to be around to take the place of old badgers like me. Besides, you're just as qualified and a little easier on the eye. They can put up with me for the other half of the lecture, one which I have named "The lost civilisation of the Essenes, DNA and the Omega Scroll".'

Allegra felt a chill. The Omega Scroll. The speculation had died down long ago and other than a passing reference Professor Rosselli hadn't brought it up. Why now, she wondered.

'Do you think that's wise, Antonio. The Omega Scroll seems to be the Essene's version of the curse of the Pharaohs.'

'Yes,' he replied. 'I'm convinced Professor Fiorini was murdered, but I'm equally convinced that was because he was about to link the Vatican to the Omega Scroll.'

'You spoke to him before he disappeared?'

'Only a brief phone call. He didn't want to say too much over the phone but he told me he had some exciting news about the Omega Scroll. He disappeared before we could talk.'

'Why are you including it in your lecture?'

'Firstly, I'm not going to mention the Vatican and secondly, my friend Professor Kaufmann, who I would like you to meet one day, has unearthed some interesting links between DNA and the

Essenes. Don't worry, I doubt the Vatican will show the slightest interest.'

Cardinal Lorenzo Petroni saw the last but one of his dinner guests to the door. The Minister for Finance, the editor of the influential *Milano Finanza* and Milano's Il Capo di Guardia di Finanza. The guest list for dinner had also included three merchant bankers and the CEO of Cologne Constructions, one of Europe's largest property developers. Petroni's remaining guest, Giorgio Felici, was enjoying a Rémy Martin Louis XIII Cognac by the fire in the Cardinal's study.

'*Allora*, I think that went fairly well, Giorgio?' Petroni said on his return.

'Some useful contacts, Lorenzo, for when you become Cardinal Secretary of State, *non è vero?*'

Lorenzo Petroni eyed the little Sicilian without expression. Giorgio Felici had his uses, and when Petroni had last been at the helm of the Vatican Bank he had persuaded the Holy Father that he should appoint Giorgio Felici as his financial adviser. The Pope had agreed and the Vatican award of 'Gentleman of His Holiness' had been promptly bestowed on the merchant banker from Milano. In the years that he'd been out of the Vatican as Cardinal Archbishop of Milano, Petroni had come to regret the arrangement intensely. The Vatican Bank holdings had become so large that Felici had acquired direct access to the Papal Apartments. Petroni had been trying to find a way to restore his own control and have Felici report through him, and now, he reflected with more than a little satisfaction, that could be done. The previous day, His Holiness had announced that Cardinal Lorenzo Petroni would take over as the Vatican's Cardinal Secretary of State. Petroni had received the news calmly. It was, he thought, part of the natural progression and he was finally within striking distance of his ultimate goal. The Pope, Petroni had noted, kept a gruelling schedule and his health seemed unusually robust, but time would tell.

'When do you plan to take up your appointment?' Giorgio asked.

'I leave for Rome next Tuesday.'

'Perhaps it is not a moment too soon, Lorenzo.'

'Oh?' Petroni replied off-handedly, but he was instantly alert.

'The new Director of the Bank, Monsignor Pasquale Garibaldi, will need to be replaced.'

Petroni's expression gave nothing away. When Garibaldi had been first mooted as a candidate he had tried to have his appointment stopped. Garibaldi had a reputation for scrupulous honesty and transparency.

'Monsignor Garibaldi has confided in me that he has found some irregularities in the accounts. It seems he may have twigged to our double invoicing scheme,' Giorgio Felici said quietly.

Petroni felt his pulse quicken but he said nothing. An earlier scheme had come perilously close to landing Petroni in gaol, but after the death of Pope John Paul I, Felici and Petroni had resurrected the scheme. Petroni had retained control of the Vatican Bank, and he had not been able to resist the thrill of millions of dollars pouring into the Papal coffers through a subsidiary bank that was jointly owned by Felici and the Vatican. Thousands of false and artificially low invoices from Felici's trading companies were sent to the Tax Office through the Bank of Italy. The false invoices attracted much less tax and the difference on the real invoices would be paid in cash by the receiving companies overseas and channelled back to Felici and the Vatican Bank. For the scheme to succeed the necessary bribes were being paid to government officials, but the Vatican Bank also had to be watertight.

'I have told Monsignor Garibaldi he is to continue his investigation, and that I am very keen for the Vatican Bank to overcome its earlier, shall we say, difficulties and that he is to report directly to me. I have bought us some time, but he will need to be dealt with quickly.' Giorgio's smile was humourless.

'You can leave that problem with me,' Petroni said, irritated by the Sicilian's superior manner. 'In the meantime, there is a more pressing issue. Professor Antonio Rosselli is planning to give a lecture next week on the Omega Scroll. I have an advance copy of the text.'

'Not provided by him,' Felici observed with a touch of sarcasm.

'You are not the only one who is well connected in Milano, Georgio,' Petroni replied. 'It is not only his lecture. I have received word that Rosselli has been in contact with an Israeli mathematician and as a result, Rosselli's investigation into the Omega Scroll is gathering pace. Rosselli has to be stopped.'

'That will attract a lot of heat, Lorenzo,' Felici said. 'It's likely to focus attention back on the Vatican and the death of Pope John Paul I, and that might be awkward.'

'These things are always temporary, Giorgio, and as Secretary of State I will be well positioned to handle any upstarts from the media. Rosselli's theories are one thing, but connecting them with the Omega Scroll is quite another. The Holy Church must be protected, and I suggest you leave the theology to me. You do your job, and I'll do mine.'

Felici smiled.

'It will be expensive,' he said, not caring too much about the reasons behind Petroni's burning desire to rid himself of the troublesome Professor at Ca' Granda. Felici's voice held a faint hint of admiration for a cold-blooded ruthlessness that matched his own.

The same day that Lorenzo Petroni took up his appointment as Cardinal Secretary of State, Giorgio Felici dressed in a pair of dirty overalls and a paint-spattered cap and headed for the University of Milano. The students and faculty at Ca' Granda took no notice as he walked into the grounds through the rear car park and up some narrow steps that led past the Faculty of Philosophy towards the main quadrangles. Felici had memorised the map of the university grounds and he made his way unerringly down the corridor that housed the offices of Professor Rosselli and Dr Bassetti. Satisfied, he made his way across to the faculty theatre where Bassetti's and Rosselli's lectures were scheduled to be held. Given the choice he decided on the theatre. The office block was too confined whereas the external fire escape from the mezzanine floor that housed the theatre projection facilities provided direct access to the car park below. The locks on the doors to the projector room were standard and Giorgio's third key fitted perfectly.

Roma

The Holy Father's first meeting with his new Secretary of State had gone well until Petroni was surprised and annoyed over a trivial matter exercising the Holy Father's mind.

'I understand that Father Donelli is presently serving in the Middle East, Lorenzo.'

'A most promising priest, Holiness. He was sent there to broaden his experience.'

'How long has he been there?' the Pope asked.

Lorenzo Petroni was on guard, but not quickly enough, and he instantly regretted the tactical slip of acknowledging the ability of the dangerously competent Donelli.

'I'm not sure, Holiness,' Petroni lied easily. 'Perhaps eighteen months.'

'I think you will find it is longer than that, if my sources are accurate.'

Inwardly Cardinal Petroni was fuming; outwardly he maintained his practised calm and said nothing, waiting for the old Pope's next move. The first Vatican Council might have agreed in 1870 that the Holy Father was infallible but the new Cardinal Secretary of State was determined to curb the Holy Father's power if it wasn't being used correctly. When it suited Petroni there could be a degree of fallibility in the infallible.

'More than five years, in fact,' the old Pope said. 'I'm not sure why we sent him to the Middle East for such a long period but I understand he's been serving in a small village that is part Christian and part Muslim. We may be able to use, as you put it, his "broader experience" here in the Vatican.'

'What did you have in mind, Holiness?' Petroni asked warily.

'The rise of Islam is an interesting phenomenon,' the Pope replied enigmatically. 'A very real threat to the true Faith. Perhaps it is time we had a closer look as to what our response to it might be, and to the other faiths, especially Judaism. It would seem that a man of Father Donelli's talent and experience might be an excellent choice for such a task. Do you think you could find a position for him? As a bishop?' His Holiness asked.

Petroni suppressed his anger. 'I will look into it, Holiness. There are probably no positions immediately vacant but I'm sure a suitable appointment can be found over time.' Lorenzo Petroni was far too adroit to make an outright refusal of the old Pope's request. Far better to accede and give the impression that the request would be actioned.

The Pope had also been around Vatican politics for a long time and he was not about to be put off by his most senior bureaucrat.

'We had hoped that we could do it more quickly than that. We are desirous of bringing the best available talent into the Vatican where it can be most effective. Islam is a very real threat and, as you pointed out at the beginning of our conversation, Father Donelli is a most promising priest. One day, Lorenzo, you and I will need to be replaced.'

Yes, Petroni thought, you have been Pope for a long time. Too long.

'Of course, Holiness, but promotion?' Petroni persisted. 'There are many others with longer experience and greater claims? Such an early promotion might cause resentment, but more importantly I would be concerned that it might actually jeopardise Father Donelli's career if we put too much responsibility on him before he is ready.' Petroni maintained a look of polite concern. In the face of the stubborn old Pope's pointed resort to the royal 'we', his mind went into tactical overdrive. He needed to appeal to the Pope's sense of fairness and get him to change direction rather than appear to be resisting.

'I have met Father Donelli and I'm sure he will handle an important policy area like inter-faith dialogue very well, and I would hardly term it an early promotion,' the Pope added meaningfully.

'Of course, Holiness.'

Comprehensively outmanoeuvred, the Secretary of State stormed back to his office, his lips compressed into a thin line of fury. Bishop Donelli would now need very careful watching.

CHAPTER TWENTY-TWO

Milano

Allegra felt a surge of excitement as she accompanied Professor Rosselli to her first major public lecture. The theatre seated over four hundred and as she and her mentor walked to the stage she realised that it was overflowing. Students, lecturers and members of the public were still filing in and sitting in the aisles.

'Not a bad turnout,' Rosselli whispered. 'Must be my good looks!'

'Radiocarbon dating,' she began, after Professor Rosselli had introduced her, 'was developed in the years following WWII by a team of scientists led by Professor Willard F. Libby at the University of Chicago. His discovery has been described as having one of the most profound impacts on our thinking and as a result, in 1960, Professor Libby was awarded the Nobel Prize in Chemistry. Not all of you are familiar with the principles of carbon dating,' Allegra continued, 'so if those of you who are will bear with me, I will start with a short summary.' Allegra switched on the overhead and took a pen from her pocket.

'Carbon is one of the most abundant elements in the universe. It was one of the first elements to appear shortly after the Big Bang, some twelve to thirteen billion years ago. The vast majority of carbon consists of stable carbon, what we call carbon twelve or ^{12}C. But carbon also exists as carbon fourteen or ^{14}C, which is unstable and radioactive, and over time decays, giving off energy in the form of electrons and reverting back to nitrogen.'

Allegra walked away from the overhead to stand in front of the lecturn. 'Some of you will be asking "so what"? How does that help us date something like the Dead Sea Scrolls, for example, something that has significant implications for the doctrine of the Church,' she added, glancing at the man in the front row in a green and yellow checked sports coat who was shaking his head vigorously.

'Professor Libby and his team discovered that carbon fourteen has a half-life of 5568 years, so if we start with 100 grams of carbon fourteen, 5568 years later we will only have 50 grams and in another 5568 years 25 grams, and so on. This standard rate of decay is the key to radiocarbon dating because the ratio of carbon fourteen to the stable carbon twelve can be measured very accurately.'

In the projection room at the back of the theatre Giorgio Felici put on a pair of fine leather gloves, opened his well-used tool box and extracted the Russian-made Vinovka Snaiperskaja Spetsialnaya sniper rifle with its integral silencer from the felt-lined interior. Unseen, he rested the barrel in one of the square wooden openings and focused the cross-hairs of the sights on Professor Rosselli sitting at the table on the stage. With a minimum of movement he swung the sights onto Dr Bassetti. Pert little breasts, he thought dispassionately, and casually wondered what she would be like in bed.

Allegra explained how plants obtained all their carbon atoms from the atmosphere and how animals and humans gained carbon from eating the plants.

'Therefore, at any one time, the ratio of carbon fourteen to carbon twelve is the same in the plants, and therefore in humans and animals, as the ratio in the atmosphere.'

To complete her introduction Allegra explained the crux of the theory. 'When a plant or an animal or human dies, the intake of carbon atoms stops, which starts up a time clock and the ratio of carbon fourteen to carbon twelve is fixed at that point. Carbon twelve is stable and the amount in the body remains unchanged. At the moment of death the amount of carbon fourteen starts to decrease, as does the ratio. By precisely measuring the ratio of carbon fourteen to carbon twelve we can get a very accurate measure of the age of a sample. It raises some interesting questions about the evolution of man over a relatively short period of hundreds of thousands of years compared to the age of the Earth, which is measured in billions.'

Allegra moved into high gear. In a dizzying array of overheads she went through the principal techniques of gas proportional counting, liquid scintillation and accelerator mass spectrometry and how the various techniques might be applied to date objects in archaeology and other fields. Forty minutes later Allegra ended her lecture to a round of spontaneous applause.

'Well done. They liked it and so did I,' Professor Rosselli whispered approvingly. 'With the possible exception of the short fellow in the front row who likes bright colours,' he added, his hand over the microphone. The man in the sports coat was again shaking his head as Professor Rosselli announced that Allegra would now take questions and his hand was first in the air.

Professor Rosselli nodded to him and he leapt to his feet, flushed and agitated.

'My name is Walter C. Whittaker the Third,' he said, introducing himself in a high-pitched southern drawl, 'and I represent the Reverend Jerry Buffett from the Buffett Evangelical Centre for Christ in Atlanta, Georgia.' The man was short with thinning red hair, a freckled complexion and a thin, wispy moustache.

'As if we couldn't guess,' Professor Rosselli whispered to Allegra in a conspiratorial aside as she prepared to move back to the lecturn.

'I think you and Professor Rosselli are seriously misguided, Dr Bassetti. I will have some questions for Professor Rosselli that will destroy his theory on the origin of DNA at the end of his lecture, but your theory that you can use carbon dating to date something like the Dead Sea Scrolls is nonsense. Carbon dating would have us believe that the world is billions of years old, but the Bible says carbon dating is just plain wrong. *In the beginning* God made them male and female, and I am quoting from Mark 10:6. If we were to take your science as true, the Bible would make no sense at all.'

'Amen to that,' someone in the front whispered loudly enough for it to be heard several rows back, prompting a titter in the audience. Unfazed, the man continued.

'It would make no sense at all to have Man appear after billions of years because the Bible tells us quite clearly that Man was in the world from the very beginning of creation. And since Man only appeared a few thousand years ago, passages from Mark only make sense if the world is also just a few thousand years old, which we know to be the case, since the Bible is the Word of God.'

Allegra groaned inwardly and shot a glance at Professor Rosselli, who gave her his trademark wink. He was enjoying the proceedings immensely and was more than a match for the man in Joseph's coat.

'Do you have an actual question, Mr Whittaker?' Professor Rosselli asked.

'I'm coming to that, sir. Rest assured, I'm definitely coming to that. The Great Flood, Dr Bassetti. Genesis clearly points out that every mountain on the Earth was covered to a depth of 6 metres.'

Which in the case of Everest makes just on 8715 metres and we got there in just forty days and forty nights, a rainfall of 225 metres a day. Some downpour, some flood, Allegra thought sceptically, now prepared to question dogma as she never had before.

'The Great Flood buried vast amounts of carbon twelve which I would point out raised, not lowered, the ratio of carbon fourteen that plants would have absorbed after the flood. Making them seem a lot older than they really are.'

'Well, if you don't mind, Mr Whittaker, you will appreciate that there are other people in the theatre and I'll now ask Dr Bassetti to comment on your assertions.' Professor Rosselli had had enough.

'I can't imagine any question that is more important than one that is concerned with a Biblical basis of truth, but I await the good doctor's response with interest.'

At last the Bible-thumping man from the Deep South sat down. Allegra glanced around the room. Many of those present, especially the undergraduates, had huge grins on their faces, but the challenge had been thrown down and she was clearly expected to answer it.

'Thank you, Mr Whittaker. You raise some interesting points. Let me repeat that carbon dating does not give a date down to an exact year.'

Walter C. Whittaker the Third smirked.

'But we do claim accuracy within a few decades, and when we are dealing with tens of thousands of years that is quite a small margin of error. In the realm of fifty thousand years or so, as accurate as carbon dating might be, we still check it, and to do that, we compare our results using tree rings or dendrochronology.' Allegra flashed up an overhead of a majestic bristle cone pine in the White Mountains of California that was more than four thousand years old.

'Trees produce one tree ring each year, and if we compare the carbon fourteen concentrations in tree rings of a known age, we can accurately check our age range for any specimen.'

Mr Whittaker looked a lot less smug but he was not done yet.

'Show me a tree that is more than six thousand years old.'

'Indeed, Mr Whittaker, there are none,' Allegra responded easily, 'but we have overcome that problem. We can extend this theory by using non-living specimens from the wood of ancient buildings where the date of construction is known quite accurately.'

'And I think there was a question up the back,' Professor Rosselli interjected pointedly.

The audience applauded, delighted that Mr Whittaker had been dispatched, along with his theory of the world being only as old as last Tuesday.

Giorgio Felici calmly adjusted the range to the 77 metres he had measured earlier and refocused the cross-hairs on Allegra's breasts as she answered more questions.

CHAPTER TWENTY-THREE

Jerusalem

Giovanni pushed open the now familiar rusty gate to the Sisters of Charity Convent in Jerusalem and climbed the steps. It had been over five years since he had first arrived in the Holy Land, although it seemed like only yesterday, and his little church in Mar'Oth had been completely rebuilt. Poor as they were, the villagers of his home town of Maratea had raised the money for two statues. One of Christ in thigh-length boots with a gnarled walking stick, and one of the Virgin Mary in blue. Very Italian and a little out of place in the Middle East but when Giovanni had unpacked the crates he had fought back tears. Patrick, who had educated him on Jerusalem and the Holy Land as no other guide ever could, had re-consecrated the church. He had seemed genuinely surprised, not only at the sight of the rejuvenated little church but at the lack of hostility and the beginnings of friendships between Muslims and Christians. When Ahmed and the whole of the Muslim community of the village turned up and stood outside the church to offer their support for its consecration, Patrick promptly moved proceedings to the front porch. Abraham would have been pleased.

There had been other highlights during Giovanni's posting. Without any reference to the Vatican, Patrick had organised an invitation for them both to attend the Conference of Latin American Bishops in Quito, the capital of Ecuador. Giovanni's paper on the Palestinians had earned him a standing ovation, and he had formed some very strong friendships in South America, including Cardinal Médici, the Head of the Church in Ecuador.

The lowlights usually came at night when he was alone, reading by the glow of a candle. There was no newspaper or television to keep him informed of things outside Mar'Oth. To the bemusement of the villagers he had rigged up an aerial, and on a good night he was able to pick up the shortwave service of the BBC, which allowed him to keep track of the world, but he longed for news of his home. When his spirits were at a low ebb, God seemed very distant, unhearing and unseeing, and Giovanni's thoughts often turned to Allegra.

Although they had kept in touch – Allegra letting him know how her research was going, and him keeping her up to date with events in Mar'Oth and the Middle East – Giovanni missed their regular discussions. He was still concerned as to why she had suddenly left the Church but he knew he wasn't going to hear her story until she was ready to tell it. He could only understand the pain and doubt she must have gone through to come to her decision. Giovanni often wondered what his life would have been like if he and Allegra had decided to stay together.

'Father Giovanni, let me take your bag, Bishop O'Hara's in the study. Come through, come through. How have you been?' Neither Sister Katherine's enthusiasm for life nor the warmth of her welcome ever waned.

'Giovanni! It's good to see you. Whiskey?' Patrick asked, not waiting for a reply and already heading for the sideboard.

'Good to see you too, Patrick, and thank you for the invitation to dinner. Sister Katherine's cooking beats mine any time.'

'And mine. It's a strange vocation, isn't it? They provide a welter of theological training and then expect you to live on your own without so much as an introduction to the kitchen. Shalom!'

Giovanni accepted the generous glass of Irish whiskey.

'I've had a letter from Cardinal Médici. You left a very favourable impression.'

'And they on me. They have some very impressive thinkers in that part of the world, speaking of which, I'm really looking forward to catching up with Yossi tonight.'

'Yes, not only a great thinker but a man with a very strong Jewish faith.'

'The more time I spend here, the more I come to realise that Islam and Judaism and the other faiths provide just as much guidance and support as our own.'

'Then your time here has not been wasted, Giovanni,' Patrick observed thoughtfully. 'Although that time may be coming to an end. As you know, I came back through Rome on the way home from South America. Your name came up in some interesting company. Care to hazard a guess?'

Giovanni raised his eyebrows. He never tired of Patrick's love of conspiracy.

'The Secretary of State?'

'Nice try but . . .' Patrick raised a finger and pointed upwards.

'His Holiness? You met with His Holiness?'

Patrick nodded. 'Il Papa. I had a private audience. Someone had mentioned to him that you were here and he wanted to know why. I gather you've met?'

'Only once. I wrote a paper on science and religion for a conference he addressed and he made a point of meeting me. He doesn't miss much.'

'Which is no doubt why he is intrigued at your posting to

Mar'Oth. Don't expect to be here much longer, I think Il Papa may want you back in the Vatican,' Patrick said, only giving Giovanni half the news.

Before Giovanni could comment, Sister Katherine showed Yossi Kaufmann in to the study.

'Yossi! Come in, come in. You're looking taller, or perhaps I'm getting shorter.' Patrick winked at Giovanni.

'Dinner will be ready very shortly, Bishop,' Sister Katherine announced from the doorway, 'so no settling in here with the whiskey.'

'Mothers me terribly. Sister Katherine would sign me up to a gym if she could.' Patrick chuckled at the thought. 'So how is the code-breaking going, Yossi?'

'Progress is slow, Patrick,' Yossi replied with a smile. 'I need a bigger computer. Eliyahu Rips found a fascinating code on DNA in the Torah, so I ran one as well and it turned up in a Dead Sea Scroll, *The Rule of the Congregation*. I've sent my findings off to Antonio Rosselli. He's giving a lecture on it tonight.'

Giovanni immediately thought of Allegra. She had written to tell him she was giving her first public lecture as part of a double act with Rosselli. It seemed that the reminders of her were constant.

'I've made some progress with the warning though. It seems to be connected with Mount Hira.'

'Islam,' Giovanni responded.

'How do you get Islam from Mount Hira?' Patrick asked.

'Every year Muhammad used to climb Mount Hira to a cave near the summit and meditate,' Yossi explained. 'It is there that he received God's revelations in his native language of Arabic. Other than the fact that there appears to be a clear countdown for civilisation, I haven't got to the precise nature of it yet, although it is somehow connected with the Christians, Jews and Muslims.'

'It's ironic, isn't it,' Patrick said, 'that one of the greatest threats faced by humankind is religion. The Islamic fundamentalists want nothing less than the entire human population to show obedience to Allah, while many in our own Church claim that salvation can only be found within the confines of the Catholic community. God is entitled to be a bit confused,' Patrick chuckled.

As if to emphasise Patrick's observations, everything in Patrick's house started shaking. It continued for about twenty seconds and the bottles and glasses in his well-stocked sideboard rattled alarmingly.

'Nothing to worry about,' Patrick said. 'Just a tremor. We get them from time to time over here but the whiskey's still intact, so it won't have damaged much.'

Patrick was only half right. The damage in Jerusalem was neg-ligible, but out amongst the marl and salt cliffs of Qumran a rock that had not moved for nearly two thousand years shifted ever so slightly. It was a movement that ultimately would have a far greater impact than any earthquake.

'What do you think the chances for peace are here, Yossi?' Giovanni asked.

Yossi shook his head. 'With the present regime? Very slim. Neither the present Israeli Government nor Yasser Arafat's Pales-tinian Authority is capable of bringing peace to this country. Neither is prepared to compromise. It will take two totally new governments and a much greater involvement of the international community before the killing stops.'

'Have you ever thought of running for prime minister?'

Yossi smiled. 'As a matter of fact I've been thinking about start-ing a new party, based on nothing more revolutionary than a just peace. It will probably take years to build the support but I think it's worth a try. Why do you ask?'

'Because there is someone I would like you to meet. Someone on the Palestinian side who shares your views. He knows how hard it will be to sell a compromise but, like you, he believes that the average person wants nothing more than to be able to live their lives normally.'

'Your opposite number?'

'Yes, Ahmed Sartawi, the Imam in my village. I'm sure you would enjoy talking with him.'

'Marian and I still have our little holiday house in Acre. Perhaps you and Ahmed could join us for a weekend?'

'There may not be time for that,' Patrick said. 'I was telling Giovanni before you arrived that Il Papa has discovered he is here and wants his talents put to work in the Vatican.'

'I doubt they'll want him back before next weekend,' Yossi said. 'Let's see if we can organise it.'

As if on cue the telephone on Patrick's desk started ringing.

'Patrick O'Hara. Guilio.' Patrick covered the mouthpiece and whispered, 'Guilio Leone, Il Papa's private secretary.'

'What crisis of state in the Vatican has you ringing me at this hour?' he asked. 'Am I at last to be made a cardinal then? Papal Nuncio in Paris perhaps?' A wicked smile spread across Patrick's face. 'But the tailors here are so reasonable, Guilio. I had my robes made up ages ago and still I wait for the call.' He winked at his guests.

'So few bishops who speak Arabic? That's what you always say, but you can be telling him yourself, he's right here.' Patrick handed Giovanni the phone.

'They hate it when I rib them,' he said to Yossi. 'No sense of humour in the Vatican.'

'Do you want to be a cardinal?'

'Good grief no! Unless it was somewhere I could do some good. Too much powerbroking in the Vatican. I might as well become a politician.'

Giovanni replaced the receiver, a slightly stunned look on his face.

'Well?' Patrick asked, feigning ignorance.

'Il Papa wants me back in Rome. He wants to make me a bishop,' was all Giovanni could say.

'First name terms at last, and about time. Congratulations, my boy. This calls for a drink.'

'Congratulations, Giovanni, well done.' Yossi stretched out his hand.

Giovanni was too surprised to resist Patrick's renewed assault with the whiskey bottle. He realised now that the Spirit did indeed move in mysterious ways.

Mysterious things were also happening in a cave above Qumran, not far from the Dead Sea, as another few grains of sand trickled through a crack in a rock wall.

CHAPTER TWENTY-FOUR

Milano

Giorgio Felici flexed his gloved fingers and steadied his breath as Professor Rosselli moved towards the lectern. He moved the cross-hairs to the centre of his quarry's chest.

'Thank you, Dr Bassetti, a most interesting exposé. Unfortunately,' he said, turning back to the audience, 'for the remainder of the evening you will have to put up with me, although I hope you will find the subject of "The lost civilisation of the Essenes, DNA and the Omega Scroll" intriguing.'

A murmur of expectation echoed through the theatre.

'In 1962 Francis Crick shared the Nobel Prize for Medicine and Physiology with James Watson and Maurice Wilkins for the discovery of the molecular structure of DNA, or deoxyribonucleic acid, which contains the genetic code for life. In 1973, the Nobel Laureate wrote a book called *Life Itself*. In it he argues very persuasively that the DNA helix is so intricate that there was insufficient time on this planet for it to have evolved of its own accord and that it had to have been introduced to our planet from a higher civilisation.'

Professor Rosselli put up an overhead of the complex double helix of nucleotides made up of phosphates, smaller deoxyribose sugar molecules and the bases, adenine, thymine, cytosine and guanine.

'As Crick describes them, DNA and its sister RNA are the dumb blondes of the biomolecular world. Exquisite to look at and good for reproduction, but unable to cope without the help of a myriad of complex proteins.' Professor Rosselli was warming up.

Felici inhaled.

'Indirectly supporting the theory of higher civilisation is the almost unimaginable number of galaxies and planets that make up the cosmos. In our own galaxy alone there are over 100 billion stars, and we need to multiply that billions of times over because there are at least 10 billion galaxies. The odds of planet Earth being the only inhabitable planet amongst billions of other galaxies must stretch the scepticism of even the most fundamental views,' he said, looking at Walter C. Whittaker the Third. 'You must now be wondering where the Essenes and the Omega Scroll fit—'

Felici exhaled, felt the first trigger pressure, held the cross-hairs on Rosselli's chest and gently squeezed through the second pressure on the trigger.

Phut. Phut. No one heard the two shots from the projection room.

Someone in the audience gasped as Rosselli fell backwards, clutching his chest. Allegra saw the bloodstain blossoming on his shirt.

'Antonio. No!' Allegra rushed to his side as Professor Rosselli lay on the floor, struggling for life. 'Call an ambulance,' she commanded. 'He's been shot.'

Giorgio Felici closed the fire escape door and quickly descended to the car park.

Roma

Cardinal Lorenzo Petroni was in his office early. The timing for terminating Rosselli's investigation into the origins of DNA and the Omega Scroll could not have been better. A massive pile-up of more than two hundred cars on the autostrada just south of Florence had killed eleven people and had pushed everything else off the front page. There had been one or two lines of speculation on the Omega Scroll, but as they had done over the death of the previous Pope, in the absence of any strong leads Petroni knew the media would lose interest.

Satisfied, he leaned back in his chair. Cardinal Secretary of State, back in the Vatican in the second most powerful position in the whole of the Catholic Church. He was getting closer and closer to absolute power and the sexual jolt it gave him reminded him of the need to arrange for Carmela, the fallen but beautiful nun, to be appointed to his personal staff in the Holy See. Her guilt was his power, the perfect way to subdue a beautiful woman.

Petroni caressed the arms of his large leather chair, savouring his power. He made a mental note to have his desk raised, then moved to look over his notes on the Vatican Bank. It was time to remove the squeaky-clean Garibaldi. A new director for the bank was needed, one who could be controlled. Despite some meticulous research, there was not a whiff of scandal about this quiet, unassuming priest with a double degree in accounting and financial management. An hour later Petroni buzzed his secretary.

'Ask Monsignor Garibaldi to come in.'

The double doors were opened and the Head of the Vatican Bank was shown in to the Secretary of State's opulent and spacious suite.

'Pasquale, how good to see you again. It's been a very long time. Please, have a seat.' Monsignor Garibaldi was shown one of three crimson couches, the soft approach.

'Thank you, Eminence,' Pasquale responded, nonplussed as to why he had been summoned on the Cardinal's second day in office.

'I was reading your report on the Latin American Bishop's Conference in Quito. Very insightful, but I fear not much has changed.'

'A sad indictment, Eminence.' Pasquale was wary but, who knew, despite Cardinal Petroni's reputation for ruthlessness, perhaps this Prince of the Church would finally give some support to the desperately poor people of South America. 'I am preparing a paper as to how we might better use the resources of the Vatican Bank to sponsor the programs they need.'

Petroni already knew that. Given half a chance this bothersome humanist priest would no doubt suggest opening a branch of the bank in downtown Bogotá.

'I would find that very interesting, Pasquale, and when you have finished it I would be grateful if you could submit it directly to my office for my personal attention. Regrettably there are some in these corridors who might oppose your plans. They guard His Holiness's vaults as if they were their own, *non è vero!*' Petroni's diplomatic laugh held not a scintilla of mirth.

'But of course, Eminence. I understand.'

'Which brings me to the reason I've asked you to see me. I think we need a closer look at the problems in Latin America. An independent view. I wondered if you would be prepared to return, as one of my emissaries?'

Pasquale was taken aback and more wary than ever. He had been Head of the Vatican Bank for less than two months.

'I don't know what to say, Eminence. Would it be for long? The bank . . . There is so much to do . . .' Pasquale had a sinking feeling that he was being comprehensively sidelined.

Petroni smiled his practised, reassuring smile. He had predicted Garibaldi's reaction and he smoothly applied his rehearsed response.

'You will forgive me, Pasquale, but for this task I need people who not only have an understanding in here,' Petroni said, tapping his forehead, 'but who really care, from here.' Petroni clenched his fist and held it to his soutane. 'Bankers are easier to find.'

'Of course, Eminence,' Pasquale responded coolly. 'Wherever I can be of best service.' It was a line Petroni himself was fond of using but when he did, it lacked sincerity. 'You mentioned emissaries. Can I ask if there are others?'

'Not initially. We have to get the right people and that will take time, which is one of the reasons I would like you to leave as soon as possible. We are making arrangements for you to travel to Peru, which I think you will agree is at the very heart of the Liberation Movement?'

Despite his misgivings Pasquale felt a strange pang of excitement. Peru! It was the home of the founder of Liberation Theology, Gustavo Gutiérrez.

'Of course, Eminence.'

'San Joaqun de Omaguas. A parish in the eastern part of the country. You will shortly receive some written directions on the more precise requirements, but I am sure you will be pleased to know that I have allowed scope for you to administer the sacraments to the local people and to gain some first-hand experience of the conditions. If only I were in your shoes instead of being stuck here in these dusty corridors, but don't tell Il Papa I said that.'

Petroni got to his feet, confident that the chances of Monsignor Garibaldi and Il Papa having a conversation in the next five years were about zero.

Pasquale left the Secretariat of State enthused about the prospect of bringing the aims of a church 'for and of the poor' to greater prominence in the corridors of power, but the uneasy feeling that he'd been 'got out of the way' wouldn't leave him. He realised that his concern over what he had found, or more to the point, what he had not found in the accounts, was well founded and disturbing, but he needed more time and more proof. Once he had left for Peru he felt sure Petroni would remove anything that might be remotely questioned. Well, he thought bitterly, at the very least the photocopier could do some overtime in the short time he had left. San Joaqun de Omaguas? He had never heard of the place and he headed in the direction of the Vatican library and an atlas. He would find that discovering details of the more remote areas of the Amazon would take a little time; places that were inaccessible by road often did.

Lorenzo Petroni put in a very long day, intermittently monitoring the news for any signs of an escalation of interest in the Rosselli case, but the carnage on the autostrada was overshadowing everything else. It was nearly midnight by the time he turned in, and he slept fitfully, tossing in the large bed in his apartment in the Vatican, trying to push back his recurring dreams.

Lorenzo Petroni's dreams were hidden memories. Lorenzo at ten, a lonely only child. His father, Emilio, was a small, bald man with a small black moustache, a small man's complex and a big, violent temper. Lorenzo's mother, Marietta, was tall, very thin and very, very timid. The Petroni family lived in a run-down house in Pianella, a small town in the foothills of the Abruzzo Apennines. Every day Emilio would travel up and down the east coast, making a meagre living selling shoes, his samples in the boot and stacked on the back seat of his little Fiat. Lorenzo was a difficult and petulant child, prone to violent tantrums followed by long periods of sulking if he didn't get his own way; and the source of constant tension between his mother and father. On rare occasions his parents would make up and Marietta would go with Emilio on one of his trips. Lorenzo would then be dropped off to stay with his bachelor uncle, Gustavo.

Petroni groaned in his sleep and pushed himself up against the wall, but it was no use. Uncle Gustavo pulled back the covers and climbed into bed with him.

Two days later he would be home again and the next morning he would creep out to the laundry to wash his sheets, terrified that his father would appear from the ramshackle outside toilet.

'*Stronzetto inetto!* You useless little shit!' his father would snarl, grabbing Lorenzo by the hair and reaching for the big strap that was kept on a nail behind the laundry shed door.

'You've wet the bed again, haven't you! Haven't you! Answer me you useless piece of dogshit!'

Lorenzo would say nothing, his bottom lip quivering as his father shoved him on top of one of the donkey's bales of hay and hit him with the heavy strap.

Thwack! Thwack! Thwack! Lorenzo would sob hysterically.

'*Stronzetto inetto!* You will never amount to anything! Never!'

'Emilio. Please . . .' Marietta would appear at the back door and plead for her son.

'*Vaffanculo! Testa di cavolo!* Butt out, cabbagehead! Or you'll be next. *Il tuo filio è un frocio!* Your son is a fairy!'

Suddenly the alarm woke him. Petroni sat up in bed, sweating, a hatred for a father and the curse of never amounting to anything burning deep within his soul.

CHAPTER TWENTY-FIVE

Acre

The waters around Acre were clear and calm. Yossi's neighbour Khalil had let him borrow his boat and the big single cylinder in the old side-valve engine chugged away contentedly, pushing the heavy boat slowly out of the harbour. The ancient stone walls caught the morning sun, lapped by the smooth green waters. A score of old fishing boats were tethered to stone jetties, nets piled underneath palm trees. A solitary lighthouse stood guard at the entrance to the harbour where the Romans had placed massive blocks of stone to protect their ships.

'Khalil has a good spot about 500 metres off the point,' Yossi said, pointing out to a placid Mediterranean. 'We'll drift around there for a while and see what we get.'

Giovanni closed his eyes and leaned back against the transom. The sun was warm on his face and bare chest.

'You're quieter than usual, Giovanni.' Yossi's energy levels were up. Fishing trips were rare and he was ready to enjoy the day.

'Just soaking up the sun,' Giovanni said lazily. 'And thinking about poor Antonio Rosselli.' Giovanni had taken Yossi into his confidence over the Omega Scroll and the murder of Professor Rosselli had not been lost on either of them. 'And reflecting. Here we are, a committed Christian, a committed Jew and a committed Muslim, and the only ones in danger are the fish!'

'If I get my way there's going to be a lot more of that,' Yossi replied, cutting the engine and reaching for the rods lying against the starboard gunwale.

'There's live bait in the bucket here, so help yourself.' Yossi had cast his rod before the other two had even baited their hooks, but despite his enthusiasm, the fish appeared to be on strike and the conversation turned to politics.

'Is there any common ground for peace talks, Ahmed?' Giovanni asked.

'There is,' Ahmed replied, 'but it needs genuine will on both sides. We are often critical of the Israelis, but we need to look at our own backyard. The PLO makes no secret of the fact that any peace deal is just the first step towards taking over the whole of Palestine. For Arafat, Fatah and the PLO it's not only the land, it's a struggle between two civilisations – one Arab, one Zionist. For them there is only one acceptable outcome: Israelis becoming citizens of a single democratic Palestinian State. A state that is an inseparable part of the Arab and Muslim homeland and that will never work.'

'Would you run for president?' Yossi asked.

'Not at the moment, but I'm thinking about it. If Arafat ever goes I will make a move, and I'm quietly building support. What about you? Giovanni tells me you're going to form a new party.'

Yossi nodded. 'Neither Labor nor Likud can bring peace to this country because first and foremost we have to convince ordinary Israelis of the need for a Palestinian State. A man without a country is a man without a soul.' It was a phrase that Yossi was fond of repeating. 'In exchange, the Palestinian people must recognise the Jewish State and her right to exist.'

'If it means peace, a lot of Palestinian people will go along with that,' Ahmed replied. 'To my mind, the other three key issues are the Jewish settlements, the return of the eight hundred thousand or so Palestinian refugees who lost everything in the wars against Israel, and Jerusalem. What would you do about the settlements?' Ahmed asked Yossi.

'That's one area where we Israelis are going to have to compromise. For years now we've had a furious building program on Palestinian land in the West Bank and Gaza. We've destroyed a lot of your olive groves and stopped a lot of Palestinians from farming their land.'

'It's a big issue, Yossi,' Ahmed agreed. 'That's been our life and our existence since way before Christ or Muhammad, or even Abraham.'

'It's a political strategy, Ahmed. Designed to take over what is left of Palestine by stealth, and it's a big mistake. It breeds untold resentment and despair and it will never work. When a man has nothing left to lose he will readily resort to violence. As painful as it might be for those we've allowed to build on Palestinian land, we are going to have to give them incentives and relocate them back into Israel.'

'And the Palestinians who were exiled in 1948 and the other wars?' asked Ahmed.

'That's an area where both sides will have to compromise. Sometimes we have to deal with reality. There is not much point in insisting that the six hundred thousand Palestinians who were forced out during the 1948 war be allowed to return to homes that no longer exist or have been occupied for half a century in Israel,' Yossi said. 'There are people on both sides who think a return to a new State of Palestine, coupled with compensation, is a sensible and workable compromise.'

Ahmed looked thoughtful. 'And Jerusalem?' he asked.

'Jerusalem. Oh Jerusalem,' Yossi sighed. 'Someone once said it wasn't so much a city as an emotion. On our side there are just as many who won't give an inch but if we're going to get out of this cycle of killing, we're both going to have to give a little. Neither side can have it all.'

'An international city?'

'Not necessarily, although to a certain extent Jerusalem belongs to the people of faith around the world and certainly any agreement has to maintain the integrity of the holy sites and allow free and unimpeded access to people of all faiths. It's bigger than just the Old City and I think the solution lies in considering Greater Jerusalem. We agree to demolish this obscene wall and recognise al-Quds in East Jerusalem as the capital of Palestine, and you recognise our capital Yerushalayim in West Jerusalem.'

'What about the Temple Mount and the Western Wall?' Ahmed asked.

'The Old City is not going to be easy,' Yossi acknowledged. 'In principle, if I'm elected the Palestinians would get jurisdiction over the Temple Mount, under al-Quds. We would get jurisdiction over the Western Wall under Yerushalayim. What would you do about the militants?'

'I think the militants would come on board if the negotiations resulted in a genuine Palestinian State,' Ahmed replied. 'It won't be easy, but if I could ever win an election I think I could get agreement to the sort of principles we're talking here. Does the Old City fall into Israel or Palestine?'

'For the moment not even you and I could sign that one away, but I would hate to see the chance for peace fall at the final hurdle. Leave the national borders as they are at present and re-visit them when there is a bit of goodwill in the tank. Baited again!' Yossi stared absentmindedly at his bare hook. 'It's theft.'

Giovanni smiled. A stolen prawn. Could these two, he wondered, steal the peace from those who had imprisoned its chances for so long.

CHAPTER TWENTY-SIX

Roma

'Giovanni. *Avanti, Avanti.*'

Cardinal Salvatore Bruno, Head of the Secretariat for non-Christians, got up from behind his desk, grabbed Giovanni by the shoulders and kissed him on each cheek. For good measure, he took Giovanni's hand in both of his.

'*Benvenuto a Roma!*'

Salvatore was a big man. Well into his sixties, his dark face was lined and his old hazel eyes were kindly and wise. When he reached eighty he would no longer be eligible to vote in any conclave and his wisdom would be sorely missed by a Church that desperately needed those who were not driven by power. Salvatore Bruno had come to Roma reluctantly, persuaded by those outside of the Vatican, Bishop O'Hara among them, that the Holy Church needed to reach out to the other faiths. Faiths that were held with equal conviction by equally decent folk. Bishop O'Hara and Salvatore had also had several conversations about the role the brilliant young Giovanni might play. Both of the older men could sense his destiny.

'I can't tell you how glad I am to have you here. *S'accomodi. S'accomodi.*'

'Thank you, Eminence. *Come stai?* You are well, I hope?'

'I can't complain,' he said, his old eyes twinkling as he patted his ample stomach. 'Now, have you given any thought as to how you might tackle this issue of the other faiths?'

'Yes, Eminence, but I will probably need some guidance. I've been out of the mainstream for a long time, and to tell you the truth, I am a little surprised at the project. I thought the Church's attitude was, well . . .'

'More rigid?' Cardinal Bruno chuckled as he finished Giovanni's sentence for him. 'I shouldn't worry too much about that. The Holy Father has always recognised the importance of the other faiths, although there's been a fierce rearguard action from the usual suspects . . .' Salvatore paused as his housekeeper of thirty-five years brought in the tea. 'Thank you, Sister Maria, I'll pour. I need to keep my hand in,' he said with another chuckle and he waited until she withdrew.

'Watch the Secretary of State. Unlike those who know you well he was not too impressed with your promotion or this project, but you have worked for him before, and I daresay you know his views on these things. He called me,' Salvatore said, smiling wryly, 'and asked me to pass on his congratulations suggesting that I have you travel widely. On the congratulations, we'll give him the benefit of the doubt. On the travel, that is my intention, although not for the reasons that drive the Secretary of State.'

'I'm not sure I follow, Eminence?'

'He wants you to spend as much time out of Rome as possible. Insecure people like the Cardinal Petronis of this world see anyone as competent as you only in terms of a possible threat to their own position.'

It was the first time Giovanni had ever heard anyone describe

Lorenzo Petroni as insecure. Perhaps the old lion knew a thing or two about the human psyche.

'While you are here in Rome there is a danger that you will come to the notice of the other Curial Cardinals and, by extension, become a potential candidate for the Keys to Peter.'

Giovanni laughed. 'I don't think Cardinal Petroni has anything to worry about on that score.'

'I hope he does, Giovanni.' Salvatore's eyes were no longer mischievous. 'The very best Popes in the whole history of this wonderful Church have been those who have never seen themselves as a candidate. John XXIII was one of those. The Curial Cardinals thought they were electing an old man they could control, and look what happened.'

'Vatican II.'

'The winds of change,' Cardinal Bruno agreed. 'Some of the older men in red have been fighting to put the genie back in the bottle ever since. I remember him with great affection. He drove the Curia to distraction, often turning up in their departments without their knowledge, just to have a chat with the staff, and il Capo di Polizia in Rome gave up,' Salvatore said, relishing the memory of the great man. 'In the time of Popes like Pius XII they used to rehearse for days for a Papal departure from the Vatican; flags, bands, bugles, honour guards, crashing cymbals. John XXIII used to just drive out.'

'You were here for the conclave in 1958?'

'I was a very ordinary priest working in the Congregation for the Clergy. Would that I was a simple priest again,' Salvatore said wistfully. 'I was here when he was elected. Roncalli – John XXIII – was their compromise candidate. They didn't know it but their Eminences had a very large tiger by the tail. *Un Terremoto!* An earthquake! I want you to promise me something, Giovanni. If they do offer you the Keys to Peter, accept.'

'Eminence I—'

'I know, I know. It's not something you would even think about, but if you are offered them, it will be for a reason.'

Giovanni left Cardinal Bruno's office, totally inspired by his new project. The Keys to Peter were the furthest thing from his mind. Fleetingly his thoughts turned to Allegra and he wondered if he should meet her in Milano, but just as quickly he decided against it. He didn't want Allegra to feel that she was being forced into telling him why she had left the Church. Giovanni decided he would wait.

It would be a long time before their paths would cross. By then the international academic community would be noticing they had a very talented Dr Bassetti in their midst, and the cardinals outside of Rome would be aware that the Holy Church had a brilliant priest within her fold. A priest that if Cardinal Bruno had his way would be elevated again, this time to archbishop. Two rising stars, on very different paths that would spectacularly intersect at the Alpha and the Omega of Jerusalem.

BOOK FIVE

2004

Ω

CHAPTER TWENTY-SEVEN

Langley, Virginia

Mike McKinnon scanned the latest intelligence reports on al-Qaeda's nuclear capability. The first came from one of the CIA's agents operating out of Kabul in Afghanistan. McKinnon skipped over the background summary. He was already depressingly familiar with the contents, including the discovery of papers that proved Osama bin Laden's nuclear intentions. After the United States had invaded Afghanistan, a group of journalists had found some chilling documents in a house in Wazir Akbar Khan, one of Kabul's more fashionable areas. The documents had included diagrams of the compression of plutonium into the critical mass required for a nuclear explosion.

The next section was headed 'Subject of interest – Dr Hussein Tretyakov'. McKinnon recognised the photograph immediately. He had met Tretyakov at a Nuclear Disarmament Conference in London. Hussein Tretyakov was short, with spiky grey hair and broad shoulders. He had a square rugged face, with a high forehead and expressionless pale blue eyes. The teeth below his thick black moustache, McKinnon recalled, were stained from years of smoking unfiltered cigarettes. Dr Tretyakov had been one of the Soviet Union's most brilliant nuclear physicists. Had been. Now he was on the Kremlin and the CIA's 'most wanted' list. McKinnon skimmed over the biographical notes. He knew Tretyakov's background well. Born in Grozny, Chechnya, in 1946. Two doctorates, one on the production of weapons-grade plutonium and the other on controlled nuclear fusion in tactical devices. A career that included stints at the quaintly named Research Institute of Experimental Physics at Chelyabinsk in the Urals, as well as at the plutonium reactor Chelyabinsk-65 at Lake Kyzltask and at Novaya Zemla, the central test site in the north of the Arctic Circle. It had never appeared on his official biography, but McKinnon and the CIA were also well aware that Dr Tretyakov had spent a considerable amount of time in the top-secret warhead production facility near Zlatoust, perfecting nuclear suitcase bombs.

Mike McKinnon stared at the colour photograph and he reflected on what had driven a man of Tretyakov's ability to the darkest side of his profession. Mike knew that with the collapse of the Soviet Union, Dr Tretyakov, along with hundreds of other Soviet scientists, had been thrown out of work. More ominously still, in 1994 Boris Yeltsin had begun to brutally suppress Chechen President Jokhar Dudayev's claim for Chechnya to become an independent state. Grozny had been bombed on New Year's Eve, but the Chechen separatist fighters had fought back tenaciously, inflicting heavy losses on the Russian tanks, armoured personnel carriers, self-propelled guns and thousands of troops. In the backlash that followed, Hussein Tretyakov had lost his wife and their three small daughters. They had been a devout and devoted Muslim family, but now that family – as an orphan, the only one Hussein had ever known – was gone. President Dudayev's threat to place the nuclear suitcase bombs on the market after the United States had ignored

Chechnya's call for independence was supported by Dr Tretyakov. He had nothing else to lose.

Tretyakov's reckless actions couldn't be condoned, but unlike some of those in the corridors of power in the Pentagon, for McKinnon it was important to understand the reason for his behaviour. President Vladimir Putin, Mike thought ruefully, had taken up the persecution of the Chechens where his predecessor had left off and Dr Hussein Tretyakov had been pushed into the arms of al-Qaeda. The report was chillingly inconclusive.

> Dr Tretyakov's present whereabouts are unknown. The last sighting of him was in Peshawar, in the north-west frontier of Pakistan. There are unconfirmed reports that he has linked up with Abdul Musa Basheer and other al-Qaeda leaders who have been seeking to purchase several of the nuclear suitcase bombs Tretyakov is known to have in his possession.

Mike McKinnon's face reflected his concern, his jaw set determinedly. Earlier that evening he had read an unclassified report on the Omega Scroll and the Islamic nuclear factor by Professor Yossi Kaufmann. Was this coincidence or connection? he wondered.

CHAPTER TWENTY-EIGHT

Milano

Allegra made her way down the familiar hallway to the Vice Chancellor's office. It had been over fifteen years since Antonio Rosselli's brutal murder but she still missed her kind-hearted mentor dreadfully. She knew Rosselli had been on the cusp of revealing the secrets contained in the Omega Scroll and that Cardinal Petroni was somehow involved. Allegra and Giovanni were more determined than ever to uncover what was in the Omega Scroll, but other than storming the vaults of the Vatican it seemed there was little they could do. That was about to change.

'You wanted to see me, Professor Gamberini?' Allegra asked at the door of the Vice Chancellor's office.

'Come in, Allegra. Have a seat.'

Professor Gamberini was immaculately groomed from his fine dark hair to his tailored pinstriped suit and polished black leather shoes. He was the antithesis of Antonio Rosselli yet his gentle and open manner reminded her, painfully, of her beloved Professor. Gamberini had taken over the role of mentor, encouraging Allegra to continue with her scientific discoveries, and he was diligently fostering her growing international reputation.

'Have you ever been to Jerusalem?' Professor Gamberini asked, coming straight to the point.

Allegra's heart skipped a beat and she immediately thought of Giovanni. She had been thrilled when he had been promoted to archbishop two years ago, and it had given her some small satisfaction to learn that their nemesis, Cardinal Petroni, had furiously opposed the promotion but had been overruled.

'No, why do you ask?' she replied, uncertain of what was coming next.

'One of the great cities of the world,' Professor Gamberini observed. 'The Hebrew University there is offering two interesting new scholarships in archaeology, the Medina Scholarships, a sabbatical for up to four years of research and study of the Dead Sea Scrolls. One for an Israeli scholar, and one for an exchange scholar from overseas. What do you think?'

'Who, me?' Allegra replied, wondering if her quest for the Omega Scroll might be taking a new turn.

Professor Gamberini looked around his office. 'There's no one else in the room,' he said with a smile. 'The chair of the selection panel is an Israeli archaeologist, Professor Kaufmann. He was an old friend of Professor Rosselli and suggested your name be put forward. I think you will like him. You've studied Hebrew, I understand.'

'I took it as an option when I was an undergraduate, but that was years ago. When is the selection panel, Professor? I will need to prepare.' Already Allegra's mind was racing ahead.

'They've already selected the Israeli scholar, a Dr David Kaufmann. Professor Kaufmann's son, so naturally enough the Professor stood aside from the panel for that one. I'm familiar with David's work and he's a very successful archaeologist in his own right, and very single too,' he added mischievously. 'In your case, Yossi Kaufmann and I have already spoken.'

'I don't understand, Professor Kaufmann and I have never met,' Allegra replied, ignoring his remark on the marital status of the Israeli academic. Allegra had buried the prospect of a relationship with a man a long time ago, and it was not something she was ready to consider.

'Your name came up in conversation during my last trip to Israel. He was very interested in your research on DNA and the Dead Sea Scrolls. I've taken the liberty of sending him a copy of your doctoral thesis and he will use that to evaluate your candidacy. I've already raised the issue with the academic board here and they're prepared to give you leave for up to four years if you're successful. Access to the Dead Sea Scrolls held in the Shrine of the Book Museum is guaranteed but for some reason there seems to be considerable opposition to any access to those housed in the Rockefeller Museum. A Monsignor Lonergan on the staff of the museum is kicking up quite a fuss. The usual academic jealousy I expect but that shouldn't bother you too much, assuming you're successful, of course,' he added with a warm smile.

Allegra left the Vice Chancellor's office with her mind in a whirl. Jerusalem, Bethlehem and the Holy Land. Who knows, her search for the Omega Scroll could continue more closely there. Giovanni would have all the contacts, she thought, then she pulled herself together.

'Get a grip, girl!' she said to herself. 'They don't give scholarships for study of the Dead Sea Scrolls to Italian scientists.'

CHAPTER TWENTY-NINE

Jerusalem

Monsignor Derek Lonergan woke with a splitting headache and waited until the room came into focus. The old metal clock indicated 4 a.m. and he stared at it uncomprehendingly, realising that he had forgotten to wind it, again. He smacked his tongue against the roof of his mouth. It felt dry and furry, as if an animal had done something nasty in it during the night. As he rolled his head off the pillow there was a loud crash and the sound of breaking glass. An empty whisky bottle had fallen on the tiled floor.

'Fuck,' he muttered.

Derek Lonergan slowly swung his legs off the bed, his feet still in his sandals, wrestling to try to gain some freedom for his ample girth among the folds of the robes he had fallen asleep in.

'Fuck these bloody cassocks,' he swore again, addressing his remarks to the long-suffering walls of his room. Putting his hand to the side of his head he got to his feet and squinted out of his dormitory window at the road that ran past the walls of L'École Biblique et Archéologique Française de Jérusalem. The sunlight caught the reddish grey of his bearded jowls and it felt hot on the pink skin at the front of his balding head. Judging by the length of the queue of the bloody Palestinians clamouring outside the cramped quarters of the Ministry of Interior on the other side of the road, and the bored looks on the faces of Israeli soldiers covering them with their Uzis, he supposed the sun was well past the yard arm.

'Fuck,' he muttered again to no one in particular. He had missed the morning meeting, as he had the morning before. This would no doubt earn him another rebuke from the director, Father 'po-face'. Father La Franci's idea of productivity was measured by the number of meetings that he could jam into a week. Dickhead. Fuck 'em. Fuck the lot of them. If the Vatican wanted him to work in this hell hole and protect their secrets and edit anything out of their bloody journals that remotely questioned their precious dogma then he would do it on his terms. Two doctorates in archaeology and geology said that he could, as he was fond of reminding anyone who tried to tell him what to do. He had friends in high places, as he was also fond of reminding them. Although Cardinal Petroni could be a right royal pain in the arse as well. Fuck him, too.

CHAPTER THIRTY

Roma

The paperweight hit the far wall of the Secretary of State's office with a resounding crash and fell soundlessly on the thick blue carpet. Two pieces of paper in his afternoon dispatches had brought the Cardinal Secretary of State close to incandescence.

The first, a confidential list of archbishops to be made cardinal. At the top of the list was Giovanni Donelli; to be made Cardinal Patriarch of Venice.

Cardinal Petroni tapped his heavy polished desk with his fingers as he considered the threat Giovanni Donelli's appointment might pose. More than one cardinal from Venice had been elected Pope in the past. Pope John XXIII had been one and Albino Luciani another. Petroni unlocked the top left-hand drawer of his desk, extracted his small black leather book, turned to Donelli and, irritably, made another entry against Giovanni's name. He grudgingly allocated him a third star and noted that Donelli was 'still B-list at best but bears watching. Not being widely canvassed amongst the Curia. Not widely known.' The last comment was a rare error of judgement. Petroni's anger was starting to get the better of him. He replaced the book, locked the drawer and picked up the next offending dispatch from his in-tray. As he re-read it he sniffed loudly. It was a letter from that infuriating Jew, Professor Yossi Kaufmann, from the Hebrew University.

> *Dear Cardinal Petroni,*
>
> *I refer to your request for the Hebrew University to reconsider the granting of the inaugural Medina Archaeology Scholarship to Dr Allegra Bassetti of the Università Statale in Milano.*
>
> *You will appreciate that such a prestigious award gives the candidate unprecedented access to those scrolls that have already come into our possession. We are also negotiating an agreement for access to the scrolls housed in the Rockefeller Museum. As a result, the Medina Archaeology Scholarship has generated intense interest worldwide and the field of candidates has been nothing short of outstanding.*
>
> *We have given careful consideration to the Vatican's sensitivities in regard to the Dead Sea Scrolls. I regret that on this occasion we cannot accede to your request for a Catholic scholar to take the place of Dr Bassetti. Although your candidate has very strong recommendations, Dr Bassetti is a brilliant scientist of quite exceptional potential and the Selection Board's decision was unanimous.*
>
> *Sincerely,*
> *Yossi Kaufmann*
> *Hebrew University*
> *Mount Scopus*

Petroni considered his options. To openly deny the troublesome woman and the Israeli scholar access to the scrolls held in the Rockefeller might be a mistake. The Tom Schweikers of this world were already proving to be a threat and it might give the Israeli Department of Antiquities unnecessary ammunition. A more cunning approach would be to instruct Lonergan to appear to be cooperating while ensuring that none of the more controversial scroll fragments were accessed. He looked at his watch. It was five o'clock in Jerusalem and there would be no point calling Lonergan now. He would be in a bar in the American Colony Hotel. Lorenzo Petroni decided to call him in the morning when Lonergan would be closer to being sober. A red haze blurred Petroni's vision briefly and he fought an urge to feel his fists against an innocent's flesh. His power was threatened and his anger was betraying his judgement. The Keys of Peter were as elusive as ever. The red haze lifted and Petroni regained his feeling of control.

Lonergan. How he detested having to deal with the pompous fat academic priest in Jerusalem. Academic priests were invariably more trouble than they were worth – always that smug satisfaction and oozing self-confidence. But for the moment it was Lonergan's academic qualifications that made him useful to Petroni. He had put the disgraced priest into the Rockefeller Museum for one reason – to ensure that the Vatican's carefully crafted 'Consensus' on the age and origin of the Dead Sea Scrolls had credibility. Lonergan was the perfect puppet, for it had been Petroni who had saved his worthless hide. That had been over forty years ago when that irksome woman in Idaho had refused the Church's generous offer of compensation to alleviate the upset over a priest playing around with young boys. The incident had been badly handled in the local diocese and eventually the fallout had threatened to overwhelm the Holy Church itself. So much so that the Vatican had taken charge and quietly arranged for a very young Bishop Petroni to take over damage control and protect the image of the Holy Church. Petroni's strategy to protect the priest had not been without risk. Many had insisted that the Church should revoke the priest's orders and accompany that dismissal with an honest apology.

'I fear that would encourage others to take similar action and expose the Holy Church to many other damaging claims,' Petroni had argued. The Cardinal Secretary of State at the time had agreed and the priest in question had been summoned to Rome. Petroni had dealt with the priest in a face-to-face interview. The personal exercise of power. It would be something he would regret.

'You will be posted to the Middle East,' Petroni had intoned dispassionately. 'To a little known parish in Mar'Oth. When this unfortunate episode has died down you will then be enrolled at L'École Biblique in Jerusalem where you will complete a doctorate in archaeology. On successful completion of your studies you will be given further instructions. It has come to my attention that this is not the first time you have offended, far from it. In the role I have in mind for you, if your past was ever exposed to the wider public, the damage to the image of the Holy Church would be quite unaccept-able. To guard against that you are to be given a new identity. Your papers are in this envelope.' With that the priest had been dismissed with an icy finality and banished to the village in the Palestinian West Bank. The Vatican had a new priest and, for all intents and purposes, he had a clean record – Father Derek Lonergan. If he was successful in his doctorate Petroni would have in place another building block for dealing with the Dead Sea Scrolls and another strategy to control any rumours that surrounded the Omega Scroll.

In the face of no comment and unable to trace the offender, the media had moved on, as Petroni had predicted they would. The only chance of discovery was a file kept in Petroni's safe. His strat-egy had worked brilliantly, and his work had not gone unnoticed by the powerful Curial Cardinals. The young Bishop Petroni's assignment to the Pontifical Biblical Commission with special responsibility for handling the Vatican's interests in the Dead Sea Scrolls had been quickly confirmed.

After two years Lonergan had been enrolled for his doctorate and assigned to L'École Biblique and the Rockefeller Museum as the Vatican's representative and a staunch public advocate for the 'Consensus'. Had he known what was happening in Lonergan's favourite bar, Petroni would have been gravely concerned. His plan was starting to unravel.

CHAPTER THIRTY-ONE

Jerusalem

The American Colony Hotel's Cellar Bar with its hundred-year-old pink stone floor and low stone arches was one of Derek Lonergan's haunts. An hour ago Derek Lonergan had been holding court with a group of visiting journalists, loudly. Now he was drinking on his own, copiously.

'Someone overheard you talking about the Dead Sea Scrolls, Monsignor Lonergan. He asked me to give you this,' Abdullah said quietly. The small, slightly built Arab barman handed over a folded piece of paper. Derek Lonergan squinted blearily at the grubby paper and the even grubbier handwriting. *Meet me outside the Damascus Gate at eleven o'clock tonight. I will be wearing a red fez. I have something you and the Vatican want.*

Derek Lonergan turned the paper over but there was nothing else on it.

'Who gave you this?' he demanded, his words slurred.

Abdullah shrugged inscrutably. 'I am sorry, Sir, he wouldn't say. He just said it was important you got the message.'

'Hrrumph.' Lonergan snorted and looked at his watch. It was a quarter to the hour. Had he been sober he might have considered such a clandestine meeting more carefully, instead he threw down the rest of his drink and lurched out of the Cellar Bar and into the night. The ancient entrance to the Old City of Jerusalem and the beginning of the road to Damascus, the Damascus Gate, was only a few minutes walk away. When Lonergan reached the gate it was eerily quiet. Only a few people were coming and going under the massive battlements that had protected it over the centuries. It was nearly ten past eleven when a small Turk in a faded red fez approached from the shadows of the old city wall.

'Monsignor Lonergan?' the man asked, his coal-like eyes darting.

'You took your time,' Lonergan replied thickly, trying to place the accent.

'You are alone?'

'Look, whatever your name is . . .'

'I asked you a question, Monsignor Lonergan,' the Turk said, ignoring Lonergan's comment. 'I suggest you answer me if you want to see what I have. Otherwise they will be lost to the Vatican for ever, which could be very embarrassing for your Cardinal Petroni.'

At the mention of Petroni's name Lonergan started sobering up. 'Yes,' he said, nodding his head.

'You will follow me, please.'

The Turk disappeared under the stone ramparts and into the Old City. Derek Lonergan struggled to keep up with the faded red fez as he moved quickly down alleys and through covered streets, and into the Christian Quarter where the Turk disappeared into a dingy narrow stone cul-de-sac, pushed open an old heavy door and beckoned for him to follow.

Struggling for breath and unused to anything more physical than raising his right arm, Derek Lonergan heaved himself up a narrow flight of stone steps, squeezed through a small kitchen and entered an inner sitting room.

'Was all that necessary?' Lonergan wheezed, collapsing into a heavy wooden chair.

'I think when you see what I have, Monsignor Lonergan, you will agree that it would be unwise for either of us to be followed by the authorities or anyone else.' The Turk lifted some coir matting and prised loose three of the old floorboards. From the cavity in the floor he removed a long olive wood box, leaving another larger box in place. He took out a faded dirty yellow linen roll and placed it on the heavy scarred wooden bench that sat in the middle of the small room.

Derek Lonergan blinked, his memory stirring. He had seen the dirty yellow linen before, around several of the Dead Sea Scrolls that had been brought to the Rockefeller.

'What do you have there?' he asked, levering himself out of the chair, his voice hoarse with excitement.

'A Dead Sea Scroll,' the Turk replied nonchalantly, noting that the panting of his quarry's breathing had nothing to do with physical exertion.

'Where did you get it?' Lonergan demanded. 'Let me see.'

The Turk ignored the question, watching while Lonergan unwrapped the priceless two-thousand-year-old artefact. He handed him an old silver magnifying glass that had belonged to his father.

For a long time Derek Lonergan looked at the faded manuscript, his heart thumping against his chest. It was in Koiné, and immediately Lonergan knew it meant only one thing. There had only been one Dead Sea Scroll that had been written in the Greek lingua franca of the day, and he checked and re-checked his translation of the ancient script. Stay calm, he told himself, stay calm. On no account must the little Turk twig to what was written on this scroll and he put his hands in his pockets to hide his trembling fingers. The Magdalene Numbers, the Essenes writing on the origin of life, and the warning of the destruction of civilisation at the hands of a new faith. It was nothing short of explosive.

The Turk remained impassive but Monsignor Lonergan's reaction had not escaped his attention. He could see the astonishment in Lonergan's eyes.

'Where did you get this from?' Derek Lonergan asked again.

'It came from a place where the sea is low and nothing lives within it,' the Turk replied cryptically. 'But measured against what is in this scroll, the exact location of the discovery is not important, Monsignor Lonergan. Fortunately for the Catholic Church, it is for sale.'

'How much?' Lonergan asked quickly, too quickly.

The Turk heard the eagerness in his adversary's voice. 'Fifty million dollars,' he answered.

'That's ridiculous,' Lonergan blurted out. 'Out of the question. It is a minor document. We would pay one million and not a solitary cent more,' he added pompously, determined not to be cornered by some shifty little backstreet dealer. Lonergan assumed there would not be anyone in the Turk's circle who could decipher the ancient text. 'Besides, you are dealing in antiquities, which is illegal.'

'As you wish, Monsignor Lonergan,' the Turk responded with a polite smile that held a touch of amusement at Lonergan's ego and naïvety. The Turk's father had sold a copy of the Omega Scroll for ten million dollars in 1978 and the Church had not blinked. Obviously this buffoon was unaware of that. 'I apologise for troubling you.'

'One million dollars is a lot of money,' Lonergan stated angrily.

'You and I both know it is worth considerably more to the Catholic Church than fifty million dollars, but for that price I would also throw in the other box.'

'What's in that?' Lonergan asked, his eyes narrowing.

'Perhaps I should have mentioned it before,' the Turk said. Had Lonergan accepted the first offer he would not have mentioned it at all.

'Show me,' Lonergan demanded.

It took the two of them to lift the larger olive wood box out of the floor cavity. The Turk unlocked the heavy brass padlock.

Derek Lonergan's eyes widened. The box was full of hundreds of fragments. He took one out and examined it carefully with the magnifying glass.

'Probably a fragment of Isaiah,' he said at last. 'Again, it is interesting but not of great value.' He took another fragment. Unlike the Great Isaiah and the Omega Scrolls, this one was written in ancient Greek. Interesting that a Gnostic Gospel should be in the trunk, he thought, although not out of the question in the murky world of the black market.

'The fifth gospel, the Gospel of Thomas,' Lonergan announced importantly.

'I see you are well versed in the languages of the ancients, Monsignor Lonergan.'

Lonergan sniffed haughtily. 'It is also of no consequence. A copy of this was found at Nag Hammadi and the translation is freely available to any scholar who wishes to access it.'

'Then perhaps you would find these more interesting, Monsignor Lonergan.' The Turk reached for a small clear plastic bag that had been taped under the lid of the box. Inside the bag were three fragments. Once they were placed on the table Lonergan's pulse raced as he began to translate the ancient Koiné.

'The Path to the Omega . . .' This time he made no attempt to hide his astonishment. The three fragments contained identical words to the scroll he had translated earlier. This was another copy of the great Omega Scroll.

'You see, Monsignor Lonergan, we have reason to believe that in amongst the fragments in this box there is a second copy of the scroll you have just declined to purchase. As you rightly point out there will also most likely be another complete Scroll of Isaiah. The Essenes were a highly organised people, Monsignor Lonergan.

You should not be surprised that their scribes ensured their library contained copies of their most precious writings. In addition, there is likely to be a complete copy of the Gnostic Gospel of Thomas. This box would be part of the purchase.'

Once more Derek Lonergan forced himself to remain calm. 'Where did these come from,' he asked again.

'As I have said, Monsignor, that is not important.' The Turk had no intention of discussing the boxes he had found under a loose floorboard after his father died and he had taken over the clutter of his antiquities store in Bethlehem.

'It is unfortunate that in the process of these scrolls coming into my hands the second copy has been allowed to disintegrate, and doubly unfortunate that the fragments have become hopelessly mixed with the other scrolls. Some of these Bedouins are not well schooled in handling ancient parchment, but they know the value of these things. As do I,' he added pointedly.

'Fifty million dollars is still out of the question,' Lonergan said. 'Even if they are genuine, the documents already exist in the wider world. The great Isaiah Scroll is in the Shrine of the Book and any other scroll in here is likely to be already under study in the Scrollery at the Rockefeller Museum,' Lonergan lied.

'Perhaps, Monsignor Lonergan, perhaps. Although given the lack of progress in the Scrollery, the wider academic community would welcome the chance to provide, shall we say, more productive scholarship on their meaning. Again, I apologise for bothering you, it's just that we wanted to give the Catholic Church first option. No doubt I will be able to find other buyers,' he said, re-taping the plastic bag underneath the lid. 'Like the fifth, sixth and seventh gospels of Thomas, Philip and Mary Magdalene I'm sure they will find the Eighth Gospel . . . the Omega Scroll most interesting.'

At the mention of the Omega Scroll Lonergan's sharp intake of breath was audible. 'How much do you know?' he rasped angrily.

'You would be mistaken to think we do not know the value of these documents,' the Turk responded, his quiet demeanour unchanged. He was used to dealing in the dark world of antiquities, a world that was full of egomaniacs, although perhaps not as pompous or volatile as Monsignor Derek Lonergan. 'And none is more valuable, or more damaging to the Christian Faith than the Omega Scroll . . .' The Turk let his words trail off as a portent of the turmoil that might follow its release.

Derek Lonergan's mind was racing. Fifty million dollars was an enormous amount but he knew Cardinal Petroni wouldn't blink at the price. Now that these other two copies of the Omega had surfaced the Vatican Bank would pay whatever was required to keep both documents out of the public domain for ever. He pursed his fleshy lips as he suddenly realised that the second box was something that Petroni need not even know about. It contained immeasurable insurance against his file ever being made public, and eventually it would fetch a considerable sum. More importantly, here was the perfect opportunity to allow him to throw off the shackles of that prick in Rome. Perhaps, just perhaps he could exact some revenge for his treatment at the hands of Petroni and the Vatican.

'I will have to consult with the Vatican,' he said finally, any pretext of the amount being preposterous suddenly evaporating. 'And I will need to confirm they are genuine.'

'Naturally,' the Turk replied. He had anticipated the request and handed Lonergan a worn leather pouch. 'This contains clearly marked envelopes with blank sample parchments from each of the scrolls. You will no doubt want to conduct carbon dating and other tests.'

'How do I contact you?'

'You don't. The boxes will now be moved to another place for safekeeping,' the Turk said. 'I will contact you in a month.'

As he headed back towards the Damascus Gate Derek Lonergan looked at his watch, wondering if the Cellar Bar would still be open.

It was after one in the morning. Probably not, he thought. The coded letter to Petroni would have to be sent via the Vatican's dip-lomatic black bag which would probably prompt a question or two from Bishop O'Hara. Fuck him. Not to mention Petroni when he got the request for fifty big ones, well fuck him too. Fuck the lot of them. He cursed again as he staggered up yet another blind alley.

CHAPTER THIRTY-TWO

Tel-Aviv

The landing gear of the British Airways Boeing 747 rumbled and thumped into place. Allegra pressed her face against the window with mounting expectation, waiting for her first glimpse of Israel. The Holy Land. She had read so much about it when she had been at the convent in Tricarico and now she was finally here. Mamma had demanded to know every detail, details that would no doubt be faithfully repeated for the benefit of La Signora Bagarella and La Signora Farini, and anyone else who might be around the cobblestone alleys of Tricarico. Papà would provide less detail, but Tricarico's only wine bar would nevertheless be kept up to date on Allegra's progress.

The big aircraft banked slowly and Allegra's first sight of the Promised Land was disappointing. The Mediterranean lapped a dirty shoreline with waves of little consequence, and the late afternoon sun couldn't do much to bring either to life. In the distance she could see Tel-Aviv and the city was equally unspectacular – a myriad of tightly packed nondescript buildings with the skyline occasionally broken by high-rise hotels overlooking what passed for a beach. The first all-Jewish city of modern Israel had been founded in 1908 as a garden suburb of Old Jaffa. Old Jaffa had been known throughout history as the pilgrims' gate to Jerusalem and one of the oldest continually inhabited places in the world. Now the tables had turned and Old Jaffa was just another part of metropolitan Tel-Aviv.

The captain applied more power and the four Rolls-Royce RB211 turbofans growled, only to quieten again as the 400-ton aircraft settled on its approach path. The purser took the intercom and commenced the customary landing spiel. 'As we will shortly be landing in Tel-Aviv . . .'

Allegra continued to stare out of her window, only to see that the surrounding countryside was as uninviting as the shoreline, a narrow plain of low scrubby greens and browns. But to the Israelis this countryside was a lot more than that. It was Eretz Israel, the land of Abraham and Moses and the twelve tribes of Israel. Nothing in the Old Testament, save Yahweh himself, was more precious.

After what seemed like an age of taxiing, clearing immigration and waiting for the luggage carousel to start spilling luggage onto the roundabout, Allegra finally reached customs.

'Open the case.' If the machine gun contrasted strangely with the attractiveness of the young customs officer, it was in perfect harmony with her eyes. Steely and suspicious.

'Is this your first visit to Israel?' Her English was crisp with only a hint of a Jewish accent.

'Yes,' Allegra replied, opening her suitcase.

'Business or pleasure?' the young Israeli customs officer demanded as she rifled through Allegra's bag with ruthless efficiency.

'I'm here on a scholarship with the Hebrew University.' The customs officer looked her up and down and snapped the suitcase shut.

'Enjoy your stay in Israel,' she said curtly and waved Allegra through. Allegra wheeled her trolley into the arrivals hall. Ben Gurion Airport was busy and there was an almost continual stream of announcements ricocheting off the terminal walls, first in Hebrew and then in English. Allegra searched the crowd for Dr David Kaufmann, scanning the dozens of faces, looking for someone who might fit the brief description she had been given. About six feet tall, olive complexion, curly black hair, blue eyes and solid-looking. With the possible exception of the curly hair it wasn't much help.

Roma

Not long after his appointment Cardinal Petroni had personally overseen the installation of secure phones for those he might need to contact. It was just as well. If what Lonergan had told him was true the acquisition of the second copy of the Omega Scroll was now nothing short of critical, and it would have to be done with the utmost secrecy. Petroni dialled his personal code, followed by the country code for Israel and finally the number for Lonergan's secure phone in Jerusalem.

Derek Lonergan winced as the telephone rang loudly and he was forced to search for it under the piles of documents and papers that covered his desk. 'Lonergan', he answered thickly, not realising it was his red phone.

'Good morning, Monsignor, this is the Cardinal Secretary of State.'

'Eminence.' Lonergan jerked his head to a more upright position and immediately regretted the suddenness of this action. 'You have my letter?' he asked, holding his head.

Petroni's voice was cool. 'Switch to secure.'

'Yes, Eminence.' Up yours, he thought darkly as he fumbled for the plastic key that switched the phone to its secure mode.

'How many people know of the existence of the Omega Scroll,

Monsignor?' Petroni asked when Lonergan eventually mastered the technology and came back on line.

'Other than the Bedouins who found them, and they would not have been able to translate it, only the antiquities dealer,' Lonergan replied. 'It stands to reason that it would not be in his interest for word to reach the authorities. I, of course, have not mentioned it to anyone.'

'Keep it that way. How much room do we have to manoeuvre on price.'

'He plays very hard, Eminence. I offered him one million dollars but he scoffed at it. It was then that he made mention of the Omega Scroll and said he would be able to find other buyers.'

'This might be a secure line, Monsignor, but unlike mine, your conversations can be overheard. Guard what you say!'

'Of course, Eminence.' Up yours again, he thought, more darkly than before. The line stayed silent until Cardinal Petroni spoke again.

'We cannot afford to take the risk. Tell him we will pay the asking price. The money will be available for collection in Switzerland and we will pay for his travel there, but once he collects the money he is no longer our problem. Monsignor Thomas will meet him in Zürich and the exchange will be done at the bank. You are to attend the meeting to attest to what we are buying. The details will be forwarded to you in a sealed envelope in the black bag and will arrive tomorrow. Is all of that clear?'

'Perfectly, Eminence.'

'Good. Now there is one other matter that requires your attention. I have received advice that Dr Allegra Bassetti and an Israeli scholar, Dr David Kaufmann, have been awarded post-doctorate scholarships at the Hebrew University.'

'Yes, Eminence,' Derek Lonergan said, wishing that the percussion section of the London Philharmonic would find somewhere else to practise other than inside his skull.

'Regrettably they will have unfettered access to those scrolls that the Jews already hold. The Hebrew University will request access to the scrolls you hold in the Rockefeller. On no account is that to occur, although outwardly you are to give the impression that we are cooperating. If necessary they can be given some office space but you are to delay that as long as possible.'

'Yes, Eminence. Although you will appreciate that Professor Kaufmann is applying a lot of pressure through the Department of Antiquities.' There was silence at the other end of the line. It had been an unwise position to take.

'I don't care how much pressure there is,' Petroni responded icily. 'As a member of the Pontifical Biblical Commission your task is to ensure that the Word of God is shielded from any errors, and you are also there to ensure that the Holy Church is protected from criticism. And while I have you on the phone I did not appreciate Professor Kaufmann's article on the codes in the Dead Sea Scrolls in last month's *Biblical Antiquities Review*. I hardly need to remind you, Monsignor, that the contents of your file would not make life easy for you if it became public. I have protected you once, I may not be so lenient the next time.'

'Of course, Eminence, of course.' Like many others, Monsignor Lonergan should have saved his subservience. The line was dead.

'*Vaffanculo!* Up your arse!' he yelled into the lifeless receiver. He got up from his desk and trod a well-worn path to the cupboard in the far wall. His trembling fingers made it difficult to get the small key into the lock and his hands were still trembling as he unscrewed the cap on the bottle. He walked back to the French windows that looked out over the gardens, drained his glass and poured himself another.

To anyone else the walled gardens would seem like an oasis in the middle of the ancient Arab capital of East Jerusalem, occupied by the Israelis since the 1967 Six Day War. Stately pine, cypress and palm trees gave shade and an air of tranquillity. Hedges, red desert flowers and sandstone steps dropped gently into leafy squares with stone seats, providing a place of escape from the pressures of the world. A short distance from the gates of the gardens, on the other side of the walls of the old stone Priory, the Old City teemed with the noise and aromas of life in the Middle East as it had done for centuries. For Monsignor Derek Lonergan, the guardian of Papal secrets in Jerusalem, the place resembled a prison.

'What you don't know, you arsehole, is that for your fifty million you get one copy of the Omega. I get the other copy, along with Thomas and Isaiah,' he muttered to himself. The sly little Turkish antiquities dealer in the faded red fez could, he felt sure, be persuaded against mentioning the second box when they went to Zürich. A commission for organising payment of the fifty million. Turks understood these things, he mused as he emptied the whisky bottle and flung it into a box in the bottom of his cupboard.

Tel-Aviv

'Dr Allegra Bassetti?'

Allegra turned to find David Kaufmann standing behind her.

'Hi, I'm David Kaufmann. Welcome to Israel,' he said with a broad smile.

'Hello and thank you,' she replied, shaking his hand. His grip was firm and confident. This tall, tanned and fit-looking Israeli was not really what she had expected. David was a gorgeous looking man and the scar on his right cheek only added to his appeal. Judging him to be in his mid-forties, Allegra had imagined that a doctor of archaeology and an expert in Greek and Aramaic languages to be a little less athletic, a little more bookish and a little older. Had she known he was in his late fifties she would have been even more surprised. Fleetingly she remembered Professor Gamberini's remark about him being very single.

'I understand you speak English and Hebrew as well as Italian? That's quite an achievement,' he said, taking her bags.

'Well, thank you, but my Hebrew is very rusty. Thanks for meeting me. I can hardly believe I am here,' she said.

'You'll soon be in the thick of it. Onslow is not very far away.'

'Your driver?'

'My car. It was given to me by a friend of mine who was the British military attaché here before he went back to London. The Honourable Onslow Harrington-Smythe – we never give the car the full title, just Onslow.'

'That was very generous of your friend.'

'You haven't seen Onslow.'

Bemused, Allegra followed her very attractive research partner to the car park where he had parked the ancient British Land Rover with 'Hebrew University' hand-painted on its front doors.

'Forgive the dust,' David said, as he opened the door and thumped the faded green vinyl seat. Powdery dust from Jericho and several other biblical cities puffed up from the seat.

David slammed his door twice before it shut and when he turned the ignition key Onslow's engine cranked uncertainly. With a belch of black smoke and a cough it fired and roared into life.

'Unless you really want to go into Tel-Aviv,' David said, raising his voice so he could be heard over the roar of the engine, 'which is nothing to write home about, I thought we might head straight up to Jerusalem. We can have a welcome drink at one of my favourite bars, then get you settled in?'

'Tel-Aviv can wait for another day,' she assured him, shouting back.

'It's the muffler or a gasket or something,' he explained. 'Must get it seen to one of these days.' David swung the Land Rover out of the car park and headed south-east onto Route 1. Allegra felt a surge of excitement at the first signpost saying 'Jerusalem'. She braced herself against the metal dashboard as David braked hard and swerved to avoid a minibus full of Arabs cutting in front of them. If the horn on the Land Rover had worked, he still wouldn't have used it. David Kaufmann was not one to get agitated easily.

'As you can see it's a toss-up as to who are the world's worst drivers. Us or the Arabs.'

'You obviously haven't driven in Italy,' she replied. 'How far is it to Jerusalem?'

'It's about 50 kilometres from here but the university campus is on Mount Scopus which is a few kilometres further on. Since this is your very first day we'll brave the traffic and take the scenic route past the Old City. Tomorrow we have a briefing at the Rockefeller, although I should warn you there has been more than a little controversy over these scholarships and they may not be too pleased to see us.'

'Does that have anything to do with the Omega Scroll?' Allegra asked, deciding to find out how much David knew.

'You know about that?' he asked, glancing sideways at her.

'A little,' she replied enigmatically, 'there's been a bit of speculation in the Italian press from time to time.'

'It may have something to do with it, not that there has ever been any proof of the Rockefeller having a copy, but it's also about the fragments of the scrolls they hold. They've been pretty choosy about granting access, and it's beginning to look as if there might be something very damaging in them, otherwise they would have been opened up to thorough scrutiny years ago.'

'Do you think it's real, the Omega Scroll?' Allegra asked, pressing for more information.

'My father certainly does,' David replied. 'Although I'm not so sure, yet it's always in the back of your mind when you're near an archaeological dig. What about you?'

'I think your father might be right and whenever people get close to uncovering it, strange things seem to happen. You heard what happened to Professor Rosselli?'

David nodded. 'A sad business. He and Yossi corresponded regularly. They never found who did it?'

Allegra shook her head. 'The file's still open but the trail seems to have gone cold. Your father is still trying to break the codes?'

'You read his article on the Dead Sea Scrolls?'

'It made the news in Italy.'

'I'm not surprised, given what he wrote. You will meet him tomorrow, after our briefing at the Rockefeller. I'll take you for a walk through the Old City and around seven-thirty-ish, if you feel up to it, we can mosey over to the Shrine of the Book. The Professor's giving a briefing on the Dead Sea Scrolls to a bunch of visiting American congressmen.'

'The Professor?'

'My father, it's a term of endearment. I've arranged our briefing at the museum for half past three so I'll pick you up about quarter past two. Ish. Just in case the Palestinians are out and about and causing havoc.' David's comment was not entirely in jest.

'Is that a problem?'

'It's been pretty quiet here for the last couple of months, but in Israel you never can tell. You get used to it. Most people are in the Reserves which is a continual reminder that the country has to be protected.'

'You're in the Army?'

'Used to be. Pretty well everyone serves in the Defense Force, unless you're pregnant or a mother. I gather you'd have to sign up,' he added, laughing.

'On both counts!' Allegra found herself responding to this interesting Israeli. She felt relaxed and at ease with a man who obviously didn't take life too seriously.

'How long did you serve for?'

'Conscription runs for three years and after that you're still assigned to a frontline Reserve unit until you're thirty-nine. If there's a war the whole country is mobilised. Buses and taxis carry troops, private planes and boats go into the Air Force and Navy and construction bulldozers and cranes go into the Engineers. All in all, we can put a quarter of a million troops into the field overnight. Back in 1973 it was very nearly not enough.'

'Were you involved then?'

David nodded. 'Pretty well everyone was. I had a gig in the '67 event too.'

Allegra smiled to herself. Somehow David Kaufmann struck her as someone who would find the discipline of the armed forces irksome.

'And your father?'

'Far more distinguished career than mine. He was one of the youngest generals in the Army, although not everyone's a fan. He has a view, and I agree with him, that fighting the Arabs is never going to solve the problem, but the High Command and a lot of politicians in this country expect their generals to be a bit more gung-ho. I don't think he's the flavour of the month with the Vatican right now either.'

'Yes, after your father's article on the codes in the Dead Sea Scrolls I can understand why the cardinal's club would not be amused.'

'That's putting it mildly. I gather the Secretary of State – what's his name – Petroli?'

'Petroni.' Allegra shivered with the memory.

'That's the fellow,' David said, pulling out to push his way past a bus that was billowing thick black smoke. Up until now the road had been dead flat, passing through ploughed fields and the rich red soils of the fertile coastal plain, but now they had reached the rocky foothills of the Judaean mountains.

'I gather he was bordering on apoplexy. I'm sorry, are you a Catholic?'

'Don't worry, lapsed, very lapsed,' Allegra replied, deciding that now was not the time to go into her time in a convent. 'You?'

'Legally I'm Jewish.'

'Legally?'

'Being a Jew can be a bit complicated. If your mother is Jewish or you convert to Judaism, regardless of where you are born, according to Jewish law you are accepted as being a Jew. It's a kind of worldwide citizenship. If you're asking if I share the religious beliefs of the Orthodox Jews then the answer is no. I suppose I'm of no fixed religion. My father has a strong faith although only God would know how he's kept it. He and my mother both lost their parents in the Holocaust. My mother's pretty normal though!'

'You seem remarkably well informed on the Vatican?' Allegra was intrigued by his earlier observations.

'My father is good friends with the bishop here, an Irish fellow by the name of O'Hara. Funnily enough he doesn't seem too religious either. Nice guy. You'll get to meet him too.'

As they reached the top of the long climb to the outskirts of Jerusalem, Allegra still couldn't believe she was actually here.

'The Old City goes back about four thousand years,' David explained, not realising just how 'lapsed' Allegra was. 'King David made it the Jewish capital about a thousand years before Christ after he beat the piss and pick handles out of the Philistines.'

Allegra smiled. She knew she would continue to enjoy David Kaufmann's irreverent turn of phrase.

'Not long after that his son Solomon built the first temple. That lasted about four hundred years until the good old Babylonians came in and knocked it over in 586 BC. Nehemiah built the second one about forty years later.' David swerved to avoid a yellow Palestinian taxi. 'Alexander the Great knocked the city off again in 332 BC, but the second temple lasted until the Romans in their inimitable style razed it to the ground in 70 AD. The Western Wailing Wall is all that's left.'

At the end of the old Jaffa Road, they reached Zahal Square and Allegra got her first glimpse of the walls of the Old City. From her research Allegra knew that the walls themselves had survived since they had been built by Suleiman the Magnificent, the Ottoman sultan of Istanbul fame, in 1537. Against the backdrop of the wall, a contrast of ancient and modern pushed Allegra's senses to their limits. A cacophony of cars, trucks, tourist buses, *sheruts* – the white Israeli minibuses – and their yellow Palestinian equivalents jostled for space on the crowded road.

'That's the Jaffa Gate and further down you can see the Citadel,' David said, pointing to the massive blocks at the base of a huge stone tower. 'Otherwise known as the Tower of David. Just before Christ's time Herod rebuilt it, and today it houses the Museum of the History of Jerusalem. When we haven't got you out searching for more Dead Sea Scrolls, you and the Old City can get better acquainted.'

'I'm looking forward to that,' Allegra said as David swung Onslow into the car park of the hotel.

Dusky lights accentuated the front of the American Colony Hotel, one of Jerusalem's most famous and stylish hotels. The architecture was typically Turkish fortress style and the rooms looked onto a beautiful old stone courtyard and well cared for palm trees, gardens and fountains.

'Would you like a table, Dr Kaufmann?' asked Abdullah, the Cellar Bar's long-serving barman, indicating a vacant alcove under one of the old sandstone archways.

David looked at Allegra and raised an eyebrow.

'I'd be happy to stand at the bar. I've been sitting in a plane for hours,' she said, smiling at Abdullah. 'I'll have a beer thanks.'

'A woman after my own heart,' David responded.

'Shalom,' David said, raising his glass after Abdullah had brought the drinks.

'David!'

David turned around to see Tom Schweiker walking into the bar.

'Tom! How are you? It's been a while. I'd like you to meet a friend of mine, Dr Allegra Bassetti. Allegra is an expert in archaeological DNA and is joining us to do some research. Allegra, meet Tom Schweiker. Tom's a journalist but don't let that put you off, some of them are actually quite decent!'

'David has very discerning taste in friends,' Tom said with an easy smile, shaking Allegra's hand. 'Welcome to Jerusalem.'

'It's good to meet you. I've often watched you covering the Vatican from Rome,' Allegra replied, struck by the open camaraderie between the two men.

'A beer thanks, Abdullah,' Tom said, looking around. 'Strange. That lard-arsed blowhard from the Rockefeller isn't here. Blessed relief.'

'Lard-arsed blowhard?' Allegra asked, intrigued.

'Monsignor Derek Lonergan,' David explained. 'He'll be doing the briefing tomorrow.'

'Lucky you,' Tom observed. 'Any progress on getting access to the scrolls?'

David shook his head. 'At the moment we're having trouble even getting an office. Every time the scandal of the scrolls is raised it makes news for a while and then you guys move on.'

'Usually because someone's blown up another bloody bus,' Tom said. 'That hardly touched the sides. Three beers thanks, Abdullah.'

'Access to these scrolls seems to have had a pretty chequered history,' Allegra observed.

'Things have eased a little,' David said. 'In 1991 the new Director of the Huntington Library in San Marino, California, discovered a long forgotten photographic record of the scrolls in a safe. Unlike the Vatican, the Huntington believes in intellectual freedom. In the face of all sorts of legal threats the Huntington published the photographs, but I have my suspicions there is still more to come. The Vatican is guarding access to the originals, not to mention the actual dates of the scrolls, with all the ferocity of bin Laden's bodyguards, and the appalling irony is that ever since the 1967 war several of the academics who do have access haven't set foot inside the country, something that Lonergan strenuously denies.'

'I think I saw him give an interview once on that very issue. Big man?' Allegra asked.

Tom grinned. 'With an ego to match. British American. David and I have already made up our minds about him, so it will be interesting to see what you think.'

'You don't like him much?'

'Not a lot,' David answered. 'An elitist academic, but the Vatican like him because he supports their line. I wouldn't be surprised if they employ him.'

Tom Schweiker was absorbing every detail of the conversation between Allegra and David. Where the Vatican was concerned he had his own reasons for getting to the truth. Not that he would ever quote David, unless they both agreed there was a reason to do so. David was a friend and Tom Schweiker always took a long-term view. David Kaufmann was far too important a source to burn in the quest for a short-term front page headline.

'The Vatican team puts the origin of the scrolls around two hundred years before Christ,' Allegra said. 'That's probably true for some of them, but from the research I've done, some have definitely been written around the time of Christ, and they reflect both his and earlier teachings. Carbon dating would solve the question simply and decisively, but the Vatican has resisted that from the very beginning.'

'I think you're right,' David said. 'Their defence is too ferocious and anyone who disagrees is likely to feel the full force of the Vatican's power, as one or two very distinguished academics have found to their cost. I have a very strong suspicion the Vatican is hiding something.'

Allegra nodded. 'I've always had the feeling that the Vatican wanted to put as much distance between Christ and the Dead Sea Scrolls as they can.'

'Why?' asked Tom.

'If it can be proven that Christ studied under the Essenes,' Allegra said, 'it would threaten the very essence of Vatican teaching, not to mention Christ's divinity, the uniqueness of his teaching, and ultimately whether he was really out to start a religion.'

David was impressed by his new colleague's willingness to question tradition, no matter how deeply rooted in history. He realised there was much more to Allegra than she was letting on. Aware that he was staring intently at her, he briskly turned towards Tom. 'To the average punter that probably doesn't matter much,' David said, 'but anything that links Christ with the Essenes is likely to give the Vatican a bad case of the vapours.'

'I wonder if the Omega Scroll will come up at the briefing tomorrow?' Allegra ventured, wondering what sort of reaction she would get from Tom.

Tom grinned. 'Lonergan will give the impression of a welcome, but don't expect too much cooperation, especially on the Omega Scroll. He'll deny it even exists and I suspect they will do everything they can to make sure you both see as little as possible. Better go,' he said. 'Ferret Face is having a bad hair day. Lovely to have met you, Allegra. No doubt we'll be seeing a lot more of you.'

'Ferret Face?' Allegra asked, curious.

'His producer. Nasty piece of work apparently,' David replied as they followed Tom out of the bar.

After they had left, Abdullah reached for the phone.

The small travel clock had a very persistent ring and Allegra fumbled for the button to silence it, blinking in the morning light coming through the big bedroom window. For a few seconds she had no idea where she was, until the fuzziness of her jet lag slowly cleared. Instead of the normal university 'cell', the Medina scholarship had provided a spacious one-bedroom apartment that was only a ten-minute walk from the Mount Scopus campus. The apartment building was nestled at the end of a quiet leafy cul-de-sac and boasted sweeping views from her bedroom and living room balconies. In the distance she could make out the Old City and greater Jerusalem. The early morning sun had caught the 35-ton golden cupola of the Dome of the Rock, the best known and most striking part of the Jerusalem skyline and the third most holy shrine in all of Islam. To the right of the Dome and beyond it Allegra could make out the drab grey cupola of the Church of the Holy Sepulchre that had been built over the reported site of Christ's crucifixion in the Old City's Christian Quarter. To the left of the Dome was the valley of Kidron and the Mount of Olives. Allegra stretched out contentedly. She had the morning free for a stroll through the university to get the university sign-up procedures out of the way, and plenty of time to get ready for the briefing with Monsignor Lonergan. She found herself looking forward to seeing David again.

Suddenly her peace was shattered as the whole building shook. When the shaking stopped Allegra got off the bed and gingerly opened the door to the bedroom balcony. The street outside was quiet and there didn't seem to be any damage or any sounds of sirens, but she wondered if there would be aftershocks.

Not being sure what 'ish' meant, Allegra was ready a little after two, but it was nearly three before Onslow broke the peace of the neighbourhood. David leaned over and pulled the wire that served as a door handle on the passenger side. 'Sorry I'm late,' he yelled, a boyish grin on his face. Allegra would learn that a time qualified by 'ish' meant just that.

'Did you get the tremor here?' he shouted, accelerating out of the cul-de-sac.

'It frightened me a little. Is there much damage?'

'Only minor. We get them here every few years although this one was a little bigger. It registered six on the Richter scale and the epicentre was near the Dead Sea but there's not much out there so I guess we're lucky.'

For the second time in two days Allegra maintained a survival grip on the dashboard as David roared across greater Jerusalem, weaving in and out between the buses and *sheruts* and anything else that stood in his way.

'You don't see the need for a horn?' she asked innocently, as another pedestrian leapt back to the safety of a streetside store.

'No point. They can hear us coming a mile off.'

Allegra raised her eyebrows but David studiously ignored her. Inwardly she smiled. There was clearly quite a lot of the 'little boy' in David Kaufmann, she thought, something that made her warm to him even more.

'Welcome to the Rockefeller.' Monsignor Derek Lonergan extended a sweaty hand to David and then to Allegra. His hand felt like a fat, wet fish. Allegra smiled politely and looked at David with a 'you should have warned me' look as they followed the Vatican's man into his office. Derek Lonergan's face was flushed and a few long strands of reddish hair waved defiantly from his pink scalp. His beard hadn't been trimmed for a very long time and his breath smelt of whisky. The cord on his cassock disappeared under the folds of his belly. David grinned as he saw Allegra struggling to keep a straight face.

'The Director sends his apologies but he's asked me to brief you on his behalf,' Lonergan said, as he cleared away the piles of papers from two old chairs and levered his ample rear onto the front of his desk, giving Allegra a glimpse of a flabby white leg as he swung it to and fro.

'The Dead Sea Scrolls is both a very difficult field, and quite a simple one,' Monsignor Lonergan began pompously. 'It is simple in that a great deal of hype has been written about what might be in the scrolls. In reality, they contain nothing of startling interest.

Biblical scrolls that contain information already available to us in the Old Testament and with very little variance from the scriptures. Most interesting, but perfectly innocuous, and they add very little to the knowledge we already have of the peaceful reclusive Essenes who chose to live in isolation in Qumran. On the other hand,' he said, looking down at Allegra, 'putting the fragments together and reaching these conclusions by deciphering the ancient script is a job that requires a considerable amount of expertise.'

'What about the date of the scrolls, Monsignor,' David asked, underwhelmed by Lonergan's pomposity. 'I see that some scholars have argued that they are more closely linked to the time of Christ than first thought?'

'You may call them scholars, Sir. I most certainly do not. There is not a shadow of doubt that all of the fragments, or at least those we have had the time to examine, are from a pre-Christian era. No doubt whatsoever.'

It was a critical slip and David jumped on it.

'So there are other fragments you have not yet examined.'

For a moment Derek Lonergan looked as if he had suddenly become very constipated. His face went crimson and he blinked several times before answering, his eyes bulging like those of a large cod.

'A very small number are still in the vault,' he replied dismissively. 'From a cursory translation they appear to be copies of one or two of the minor books of the Old Testament.'

'And the dating of those?' Allegra asked.

'That has yet to be determined but given the overwhelming evidence that we have obtained from the fragments already analysed I have no doubt they will also date between 200 and 100 BC.'

'Does the analysis include carbon dating, Monsignor?' Allegra asked with an almost nonchalant look on her face.

Constipation set in again. 'I need hardly remind you, Dr Bassetti, that these scrolls are priceless. We are not about to chop them up to provide samples for chemists. The linen they were wrapped in has already been subjected to that type of analysis but,' he said, pausing for emphasis, 'when you have spent as many years as I have in this field you will come to realise that there are many other methods of dating that are just as accurate, if not more so. The coins found at Qumran for a start, not to mention palaeography.'

'Palaeography?'

'The science of the comparative study of ancient calligraphy or more simply, changes evident in the evolution of handwriting that can be dated according to style,' Lonergan said patronisingly, as if Allegra was a particularly thick school student.

'I know what palaeography is, Monsignor,' Allegra retaliated evenly. 'It's just that in my experience using palaeography to obtain accurate dates is, at best, somewhat tenuous?' Allegra's smile infuriated Lonergan.

'When you *have* some experience, Dr Bassetti, perhaps we might discuss the issue,' he spat back, making no attempt to hide the contempt in his voice. 'Now, if you will both follow me, I will give you a tour of the museum.'

'Nice arse,' David whispered as they followed the waddling off-white cassock down the corridor that led to the Scrollery. Allegra struggled to hold back a giggle.

The Scrollery was a long rectangular room with three rows of trestle tables running along almost its entire length. On top of these, dozens of thick square sheets of glass provided the only protection for the thousands of scroll fragments that had been assembled by the small international team dominated by Vatican scholars.

'This,' Lonergan announced unnecessarily, 'is the Scrollery. Please don't touch any of the glass covers. As you can see protestations of secrecy are entirely unfounded. Any member of the international team is free to move around the Scrollery and observe what other members are doing.'

David refrained from commenting. Since there was no one

actually in the Scrollery, 'doing' seemed a moot point. Both David and Allegra were somewhat bemused to find that for reasons best known to himself, Lonergan gave them a detailed tour of the administration areas; room after room of filing cabinets and computers. Finally they reached the basement area that housed the photographic dark rooms.

'Is that the vault?' David asked innocuously, as they passed the very same heavy steel doors he had come across during the 1967 Six Day War.

'Only the Director has the combination I'm afraid,' Lonergan lied easily, not even breaking the rhythm of his waddle.

'The fragments in the vault that have yet to be analysed. Perhaps we may be able to assist you in that area?' David suggested.

'Out of the question,' Lonergan replied emphatically. 'They have already been assigned. And,' he said meaningfully, 'the suggestion you might be attached to the Rockefeller has yet to be approved. Whilst we congratulate you both, most of the work of translation has already been done, and we were somewhat surprised when the Department of Antiquities saw fit to put more resources into a field that is already fully allocated.' The use of the royal 'we' seemed to underline the 'them' and 'us' approach that David had predicted.

'Have you any idea when approval might be forthcoming?' David persisted, as they arrived back at Lonergan's office.

'That will be up to the Director,' Lonergan replied vaguely. 'Now, I'm afraid you will have to excuse me. I have another appointment,' he said, looking at his watch. Across at the American Colony Hotel Abdullah was about to open the Cellar Bar.

'What do you think of our man Lonergan?' David asked as he and Allegra climbed back into Onslow.

'I thought if I saw another filing cabinet I'd scream. Are the academics here all like that?' Allegra asked, shaking her head in disbelief.

'In the pompous fart stakes he probably tops the list but I think we've just been given a taste of how far they will go to prevent us seeing anything of value in the Rockefeller.'

'He wasn't too keen to let you get into the vaults,' Allegra ventured.

'You noticed. Makes me wonder what's in them. I thought he was going to give birth there for a while, especially when he let slip there were more fragments.'

'You nearly brought me undone with your "nice arse" comment.'

David laughed. 'It's amazing what some people do to their bodies. How would you like to get into bed with that lot? You'd have to go looking for it,' he said, trying to keep a straight face.

'Ugh,' Allegra shuddered. 'What an awful thought!'

David found a place to park Onslow not far from the New Gate and they walked towards the Old City Walls. Allegra's faith, or at least the Catholic form of it, was now only a distant memory, but like most people who visit Jerusalem for the very first time, Allegra looked around with a certain amount of awe as she walked on the very same cobblestones that Christ and his disciples, Pontius Pilot, King David and a host of others had walked on so many years ago. David and Allegra paused for a moment inside the Church of the Holy Sepulchre that covered Christ's tomb. Then they walked on towards the eastern end of David Street and the Central Souk; three parallel streets covered with stone arches that dated back to the Crusaders. Allegra soaked up the atmosphere as they wandered into Souk el-Lakhamin, the butchers' market, where freshly slaughtered meat and chickens were hanging on big hooks in front of white tiled alcoves, a scene that looked like it had not changed for hundreds of years. Further on in Souk el-Attarin and el-Khawaiat, Arabs had crammed their wares into tiny stone Crusader vaults and were bent over dirty blue and green plastic buckets, full to overflowing with green and black olives. Nutmeg, ground peppers, cumin seeds and a hundred other spices were piled in wooden boxes or wrapped in plastic. Oranges from Jaffa, together with eggplants, custard apples, tomatoes, beetroot, cabbages and a myriad of other fruit and vegetables tumbled onto the smooth stone pavement. They walked past a corner bakery where sweet breads and pastries were piled on wooden trays.

'The history of this city is amazing,' Allegra said. 'I can hardly believe I'm walking around here.'

'One of the great cities of the world,' David agreed. 'The only city in the world where the three great monotheistic faiths of Judaism, Christianity and Islam meet.'

Jerusalem. It was one of the great sticking points of the Middle East but one of the keys to any solution to the Palestinian–Israeli problem. Sacred to the Jews, the place where King David had thrown the Jebusites out of an otherwise inconsequential city a thousand years before Christ, declaring it to be the Jewish capital. Sacred to the Christians, the place where their Saviour had been crucified and buried. Sacred to the Muslims, the place where Muhammad had ascended to heaven from Haram al-Sharif, the Dome of the Rock.

Three great religions, all competing fiercely with one another, all with the same God, Allegra mused, as they made their way back to Onslow.

The Shrine of the Book, part of the Israel Museum, was to the west of the Old City and not far from the National Library and the Knesset. It had been built in 1965, specifically to house the Dead Sea Scrolls that were held by the Israeli Government. The building had a unique appearance influenced by the scrolls themselves. The roof was a white dome in the shape of one of the lids of the jars in which the scrolls had been found. At the entrance, a black granite wall had been erected, the contrast of black and white a reference to the War Scroll and its description of a forty-year titanic struggle between good and evil that civilisation had yet to witness

– a struggle between 'the Sons of Light' and 'the Sons of Darkness'. A struggle that would herald the return of the Messiah.

David bounded into the entrance vestibule with Allegra at his side.

'Good evening, Yitzhak,' he said, addressing the man at the security desk and flashing one of several ID cards he kept on a chain around his neck.

'Go on through, Dr Kaufmann, Professor Kaufmann is about to begin. Welcome to Israel, Dr Bassetti.'

'Thank you,' she said, a little surprised that the guard knew who she was.

'Do you know everyone in Israel by their first name,' she demanded when they were through the magnetometer.

'Only the important ones. The security guards and the typing pool,' David said with a laugh, and led her into a long, subtly lit passage way.

'This is a reconstruction of the caves. They depict the Essene community and the area around Qumran where the scrolls were discovered. They were a very advanced civilisation,' he said, pointing to the orrery, a bronze model of the solar system. In the middle, a large bronze ball spinning on top of an iron rod represented the sun. Around it, the planets of the solar system were depicted by smaller bronze balls that were spinning and moving around the larger sun in elliptical orbits.

'There are ten planets in this model,' Allegra observed. 'A very recent discovery.'

'Interesting, isn't it.'

In 1999 two teams of scientists – one at the University of Louisiana at Lafayette and one at the Open University in the United Kingdom – reported that the orbits of the most distant comets in the icy wastes of the solar system were inexplicably clumping together into highly elliptical orbits, suggesting the influence of an unknown planet. Both teams had put the possible tenth planet at three trillion miles out.

'If this model was to scale,' David continued, 'and our farthest known planet Pluto was placed a metre from the sun, the tenth planet would need to be positioned a kilometre away.'

'Which explains why none of our telescopes have been able to pick it up,' Allegra reflected. 'The Essenes couldn't have known that?'

'No, although I think there is probably more to that community than we first thought. The model is based on a diagram that was unearthed from the Qumran library. They certainly had a strong interest in astronomy,' David said, indicating an ancient telescope in the display case.

'I thought the telescope wasn't invented until the seventeenth century?'

'Galileo,' David agreed, 'but archaeologists have long been puzzled by crystal lenses that pre-date even this one. One is in the British Museum and was found in a tomb in Egypt and the other is dated at 7 BC from Assyria. Both were mechanically ground to a complex mathematical formula. There is a theory that the Essenes discovered the telescope well before Galileo. The second Essene model is more interesting still,' he said, moving past the orrery and the telescope.

'It looks like a DNA helix,' Allegra said, her thoughts going back to the theories of Francis Crick and Antonio Rosselli.

'It is. That model is also based on a diagram found in the Qumran library. The Romans may have destroyed one of the most advanced civilisations of the ancient world when they sacked Qumran, but we'll see the ruins tomorrow morning. By the way, is nine too early?'

'Ish?' Allegra asked.

'Definitely "ish",' David answered. He could hardly believe he'd known Allegra for only a couple of days. She was definitely someone quite special and he felt his heart skip a beat. His instinct was to move closer to her, but instead he took a breath and moved quickly towards the entrance of the main room. Allegra, surprised by David's slight change of mood, followed him.

They emerged from the passageway into a huge chamber. The dome was bathed in a stunning green and soft orange light and beneath it a large circular podium dominated the room with what looked to Allegra like one end of a huge rolling pin protruding through the centre. As they entered, a tall, distinguished looking man detached himself from the group of senators.

'Almost on time, Dr Kaufmann, you can't be feeling well.' Yossi Kaufmann winked at Allegra and held out his hand. 'You must be Allegra. Welcome to Israel. You have my sympathies for whatever you might experience at the hands of David and Onslow,' Yossi said with a smile that reminded Allegra of David; the same confidence, the same laughter lines around the eyes. Like father like son.

'David has been most kind, Professor Kaufmann. It's an honour to meet you.'

'Please, call me Yossi because I intend to call you Allegra. Now, if it's OK by Dr Kaufmann here,' he said putting his arm around David, 'I will introduce you to our American friends and we'll start. But first, there are a couple of people here. Tom Schweiker from CCN, who I think you've met already?'

'Good to see you again, Allegra.'

'Bishop Patrick O'Hara,' Yossi continued, 'who is insisting that we all go back to his place after this for a drink, which I can warn you from personal experience can be a hazardous under-taking.'

'Patrick,' Allegra said. 'I've heard so much about you from Giovanni, I feel I know you already.' Patrick was just as Giovanni described him: thinning grey hair, twinkling green eyes, a cheerful face, his large Bishop's sash encompassing a body that reflected a love of people, food and whiskey. Allegra reflected on Giovanni's assessment that Patrick O'Hara also possessed one of the great intellects of Catholicism; a man who was prepared to question and debate.

'Welcome to the Promised Land, Allegra. And I wouldn't be believing all you've been told either. It's a lot worse than that,' he said with a chuckle.

'And last but by no means least, my wife, Marian.'

'Congratulations on your scholarship, Allegra. Yossi has told me a lot about you.'

'Thank you, Mrs Kaufmann . . .' Allegra got no further.

'Marian. You are part of the family now.'

'Steady on.' David protested. 'We're not even married.'

'David Kaufmann.'

Allegra smiled at the warmth in Marian's rebuke.

'I gather you got acquainted with Monsignor Lonergan today?' Yossi Kaufmann said.

'David assures me they're not all like that,' Allegra replied diplomatically.

'Don't be too certain. They may not all be as full of booze and bad manners,' Yossi said, giving Allegra some inkling as to where David might have learnt his colourful language, 'but collectively they're dangerously out of touch with reality. They still haven't approved your access or office space, but we'll keep at them. In the meantime the Hebrew University has allocated you a laboratory in the biochemistry complex. It's small but the equipment is state of the art. Some things are outside the control of the Vatican,' he added with a whisper of conspiracy. He excused himself to take his place on the steps of the podium. The dark-haired Cohatek technician signalled to Yossi that the sound system was ready to go.

'Ladies and Gentlemen,' Professor Kaufmann began. 'Welcome to the Shrine of the Book. Behind me in the display cases is the Great Isaiah Scroll, all sixty-six chapters and 7 metres of it.'

Recovered from the library of the mysterious Essenes in

Qumran, the priceless document had been written over five centuries before Christ. The senators listened attentively while Yossi described how the scrolls had been discovered, and how some of them had eventually found their way into Israeli hands.

'Many of the scrolls were not acquired by Israel until the Rockefeller Museum was liberated by Israeli forces during the 1967 Six Day War. For anyone who is interested, Dr David Kaufmann can give you far more information than I can. He was personally involved in their capture.' Yossi nodded towards his son with an unmistakable look of 'well done'.

'Isaiah contains a dire warning for civilisation,' Yossi continued. 'It's perhaps best summed up by Isaiah when he says, "The earth shall be utterly laid waste and utterly despoiled." Isaiah, Daniel, Enoch and Revelations and the more recent prophecies of Nostradamus and Edgar Cayce all point to an increase in wars, a growing gap between rich and poor, a change in weather patterns and problems with water, and a striking increase in the number and severity of earthquakes. My own research on the codes contained in the Dead Sea Scrolls is giving clues to the final countdown, the key to which is in a scroll known as the Omega Scroll.'

'I thought that was a myth?' the Republican senator from Alabama suggested.

'And you would not be alone in thinking that,' Yossi answered with a smile, 'but there is irrefutable evidence in the War Scroll, the Manual of Discipline, the Temple Scroll, Isaiah and others that points to its existence and within it, the key to ours. We have become immune to the prophecies of the ancients, but my hope, Senator, is that we can find the warning contained in the Omega Scroll before it is too late. If you would like to follow me, we can examine these prophecies close up.'

'Did you actually capture the Rockefeller Museum?' Allegra whispered, realising there were many things about David that she knew nothing about. Her interest was piqued and she wanted to find out more, much more, about him.

'I wish he wouldn't say things like that. We'll be here all night.'

Roma

Cardinal Petroni answered the intercom.

'Petroni!'

Monsignor Thomas had grown used to his cardinal's irritability and complete lack of telephone manner. It came with the territory. Nor did he question the frequency of calls from the CCN studios in New York. There were some things about his cardinal's rituals and habits that were not discussed.

'Daniel Kirkpatrick from CCN is on line four, Eminence.'

Impatiently Cardinal Petroni clicked off the intercom.

'Daniel. Good to hear from you. How are things in New York?'

'Very well, Lorenzo, and you?'

'Can't complain. How can I help?'

'It's more the other way round this time. I just wanted you to be aware that there will be a program on the Dead Sea Scrolls next week. The reporter is one of our news journalists and I've tried to have it canned, but *International Correspondent* is not really in my area and they're sticking to their guns.'

'Schweiker?'

'Got it in one. I'd get rid of him if I had my way, but it's not that easy to shift the big guns. I don't have your weight to throw around, though I wish I did! Things would be a lot different around here.'

'That will come, Daniel, that will come. In the meantime, do we know the contents of the program?'

'I've sent you an email. Essentially it's the old line of questioning the dates. Nothing new and I wonder why they bother, although there seems to be a bit of pressure from the Israeli side. A Professor Kaufmann?'

'I know him. Jewish, which is enough said. I'll get our man in Jerusalem primed. Stay well.'

For a long while after he had hung up the phone Cardinal Petroni stared out of the window at the lights of Rome. Know your enemy. Was it just Kaufmann or did Dr Bassetti have something to do with this renewed pressure on the dates of the scrolls, he wondered. Tomorrow he would put a call in to Lonergan.

Jerusalem

'Get fucked,' Derek Lonergan muttered as he used his free hand to reach for the red phone, supporting his aching head with the other.

'Good morning, Eminence.'

'I have had a call from CCN in New York,' Cardinal Petroni said, dispensing with the need for any greetings. '*International Correspondent* have put a program together that will raise the usual allegations over the dates of the Dead Sea Scrolls and Vatican involvement. Do you have any idea where this might be coming from?'

'No, Eminence, although as I have explained, there may be some pressure being applied from Professor Kaufmann's office.'

'We don't deal in "maybe's" here, Monsignor. Find out.'

Up yours, Lonergan thought, but he said nothing.

'They'll want to interview you, so stick to the usual consensus. To avoid any embarrassing questions on access for the two academics, you can finalise their secondment but make sure what they see is perfectly innocuous.'

'Do we know who the journalist is, Eminence?'

'Schweiker. Their Middle East correspondent. At times he can be useful, but for the most part he is a thorn in our side.'

Lonergan took a deep breath. Schweiker had seen him often enough in the Cellar Bar but Lonergan had always avoided talking to him. Schweiker, he felt sure, had been none the wiser, but an interview would be an entirely different matter. The name Schweiker was a reasonably common one in the United States and clearly the Cardinal had not put two and two together. Lonergan's ego kicked in. It had been over forty years ago and he didn't look anything remotely like he did back then.

'I expect an answer on where this pressure is coming from, Monsignor. The Holy Church is to be protected with something better than "maybe".'

The line went dead.

CHAPTER THIRTY-THREE

Qumran

Allegra groped for the alarm and sat up bleary eyed. After Yossi's briefing and a mandatory drink at Patrick's, Allegra and David had gone out for dinner. Allegra could feel all her resistance disappearing, and for the first time she was secretly pleased that David was so 'single'. They talked late into the night, scarcely aware of the time. Driving her home after dinner, the usually talkative David became very quiet. As he leaned over to open Onslow's dodgy passenger door to let her out they had both felt awkward. David broke the silence.

'Next time I'll cook you dinner at my place. Sleep well,' he said, and he kissed her lightly on the lips. As he drove off, he blew her another kiss.

She'd hardly slept. Allegra had tossed and turned, thoughts keeping her awake all night. Perhaps a relationship with another man might be a possibility after all. Ever since that terrible night in Milano she had buried herself in her studies and her research. Until now. From the day she had met David he had made her laugh and gradually she had been able to relax and not take life quite so seriously. Dinner at his place. Maybe it was time to trust again.

'Sorry about the early start,' David said as Onslow ground up the Mount of Olives towards the Jericho road. 'It gets bloody hot out here so it's best to do our walking around before the sun gets too ferocious.'

'I'm surprised you're on time,' Allegra responded.

'Hurtful and unnecessary.'

'So what are we going to see today, "tour guide"?'

'Qumran, Ladies and Gentlemen. Gateway to the Dead Sea and the site of much mystery and intrigue. Don't give up my day job?' he asked, feigning a downcast look as Allegra rolled her eyes.

'I shall make that assessment at the end of the day, David Kaufmann. Is Qumran really full of that much intrigue or is it just Vatican spin?'

'I suspect it's a bit of both, although there's certainly a healthy dose of the latter, and locking the scrolls away from public view for a quarter of a century hasn't helped.'

'Do you really think they're hiding something?'

David nodded. 'I think so. Judging from the enormous effort they've gone to in disguising the dates, I think it's something pretty serious.'

Onslow roared past the Bedouin Arabs' dirty white tents clumped amongst the sand dunes by the side of the road. David and Allegra reached the last crest and started down the long, steep winding road that dropped 1200 metres to the shores of the Dead Sea, the lowest place on earth, 400 metres below sea level. The air was not only hot, it was thick and oppressive and the morning sun had a fierce bite to it. The heat haze was rising and through it Allegra could just make out the wadis and cliffs of Jordan on the far shoreline. Big trucks thundered past carrying cargoes from Israel's southernmost settlement of Eilat along the lifeline to Tiberias in the north, protected by Israeli military patrols, armed to the teeth and moving slowly up and down the road, suspicious of everyone and everything that moved in the West Bank.

'Is the sea very deep?' she asked David.

'Not down south. It's only about 6 metres or so but the northern basin up here is very deep, over 400 metres in parts. The sea lies on a fault line that stretches from here all the way to the Zambesi River system in East Africa, and the salinity is so high that if the fish happen to get washed into it from the Jordan River they die instantly.'

'It makes you wonder why anyone would have wanted to live out here,' Allegra mused.

'It's not my cup of tea but the Essenes seemed to like it.'

'And I seem to remember that Sodom and Gomorrah were not far away.'

'They've never found any evidence of those two cities but there's a very strong theory they were buried in a violent earthquake about four thousand years ago.'

'Around the time of Abraham,' Allegra said, remembering the description in Genesis 19 of a destructive earthquake at the same time the father of the three faiths of Judaism, Christianity and Islam was treading the very desert they were venturing into.

'I guess so,' David said. 'In any case the archaeology supports the story because there is evidence of a big quake around 1900 BC that destroyed the cities on the Moab plain and the ruins are probably somewhere beneath the waters of the southern basin.'

Once they passed the turnoff to Jericho the main road continued on to the Jordan River and the site of Christ's baptism, but before they reached the river itself, David turned off and headed south towards the arid orange-yellow cliffs that soared 365 metres to the Judaean plateau above. At the base of these cliffs stood Qumran, about 30 metres above the road on the side of a rocky ravine.

A wadi that was scarred and barren. In amongst the rocks and the cliffs Allegra managed to pick out some of the caves that had hidden the scrolls from civilisation for so long.

If they had been around at the time of the discovery of the Dead Sea Scrolls, David and Allegra would have had to grind their way up an old Roman road that led towards the ancient settlement. Now there was a car park for tourist buses and the inevitable air-conditioned coffee house packed to the gunwales with T-shirts, key rings, wooden statues and every other conceivable biblical trinket that a passing tourist might be enticed to buy for ten times what it was worth. Today, save for one car, the car park was empty, its driver the only visitor in the coffee house. Yusef Sartawi buried his head in his newspaper. The waves of killing that had engulfed the modern successors to the Israelis and Palestinians of the ancient biblical lands had made tourism a high-risk business and the tourists were staying away in droves.

As Allegra and David got out of the Land Rover two American-built F-16 fighters screamed in low over the Dead Sea, the pilots clearly visible as they patrolled the border with Jordan.

'No tourists. We're in luck,' David said, shrugging a faded canvas backpack onto his shoulders.

'What's in the bag?' Allegra asked.

'Normally I carry all my equipment. Today, just a small pick and a brush, and lunch. Smoked salmon and chicken rolls and a bottle of Israel's finest chardonnay. All chilled with an ice pack,' he yelled over his shoulder as he set off for the ruins.

Allegra followed David up the narrow rocky path to the top of the salty barren outcrop the Essenes had chosen for their settlement. It overlooked the hazy shores of the Dead Sea a couple of kilometres in the distance.

Yusef Sartawi picked up his mobile, dialled a preset encrypted number and gave a quick update. 'Subject has arrived at the ruins.'

When they reached the top they climbed onto the remains of an old stone wall and Allegra looked around.

'The Romans sacked this place in 68 AD on their march to attack Jerusalem and destroy the second temple,' David explained. 'If you look around the ruins you can still see the layout of the stone walls and the inner courtyards. Over there is the big defence tower that dominated the landscape and closer to the wadi is the cistern that held their water.'

For the next two hours David and Allegra walked around the ruins that had been excavated by Roland de Vaux and others from the international team, the authors of the Vatican's consensus on the dates and origin of the scrolls.

'They really have gotten away with archaeological blue murder here,' David muttered as they walked into a long oblong area enclosed by rough stone walls. 'When they dug here, I suspect the Vatican already had their consensus well planned and it became a case of making the site fit the dogma. When L'École Biblique finally got their act together and published the raw material from the dig, we discovered that none of the rules of stratigraphy had been followed. Qumran had been occupied for a long period of time, so they should have known that the layers of civilisation had to be pretty carefully labelled and correlated.'

'That's about as damning as it gets,' Allegra agreed. 'How could they date the occupation without it?'

'They couldn't, but then I don't think dating was something the Vatican was too keen on. Not only has the Vatican refused to budge from their line that the scrolls date well before Christ, but the boys from the Vatican have always insisted the Qumran Essenes were peaceful, remote and celibate à la those described by the ancient historians Josephus, Philo, Pliny and company. If you have a look over here,' he said, taking her through a small passageway near the defence tower, 'you can see the remains of a pretty substantial forge. And here are the remains of the water supply they used to temper the metal. You could argue that they needed it to make tools, but that wouldn't explain a heap of arrowheads that were found inside the fortress.'

'The Vatican has never been able to hide the fact that John the Baptist might have been associated with the Essenes and he baptised Christ not far from here where the Jordan enters the Dead Sea,' Allegra said. 'I agree with you, the peaceful and celibate description was probably manufactured to fit the dogma.'

'Got it in one,' David said with a grin. 'If you have to allow John the Baptist to be part of a sect like the Essenes, you wouldn't want a story circulating that has him wandering past the forge and asking his mates how the weapons were coming on. In reality, when they were provoked, the Essenes were fierce fighters. Over there,' David continued, 'you can see the cemetery. It contained over twelve hundred graves, many of them women and children, which tends to make the consensus on celibacy look a bit shaky. I reckon if they'd had them back then we would have found a few used condoms in the rubble!' he said, chuckling to himself.

'You are incorrigible!'

'The Essenes detested the priests and the corruption in the second temple in Jerusalem,' David said as they walked into the stone surrounds of an ancient courtyard. Brilliant red and yellow flowers that had bloomed after the desert rains were clustered around several palm trees, fronds rustling defiantly against the hot wind that blew in from the Dead Sea. 'They dressed in long Pythagorean robes made from white linen and these courtyards were built for meditation. There is quite a bit of evidence pointing to Christ being part of this community, which would explain his provoked aggression in overturning the tables of the temple moneychangers. Yossi thinks that the Omega Scroll might prove Mary Magdalene was here as well, but I'm not so sure.'

'I think if Jesus studied his early philosophy with this group, which stands to reason if John the Baptist baptised him here, then there would be little doubt that Mary Magdalene would have been here as well.'

'Why do you say that?' David asked, intrigued as to why Allegra would be so sure.

'You're going to find out eventually, so I may as well tell you now. In a former life I was a nun.'

'That lapsed, eh.' David's grin was wicked. Their eyes met, each wondering what the other was thinking.

'There's quite a lot you don't know about me,' Allegra said, 'but in time, all will be revealed.'

'I'm looking forward to seeing that.'

'I will ignore that remark,' she said with a smile. 'When you piece together the story of Mary Magdalene it says a lot more than the Church would have you believe. Some argue differently, but I'm with those who think Mary Magdalene and Mary of Bethany were one and the same. When her brother Lazarus died, under Jewish custom a sister was required to stay with the body and "sit shiva". The only exception that allowed her to leave was if she was required by her husband. There's a little-quoted passage in *John* where Mary Magdalene's sister tells her that Jesus wants to see her and she gets up immediately. And there is a second Jewish custom in which a bride is required to anoint her bridegroom's feet. It is Mary Magdalene who does that for Jesus.'

'You think they were married?'

Allegra nodded. 'I think there's very strong evidence. I used not to,' she said, as she remembered her days in Tricarico. 'Mother Superior would not have approved, but when you're allowed the freedom to think, the evidence has always been there. It was Mary who went to the tomb with the other women, and in a strong Jewish society, only a wife would do that, but the most persuasive evidence is in the copies of the Gnostic Gospels that were discovered at Nag Hammadi on the Nile.'

'Which might explain why the early Church Fathers tried to have them all destroyed,' David ventured.

'Exactly. Apart from the sayings of Jesus in the Gospel of Thomas that threatened the power of the priesthood, Mary wrote her own gospel after the crucifixion, and in it she explains how she had to give the disciples a pep talk. If I remember it correctly, Mary Magdalene says, "Do not weep, and do not grieve, and do not doubt, for his grace will be with you completely, and will protect you." In a patriarchal Jewish culture, only a very powerful woman would give directions to men, and then there's the Gospel of Philip.'

'Ah yes,' David said mischievously, 'where the disciples are all a bit pissed off because Jesus keeps kissing Mary on the mouth.'

'That's one way of putting it,' she said, shaking her head. Allegra knew the quote from the Gospel of Philip by heart:

> . . . the companion of the Saviour is Mary Magdalene. But Christ loved her more than all the disciples, and used to kiss her often on the mouth. The rest of the disciples were offended . . .

'In Judaic culture men were expected to marry,' Allegra said. 'Jesus was charismatic, fun, charming and attracted to the company of women.'

'Sounds a bit like me really.'

'Well, he was also a thorough gentleman and I doubt that "pissed off" would have been in his vocabulary,' she said, her dark eyes sparkling. 'Perhaps the Omega Scroll might throw a bit of light on all of this.' Allegra was still reluctant to tell David everything, but in time she knew she would. If the scroll was ever found and the number 153 appeared amongst the Magdalene Numbers, that would be the decisive proof.

CHAPTER THIRTY-FOUR

Langley, Virginia

Mike McKinnon put down the file 'Nuclear Fallout – Medical Issues' and shook his head. Even if al-Qaeda issued a 30-minute warning and the emergency broadcast system was activated over TV and radio, only those few who had immediate access to a nuclear fallout shelter would be able to react. Even those who survived the devastating blast would suffer terribly. The radioactive cloud, Mike knew, could cover hundreds of square miles, especially if the wind and weather conditions were unfavourable. The brain cells in people subjected to any more than a few thousand of what were known as rads or radiation doses would be so damaged they would immediately start to swell. After a day of vomiting, excruciating headaches and seizures, tens of thousands would die. Even after a few hundred rads, half those exposed, perhaps a million people in the larger cities, would experience intense abdominal pain as the cells of their intestinal lining were destroyed. Their hair would drop out, bleeding would occur from the gums and anus, and death would occur within days.

Those who staffed the city hospitals would themselves be part of the death toll. The countdown for civilisation had begun the day that man split the atom, Mike thought bleakly. As soon as they were ready, he knew the Islamic fundamentalists would not hesitate.

Mike reached for Professor Kaufmann's paper on 'The Omega Scroll and the Islamic Nuclear Factor' and again he wondered whether there was a connection between the nuclear suitcases now in the hands of al-Qaeda and the ancient Dead Sea Scroll. Kaufmann had argued persuasively that in monotheistic religions there had been three revelations, the first to the Jews, the second to the Christians and finally to the Muslims, and he had now deciphered the ancient codes that seemed to make a connection with the third revelation, Islam and a coming atomic holocaust.

CHAPTER THIRTY-FIVE

Qumran

Another pair of patrolling Israeli F-16s shrieked over the ruins of Qumran and Allegra and David watched them disappear, twin trails of hot exhaust drifting down over the Dead Sea border with Jordan.

'Where does the DNA model fit in with the Essenes?' Allegra asked David, determined to find out as much as she could about the second element of the scroll.

'Those models in the Shrine of the Book were made from diagrams found in the Qumran library. Your Professor Rosselli from Ca' Granda was starting to investigate further when he was shot. Did you know him well?'

'Pretty well,' Allegra said sadly. 'He was a mentor.'

'I'm sorry. It didn't get much coverage here but Yossi was shocked. He confided in me at the time that he thought someone didn't want Rosselli to get too close to the truth. Did Rosselli talk much about his theories on the origin of DNA?'

'He was pretty wary. I think someone had warned him, but he

had a lot of time for Francis Crick. I read his book but to be honest, I still have an open mind about DNA being introduced from a higher civilisation.'

'So do I, and in the 1970s suggesting that a higher civilisation had sent rocket probes here would have qualified Crick for a padded cell, but when you think about it, we've got space probes headed for the icy wastes of our own galaxy and in the billions of others, it's absurd to think we're the only planet with life.' David's face grew serious. 'Yossi has an open mind too, although his code work indicates that the Omega Scroll might confirm Crick's theory.'

Allegra was seeing another side of this fun-loving man with the boyish good looks and impish sense of humour; the serious side.

'Feel like lunch?' David asked. 'There's a cave over there,' he said, pointing to an opening halfway up the other side of the wadi. 'For that one we won't need climbing spikes.'

'Sounds good to me,' Allegra said, following him out of the ruins.

It took them nearly half an hour to negotiate the same rocks that the young Bedouin boy had scrambled over fifty years before, searching for his goat, but it was worth the effort. Allegra followed David into the same long narrow chamber where the Bedouins had discovered the first of the scrolls.

'It's a pity the two Bedouin boys didn't know what they'd found,' Allegra said. 'It would have been an incredible feeling to have known you were the first person in here after nearly two thousand years.'

'Not the case now though,' David replied ruefully. 'It looks as if an army's been through here.'

Even an army of people could miss something critical if it had been deliberately sealed from view. Another tiny sprinkle of dust fell from the high ledge concealed just inside the entrance to the cave, but neither David or Allegra noticed it as they found a place for lunch in the shade of the cave opening.

'Chardonnay?'

'Why not. I'll bet you didn't bring anything else.'

'Did too. Water is the lifeblood out here.'

'Then I'll have some of both. I wonder what Lonergan is hiding in that vault,' Allegra mused, accepting a smoked salmon roll.

'It will take a bit of finding out. They haven't even given us access to the museum yet but Yossi's on his case and from experience I know my father doesn't give up on things without one hell of a fight.'

'Is it hard having a famous father?'

David smiled. 'You get used to people saying "Oh, you're Professor Kaufmann's son", but Yossi has always encouraged me to do my own thing and he makes it pretty easy. Even when we served in the Army together the father–son thing wasn't really a problem.'

'What's it like? Fighting a war.'

'I think when you're young there is a feeling of excitement. Until someone starts shooting at you and you realise you need a spare set of underpants.'

Allegra laughed.

'Some of the politicians milk war for all they're worth,' David continued, 'especially if they think it will go down well with the public. But when you've been involved in one, you realise how utterly senseless and what a terrible waste it all is. I guess it took the death of my brother Michael for it to really hit me.'

'I had no idea,' Allegra said apologetically. 'I shouldn't have asked.'

'That's OK. It took a while to come to terms with his death but there is hardly an Israeli family, or a Palestinian one, who haven't lost loved ones. Part of the price of war. I was very angry for a while, and I still miss the crazy bastard.'

'I'm so sorry, David. These days we seem to turn to war as the first solution to a problem.'

In the car park below Yusef Sartawi answered his mobile. 'Yes, I am in position. They are at the entrance to Cave One.' The message was deliberately short and cryptic.

'We all have a defined time span and we should make the most of it,' David said, getting to his feet, 'but a lot of us spend our time killing each other and manoeuvring for power. Take this cave.' David wandered back inside. 'What they found in here is for the whole of humanity, not just a few privileged Catholic academics, yet we're still fighting the Catholic Church tooth and nail to try to get to the truth.' He brushed at what he thought was a bug in his hair. Another fine sprinkle of sand fell on his neck and he brushed at it again, but this time he stopped and looked up as he felt the sand trickle down his back. Above his head he could see what looked like a small crack in the rough rock of the overhanging wall. He turned to Allegra, who was still standing in the entrance.

'Come and have a look at this.'

'What,' she said, stepping back into the cave.

'There's a crack in the rock here.'

Together they peered at the crack as a few more grains of sand trickled out of it. David retrieved the small pick from his backpack and started to scrape at the fissure. The ancient mortar that had finally succumbed to the same tremors that had rocked Bishop O'Hara's whiskey bottles and Allegra's apartment in Jerusalem came away easily. David's pulse quickened.

'This is mortar,' he said excitedly. The pick started to come up against the rock of the cave and the straight edge of what looked like a small sealed cavity started to appear.

Working more slowly David picked at the mortar, edging his way around the extent of the cavity opening. The cavity was only about 60 centimetres square and the entrance had been ingeniously blocked with rock that had been chiselled from the cave wall. The mortar had been carefully mixed to match it.

'Whatever is in here the Essenes obviously wanted to hide it from the outside world,' David said as he slowly scraped away at the last of the mortar. Suddenly he stepped back and covered his nose.

'Ugh!' The air escaping from the cavity was foul.

'Cover your face,' he said quickly, signalling for Allegra to get out of the cave.

'*Cryptococcus neuromyces?*' Allegra asked, giving the fungus spores that had killed more than one unwary archaeologist their scientific name. The lung disease caused by it would start with headaches and a fever coupled with difficulty in breathing. The bleeding would follow and the toxins would be transported to the brain, where they would attack the meninges and the victim would hallucinate and die.

'I don't think we're faced with an Essenes' version of a curse of the Pharaohs,' David replied. 'The air here has a very low humidity so it's unlikely to have any nasties in it, but let's be careful just the same. Whatever's in that cavity has waited for two thousand years. It can wait another few minutes.'

David was right to be cautious.

CHAPTER THIRTY-SIX

Langley, Virginia

In the basement below Mike McKinnon's office the massive Cray mainframe computers hummed quietly, collecting and collating thousands of reports from all over the world. Reports from station chiefs in over a hundred countries; analysis from seismic listening devices and satellite imagery; results from bugs placed in embassies and offices and reports from dozens of other sources, both human and electronic.

Mike McKinnon's initial views on being assigned to a presidential search for some ancient scroll had been unprintable, liberally sprinkled with a four-letter word for intercourse, but true to his years of training he had put together a plan that might turn up even the smallest clue. Kaufmann's paper on the Dead Sea codes had been caught in the net, and now Echelon was producing results as well. Echelon was the codename for the National Security Agency's system for intercepting phone calls, emails, faxes, telexes and any other electronic emission from anywhere around the globe, but the Echelon file on the Omega Scroll posed more questions than it answered.

Some things were not adding up, Mike mused. Why would the Vatican put out a surveillance contract on an internationally renowned expert in archaeological DNA? Her presence at some ruins was normal enough, but which one. 'At the entrance to Cave One' wasn't much help. It was like looking for a needle in a haystack. And why was Hamas involved? And who was this fellow Lonergan who kept getting a mention? McKinnon decided it was time to get a little closer to the action by relocating to Israel. He would be able to monitor the report collection from the CIA cell in the American Embassy in Tel-Aviv.

CHAPTER THIRTY-SEVEN

Qumran

Neither David or Allegra could contain their excitement any longer and David eased the rock from the front of the cavity in the cave wall. Both of them gasped.

'My God, David. It's another urn.'

The rough clay pot had stood on the concealed shelf since the destruction of Nehemiah's Temple. David carefully lifted the urn and gently placed it on the floor of the cave. Not quite 30 centimetres high, it had been sealed with the same bowl-like lid as the others that had been found over forty years before. David took his penknife and carefully sliced through the seal of soft black pitch. He reached into the jar and took out a roll of faded yellow linen that had started to disintegrate. Inside was a leather bundle.

'Allegra! It's another scroll.'

Allegra nodded, speechless. The earlier discovery of the Dead Sea Scrolls had been hailed as the greatest archaeological discovery of the twentieth century. Allegra wondered whether this might be its equal in the twenty-first.

'Someone's gone to an awful lot of trouble to hide it,' Allegra said, her heart rate slowing.

'The problem is,' David mused, 'how do we get it out of here without someone seeing us.'

'Interfering with the property of the State?'

'I'm more concerned that we don't start a stampede of Bedouins out here armed with pickaxes and mattocks. I'd rather keep it quiet until I've done the translation and we can see what's in it.'

'What if one of those Israeli patrols stops us on the way back. If they search the vehicle . . .' Allegra said, thinking out loud.

'We can't leave it here!' they said together.

'Snap!' David said with a grin. 'I guess we'll just have to risk it and hope that Captain Shagnasty and his boys out there aren't in too much of a checking mood. In the meantime, we'd better try and make this cavity look as if it was part of the original find,' he said, reaching for his brush.

They certainly would not have been done for speeding. David's driving was uncharacteristically sedate as Allegra cradled the priceless cargo. Yusef Sartawi followed at a discreet distance, allowing a big truck to get between him and his surveillance targets. One thing was puzzling Yusef. When the pair had returned from the ruins, the Israeli had seemed extremely cautious in handling his satchel.

As David and Allegra passed the turnoff to Jericho an open-backed Israeli truck loomed from the opposite direction, two heavy machine guns trained on Onslow's windscreen. Allegra held her breath. The truck cruised slowly towards them, the Israeli soldiers suspicious and alert, then just before the soldiers drew level they seemed to relax and the truck went past.

'Israeli plates help,' David said. 'Not to mention my stunning artwork on the doors, although just because it says Hebrew University is no guarantee. These guys have learned to take absolutely nothing at face value.'

Six more Israeli trucks scrutinised their progress but surprisingly none of them stopped. Just the same, Allegra was very relieved when they reached the Mount Scopus campus and they got their priceless cargo safely into their office in the laboratory.

'It's in Aramaic,' David said after they had carefully laid the scroll out on the desk. A look of confusion shadowed his face. 'It looks like an inventory. Why would the Essenes go to such lengths to hide an inventory?' His confusion was replaced with astonishment as the reason for the urn being hidden from the rest became apparent.

'Allegra,' he said, looking up from his magnifying glass. 'This is not only the complete list of scrolls, this scroll contains the precise locations of all the caves in Qumran that the Essenes used to store their library.'

'That explains why it was so well hidden,' Allegra said. 'If anyone found this it would automatically lead them to all the other documents.'

'Exactly.' David's grasp of Aramaic was unequalled by anyone else in the field and he translated it as easily as he might have from Hebrew into English. He frowned as he read the titles and locations of the scrolls, and then he whistled softly. 'The Omega Scroll! There are three copies listed here.'

'Which makes it far more important than any of the others,' Allegra said.

David rubbed his eyes. After two hours spent deciphering the inventory in the scroll his initial exhilaration was replaced by disappointment.

'The three copies of the Omega Scroll are listed, but from what I know of Qumran and the caves, all of the caves on this list have been thoroughly explored already. How many were taken by the Bedouin and traded on the black market is anybody's guess,' David said. 'This inventory just completes part of the puzzle. We've no idea where any of the copies of the Omega Scroll might be now, or even if they still exist,' David said dejectedly.

'But we do know they *were* written. Professor Rosselli knew and someone killed him before he got too close, and the Vatican has been pretty ferocious in keeping the scroll secret,' Allegra said, thinking back to her conversations with Giovanni.

'That protection might be as much to distance Christ from the Essenes as anything else,' David said, still pessimistic. 'It's not widely known, but Christ's use of the Beatitudes in the Sermon on the Mount was not original. "Blessed are the meek" has an earlier form in an Essenes scroll, and "Blessed are the poor in spirit: for theirs is the Kingdom of Heaven" came from the War Scroll found in Cave One. Christ's Beatitudes of the Gospels were built on the Beatitudes found in the Dead Sea Scrolls. Christ's message in the Bible is not unique, and the Vatican will do anything to prevent that from coming to light.'

'I agree with you,' Allegra said, 'and that is something carbon dating can resolve.' She decided it was time to declare her hand. 'The duplication of the Beatitudes would be enough to explain the Vatican's extraordinary efforts to distance Christ from Qumran, but there is another reason. When I said to you earlier today that all would be revealed, it wasn't me you thought you'd see.'

David grinned. 'I thought my luck had changed there for a while.' His face became serious as Allegra continued.

'As damaging as Christ's relationship with the Essenes and Mary Magdalene might be to the dogma, it is the Omega Scroll the Vatican fear the most. What I'm about to tell you will put someone's life at risk, so it can't go past us.'

David nodded.

'You remember Giovanni Donelli?'

'I met him at dinner at Patrick O'Hara's. Is he still in the Vatican?'

'He's now the Patriarch of Venice. It's his life that is at risk.'

David shook his head in disbelief when Allegra finished recounting Giovanni's time with Pope John Paul I and his suspicions over Petroni.

'They don't muck around, those guys in scarlet. I won't mention it, but when you're ready you might think about bringing Yossi into the loop. He will give Giovanni every protection.'

Allegra nodded. 'I'm sure he will and I'm sure he already knows that any challenge to the uniqueness of Christ or the dating of the scrolls in the Rockefeller will be denounced by Lonergan and the Vatican. The Omega Scroll is *not* a myth, and its existence will be met with a sustained fury and passed off as a total fraud. If we ever do find it, it might be better to have one of the Vatican's own onside before any announcement.'

David laughed. 'That's a bit radical. Does such a creature exist? Apart from Patrick O'Hara?'

'Patrick would do it, but they'd crucify him. He hasn't got the academic cred, although he'd run rings around a lot of their Gregorian University types. But there is one who might.'

'And where might they be hiding him? I presume it's not a her!'

Allegra smiled. 'No I think the old men in scarlet are threatened by women who go to university. Incongruously enough,' she said, 'it's Giovanni who would do it.'

'What makes you think the Patriarch of Venice would be part of any announcement, especially if his life's at risk?'

'It's a long story but he's a very wide thinker, and in a way it would give him some protection. If the Vatican wanted to get rid of him, they would have to think twice and not risk the heat of the inevitable inquiry uncovering the truth of the Omega Scroll,' Allegra replied. 'Giovanni has a towering intellect, although he hides it pretty well. Any more relaxed and he'd fall over.'

'If you think he would do it, it's worth a try because if we ever do find the Omega Scroll those bastards in the Vatican will pay whatever it costs to get hold of it before any theologian could comment on it, then it will just disappear into the depths of the Secret Archives,' David said. 'I guess we can hold off on announcing this inventory and that'll keep Lonergan and the Vatican in their place, at least until we're ready, although I'd love to know what's in the Rockefeller's vaults that made Lonergan so jumpy.'

'I don't think there is much hope of finding out,' Allegra said.

'I don't know . . .' David let his thoughts trail off, a conspiratorial look on his face. He carefully wrapped up the scroll and locked it in the office safe before they both headed off to David's apartment for the dinner he had promised Allegra. Both were silent, acutely aware of the powerful consequences of their discovery.

David's apartment was in Levi Eshkol Boulevard, not far from the Old City. It was on the top floor of an older stone building and had sweeping views across the lights of greater Jerusalem, out to the ramparts where King David had once governed.

'I'm impressed, David. You're quite the chef,' Allegra exclaimed as David placed the dish on the table with a flourish.

'Pesach cholent with stuffed eggplant.'

'Pesach cholent?'

'What I hope is very tender steak that has been slowly cooked with potatoes and eggs. Shalom,' he said, raising his wine glass.

After dinner David and Allegra headed out onto the balcony with their coffee. The city was golden-hued and the inkiness of the night made the scene seem otherworldly. They leaned on the railing, relaxed and joking about getting on with their research and thinking of ways to infuriate Lonergan, making a deal that whoever got him to explode first had to buy the other dinner.

David bent low over Allegra's hand making a show of sealing the deal with a theatrical kiss on her upturned palm. Allegra caressed his cheek and gently brought his face up to meet her gaze. David's lips brushed hers and Allegra responded with an intake of breath. Her fear and apprehension of loving a man evaporated into the night air as David gently wrapped his arms around her body. She closed her eyes, capturing the moment. David's lips pressed against hers and Allegra lost all sense of place. It was as though they belonged to each other and he knew how to make her head swim. His hands slid from her waist to her hips and he pressed her body against him. She began to kiss him back, urgently, passionately. David's heart felt like it was beating in his throat, and he lost the power of speech. Keeping her close, David led Allegra back into the apartment towards the bedroom, the scent of her hair heightening his desire.

'I haven't done this for a very long time, David,' Allegra whispered. Her body arched against his and they both melted into each other as they collapsed to the floor.

Allegra smiled as the message popped up on her computer screen. An email from Giovanni.

Buongiorno

Ho una sorpresa. I am coming to Jerusalem.

I will be in Jerusalem for a few days next week. There is an interfaith dialogue conference where I will formally, if belatedly, hand over the reins to my successor and I'm to present a final paper on the Catholic Church's response to Islam and Judaism. You will no doubt remember the Vatican politics. They're still the same and the Veneto is a wonderful change. I had an email from my old friend Patrick O'Hara singing your praises – he says you're doing brilliantly – nothing less than I expected. Dinner?

Best wishes from your old friend, Giovanni.

After all this time they would finally catch up face to face. There had been plenty of emails but so often they had missed each other by a few weeks in different countries around the world. It was as if the universe had been keeping them apart. Allegra eagerly typed in her reply.

Dinner would be wonderful. Would you like me to pick you up at the airport?

Giovanni's reply came back immediately.

Thanks but Patrick already has that in hand (no doubt in the other he will have a bottle of Irish whiskey). If you're free on Wednesday night – I'll let you choose the restaurant.

'What are you up to?' David asked as he came in. He bent down to kiss her shoulder.

'Giovanni's coming to Jerusalem,' Allegra replied, turning her head towards him.

'That's great news. When does he arrive?'

'Patrick's picking him up from the airport next week and I've organised dinner for Wednesday night. Can you join us?'

'Not for dinner. You two haven't seen each other for years and you both need time to catch up, but I can drop you off in Onslow and I'll join you for a drink. It will be good to see him again.'

'I'm not sure he'll be thrilled about a ride in Onslow but he's Italian and I've always had a strong suspicion that's where you learned to drive.'

Numero Venti was still only half full as Elie showed Giovanni and Allegra to their table by the window. A moment later a well-dressed Arab smiled politely to Elie and indicated he would like the table behind them.

'David is a very charming man,' Giovanni said, a touch of wistfulness in his voice.

'And like you, he has many talents,' Allegra said. 'He hasn't made up his mind but he told me the other night he is thinking of running for election in Yossi's party.'

'If he's anything like Yossi he will be very successful,' Giovanni said. 'Yossi is probably one of the few politicians in Israel who can see that the present policy is never going to work.'

Allegra nodded. 'Your friend Ahmed Sartawi has similar views and it seems that ordinary Palestinians are coming around to his way of thinking. Provided he can deliver a Palestinian State, he thinks the militant groups can be brought onside as well.'

'In a way the death of Yasser Arafat was a circuit breaker,' Giovanni observed. 'Ordinary Palestinians are sick of the violence, as are the Israelis. Someone like Ahmed Sartawi would be a genuine hope for peace, as would Yossi.' Giovanni thought back to the fishing trip. 'I sent Ahmed my best wishes for the Palestinian elections and I've been praying for him.'

'Will you see him while you're here?'

'I'd like to, but some of his more fanatical opponents might use it against him. Mar'Oth was an example of what can be done between Muslims and Christians but even there the change was gradual and people have to be given time to adjust. Are you sure David didn't want to join us for dinner?'

'Positive. He knows we needed some time alone to catch up.' Allegra placed her hand on top of Giovanni's. 'I owe you an explanation, after all we've been through together. I feel that I've let you down as a friend.'

'Well, you shouldn't,' Giovanni responded. 'Especially after what happened.'

'I hope you don't feel guilty about that. It was a wonderful moment.'

'I feel guilty that I wanted a lot more moments like that,' Giovanni said with a lopsided grin. 'I know you denied it, but I felt guilty when you left the Church so suddenly. Was that the reason?'

'No, it wasn't,' Allegra said, the memory flooding back.

Giovanni's smile disappeared as Allegra recounted the events of her dreadful night in Milano.

'I'm so sorry,' Giovanni said softly when Allegra had finished. 'Why didn't you tell me?'

'I was in shock, Giovanni. I thought I'd let you down. It took a long while to put it all in perspective.'

'Petroni must be punished for this. We've been hiding this sort of thing in the Church for far too long.'

'I wish he could be, but it would be my word against the most powerful cardinal in the whole of the Catholic Church. The Vatican's spin would be horrific.'

'Yes, but more and more people are now coming out. Look at what has happened in Boston. The Church has been protecting paedophiles and other sexual deviants for years. Ultimately the rank of cardinal is not going to absolve anyone from responsibility. Would you be able to take the heat?'

'If I thought we could bring him to justice, of course,' Allegra answered defiantly.

'Then we should give some thought to how that can be done. In the meantime, I may be able to get him on another front.'

It was the first time in all the years she had known him that Allegra had ever heard Giovanni plan to 'get' anyone.

'Petroni and the Vatican Bank have been up to their old murky dealings,' Giovanni said. 'Do you remember I told you that just before he was murdered, Pope John Paul sacked his Cardinal Secretary of State?'

'And was about to sack Petroni and investigate the Vatican Bank,' Allegra said. 'I remember it well.'

'At the time, the Head of the Freemasons Propaganda Two was one Giorgio Felici, a Sicilian thug operating as a Milanese banker. He's now the Head of P2's successor, P3, but he's also been expanding his banking business. We used to have a very profitable small bank in the Veneto, the Banco del Sacerdozio.'

'The Priests' Bank?'

'It was set up after the Second World War by a group of wealthy Catholic Venetian bankers to provide low interest loans to struggling workers in the vineyards and it also provided loans for centres for the handicapped and destitute in the Veneto. Banco del Sacerdozio was one of the best run and most profitable banks in Italy and it was protected from takeover by the Vatican owning 51 per cent of the shares. Last month the shares were sold to Giorgio Felici and he has foreclosed on all the loans.'

Anger flashed in Giovanni's eyes as he remembered the meeting he had attended the month before in a little vineyard, one of dozens nestling in the southern foothills of the craggy, snow-capped peaks of the Dolomites. A meeting that revealed the desperation and hopelessness that the locals were feeling, faced with the prospect that their livelihood and support of their families would be callously ripped away from them by a faceless conglomerate.

'Had I known, I could have gone to the Pope and had the sale postponed,' Giovanni said.

'Can't you still go to him now?' Allegra asked.

Giovanni shook his head. 'Several years ago Petroni was instrumental in Giorgio Felici being appointed as the Pope's financial adviser so I need proof. I've started my own internal investigation and when I have enough evidence I will go to the Pope and insist on a full-scale investigation of the Vatican Bank.'

'The Pope may resist that,' Allegra observed. 'Especially if he's being advised by Felici.'

'Felici has strong connections to the Mafia and the Church should sever any dealings with him,' Giovanni said, a hint of steel in his voice. 'In the past the Church has owned companies that have manufactured bombs, bullets and tanks, as well as contraceptives. The only criteria for owning shares has been profitability and I suspect we're at it again. If the Pope will not do what is necessary to clean out this cesspool in his own backyard I will call for a public inquiry.'

For Giovanni it would be a last resort, but Allegra knew he wouldn't hesitate.

'The Lord sometimes moves in strange ways,' Giovanni said grimly. 'And who knows, if an inquiry were to result in Petroni being removed we might even be able to quietly prise the copy of the Omega Scroll out of its hiding place in the Secret Archives. After what he did to you he deserves to be imprisoned. Bastard.'

It was the first time Allegra had ever heard Giovanni swear. 'Well, you wouldn't want to know what I had to say to God,' she said.

'I think he's heard it all before,' Giovanni said, his smile recovering some of its warmth. 'It cost you your faith?'

Allegra nodded. 'Although just lately I can't help but think there is something quite powerful around me. It's just not Catholic.'

Giovanni smiled. 'You haven't lost your faith, it comes in many different forms.'

Allegra looked at Giovanni quizzically. 'That's a very strange thing for a cardinal to say,' she said, smiling. Suddenly it was like old times at La Pizzeria Milano and they began to relax into each other's company.

'Not really. I've changed a lot since we were in Milano. My time here in Jerusalem and the Middle East gave me time to think and has taught me a lot. I met people like Ahmed who made me realise that they hold their faiths just as dearly as Catholics hold theirs. I think our doctrine of the Catholic faith being the "only true path" has done a lot of damage. By the time I left here I came to the conclusion that there is more than one path to the Omega and Eternity, and the Bible is but one of the guides.'

The Spirit smiled.

'I did a lot of thinking too after Professor Rosselli was shot,' Allegra said. 'He was a great loss, not only to Ca' Granda. What did you think of his theory on the origin of DNA?'

'On the scientific evidence it's more than possible, it's probable, but like many of the world's truly great thinkers, Crick and Rosselli were way ahead of their time. Most people get so caught up in their own problems that it is difficult for them to imagine other parts of our own planet, let alone that there might be higher civilisations somewhere in the billions of other galaxies.'

'Capable of delivering one or more vehicles to other planets in the cosmos in the hope of starting life,' Allegra responded. 'I agree with you, when people are pushed out of their comfort zone they feel threatened and their immediate reaction is to denounce it all as nonsense.' Allegra leaned forward and lowered her voice. 'When you realised you could never prove that there was a copy of the Omega Scroll in the Vatican, you said to me "the truth will always out". When Professor Rosselli was murdered, the pursuit of that truth became a quest for me, and now there has been a small frustrating step forward. I know you will keep this to yourself, but David and I have found another Dead Sea Scroll.'

Giovanni listened as Allegra quietly brought him up to date on their discovery.

'That's wonderful news,' Giovanni whispered. 'Even though it is an inventory, the confirmation that more than one copy of the Omega Scroll exists is a wonderful find within itself.'

'The problem is, Giovanni, even if we do find another copy of the Omega Scroll, the Vatican will fight tooth and nail to get hold of it. And if they do, they'll bury it. At the very least there will be a furious campaign to dump it as a fraud, and a lot of people will believe them.'

'They will, so let me make you and David an offer. If you find it I will be more than happy to be with you at the announcement, wherever that might be, and I will personally ensure it gets an open debate in the Church. Later, when the Vatican least expects it, if the copy in the Secret Archives can be found, the Vatican will be forced to debate the truth.'

Allegra felt a little stunned. It was the very thing she and David had talked about and she had been wondering how she might raise such a delicate issue. Giovanni had come straight out with it. If anything, she had underestimated the intellect of this man, and just fleetingly, Allegra gave David cause to be jealous.

'Won't the Petronis of this world prevent you doing that?' she asked.

'Not if I just do it. It is time for the Church to allow intellectual freedom, otherwise the real message of Christ will be lost for ever.'

As Giovanni and Allegra left the restaurant and headed for the Old City and a nightcap at Patrick O'Hara's, they were followed a little while later by the well-dressed Arab.

A short distance away Tom Schweiker was about to do a cross for the mid-afternoon bulletin in New York. The Vatican was showing no signs of giving ground on either the Dead Sea Scrolls' dating or access to those who might be able to prove the truth.

'Ten seconds, Geraldine . . . and live . . .'

'And we're joined now by Tom Schweiker in Jerusalem. Pressure seems to be mounting on allowing more light on the Dead Sea Scrolls, Tom.'

'On two fronts, Geraldine. First, the dating of the scrolls and secondly, access. Earlier this week I put those questions to one of the internationally recognised academics in the field, Monsignor Derek Lonergan.'

For such a pompous blowhard, Derek Lonergan had seemed oddly reluctant to give an interview, but Tom had persisted, subtly appealing to Lonergan's ego and suggesting that it would be a great loss if only one side of the story was heard. Lonergan's ego was an easy target.

'Monsignor Lonergan, for many years now you've been resolutely defending the Vatican's dating of these scrolls as being two hundred years before the time of Christ, but the basis for that consensus is now coming into question. Do you still stand by those dates?'

'Not a shadow of a doubt, my man. These scrolls are most certainly from the second century before Christ. Not a shadow of doubt at all.'

'One of the planks that you have used for dating is based on the coins that were found in the area of Qumran?'

'Certainly.' Lonergan raised his chin and sniffed patronisingly at the camera as if it was a question to which any fool would know the answer. For an instant, the angle of the bright camera lights exposed the purple welt of a scar hidden under Lonergan's unkempt beard.

'Yet the first Director of L'École Biblique claimed to have found a coin with the insignia of the tenth Roman Legion on it but when it was examined by impartial experts not only was it found to be not from the tenth or any other legion, but from Ashkelon dating at 72 AD?'

Derek Lonergan's face started to match the colour of his scar. He was visibly furious at both the question and having to answer it.

'That was an unfortunate oversight and obviously a coin that had been dropped in the ruins much later by a passer-by,' he responded angrily.

'Really? Nevertheless something the Director of L'École Biblique took over five years to correct?' Tom maintained a polite, calm, almost nonchalant approach which got the result he wanted. Lonergan was bordering on exploding.

'One final question, Monsignor. Is it true that it has taken nearly six months to finalise the secondment of two scholars to the museum?'

'The Israeli and Italian academics you refer to are being shown every courtesy,' he replied, his obvious anger making his response even more unconvincing.

'Monsignor Lonergan, thank you for joining us on *International Correspondent*.'

Tom unhooked his microphone and walked back to the car park of the Rockefeller. He wondered how much pressure it would take to make Lonergan crack and, in turn, force whoever was instructing him to relent on the issue of access to the scrolls. Tom was also troubled by the sense that he had met Lonergan before, a sense that was getting stronger from the moment he spotted the scar on Lonergan's cheek. The journalist in him came to the fore and he was determined to find the missing pieces.

CHAPTER THIRTY-EIGHT

Roma

Lorenzo Petroni read the surveillance report on Dr Bassetti and Cardinal Donelli's dinner in the Jerusalem restaurant with a growing sense of desperation. Timing was everything and it was running out. Soon he would gather the Curial Cardinals for a brief on the Pope's failing health and the possibility of resignation. Faced with the possibility of a Pope, and as a result, the Holy Church in a coma, Petroni felt sure the Cardinals could be manipulated into agreement, but all of that would come to nothing unless his own candidacy remained absolutely untarnished.

Petroni paced his office. He knew that his life's ambition could be damaged by any number of factors, and until now he had been confident they were all under control. At least the woman had not found the actual Omega Scroll but she would need to be kept under continued surveillance. As far as the allegations of rape were concerned Petroni was confident they could be quashed with a straight denial. Perhaps the allegations could be turned to his advantage, invoking sympathy for a cowardly and totally baseless attack on an upright member of the Church. If necessary, money could create witnesses, he mused, and he began to develop a theme, one of Bassetti leaving her Order for a life of loose living and sex, wanting to attack those who maintained a chaste existence.

Donelli was another matter. Petroni knew that if Donelli was successful in starting an investigation into the Vatican Bank it would finish him. It was high risk, he mused, but so were the stakes for the Keys to Peter and Petroni's adrenaline surged as he made up his mind. The 'Italian Solution' would need to be applied to Donelli. Suddenly, the buzzing of his intercom interrupted his thoughts.

'Petroni.'

'Daniel Kirkpatrick from CCN is on line two, Eminence.'

'Lorenzo. *Come stai?*'

'*Bene, grazie, e tu?*' Petroni replied smoothly, automatically switching to diplomatic mode.

'Well thank you, Lorenzo.'

'What have you got?'

'It's Schweiker again. He's making inquiries into the background of Monsignor Lonergan, your representative in Jerusalem.'

Petroni's eyes narrowed. 'What sort of inquiries?'

'My sources are good here, Lorenzo. He seems to think Lonergan went by another name in a parish in Idaho?'

'I would find that very hard to believe, Daniel, but let me look into it and I'll get back to you.'

'I'd be much obliged, Lorenzo. This sort of speculation can be very harmful to the Church.'

Petroni's mood darkened as another factor from his past threatened to destabilise his lifelong grab for the Keys to Peter, even before a Conclave and election could be manipulated. First, Donelli's investigation into the Vatican Bank, now this. It was as if the winds of the cosmos were massing to destroy his control and his mind raced as he sought a means of restoring it. Petroni unlocked the top drawer of his desk and took out the .38 Beretta Cheetah pistol that he kept in a leather box. He aimed it at the far wall of his spacious office. Like Donelli's proposed investigation into the Vatican Bank, any investigation into Lonergan that exposed Petroni's own involvement might also derail his candidature for the Papacy and that could not be allowed to happen. It might not be necessary to kill the journalist just yet, but if he got too close, like Donelli, he would have to go. Given what was at stake, Petroni resolved to talk with Felici in the morning. He smiled inwardly at his choice of meeting place. Felici could come to the Vatican, but not to his office.

The Church must be returned to pre-Vatican II days where her authority was not questioned. Neither Donelli nor Schweiker could be allowed to succeed; whatever it took. In the end there was only one solution that was guaranteed.

Petroni entered the Basilica San Pietro from below, through the labyrinth of underground passages that accessed the grottoes beneath the most famous church in all of Christendom, unobserved by the crowd of tourists. Emerging behind the row of confessionals he moved to the one at the end that had been reserved for his use and he slipped through the door at the rear. Drawing the curtain and the '*Occupato*' sign he settled down to wait.

Outside the tourists thronged backwards and forwards across the Piazza San Pietro and through the massive bronze doors of the Basilica that Filarete had decorated with biblical reliefs in 1439. Outside Giorgio Felici looked at his watch, grateful for the anonymity the tourists provided. For some strange reason he was uncharacteristically nervous. Felici had understood the need for a meeting outside of Petroni's office and had admired the ruthless Cardinal's audacity. Even if the meeting was somehow discovered, which was extremely unlikely, it could be put down to a request for confession. Perhaps that was the cause of his nervousness. Felici hadn't been anywhere near a church since he was a boy, much less visited St Peter's. Giorgio joined the queue to go through the magnetometers and a possible physical search. No guns today.

The sign above the small dark panelled confessional was in position as Giorgio knew it would be. He glanced around casually. No one was taking the slightest interest and he slipped onto the kneeler.

'Forgive me Father for I have sinned,' he said softly, echoing the agreed passwords, ending with, 'and many of mine have been the sins of Mammon.' Petroni, Giorgio thought darkly, had a peculiar sense of humour.

'We have two new problems, either of which can destroy control here,' Petroni began, cutting straight to the chase. 'There is a journalist, Tom Schweiker . . .'

Giorgio listened intently as Petroni outlined the contract on CCN's Middle East correspondent, and as he listened his nervousness disappeared. Sensing a desperation in Petroni, his old cunning returned and he wondered why a journalist would pose such a threat to the Vatican.

'It is perhaps fortunate,' Giorgio Felici responded evenly, when Petroni had finished, 'that in this era of mobile phones, surveillance is easy. Should we need to take the final step, murders are quite commonplace in Jerusalem, although the journalist is a very prominent international figure and this will not be easy.'

'*Si*. The second assignment is even more difficult,' Petroni warned.

'The second assignment is indeed far more difficult,' Giorgio agreed when Petroni had finished issuing the second contract. In the circles of assassination and intrigue in which the members of P3 moved, Giorgio Felici had learned not to be surprised by the various threats that had to be eliminated, but it was the first time he had ever been asked to assassinate a cardinal.

'On occasions we have had to deal with leading bankers and industrialists who have misbehaved, but we try to avoid it.

Assassinating powerful people can make life very uncomfortable and assassinating a cardinal would be no exception. The heat would be intense.'

In the silence that followed Felici wrongly concluded that Petroni's concern was a simple case of him making certain of the Keys to Peter. Elimination of rivals was something the little Sicilian was well practised in, as the members of the Bontate and Buscetta families had found to their cost in Palermo. Felici now perceived a vulnerability in Petroni on the other side of the confessional, and his green eyes glinted in the half light. With a touch of condescension he said, 'Should you lose the conclave, you will still be very useful to us as a cardinal.'

Petroni smiled thinly. Giorgio Felici was a piece of work, a particularly nasty one at that, but Petroni was ready for him.

'Be that as it may, Giorgio, it is not only a matter of what happens in the conclave – your own survival is at stake here.'

'For you to lose an election, even to someone like Cardinal Donelli, might be awkward but I doubt it will affect me.'

'But the Vatican Bank does affect you and the reason for this contract is that Cardinal Donelli has commenced an investigation into your acquisition of the Banco del Sacerdozio. If he is elected Pope that investigation will certainly probe into the depths of the Vatican Bank itself.'

Giorgio Felici felt as if he'd been hit by a combination left and right from Mike Tyson at his peak. He shifted uncomfortably on his knees, detesting the subservience of the confessional.

'That must never be allowed to happen,' he hissed.

'The takeover of the Priests' Bank in the Veneto may have made you a lot of money, my friend, but your cancellation of the low interest loans is coming home to roost.' Cardinal Petroni would normally not have given a second thought to the Patriarch of Venice's constituents, but now it had become necessary to grind the little Sicilian's face in his own greed. Petroni knew that the contract on Giovanni Donelli might be difficult to enforce unless Felici was in a corner, and Petroni wanted that corner to be as tight as he could make it.

'Cardinal Donelli must be the victim of an unfortunate accident,' Petroni said calmly, as if he was making the decision to put a dog out of its misery.

'The journalist is difficult enough but assassinate a cardinal? Are you out of your mind?' Giorgio was angry now, and wary, like a rat that had been cornered, looking for a way out. 'Have you any idea how much that will cost? You're looking at a price tag in the millions.'

'Cost is not an issue, my friend,' Petroni replied. 'The Vatican Bank will pay, but if it ever gets to the stage where independent authorities open up the bank's books, you will be looking at spending the rest of your life in a cell.'

Giorgio Felici was silent for the count of quite a few heartbeats. 'Let me get back to you,' he said finally. 'This is going to be extremely difficult.'

CHAPTER THIRTY-NINE

Jerusalem

'Welcome to the Rockefeller Museum. Or should I say welcome back.' Derek Lonergan had a habit of smiling without exposing his teeth.

'We've been a little bemused by all the fuss in the media but that's politics, I suppose,' he said over his shoulder as David and Allegra followed 'the waddling cassock' down the corridor to his office.

'Don't,' Allegra mouthed at David, who wore a look of innocence. She instinctively knew he was going to come up with another of his 'nice arse' comments that would bring her undone.

'As I understand it you will be working with us for the next six months or so.'

'It's a four-year research project,' David said.

'Is it really? That's even better, I hadn't realised you would be here that long,' Lonergan lied. 'We're still finalising your tasking so we can take that into account.'

'What scrolls do we have access to?' David asked abruptly, determined to nail Lonergan to something concrete.

'As it happens, I'm due to leave this week for a five-month lecture tour of Europe,' Lonergan replied evasively. 'Blasted nuisance but as I'm the acknowledged expert on these things it's only natural that the great universities of this world are going to want a fair slice of my time. That should provide plenty of opportunity for you to settle in and start reading up and we can discuss the details of your task on my return.' Lonergan looked at his watch. It was twenty to five. 'If you'll excuse me I have another appointment. I'll get someone to show you to your office space.'

Derek Lonergan had the trip to the nearby Cellar Bar down to a fine art. Within fifteen minutes of leaving the Rockefeller he had launched himself into the vaults of the American Colony Hotel.

'Another whiskey, Dr Lonergan?' Abdullah asked politely as Derek Lonergan threw the first one down.

'Certainly, Abdullah. I thought you'd never ask.' Derek Lonergan was in high spirits. The great academic halls of Europe were awaiting his presence.

'A fresh glass,' Abdullah said, replacing the empty one and pouring a generous shot of Tullamore Dew.

In the room behind the bar Abdullah carefully put Lonergan's first glass on a shelf out of reach. He had no idea why the American journalist wanted a glass used by Lonergan but he had long ago learned not to ask questions and had simply pocketed the 200 shekels with a polite smile.

A week later, after Lonergan had left for Europe, David decided to try to find out what Lonergan might be hiding in the vaults of the Rockefeller. It was high risk, and would mean his career if he was caught, but he had faced higher risks in the past and he had a strong feeling that whatever Lonergan had, it was important.

David greeted the security guard with a smile as he headed out to join Allegra in the museum's courtyard for lunch.

'Morning, Hafiz!'

'Morning, Dr Kaufmann.'

'How are the children?' David asked.

Hafiz had been working at the museum for twenty years and David had a genuine affection for the old Palestinian. Hafiz had four children and for all of those years he had pulled double shifts to get the money together for their education. From eight until three he did duty at the front desk, and on top of that, three nights a week he drove a security car on mobile patrol, a routine he still followed. Hafiz considered himself to be one of the lucky ones, as not many Palestinians in Israel had jobs.

'Fine thanks, Dr Kaufmann. Abdul has been accepted for university,' he said with a proud smile.

Allegra watched as David chatted amiably with the old guard, oblivious to the tourists streaming in and out of the museum's exhibitions. She had a sneaking suspicion that she was falling in love with David. They had become so close in such a short amount of time, it seemed that they often knew exactly what the other was thinking.

'I'm very fond of Hafiz and you can sometimes find out a great deal from security guards,' he said, answering her question before she could even ask what he was up to. He leaned over, making a show of nuzzling her neck while he outlined the plan he had in mind.

'David,' Allegra replied in a soft whisper. 'Do you think we can pull it off?'

'I'm not going to put you to that sort of risk,' David said, 'but I've got to get to the truth here.'

'Point one,' Allegra said. 'We do this together, so start talking in terms of "we". Point two. How do we avoid all the security cameras?'

'We work back and do it after the security desk is closed for the night and the external patrols take over. There's only one camera down there and that can be disabled. Talking with security guards is not all idle chat you know.'

Allegra's dark eyes flashed with excitement. 'Do you really think we can crack the vault?'

'If Private Silberman were around that wouldn't be an issue, but like all good students I've been practising.'

The red movement sensor high on the far wall clicked on as David checked the lobby to see that Hafiz had left. Satisfied, he returned to collect Allegra and the small bag he had brought into the office that morning.

'Got your gloves?'

Allegra nodded, her initial excitement giving way to nervousness.

'They've put the security camera in a really dumb position,' David said when they stepped into the same corridor he had headed down with a gun in his hands all those years before. 'We can approach it from behind and I can reach it quite easily.' David took a piece of black cloth from his bag and climbed onto one of the wide ledges directly beneath the camera and threw the cloth over the lens.

'Won't they suspect something?'

'They might, but what if they do? They'll check the vault, find nothing missing and assume it's malfunctioned. They haven't changed this vault since 1938,' he said. 'I don't think security is their long suit.'

Allegra watched as David pulled a stethoscope out of his black bag. Joseph Silberman had given David the stethoscope, along with a set of lock picks, as a memento when he had left the Army to join Mossad. David spun the dial to the left to clear the tumblers and rolled it one revolution to the right until he picked up the click of the cam and lever mechanism, just as Silberman had shown him.

'Twenty-five is still the last number,' he said, 'and it's only got three tumblers.' It took David about twenty minutes until he picked up the soft 'nikt' of the last tumbler slot being lined up.

Twice the time that Joseph Silberman had taken but David was pretty pleased with himself as he turned the wheel and the big retaining bolts slid aside. Allegra's heart was pounding. David was calm but the excitement of discovery was reflected in his eyes as he clicked on the lights and looked around.

'Look! In the far corner,' he said, pointing towards a battered red trunk marked 'Lonergan' and 'Personal', secured with an old brass padlock. David chose a torque wrench and a small half-diamond shaped shallow angle lock pick from his bag. He inserted both and without applying any torque on the lock's plug, pulled the pick out to get a feel for the stiffness of the pin springs. Satisfied, he applied a light torque and using Silberman's scrubbing technique, moved the pick backwards and forwards, gradually increasing the torque so that each of the driver pins set on the sheer line. One by one the pins set until he was able to turn the plug and the 'U' of the lock popped free.

'I'm getting better at this,' he said, grinning as he swung the trunk lid open.

Allegra just shook her head and smiled. Inside the trunk was the olive wood box Lonergan had secured as his 'commission' for arranging the Vatican's fifty million dollar purchase of the intact copy of the Omega Scroll.

David let out a low whistle. 'Fragments,' he said. 'Hundreds of them.'

'What are they?' Allegra asked, pointing to the three fragments in the small plastic bag taped to the inside of the lid.

'Don't know, but there's only one way to find out.' David took a pair of tweezers from his bag and put the three fragments on top of a trunk nearby.

David recognised the ancient Koiné immediately. 'Allegra! The Omega Scroll. It's here!' he said, staring at the three fragments. 'These are in Koiné and the Omega was the only Dead Sea Scroll to be written in that language. The Omega's messages were meant for the wider world,' David said. 'Koiné was the dialect of Greek spoken in the Roman Empire in the East.'

The three fragments were a clear indication that the rest of the scroll was to be found in amongst the others, but they could only be pieced together by someone with extraordinary skill, and time.

'That bastard Lonergan has known about this all along,' David said, deep in thought.

'Trouble is,' Allegra said, 'how do we get this box out of here?'

'We don't,' David replied finally, taking out some large plastic envelopes from his bag. 'We leave the box in the trunk. We put the fragments in the safe in our office tonight and tomorrow we get them out in broad daylight.'

'Isn't that a bit risky?'

'Not as risky as being stopped by the night security patrol.'

David carefully transferred the fragments into the envelopes, re-locked the trunk and closed the big vault door. He removed the black cloth from the camera and they slipped back up the corridor.

As they walked to the car park a figure loomed out of the shadows.

'Working late, Dr Kaufmann?'

Allegra felt her blood freeze.

'No rest for the wicked, Hafiz,' David replied with a smile.

'I'm sorry to have to ask, Sir, but do you mind if I have a quick look in your briefcase. We've had some petty theft in the museum lately and, while I'm sure you're not stealing the biros and paperclips, they are insisting we make random checks of all people leaving the building.' Hafiz was clearly embarrassed, torn between doing his duty and loyalty to David.

'Not at all, Hafiz, not at all,' David replied, opening his briefcase on Onslow's bonnet.

CHAPTER FORTY

Jerusalem

The biochemistry laboratory that the Hebrew University had made available was equipped with the latest technology for DNA analysis.

'Fire away, Teach.' David's grin was irrepressible.

'Twenty years ago we couldn't have done this,' Allegra said, standing in front of a whiteboard. David had asked for an explanation of how DNA analysis might help unlock the secrets of the Dead Sea Scrolls.

'DNA or deoxyribonucleic acid looks like this,' she said. Allegra then drew the long spiralling ladder-like helix on the board. 'The goatskin parchment the Essenes used to prepare their documents is so old that any DNA has deteriorated to the point where there are only very short sequences and not enough to analyse,' she said. 'But in 1983, an American biochemist, Kary Mullus, developed a technique called polymerase chain reaction which makes copies of DNA so that we have enough to test.'

'So even though the fragments in the trunk don't contain much DNA, you can manufacture more from what's left?'

'Precisely. And it may not be as difficult as I first thought. If you're right and there are only three scrolls, one of which is Isaiah, one the Gospel of Thomas and the third being the Omega Scroll, the chances are there will only be three sets of goat DNA. And that will separate the thousand-piece nightmare into three much smaller puzzles.'

'Always assuming they've only used three separate goatskins,' David observed.

Allegra looked thoughtful. 'Even if we turn up a fourth or a fifth skin and we can identify what scroll it comes from, we will only have to worry about it if it's part of the Omega Scroll. And we already have a great start because we've got the DNA of the Omega Scroll from the envelope inside the lid of the trunk.'

'Lonergan will be back in a bit over four months. Are we going to have enough time?' David asked.

'Because there are so many fragments, we're going to have to put in some long hours in here, but four months should be enough. With the equipment in the lab we can process nearly four hundred samples simultaneously. That will generate nearly three million bases a day and we're only talking picogram amounts here.'

David pulled another face.

'To give you peasants an idea,' Allegra said with a smile, 'there's enough DNA in one-tenth of one-millionth of a litre of human saliva to identify a genetic sequence as human. So we won't need to damage any of the script on the fragments. We'll only need microscopic amounts for copying the sequences and analysing them.'

Allegra took David through the process step by step, explaining how the samples were cooled so that the paired strands would form again with the help of primers and how enzymes were added that could read the sequences and extend them in a chain reaction replication.

Even with David acting as the junior lab assistant, it was going to take time. Time they might not have.

Mike McKinnon walked into the Cellar Bar as Tom Schweiker was ordering a beer.

'Mike! Welcome back,' Tom said, stretching out his hand. 'Make that two beers, thanks Abdullah.'

Beers in hand, the two men headed towards one of the vacant booths, neither missing the two striking women chatting at the end of the bar.

'Nice legs,' Mike said, glancing back towards the bar. 'Wonder what time they open.'

'You haven't changed. Looks as if they're on their own, too.'

'Let's hope so. Cheers!'

'Good health!'

'Have you got any contacts in the FBI, Mike?' Tom asked when he'd taken a swig of his beer.

'A barnful. Depends what you want them for,' Mike replied.

'I need a favour. Some fingerprints need checking. I've got a suspicion they belong to someone I've known in a previous life.'

'That shouldn't be too hard,' Mike said. 'Give me the prints and I'll send them back in the black bag to a buddy of mine.'

'Thanks, I appreciate it. How's Washington?' Tom asked.

Giorgio Felici slid into the bar and, keeping a large pillar between himself and his targets, he unobtrusively manoeuvred himself into the next booth.

'Every bit as bad as I remember it,' Mike replied ruefully, and he brought Tom up to date. 'I've never seen the Agency in worse shape in all the years I've been part of it. Intelligence has become irrelevant to the politicians. The "Baghdad or Bust" brigade over at the Pentagon changed anything I came up with to fit the decision to invade that they'd already made.'

Over the years the two men had built up a trust that was highly unusual between a CIA agent and a journalist, and it was as valuable to both men as it was curious. Tom could check the information that he had from other sources, as well as getting the inside running on what was really going on inside the CIA, and Mike gained equally valuable information from Tom. Neither had any time for self-serving politicians, and neither would ever disclose their source.

'A bit like the Brits and their "forty-five minutes until an attack on Harrods", which turned out to be the time it would take for Saddam to get his fucking mortars into action,' Tom said with a grin. 'The military operation in Iraq's been such a ham-fisted, club-footed cock-up that we've managed to kill more than a hundred thousand civilians. Most Iraqis will be glad to see the back of us and the Islamic fundamentalists are having a field day,' he added more grimly.

'I saw your piece on the Omega Scroll. Do you think there's any connection between the fundamentalists operating in the Middle East and the scroll?' Mike asked.

Tom nodded. 'Yes, and not only in the Middle East. There are a couple of mathematicians here who have been doing some work decoding biblical manuscripts. Rips has been working on the Torah and Yossi Kaufmann has been working on the Dead Sea Scrolls. Kaufmann thinks that the rise in Islamic fundamentalism and the Omega Scroll are definitely connected.'

'You think these codes are real?'

'I think so. The technique involves isolating every third or fourth letter of the old text, what Rips calls a skip code. I used to think you could do a skip code on the dictionary and get the same result, but these guys are nobody's fools and Kaufmann thinks there is a catastrophic warning in the Omega Scroll that involves fundamentalist Islam,' said Mike.

'Any word on that Russian scientist?'

'Tretyakov?' Mike shook his head. 'Last we heard he was in Peshawar. We've also had reports that one of bin Laden's top lieutenants, Abdul Basheer, has been sighted on the border of Afghanistan and Pakistan, so if Tretyakov's linked up with al-Qaeda he could be well into the Hindu Kush by now.'

'Basheer is a master strategist. Kaufmann might be closer to the truth than he realises,' Tom reflected.

'Kaufmann's the guy who is running against Sharon and Peres with a new platform. What's it called – the Liberal Justice Party?'

'That's the one. For a politician, he's very different and between you and me, his Liberal Justice Party has got a pretty good chance of getting up. Sharon's approach borders on thuggery, and ultimately this wall he's built will do more harm than good. Ordinary Israelis are starting to realise this and they're looking for someone who can give them some hope.'

Mike nodded. 'Yeah. You can't go round ripping up hundreds of olive groves and expect to win the hearts and minds campaign. The election's coming up soon?'

'Yes, in early January. There is some hope on the Palestinian front as well. Ahmed Sartawi who won the Palestinian election knows Kaufmann pretty well and their peace plans are already well advanced. Between the two of them they might just make it in the peace stakes. Even the militants might come onside if these two can achieve a Palestinian State, although I'm not holding my breath.' The sceptical journalist in Tom had seen it all before.

'What do you think the chances are of finding this scroll?' Mike asked, nonchalantly turning the conversation back to his mission.

Tom shrugged. 'Hard to say. Yossi's son David is an archaeologist and he seems keen on finding it, as does his partner, Dr Allegra Bassetti. They were down at Qumran a couple of weeks ago. I don't know what she's like as a sleuth, but she's an absolute stunner to look at, lucky bastard.'

Mike got up to order more beers. The trip had already been worthwhile. The 'ruins' were more than likely Qumran and the Omega Scroll was more than likely real, and if he played his cards right his visit to the Holy City might be even more worthwhile, he thought, as the two women at the bar returned his smile.

'Staying in Jerusalem long?' he asked.

CHAPTER FORTY-ONE

The Hindu Kush

The wind howled viciously outside the heavily guarded cave complex, high in a remote area of the Hindu Kush on the border of Pakistan and Afghanistan. The majestic snow-capped peaks soared to 6000 metres and beyond. Today the temperature had dropped to 15 degrees below zero and visibility was down to a few metres. Dr Hussein Tretyakov placed the heavy metal suitcase in the centre of the cave and rubbed his hands vigorously. It was one of several for which his new employer had paid ten million dollars each. Most of the others were already with the sleeper cells in the United States, Britain and Australia.

The small group of Arabs gathered around the bomb. They were led by a man in his mid-fifties dressed in a nondescript but expensive robe and a spotless white turban. Hussein Tretyakov had come to know and like the Egyptian lawyer, Abdul Musa Basheer, and his gentle sense of humour. Both men were now on a similar path and Abdul Basheer was one of bin Laden's most trusted lieutenants and strategists. The former member of the

Egyptian Islamic Jihad was a man of extraordinary ability and the West had every reason to be worried. If anything happened to either bin Laden or himself, Basheer had recruited some of the finest engineers, soldiers, lawyers and doctors in Islam to carry on the struggle.

'The original nuclear bombs were fission bombs where atoms were split, giving off an enormous amount of energy in the form of heat, neutrons and gamma rays,' Hussein explained, waiting for the interpreter to translate.

'Neutrons and gamma rays penetrate the body and destroy the body's cells, resulting in hundreds of thousands more deaths than might be achieved from just the blast and heat of a nuclear explosion,' he continued. 'Plutonium has a half-life of about twenty-four thousand years. Together, the heat and force of a nuclear suitcase bomb, coupled with the radiation, will render the Western cities unusable for a very long time.'

The Arabs exchanged glances. Praise be to God, the infidels could now be dealt a blow that would make September 11 look like child's play.

Tretyakov opened the lid of the deadly nuclear bomb. 'As you can see, this suitcase contains a heavily shielded cylinder in which the fuel is kept in what is called a sub-critical mass so that it won't detonate prematurely. On detonation the plutonium inside compresses and when it reaches a critical mass we have our nuclear explosion.'

Dr Tretyakov passed around a sheet of paper with a diagram of the inside of the cylinder and its plutonium core.

'In the 1950s, despite the carnage in Hiroshima and Nagasaki, scientists found that fission bombs were inefficient,' he explained. 'Fusion bombs, which we call thermonuclear bombs, can do a lot more damage.'

Again there was an exchange of glances as the interpreter translated.

'For the last twenty years Russian scientists have been working to perfect small thermonuclear devices which will destroy any known city. Most of the radiation from a fission bomb is in the form of X-rays,' the Chechen nuclear physicist said. 'The X-rays from a fission bomb can be used to produce the very high temperatures and pressures that are required to trigger a fusion reaction. Thermonuclear bombs work with a fission bomb being first imploded inside a casing to compress a fusion fuel of lithium deuterate and a rod of plutonium-239.'

Hussein handed out another sheet of paper with a diagram of the fission bomb and fusion bomb inside a casing of uranium-238 and the sequence of events that produced an ever increasing series of neutron emissions, culminating in the lithium deuterate and plutonium-239 fuel of the fusion bomb producing even more neutrons and heat, and a nuclear explosion that was a hundred times more powerful than Hiroshima.

'The first three targets are New York, London and Sydney,' Abdul Basheer said quietly. 'God willing, we will also be able to attack other cities like Washington, Chicago, San Francisco and Los Angeles.' His eyes were clear and his manner chillingly calm. 'If the British and Australians continue to support the United States killing innocent Muslim women and children around the world, then we will also attack cities like Manchester and Melbourne. What would be the effect of such a bomb?'

Dr Tretyakov had prior knowledge of the initial targets and he produced simple travel maps of the Western cities. 'The thermonuclear suitcases will destroy any of your targets,' he explained to the al-Qaeda command group. 'In New York, the Brooklyn, Manhattan and other bridges would twist and melt into the East River. The skyscrapers would implode and Wall Street and the financial district would be razed to a smoking ruin. Lower Manhattan would be totally destroyed, as well as the rest of the city including 5th Avenue, Broadway and the area around Central Park. In London,

Trafalgar Square, Westminster Abbey, Big Ben and the Houses of Parliament, Buckingham Palace and Westminster Bridge, together with everything else around them, would be wiped off the map. Permanently.'

Jerusalem

In a safe house in the Old City, Yusef Sartawi pored over the photos of the Hebrew University and the biochemistry laboratory with its trademark fume cupboard venting on the roof. The safe, he had been assured by the laboratory technician, was rudimentary. It was an old free-standing Chubb and old safes sometimes needed to be repaired. Yusef checked the letterhead on the invoice. *Leibzoll Safes and Security, 84 Ben Yehuda Street, Tel-Aviv*. The blanks had been stolen from a security company that specialised in safes. He'd lined up one of his most experienced drivers for the job and a sign-writer had almost finished preparing the van. Now the only thing preventing them from putting the plan into action was the final approval for repair, and that had to come from within the bureaucracy of the university administration. The delay was frustrating, Yusef mused, but if Allah willed it, the approval would eventually be forthcoming without arousing any suspicion.

CHAPTER FORTY-TWO

Roma

The new year had begun badly for Cardinal Petroni. The laboratory technician at the Hebrew University had not only sold information to Yusef Sartawi. The Director of L'École Biblique, Father Jean-Pierre La Franci, had also been startled to learn of Dr Allegra Bassetti's DNA analysis on fragments of a Dead Sea Scroll. With confirmation of the woman's involvement and the news that the fragments might be the legendary Omega Scroll, Cardinal Petroni had not hesitated. Allegra Bassetti would have to be eliminated and the Dead Sea Scroll recovered. Now, with his customary ruthlessness, Lorenzo Petroni had turned his attention to the more urgent matter of the Pope's health.

The intercom on Cardinal Petroni's desk sounded quietly.

'Yes, Father Thomas?' The Cardinal Secretary of State's politeness could only be attributed to the presence of the Papal Physician, Professor Vincenzo Martines.

'The cardinals have assembled in the Borgia Chamber, Eminence.'

'Thank you, Father Thomas. You may tell them Professor Martines and I are on our way.'

'As you can see, Vincenzo, it's a very delicate issue,' Petroni continued, sinking back into one of the crimson couches. 'The resignation of a Holy Father is not without precedent but fraught with difficulty and some of my colleagues will be loathe to even consider it.'

'I can understand that, Lorenzo. After all, the Holy Father's faculties are still quite sharp.' The Papal Physician kept his fears that the Pope's condition was far more serious to himself.

'Yes, and he is determined to bear the burden of his debilitating condition until the end. Between you and me, Vincenzo, the Church's greatest nightmare would be for a reigning Pope to become unconscious for any prolonged period. I don't mean any disrespect to your profession but, in the case of a Pope, modern medicine brings mixed blessings. A hundred years ago the physician's remedy was often more dangerous than the affliction, now we keep people alive for a very long time. To the ordinary man that can either be a comfort or a curse. A Pope is different. If he slips into a coma, the Holy Church slips into a coma with him. I can run the day-to-day business here, but unless His Holiness delegates specific authority, bishops can't be appointed and major policy decisions can't be made. A Pope on life-support can spell serious trouble for the Church.'

'And who amongst the Curial Cardinals will have the courage to turn off the life support of a Pope,' Professor Martines mused. It was a statement rather than a question. Vincenzo Martines again reflected on his diagnosis of Petroni and the cardinal's judicious use of charm, manipulation and intimidation to achieve total control. Martines wondered if that would stretch to violence should the need arise. There was a coldness about this Prince of the Church that was the antipathy of Christ, along with a ruthless ambition that hid what Martines suspected was an inner insecurity. But it was not his role in life to make judgements on the fitness or otherwise

of a candidate for the Keys to Peter. His task was to brief the Curial
Cardinals on His Holiness' condition, although he was under no
illusions as to what was driving Cardinal Lorenzo Petroni.

'Who indeed, Vincenzo. Perhaps it is time my Curial colleagues
were given all the facts. Shall we?'

'I know you all have busy schedules,' Petroni began when he and
Professor Martines had taken their places at the heavy polished
table in the Borgia Chamber, 'and I am grateful to each of you for
your valuable time.' It was a vintage Petroni opening. He knew
full well that not one of the Vatican's Cardinal Prefects would
have dared miss such a meeting. In the secret mazes of the Curial
bureaucracy, knowledge was power, and as always, Petroni's own
ruthless power was paramount but it was masked with a velvet
glove of courtesy and silken diplomacy.

'I have asked Professor Martines to join us this evening because
I think the time has come for you all to be given a forthright assessment of his Holiness' condition. As this is an informal meeting
and not a consistory, no notes will be taken. It goes without saying
that what is said here tonight is to remain in this room.' Cardinal
Petroni nodded politely towards the Papal Physician. 'Professor
Martines, we are indebted to you.'

Professor Martines cleared his throat and adjusted a pair of
horn-rimmed glasses on his large aquiline nose.

'I am happy to be of service, Eminence; I only wish it was under
better circumstances,' he said, looking out at the sea of scarlet
around the table.

'As you know, Eminences, the Pope has been suffering from
Parkinson's for some years, and as you are also aware, Parkinson's
is a progressively degenerative neurological disorder that affects
the control of body movements.'

'Is there a cure?' The question came from Cardinal Castiglione,
one of the longest serving of the Curial Cardinals and Prefect of

the Congregation for the Causes of Saints. Giulio Castiglione came from the old school. He was already past the normal retiring age of seventy-five, and when he turned eighty in two years time, he would no longer be eligible to vote. The Holy Father had extended him in his appointment and no one present at the meeting tonight was in any doubt where his loyalties lay. The 'old bull' was clearly not happy.

'Unfortunately not.' Professor Martines confirmed what most already knew. 'There is an enormous amount of research being conducted, but the present treatment is restricted to reducing the effects of the disease, not to alleviating the disease itself.'

'I thought there was some promising research coming out of the United States.' This time the question came from Cardinal Rinato Fiore, Cardinal Prefect of the Congregation for Bishops.

'Eminence, I assume you are referring to some work done at the University of Colorado and the Columbian University where they are assessing whether or not cell transplants can restore the dopamine function.' Professor Martines chose his words carefully. 'Medical scientists in the United States have shown that dopamine-producing cells can take root, survive and function after a transplant. That gives us some useful clues for further research, but I'm afraid that while the work has shown some promise, implanted cells cannot be fully controlled. An overproduction of some chemicals can trigger involuntary movements which can be quite disturbing.'

'And the Holy Father's present condition?' asked Cardinal Fumagalli, Prefect of the Congregation for the Clergy.

'You will appreciate, Eminence, that the Holy Father has been on medication for a very long time. One of the characteristics of Parkinson's is that over time, its effects become commensurately more severe. His Holiness' stooped posture is, I'm afraid, just one symptom of that. As the illness progresses, more and more medication is required and unfortunately the side-effects become more pronounced.'

'I understand that in time, Professor Martines, medication might no longer be effective?' Petroni's interjection was designed to ultimately force the direction of a decision in his favour.

'Sadly, we are probably close to that point now, Eminence. To be blunt, apart from his problems with movement and writing, and sometimes with speech, His Holiness is suffering increasingly from nausea and vomiting. He is not sleeping and he is becoming progressively more tired as his dosage of levodopa is increased. There will come a time when the drugs will no longer be effective and appearances in public may be difficult, if not impossible.'

'And what of the Holy Father's mental state?' Cardinal Fiore had ventured where no one else had so far dared, but this was too much for Castiglione.

'Someone should rule that question out of order!' Castiglione spluttered, looking directly at Cardinal Petroni. 'It is not up to us as cardinals to sit here and discuss the Holy Father's mental capacity as if he were some priest we're considering putting in a home.'

'I can understand that some of us, all of us, find this distasteful,' the Secretary of State responded calmly, 'but it is not the first time that the Church has had to face this sort of difficulty.' The Secretary of State turned to face Cardinal Castiglione. 'There is a lot of experience around this table and none of us have more than you, Eminence, but if the stewardship of the Church should pass into our hands, we need to be prepared.'

'You make it sound as if His Holiness is half-dead already,' Castiglione snapped.

'Forgive me, Eminence, I don't mean to. Please continue, Professor Martines,' Petroni said, coldness creeping into his voice.

'If you are asking me whether or not His Holiness comprehends what is going on around him, the answer is unequivocally yes. His mind is still very sharp. However,' Professor Martines warned, 'some patients have difficulty with short-term memory and, for some, complex issues are increasingly more difficult to grasp. His

Holiness has been accustomed to a very full working day, which is no longer possible. This is causing him a degree of stress which further lessens the effectiveness of the pharmacological intervention.'

Petroni scanned the faces of his fellow cardinals. The reality was that modern medicine could not provide a recovery, nor could it provide a peaceful death. In a way, the cardinals were also refusing to face their own mortality, grimly hanging on to the old inflexible Church they loved. Petroni was determined to press them for a decision on the Pope's resignation, but tonight was not the time.

'Thank you, Professor Martines,' Petroni said, bringing the meeting to an end. 'You have given us all much to think about and again we are indebted to you. I propose, gentlemen, that over the coming days we should all devote some time, thought and prayer to this serious issue with which the Holy Church is now faced.'

As Petroni walked back to his apartments he thought about how close he was getting to ultimate power. Nothing could be allowed to stand in his way – not Donelli, not Schweiker, and especially not the woman.

CHAPTER FORTY-THREE

Tel-Aviv

Mike McKinnon had dinner on his own in a small restaurant near the US Embassy in Tel-Aviv and then went back to work. The Omega Scroll was proving more elusive than ever and he wearily punched a six-digit code into the keypad on a reinforced door in the basement, behind which worked the 'declared' and 'undeclared' agents of the CIA in Israel. It was the last of five security checks that had started with the guards on the entrance to the embassy and the magnetometer check. Sitting down at his desk he flicked on CCN to catch up on the Israeli election. The CCN anchor, Geraldine Rushmore, appeared on his screen.

'Tonight on *International Correspondent* we look at the changing face of politics and the possibility of renewed hope for peace in the Middle East. Following a convincing win for President Ahmed Sartawi's Democratic Islamic Party in the Palestinian elections, Professor Yossi Kaufmann has claimed victory in the Israeli poll. We now cross live to Jerusalem and our correspondent Tom Schweiker. Tom, a surprising result?'

'Yes and no, Geraldine. Yes, in that Ariel Sharon's Likud Party and Shimon Peres' Labor Party have both suffered a major loss of support. No, in that Professor Yossi Kaufmann and his Liberal Justice Party have campaigned on only one issue – a just peace, which has struck a chord with ordinary Israelis in the same way Sartawi did with ordinary Palestinians. A lot of people on both sides are sick of the killing and the violence, and these two men represent a genuine hope for a peaceful co-existence. Here's what Professor Kaufmann had to say when I interviewed him a few minutes ago.'

The vision cut to the Israeli who would soon be Israel's next Prime Minister.

'Israelis have had the chance to vote for peace, and they have done so in overwhelming numbers. It is time to end the killing, it is time to end the violence, and as I've said throughout this campaign, peace can only be achieved if there is justice for both sides. Neither side will get everything they want, but all of us, Israeli or Palestinian, Jewish or Muslim, all of us have the right to pursue our lives in a country that is peaceful and secure.'

'And you're serious about cutting defence spending?' Tom asked.

'Continual warfare and killing has devastating consequences,' Yossi replied. 'The Iraq war is costing a billion dollars a week, and here, we went into debt to the United States for over four billion dollars on defence last year. If we can achieve peace, and I am confident that together with the new Palestinian President, Ahmed Sartawi, we can, it will mean construction of the wall can be stopped and other defence expenditure can be lowered dramatically. That money can be channelled towards education, health and the environment so our children can live to realise their potential. President Sartawi has already rung to congratulate me and we have agreed to issue a draft peace plan in the very near future.'

Tom smiled. 'Good luck and thank you for talking to CCN, Professor Kaufmann.'

'That was Tom Schweiker speaking with the next Prime Minister of Israel. Now to the continuing war in Iraq . . .'

Mike McKinnon turned the TV off. Perhaps these two might bring an end to the bloodshed, he thought. He turned back to his computer and entered a series of codes. The first email headed 'Top Secret – Omega' was from the Director.

> For McKinnon from DCI. The President is meeting with the Reverend Buffett tomorrow and has asked for an update on the search for the Omega Scroll. Please provide by 1700 hours.

'Fuck me,' Mike muttered grimly. 'Osama bin Laden and his mad mullahs are running around with enough plutonium and deuterium to destroy the financial capitals of the Western World and the White House is still carrying on over a Dead Sea Scroll.' He smiled to himself. At least the result of the Israeli and Palestinian elections would give them something else to think about. The State Department, Pentagon, Finance and a dozen other departments around the beltway would be cutting down another forest of trees to produce a flurry of 'impact statements' on how the elections might affect US interests. If Tom Schweiker was right about Kaufmann and Sartawi knowing each other well, and they were already drafting a peace plan, Washington would be reduced to observing the process from the sidelines. Probably not a bad thing, he thought as he opened the next report from Echelon.

In the time he'd been in Tel-Aviv Mike McKinnon had made a little progress, particularly with the phone intercepts. 'Cave One' was almost certainly at Qumran and Tom had been more than happy to fill him in on Lonergan who, he had noted, was now overseas and headed for Florence, but 'Free-standing Chubb circa 1950' had him intrigued. Was it possible that there was something in a safe in the quiet surrounds of a biochemistry laboratory in the Hebrew University, something so sensitive that someone was going to extraordinary lengths to remove it? Safecracking and lock picking were just two of McKinnon's many talents. The boys in the basements at Langley were among the best in the business and Mike had taken the trouble to hone his skills. He had also spent many hours on the indoor range before he had satisfied himself that he was back up to scratch with his weapon of choice. Rather than the .22 that most agents used, Mike preferred a Heckler-Koch Mark 23 .45 ACP calibre with a silencer and a laser aimer that had been developed for US Special Forces. He had a feeling he would need it.

Venezia

'Giovanni here.'

'The Prime Minister of Israel, Eminence,' Vittorio announced.

'Thank you.'

The line crackled and the distinctive voice of Yossi Kaufmann could be heard.

'*Buongiorno* Giovanni, it's Yossi.'

'Yossi. Congratulations! How is it going? I've been praying for you.'

'Thank you, Giovanni! It's almost going too well. I'm meeting with Ahmed in a week's time and our draft on the peace agreement is pretty well agreed, at least by us, although I don't want to get ahead of ourselves,' Yossi said. 'There is still furious opposition from some of the settlers on our side, even though the compensation package is very generous. Where we can, we will let them stay and compensate the Palestinians with Israeli land, and I think they're coming around.'

'What about the fundamentalists?' Giovanni asked.

'The key to getting Hamas, Islamic Jihad and the Al-Aqsa Martyrs Brigade on our side is the promise of a Palestinian State, Giovanni. Some of their members will never renounce terrorism, but if we can get the bulk of them on board, including the leadership, the fanatics can be marginalised. Ahmed and I are both confident we can pull this off and we're going to strike while the mainstream enthusiasm is there. When we have a date, what would your reaction be to taking a small part in a peace ceremony? We don't plan to mix religion with State here, so it would be a personal rather than an official invitation. When we've ironed out the details, the signing will take place underneath the Damascus Gate between a Jew and a Muslim. It seems to me that Abraham would not object if we got the support of Christianity as well?'

Giovanni laughed as he thought back to their fishing trip.

'I'd be delighted,' he said.

CHAPTER FORTY-FOUR

Jerusalem

Yusef Sartawi opened the door of the safe house at the sound of the pre-arranged knock. Despite the mission that was being planned, Wasfiheh Khatib looked calm and untroubled, almost peaceful. Just nineteen, the striking young woman was studying sociology at the Palestinian Al-Quds University in Ramallah. To make ends meet she drove an ambulance on weekends and it was this that had pushed her to a state of utter despair. When her ambulance had been shot at by Israeli soldiers she had put it down to a mistake, but in the past few months it had happened repeatedly and she had been wounded twice. The Red Crescent uniform made no difference to the Israeli soldiers. Too many times Wasfiheh had cradled a dying child in her arms, and too many times she had tried to stem the lifeblood of many others who had lost a leg or an arm at the hands of the Israelis.

Yusef checked beyond the doorway and ushered Wasfiheh inside.

'The restaurant is Numero Venti,' he said, pointing to King George V Street and Ha Histradrut in a street directory. 'It's an upmarket restaurant and the targets often dine there. You have a booking to eat there next week,' Yusef said, handing Wasfiheh an envelope. 'Familiarise yourself with the layout and wear something stylish but nondescript. Once we are happy that you know the target and you are thoroughly familiar with wearing the explosives we will put you on standby. You will have to be able to respond quickly as we sometimes only get one or two hours' notice of a booking.'

Wasfiheh nodded calmly.

Yusef pulled two photographs out of a folder. They were the standard Hebrew University mug shots that were taken of all lecturers and staff.

'Memorise the faces of the infidels so that when the attack is finalised you can get as close to their table as possible before you detonate the belt.'

'Mine will be the last face they will see.' At last Wasfiheh felt empowered and the lives of the innocent would be avenged.

Tel-Aviv

Mike McKinnon waited for the encryptions to boot up on his computer and for the latest report from Echelon to appear on his screen. Two days before he'd had a breakthrough. An Echelon report had provided a printout on a mobile that had been tracked by satellite to a laneway off Yehuda ha-Yamit, not far from Tel-Aviv's port of Old Yafo. Armed with the necessary diplomatic clearances for any roadblocks, Mike had found the laneway and an old garage under an ancient stone building, but his reconnaissance had yielded nothing more. Now, as the most recent intercept appeared, it looked as if he'd hit paydirt.

Operation Omega. Echelon Intercept Tel-Aviv. 261200Z hours. 'Repair of safe approved and clearances in place. Proceed 1500 tomorrow.'

Mike checked the date/time group and then the number of the mobile. It matched the 'Yes, I am in position – they are at the entrance to Cave One' intercept. It seemed that whatever was in the safe was associated with the surveillance on Dr David Kaufmann and Dr Allegra Bassetti. Might that mean, he wondered, that the pair had found something quite significant, significant enough for Hamas to dispatch someone to retrieve it?

The next day, just after 2.30 p.m. Mike parked his beige Renault Clio sedan where he could see down the laneway and waited. He was on his own, acutely aware that he was making decisions that the Director of the CIA would rightfully deny. Worse still, with the intercepts posing more questions than they answered, there were gaping holes in the intelligence. Mossad would not take too kindly to any attempt to steal a scroll and without their help Mike had been forced to put together a plan that was based on instinct – follow the Hamas operative and wait for an opportunity.

A little further along the road Giorgio Felici put down his binoculars and wondered why the CIA would have an interest in a Dead Sea Scroll. Hamas might need a little help, he mused, absentmindedly feeling for his Beretta Cougar hidden under his Armani jacket.

At 1500 hours, a swarthy-faced Arab emerged from a side gate. The garage doors underneath the old stone house were not the usual tilta-door or roller variety. They were big, heavy wooden doors that opened like a concertina and Mike watched as the stocky Arab began, with some difficulty, to force them apart. Shortly afterwards the Arab drove out in a dark green van, its sides painted with gold lettering: Leibzoll Safes and Security, 84 Ben Yehuda Street, Tel-Aviv.

The lane was quite a distance from Ben Yehuda Street and Mike McKinnon concluded that although Leibzoll Safes and Security were probably a legitimate company, this van was one they didn't know they owned.

The van driver didn't seem in any hurry as they negotiated the traffic in Tel-Aviv but once they got onto Route 1 and the freeway to Jerusalem the van sped up with Mike following at a distance. Three roadblocks, which the van took far more time to get through than he did, and an hour later, the 'safe man' reached the Mount Scopus campus of the Hebrew University. After a brief discussion where the guard on the entrance appeared to be giving directions, the Arab was waved through. Sometimes the Israelis could be very cooperative Mike thought grimly, wondering whether he should follow the van onto the campus. That, he thought, would only attract attention and he settled down to wait in a side road where he could watch the entrance.

Jerusalem

David called in to see Bishop O'Hara and then headed off to meet Allegra at Numero Venti, reflecting on Allegra's stunning results. The carbon dating had been easy – 20 to 40 AD – but even with David helping out, it had taken Allegra nearly two months to complete the initial task of analysing two thousand fragments into parcels of DNA. At least the Essenes had only used three goatskins, David thought. Allegra's analysis had enabled fragments of the Gospel of Thomas, the Great Isaiah Scroll and the Omega Scroll to be separated into three large plastic bags but the extraordinarily difficult task of piecing together the fragments of the Omega Scroll still lay ahead of them.

'Congratulations, David!' Allegra raised her champagne glass in a toast to the country's newest member of the Knesset just as Elie appeared with the menus.

'Congratulations on your election, Dr Kaufmann,' Elie said, adding his own best wishes to those of Allegra. 'At last there seems to be an opportunity for peace.'

'I hope so, Elie, I really hope so, and thank you.'

A short distance away in the Muslim quarter of the Old City, Yusef Sartawi made the final adjustments to the thin explosives belt that he had packed with ammonium nitrate. To maximise the casualties, more than three hundred nails and steel bearings had been packed in with the explosive. Wasfiheh raised the top of her elegant jacket and he strapped the belt firmly around her slender waist.

'Keep the detonator in your pocket until you have to use it,' Yusef instructed, making sure Wasfiheh's top covered the wire running from the belt. 'And here is 100 shekels. Make sure you catch a taxi, clients of Numero Venti don't travel by bus.'

Mike McKinnon weighed up his options. The freeway was unlikely to provide an interception opportunity, he mused – too much traffic and too many Israeli patrols. It would be better to follow the Arab driver back to Tel-Aviv. Any further consideration was cut short by the re-appearance of the van at the university entrance. Mike McKinnon started his car and eased out of the side street.

Just before they reached Nablus Road they encountered the first of what would be a number of random checkpoints and Mike waited uneasily while the van driver handed over his papers. If his suspicions were correct, and the Omega Scroll was in the safe and the Israeli soldiers found it, it would spell disaster. The Hamas paperwork must have been very professional, Mike thought as he watched the Uzi-wielding Israeli soldiers let the van pass.

By the time they reached the freeway to Tel-Aviv, Mike realised that his earlier assessment had been correct. Interception on the freeway was out of the question. The traffic, apart from two more checkpoints, was free flowing and the van's tyres could have been shot out easily enough but the Israeli patrols were everywhere and he forced himself to remain calm as he followed. When the traffic slowed on the outskirts of Tel-Aviv and darkness descended, Mike closed on the van, not wanting to lose his quarry in the traffic snarls of Tel-Aviv. Thirty minutes later Mike watched the van turn off into the lane and he parked as close as he dared. Normally Mike didn't wear driving gloves but this time they served another purpose and leaving them on he retrieved his Heckler-Koch from the glove box. Glancing up and down he was relieved to find that the road was empty and he was grateful for the sparseness of street lighting in this part of Tel-Aviv. Moving quickly, he melted into the shadows, keeping the parked cars between him and his target as he moved silently down the lane.

The van had pulled up in front of the garage and his quarry was once again having trouble forcing the heavy doors apart. Using the van as cover, Mike moved silently along the side until he was only two steps away from the Arab who was now cursing loudly. Judging that he would not have a better chance, Mike reversed his grip on his Heckler-Koch to bring the butt down hard on the Arab's head, but as he did so the Arab lost his footing in the dirt and slipped forwards. Mike's pistol butt cracked against the Arab's back instead of his head. The Hamas man had been trained to deal with a surprise attack from behind and dropped to his knees. With a powerful backward thrust he flung Mike into the air. Instinctively Mike hit the dirt entrance of the garage and rolled, weapon in hand, in time to see the Arab draw his own weapon.

Pfunk. Pfunk. Pfunk. The silenced .45 sounded incredibly loud as Mike squeezed off three quick shots in succession. The Langley training had not been wasted. The Arab clutched his chest, his gun tumbling harmlessly underneath the van. Mike watched his quarry sink in what seemed like slow motion to the garage floor, his lifeblood ebbing away, hatred visible in his eyes, but fading. Calmly, Mike McKinnon dragged the body into the back of the garage and drove the van inside. He picked up the three spent cartridges and pocketed them.

With the aid of the small microphone and earpiece that the boys in the basement had provided, Mike listened to the final tumbler fall into position. After he opened the door of the old Chubb safe he scanned the contents. There was one envelope, and the only outside marking was in thick black pen: Ω.

Giorgio Felici had followed Mike McKinnon on the opposite side of the lane. The Hamas operative would be more than a match for the American, he thought, but he would get in close, just in case.

For a brief moment Felici lost sight of the other two men behind the van. Then he heard three shots from a silenced .45 and knew he'd lost his Hamas man. Deciding against taking on the American in a confined space, Felici waited. As the CIA agent drove the van into the garage, Felici crouched low. Moving past the garage he took cover behind a parked car.

Fifteen minutes later the CIA agent emerged carrying a plastic envelope. Felici watched as his target looked around quickly before moving up the lane towards his car. Felici drew his Beretta and silently followed.

Mike McKinnon heard a noise and immediately reached for his gun as he spun around towards the sound. A single bullet hit him between the eyes and he crumpled silently to the footpath.

CHAPTER FORTY-FIVE

Jerusalem

'Yossi will make a wonderful Prime Minister, David,' Allegra said as Elie headed off with their order, 'but I worry for both of you. Some of the ultra-orthodox Jews and the settlers are seething.'

As David and Allegra clinked their glasses in a toast to peace, two young men deep in conversation near the entrance to Numero Venti stopped talking and stepped aside to make way for a beautiful young woman. Wasfiheh Khatib walked confidently into the crowded restaurant and moved towards David and Allegra.

Elie moved out from behind the bar. He had seen her once before and it was not the young woman's striking looks that prompted him, it was his years of training and a sixth sense that something was not quite right; none of his guests were expecting anyone and all the tables were full.

'May I help,' Elie asked with a polite smile, tapping her on the shoulder. As she turned, the brief look of concern in the girl's dark eyes did not escape the old waiter. She put her hand in her pocket and Elie saw the wire. Instinctively he spun the girl around and wrapped both arms around her, but he was too late. Wasfiheh pressed the button, detonating nearly 2 kilograms of ammonium nitrate. A blast of flying nails, smoke and deadly shards of glass shattered the restaurant and the shock waves thundered off the old stone walls.

'Allegra!' David shook his head and staggered to his feet. Blood was streaming from a deep cut on the side of his head. Allegra had been closer to the girl and was now lying motionless in a pool of blood. In the distance the all-too-familiar sound of approaching sirens could be heard, the vision of which would be carried on news bulletin updates around the world.

'We open this bulletin,' Geraldine began, 'with another tragic bombing in Jerusalem, with the first reports indicating that up to five people have been killed and a dozen more injured, some critically.'

Normally it would have been just another set of statistics to which the world had become anaesthetised by their sheer regularity, but this time the bombing had struck at members of Prime Minister Kaufmann's family, and the footage showed scenes of ambulance workers trollying the wounded against a backdrop of destruction and the eerie hue of red and blue flashing lights. The picture faded to the entrance of the Hadassah Hospital at Ein Karem, with the pale face of a visibly shaken Tom Schweiker in the foreground.

'Tom, what's the latest there?'

Despite his personal connections to David and Allegra, Tom's voice was calm and measured.

'Another shocking tragedy for the people of Jerusalem with the bombing of one of the city's most popular restaurants, Numero Venti,' Tom began. 'The casualties have been heavy and include the Prime Minister's son, Dr David Kaufmann, and one of the world's foremost scientists in the field of archaeological DNA, Dr Allegra Bassetti.'

'Is there any word on their condition?'

'It's understood that David Kaufmann has been treated for cuts and abrasions but Dr Bassetti is still in surgery and as yet there is no word on her.'

In Rome the Cardinal Secretary of State, with prior warning of the bombing, was glued to the live broadcast, his anger growing at the mention of the woman's name.

'Will this affect the peace process, Tom?'

'As tragic as it is, I don't think so, Geraldine. A short time ago Prime Minister Kaufmann made a statement to that effect. Here's a bit of what he had to say.'

The Prime Minister of Israel walked into the hospital foyer, and with a sad look he nodded to the waiting media.

'Tonight we have together suffered another tragedy in what has for too long now been a cycle of bloodshed and violence. I want to convey my deepest sympathy to those who have lost their loved ones in this senseless attack on innocent people. I want those responsible to know that it only deepens our resolve to find a just peace. For both sides.' It was a measure of the vision of Yossi Kaufmann that even in the middle of a personal tragedy, he could avoid the revengeful invective of previous administrations. 'I want all Israelis to know that President Ahmed Sartawi of Palestine was one of the first to call me and offer his condolences to the people of Israel.'

'How will this affect the peace process, Prime Minister?' The question came from Tom Schweiker. He had got to know and admire the Israeli statesman, but the tough questions still had to be asked.

'Two weeks ago, President Sartawi and I issued our draft peace agreement. Nothing has happened today that alters our resolve and both sides are very close to reaching agreement. This agreement allows for the establishment of a Palestinian State, and it lays out a timetable for the withdrawal of our own settlers from the Gaza Strip and the West Bank, back into Israel proper. I have already acknowledged the pain this will cause some Israelis, but it is essential that we keep our land from the agreed pre-1967 borders and the Palestinians theirs; and the relocation of the settlers will be done under a very generous taxation and incentive scheme. The agreement also specifies compensation for nearly eight hundred thousand Palestinian refugees who will be able to return to the new country of Palestine. We have established a Joint Council for the government of the Old City of Jerusalem with a guarantee of religious freedom and access, with recognition of the Israeli capital of Yerushalayim centred on the present capital in West Jerusalem and recognition of the Palestinian capital of al-Quds in East Jerusalem. We have also agreed on a timetable for pulling down a wall that, like its counterpart in Berlin, has proven to be a divisive mistake.'

Many of the journalists were mesmerised by the moment. It felt like history in the making.

Now,' Yossi said, wrapping up the interview, 'I know you will excuse me if, on this occasion, I don't take questions. I will be more than happy to do that next time.' Not one question was thrown at Prime Minister Kaufmann as he walked out of the room full of journalists, a mark of respect for a true statesman.

'Has there been any international reaction to this proposed agreement, Tom?'

'The Kaufmann/Sartawi plan is visionary, Geraldine. It is not only a peace agreement, it has a much wider context. Hundreds of millions of defence dollars will now be channelled into one of the most sweeping Middle East investment programs in history, and if they're successful in creating a stable environment both men are confident that there will be support from the international community, especially the European Union. Thousands of jobs will be created in water, transnational railways, canals, roads, de-salinisation projects, education and health. Prime Minister

Kaufmann and President Sartawi have a vision for all the Middle Eastern States to work together with membership of a consultative council that will be similar in form to the European Union. The European countries have already been very strong in their support, especially France and Germany, although the United States has been less emphatic, and seems to be reserving judgement. Most interesting is the strong support coming from the Catholic Church.'

'The Pope?'

'Not quite, but still from a very senior level, the Cardinal Patriarch of Venice, Giovanni Donelli. The word is that Cardinal Donelli has accepted an invitation to be at the peace ceremony which will be held under the Damascus Gate.'

'Professor Kaufmann is certainly showing people hope, Tom, but has anyone claimed responsibility for this latest bombing?'

'Yes, Geraldine. Hamas has been quick to issue a statement to that effect, threatening further bombings, although that may well backfire on them. Even the Palestinians seem to want Kaufmann and Sartawi to succeed.'

'Tom, thanks for joining us on *International Correspondent*. Now to the nuclear build-up in North Korea . . .'

Petroni's fury was blazing. He tried to order his swirl of thoughts and calm the beginnings of panic he hadn't felt in years. He took out his snub-nosed Beretta Cheetah and put his cheek against the soothing cool of the metal. Donelli was still very much alive, possibly the woman was as well. The remaining copy of the Omega Scroll was still out of reach, and Petroni knew that the journalist's investigation into Lonergan was gathering pace. At least the doddering old Pontiff's health was deteriorating, he mused; and if nothing else, Donelli's visit to the Middle East could be cancelled and a media release issued to the effect that Vatican protocol had not been followed. If it wasn't possible to eliminate him immediately, he would have to be kept away from the spotlight. Donelli's presence at the signing of an international peace treaty with these Muslims, Petroni thought bitterly, was the sort of international recognition that might sway a conclave. Petroni gripped the Beretta more tightly. He hated not being in control, hated it with a passion, and he was now more determined than ever to get the results he wanted.

CHAPTER FORTY-SIX

Tel-Aviv

Back in his Tel-Aviv hotel, Giorgio Felici watched a re-run of the interview between Tom Schweiker and the CCN anchor on *International Correspondent*. There was still no word on the condition of the Italian scientist. He thought back to the time he had those pert little breasts in the cross-hairs of his sniper sight. It would be a pity if she survived, but the announcement that Donelli was attending the peace ceremony had given Felici an idea. He had been wrestling with the problem of how to eliminate Cardinal Donelli and at the same time avoid getting caught up in the aftermath, and this plan might just work. If a cardinal was to die as a result of an attack on the Prime Minister of Israel, the inevitable investigation would remain focused on the death of Prime Minister Kaufmann. The death of Donelli would be dismissed as an unfortunate coincidence. Giorgio knew that Yusef Sartawi had a deep-seated hatred of the Israelis but was it enough to kill the Israeli Prime Minister, along with Donelli? Of all the countries in the world, Israel had to be one of the toughest in which to carry out an assassination.

Felici picked up his mobile and punched in the code to the Cardinal Secretary of State's secure phone, anticipating that the Cardinal would be in a black mood. He was not disappointed.

'Petroni!'

'Giorgio Felici here, Lorenzo. I have just seen the announcement that Cardinal Donelli has been invited to the signing of the Peace Treaty at the ceremony in Jerusalem,' he said, keeping the recovery of the Omega Scroll to himself.

'An invitation that he will not be keeping, Giorgio. It hasn't been approved by the Holy Father and it certainly hasn't been approved by me.' Petroni was livid and his words hissed over the phone line.

'I would suggest you allow the visit to go ahead, Lorenzo,' Giorgio replied evenly. 'It will give me an opportunity to enlist the support of those I need to meet our requirements.'

Petroni didn't answer immediately. He was in a corner and unable to do anything about it. 'Judging from the results of your efforts so far, Giorgio, I have no option,' Petroni replied acidly, and he slammed the handset on to the phone's cradle.

Giorgio smiled. Petroni would be useful as Pope, but if not, there were others on P3's list. In the meantime, he took great satisfaction from letting the ruthlessly ambitious Petroni stew for a little while longer over the whereabouts of the Omega Scroll.

David reached the third-floor ward of the vast Hadassah Hospital and knocked on the small outer office.

'For me, Dr Kaufmann. You shouldn't have!' The ward sister smiled at the handsome visitor. His head was lightly bandaged and he held a dozen roses.

David returned the smile. 'How is she?'

'Much better this morning. Still a bit shaken so we'll keep her under observation for another night but you should be able to take her home tomorrow.'

'I know it's not visiting hours but could I see her?'

'Of course.'

David followed the ward sister down the corridor. A Shin Bet security agent was sitting unobtrusively near Allegra's private room. Shades of things to come, David thought ruefully.

Allegra's face was bruised and flecked with small cuts. Her arms were heavily bandaged, as were her feet. Fortunately her wounds looked much worse than they actually were. She still managed a smile for David as she supervised him with the roses and a vase. Arranging done, he gently kissed her unscarred lips.

'David, the roses are beautiful. Even I didn't think you were that romantic,' she joked, then her mood became serious.

'How is Elie's family?' she asked. 'Is there anything we can do to help?' Allegra's heart ached for Elie, she owed him her life.

'I spoke to his wife,' David replied softly. 'She's coping as best as she can. Are you sure you still want to be part of this?'

Allegra pushed herself off the pillows and leaned towards David, taking his hand. 'If you were like those who wanted to fight violence with violence and you thought that there was no other way, I might have second thoughts. I whole-heartedly believe in the peace that you, Yossi and Ahmed are brokering. I also know that I love you very much, and I won't let you go that easily.'

David's eyes were misty as he looked at Allegra, smiling across at him. There would be time enough to tell her about the break-in at the university when she was fully recovered.

CHAPTER FORTY-SEVEN

Nablus

Yusef Sartawi struggled against the suffocating force of someone holding him down. He tried to get free and called out
twice before he woke up, soaked in sweat. Tears fell again as he
relived the massacre of his family.

Yusef looked at his watch. Four. He woke at this time most morn-
ings, and knowing that he would not get back to sleep he made some
coffee and once again pondered the capitulation of his brother to the
infidels. September 11 had shown what Islam was capable of, Allah
be praised. Now the prospect of a peace deal with the Israelis tormented his soul, but the peace deal was not the only thing that was
bothering him. He had to meet with Giorgio Felici and he was not
looking forward to it. Felici, Yusef knew, would not have taken too
kindly to the botched grab on the scroll or the survival of the scientist, but the plan for the journalist was in place and they would try for
the scientist again. Yusef had suggested they meet in a park where
it would be hard for anyone to eavesdrop, and a meeting under the
shadow of the Knesset held a nice irony.

'My clients in Rome are very unhappy about the loss of the Omega Scroll,' Felici said darkly. Now that he had the scroll, Giorgio Felici had no intention of handing over any of the Vatican's money.

Yusef's lean, tanned face and dark eyes remained inscrutable.

'And they are even more unhappy that you have so far been unable to dispose of the Italian scientist.'

'This target is not easy to hit. She is part of the Prime Minister's circle now, although our girl got very close and the scientist will not be so lucky next time.'

'And you have the journalist under surveillance?'

'His SIM card is now inside an identical phone that's packed with explosives. If it becomes necessary, the journalist can be eliminated easily.'

Giorgio Felici sniffed derisively. 'The contract on the Omega Scroll will not be paid out until you deliver, but there is a way for you to redeem yourself and an opportunity for you to secure even more funding for your cause.'

Yusef listened while Felici gave him the details of the new contract on the Italian cardinal. 'But there is a condition,' Felici warned. 'It must be carried out as part of an attack on the peace ceremony and the Israeli Prime Minister.'

Yusef did not respond immediately. Unbeknown to Giorgio Felici, Yusef had already given the assassination of Prime Minister Yossi Kaufmann a great deal of thought, including the possibility of destroying the peace ceremony, and he already had the beginnings of a plan. Up until now he had lacked the critical resources to ensure its success.

'Such a contract would be extremely difficult and very expensive,' Yusef said, knowing better than to ask why the infidels would want one of their clerics assassinated. 'Security will be very tight. The area around the Damascus Gate will be locked down tighter than Ben Gurion Airport. With the right explosive I might get a suicide bomber in past the cordon but I doubt a suicide bomber would get close enough to the main party before being brought down. Just killing a few Israeli soldiers would be a failure.'

'A light aircraft?' Felici asked.

Yusef shook his head. 'I have considered that. We have a pilot who is more than willing to avenge the death of his wife but I am keeping him for another day. The Damascus Gate target is too well guarded for that. Our aircraft could only take off from either Lebanon or Jordan. There is an air exclusion zone around Jerusalem and as soon as our man deviated from his approved flight plan the Israeli's F-16s would shoot him out of the sky.' Yusef almost spat out the words, then he paused, a thoughtful look on his face. Now that his brother had joined the infidels, if the opportunity presented itself, Yusef had decided to kill him. This plan might achieve that as well, but Yusef knew he would have to be in close, which meant that he might be killed too. He also knew that his plan would only work if he could get the right explosive, an explosive that was very hard to source. Now, Allah be praised, perhaps there was a possibility and Yusef would earn his place in heaven.

'This can still be done,' Yusef said finally, 'but it will be a very high-risk operation. There will need to be substantial compensation.'

'Of course,' Giorgio responded. 'What did you have in mind?'

'I will need at least six kilograms of Semtex.'

'Does it have to be Semtex?'

Yusef nodded. 'It's the only explosive that I would have any hope of getting in, and even then my plan will require some subterfuge,' he said, without elaborating. 'Semtex is extremely stable and it is hard to set off accidentally. It can be moulded into virtually any shape you want, which in this case will be critical. Most importantly, it is odourless so sniffer dogs can't detect it.'

'Can it be detected at all?' Giorgio asked, impressed by his

Palestinian contact's professionalism but already thinking ahead to the problems of getting explosives into Israel.

'Yes, if you bathe it in neutrons. The equipment for that is very expensive and unless the Israelis have some intelligence it is unlikely to be present, even for the peace ceremony.'

'How tightly are your plans held?'

'This particular plan is held strictly on a need-to-know basis. You have a rough outline because without you I can't get the Semtex,' Yusef responded coldly.

Giorgio Felici had only known the Palestinian through coded messages, but he felt a growing respect for the man.

'Anything else?' he asked.

'Twenty million dollars. Over and above expenses and payable in advance,' Yusef answered.

'That is a very large amount, my friend.'

'It's in keeping with a very large risk,' Yusef replied, his face expressionless. 'Hamas is no different from any other organisation. If we are to continue to fight, we need funds.'

'The Italian scientist is likely to be at the peace ceremony?' Felici asked, returning to the original target.

'In the front row,' Yusef replied. 'It is possible that we may catch her in the net as well,' he added, reading Giorgio's mind.

Before Giorgio Felici left for Rome he left a coded message for Cardinal Petroni. The Semtex would need to be provided through one of the Vatican's companies that manufactured explosives and delivered in the black bag.

Jerusalem

'A big concession,' David said as he waved to the well-wishers in the hospital foyer and escorted Allegra to the waiting government car. 'I've given Onslow the day off.'

'You said that almost wistfully,' Allegra chided him.

'Well, half a day. We'll pick him up at my place.'

'Our place!' Allegra whispered, elbowing him in the ribs.

'How do you feel? Fully recovered, I'd say,' David said, massaging his midriff.

'Raring to go. The laboratory after lunch?'

'Well, sort of,' he replied with his trademark grin.

After lunch they drove towards the Old City heading for Bishop O'Hara's.

'Where are we going?' Allegra asked, when she realised they weren't heading for Mount Scopus.

'All will be revealed,' David said with a strange look on his face.

They were met at the door by the irrepressible Sister Katherine.

'David! Allegra! Come in, come in. I'm so glad you're all right, Allegra.' The words tumbled over one another as she led them up the stairs.

'Allegra!' Patrick greeted Allegra with outstretched arms. 'We've all been worrying sick. Sister Katherine and I were coming to the hospital today but they said you were fine. It does my eyes good to see you on your feet.'

'I was very lucky, Patrick, thank you. Not my turn to go, I guess,' she added with a smile. 'Although I'm a little puzzled as to why we're here when there's so much work to do.' Allegra looked quizzically at David.

'May I, Patrick?'

'To be sure, David. It's been as safe as houses here.'

David walked over to the large painting on the wall and lifted it gently onto the floor, revealing an ancient wall safe. He dialled the combination and took out two large envelopes that Allegra recognised instantly.

'Only two?' she asked, a look of concern on her face.

'The Gospel of Thomas and the Omega Scroll.'

'I don't understand. What happened to the Isaiah Scroll?'

'The morning of the bombing I got a call from Yossi. One of his contacts in Mossad let him know that it was possible the scrolls were under surveillance at the laboratory so I enlisted Patrick's help and brought him into the loop.'

'Giovanni and I talked about the Omega Scroll often, Allegra,' said Patrick, 'and he told me about what happened to John Paul I. The fragments were never going to be safe at the university, there are just too many people who have access to the laboratories.'

'The shifty-eyed lab assistant?' Allegra asked, turning to David.

David nodded. 'Found dead in a garage in Tel-Aviv, interestingly enough, along with a CIA agent. A Mossad car was shadowing them both but was hit by a truck when it ran a red light. Whoever has the envelope with the Isaiah Scroll in it thinks they have the Omega.'

'So there is more than one group after this,' Allegra observed.

'Yes, and while any one of them thought we had it, they would be watching us like a hawk. I marked an envelope with the omega symbol but I had to have something to put in it, something that would fool them as long as possible, so I sacrificed the copy of Isaiah. We had hoped that Mossad would retrieve it, but . . . well, no security service is perfect, I guess,' he said, a note of disappointment in his voice, 'but at least the original Isaiah is still in the Shrine of the Book.'

Allegra smiled. 'Quite the conspirators, you two,' she said. 'This is probably the last place anyone would think of looking.'

'In a previous life I was one of Nebachadnezzar's spies,' Patrick said with a chuckle. 'I'd love to stay but I've got an appointment across the road,' he said, inclining his head towards the Church of the Holy Sepulchre. 'Although I'm looking forward to finding out what's in the Omega Scroll.'

'That's going to take a while, Patrick,' David said. 'Thanks for making your lounge room available.'

'It's interesting that more than one group is after this,' Allegra said after Patrick had left. 'Although I've got a fair idea who one of the groups is.'

David nodded. 'Petroni and his boys. They may still be watching us, so we'll dummy up some stuff so that it looks as if you're still working on fragments in the lab, although if they think we've no longer got the Omega, the heat will be off for a while.'

'How long will it take to put the Omega fragments together?'

'Hard to say, but now that the scrolls have been separated, our task will be a lot easier. Yossi tells me they're planning the peace ceremony for two months' time, which is still well before Lonergan gets back, so hopefully we'll be close by then.'

'Should we get the other fragments back to the vault?'

'Plenty of time. I'd rather wait until we can replace the three pieces of the Omega Scroll that were taped to the lid of the box and do it in one hit. I have a friend who restores old books and parchments. One of his skills is copying documents and making them look old. In this case very old.'

'You have some interesting friends,' Allegra said, rolling her eyes.

CHAPTER FORTY-EIGHT

Jerusalem

The media had had the story for nearly two months. The murder of Mike McKinnon had been embarrassing for both Israel and the United States, and the CIA categorically denied McKinnon had any authorisation for involvement with what was now suspected to be the theft of an Israeli antiquity. Mossad wasn't buying any of it. Eventually a compromise was reached. Provided the name of 'the man in his fifties' or his relationship with the CIA was not disclosed, an increasingly restive media would be allowed to report on the double murder in the laneway off Yehuda ha-Yamit and publicly air the speculation on the Omega Scroll that had been swirling around Jerusalem and Tel-Aviv for weeks. Four billion dollars worth of defence equipment bought a certain amount of cooperation, even from the Israelis. The first report appeared on the front page of the *Jerusalem Post*, alongside a report on Pope John Paul II's throat surgery and his deteriorating condition.

Hunt for the Omega Scroll Goes On

Tel-Aviv police are baffled by a robbery at the Hebrew University several weeks ago, and a subsequent double murder in a laneway off Yehuda ha-Yamit, the police officer in charge of the case, Chief Inspector Amos Raviv, admitted today. In a daring raid on one of the university's laboratories, a suspected Hamas operative driving a van carrying the signage of a local security company stole a safe pretending to collect it for repair. The driver of the van was found shot dead in a garage near the Old Yafo Port area along with another male, believed to be in his fifties, whose name has not been released.

'At this stage we still have no idea what interest Hamas might have had in the safe,' Inspector Raviv said, acknowledging there were rumours that it might have contained the Omega Scroll.

The Hebrew University has dismissed the rumours as speculative nonsense.

'To the best of our knowledge the safe was empty,' a spokesman for the Hebrew University said, denying that the university had any involvement with the Omega Scroll.

The Rockefeller Museum has refused to comment.

'We have no significant leads at present and we are appealing to anyone who may have seen anything to come forward,' Chief Inspector Raviv said. – Associated Press

The Director of the Rockefeller's 'refusal to comment' had focused the media's attention on what the museum might be hiding and a worried Jean-Pierre La Franci telephoned Cardinal Petroni with the news.

'We are getting calls here as well, Eminence, and unless someone says something, this is not going to die.'

'Leave it with me,' Petroni said icily. Lonergan had been away long enough, he decided. It was time the fat academic stopped swanning around the world and got back to doing what he was paid to do, protecting the Church's interests. Petroni buzzed his private secretary.

'Eminence?' answered Father Thomas.

'Do we know where Monsignor Lonergan is?'

'Somewhere in Europe on a lecture tour, Eminence. Possibly Florence.'

'Possibly is not good enough, Father Thomas. Find out and place a call.' The Cardinal Secretary of State switched off his intercom with an irritated flick.

Firenze

At Il Museo Archeologico in the Italian city of Florence, Derek Lonergan brought his lecture on the Dead Sea Scrolls to its conclusion.

'I reiterate, there is not a shadow of doubt,' he said, raising his chin and almost closing his eyes, 'that the Dead Sea Scrolls are dated two hundred years before the birth of Christ.'

The 'crowd' of eighteen people applauded politely, and one by one they made their excuses, leaving Monsignor Lonergan in the hands of the museum's hapless director, who eventually managed to put him in a taxi and send him in the direction of his hotel on the banks of the Arno, facing the Ponte Vecchio.

'A triple scotch, barman. My vocal chords need oiling,' Lonergan said as he sat on a bar stool, belching loudly.

More than one eyebrow was raised among the occupants of the white lounge chairs scattered around the elegant surrounds of the Hotel Lungarno's main bar.

'*Certamente, Signor,*' the barman replied. 'You are a singer?' he asked with a smile, his English pronunciation less than perfect but streets ahead of Lonergan's Italian.

'Good God, man. Are you all mad over here? I have been lec-turing to a very large and appreciative audience on the mysteries of the Dead Sea Scrolls. You've heard of the Lonergan Lectures? They're quite famous.'

'Ah! Monsignor Lonergan.'

'The very same.'

'There is a message for you.'

It did not occur to Derek Lonergan that the barman's recognition might be due solely to the name written on the phone message which said, 'Urgent you return to Jerusalem immediately. La Franci.'

'*Lei è va bene, Signor?*' the barman asked, a concerned look on his face.

CHAPTER FORTY-NINE

Jerusalem

The day of the peace ceremony had dawned fine and warm, and Cohatek's chief sound engineer had spent the day supervising the preparations. It was late afternoon and Yusef leaned against one of the scaffoldings and looked around the sanitised Damascus Gate, now sealed off by the Israeli Army, minus the usual tanks and armoured vehicles. Much to the chagrin of some in the military, the Prime Minister had directed that 'all life was to be respected' and a new policy of absolute minimum force had been applied.

Despite this, not everyone was in favour of the peace agreement and the minimal presence was still visible. Every chair, table, box of equipment and even the outdoor toilets had been subjected to rigorous searches by hundreds of ordinary soldiers, bomb squads and sniffer dogs. Banks of magnetometers had been set up at all of the entrances and young Israeli soldiers guarded the checkpoints nervously. All but the prime ministerial parties and cleared VIPs would have to pass through these if they wanted to watch the ceremony. Lengthy queues were already forming.

Even with all those defences in place Yusef knew that a determined attack could still succeed and he nodded to the young Palestinian who had been put on the payroll. The false papers had passed scrutiny and Yusef watched as the young man slid behind the wheel of the forklift. Suddenly the forklift lurched backwards into the speaker's lectern, the one with the specially constructed motifs on the front. The grinding crunch caught the attention of everyone in the area and Yusef rushed over to the hapless driver, shaking his fist.

'You stupid fucking idiot!' he swore. 'Look what you've done!' Yusef stared at the shattered remains of the lectern with a look of despair on his face. He was quickly joined by two Israeli officers, one of them Brigadier General Avrahim Mishal, the man tasked with the security for the peace ceremony.

'Do you have another one?' General Mishal asked.

'Yes, but we don't have much time. At least these haven't been damaged,' Yusef replied, running his hands over the symbols of Israel and Palestine. 'Would it be possible to provide an escort, General?' he asked. 'Our warehouse is in West Jerusalem and I'm not sure we'll get a replacement through the traffic in time.'

Brigadier General Mishal spoke to the young captain at his side. 'Get this man a truck and an escort and get the replacement back here as soon as you can.'

An hour later Yusef watched as the soldiers at the checkpoint on Nablus Road stopped the Israeli Army truck with the replacement lectern strapped in the back. A short conversation followed between the captain in the front of the truck and the soldier manning the checkpoint and the truck was waved through.

It took Yusef twenty minutes to re-attach the national symbols and re-wire a new microphone to the system on the podium under the Damascus Gate. His voice boomed over the Old City of Jerusalem.

'Testing . . . testing . . . testing . . .' Satisfied, he switched the microphone off.

'Everything OK?' General Mishal asked, coming over from where he had been standing watching the crowd fill the area in front of the ancient gate.

'Fine, thank you, and thank you for the escort. I don't think we could have got the replacement here without it,' Yusef replied.

'Happy to help,' General Mishal said with a smile.

Deciphering the Omega Scroll had taken two painstaking months, and now there were only ten pieces left. On the afternoon of the peace ceremony David and Allegra packed up their finery for the evening and headed over to Patrick's.

'Did you see the article in the *Jerusalem Post* on the safe murder a couple of days ago?' Patrick asked. 'Odd that it's taken this long to reach the press.'

'It probably had something to do with the American man. Tom tells me he was a CIA agent, and there was a suppression order on the media, which makes it all murkier still.'

'It's a pretty vague article,' Allegra said. 'They've yet to identify him, and after what happened to John Paul I, I wouldn't be surprised if the Vatican's gorillas have something to do with it.'

'Trouble is it's stirred up another bucket load of media interest in the Omega Scroll, so I hope whoever thinks they've grabbed it doesn't look too closely at what they've got,' David said, easing another fragment into place. Just four more to go. Already the messages on the Magdalene Numbers and DNA were very clear. The warning was almost complete.

'And two revelations will ridicule a third,' he said, translating the Koiné, 'though the revelations be from Abraham, all of them.'

'It's beginning to look like Yossi was right about the clash of civilisations,' Patrick observed sombrely. 'It's nearly half past six though, perhaps we'd better be leaving this for tomorrow.'

'Yes,' David said reluctantly. 'By the time we walk down there and get through security the orchestra will be well and truly warmed up. This has waited two thousand years, it can wait another day.'

David's mobile rang and he picked it up from the table.

'David Kaufmann.'

Allegra knew instinctively that something was not quite right and she waited anxiously for him to hang up.

'That was Hafiz,' David said, his mind racing. 'He's just got a message to say that Lonergan is due in from Europe later tonight. He's going to the museum straight from the airport and the Director is meeting him at nine. Hafiz has been told to stay on duty in case he's needed.'

'He's not due back for another month!'

'He's supposed to be speaking to the London Archaeological Society next week. Lonergan wouldn't be missing a gig like that for the world,' Patrick observed.

'Not to mention working after hours. He's normally at the bar by five,' Allegra said, realising that time was running out.

'It can only mean one thing,' David said. 'Someone's ordered him back, and I'll wager it's because of that article on the Omega Scroll.'

'Lonergan will be worried that the fragments might have come from his trunk and if he's going straight to the museum he'll be wanting to check it before he meets with the Director,' Allegra said.

'You're right, I wish I'd put the Gospel of Thomas back when we got the three duplicates of the Omega fragments. A bit late now,' David reflected ruefully, 'but we can't afford to take the risk. I'll have to get the fragments of the Gospel of Thomas back into the vault now. Hopefully Lonergan won't search his trunk too closely.'

'What about the ceremony, David. We'll miss it!'

'You go with Patrick, I'll join you both later.'

'No you don't, I'm coming with you. If we get to the vault in time, maybe we can still catch some of the ceremony later.'

'What about the external security patrols?' Allegra asked as they drove into the museum car park.

'We'll have to chance it,' David said.

Allegra's heart sank as the security patrol car drew into the car park behind them.

Roma

Cardinal Petroni flicked the television on. Two items were dominating the world's media: the Pope's failing health and the peace ceremony in Jerusalem. Petroni watched as the network recapped the events of the last month, showing a clip of the ambulance carrying the ailing Pontiff arriving at Rome's Gemelli Clinic. The Pontiff waved feebly from his stretcher and Petroni sniffed derisively. When the Pope's breathing had worsened, necessitating a tracheotomy, Petroni had approved the Vatican's media releases that were designed to reassure the faithful. Now, in the Papal apartments directly above, the old Pope had suffered a heart attack and his kidneys were failing. Petroni had been angered when the Papal Physician had kept the true state of the Pope's health to himself, but now the Pope's condition was terminal and he had perhaps forty-eight hours left. Petroni allowed himself a smile of satisfaction. Given his legendary stubbornness, the Pontiff might hang on for a little longer, but seeking his resignation would not be necessary. Petroni had instructed a reluctant media office to prepare a media release 'should he be called by the Lord' and that was now ready for signature. Petroni leaned forward in his chair as the scenes of the lights in the Papal apartment windows faded, to be replaced with the Golden Cupola of the Dome of the Rock.

CCN, along with the world's media, were covering the momentous peace ceremony in Jerusalem. The international journalists had been allocated an area on top of the old Wall, off to one side, and Tom Schweiker was giving a background brief on the lead up to the signing and the hope it held for the future. Not for you, Petroni mused. A contact in Washington had let him know that Schweiker's investigation into Lonergan's past had reached as far as the FBI and Petroni had told Felici to execute the next level. That would be done at the same time as the assassination of Donelli.

Jerusalem

Cameras, from which the feed was being pooled, were positioned at several points near the front of the podium. President Ahmed Sartawi would speak for the new State of Palestine, and as a cleric, he would also speak of the way ahead for Muslims in Palestine, supported by the presence of the Imam of Jerusalem on the dais. Prime Minister Yossi Kaufmann would speak for the State of Israel, and as a devout Jew, he would speak to the Jewish faith, supported by the presence of the Chief Rabbi of Jerusalem. Cardinal Giovanni Donelli, the Patriarch of Venice, would add the support of Christianity, the third great faith of Abraham. Giovanni would speak first, followed by Ahmed and then Yossi. Three leaders, three statesmen, three men of vision. Once the speeches were over, they would move to the table beside the lectern where the Prime Minister of Israel and the President of Palestine would sign the agreements handed to them by Giovanni.

Under the direction of the internationally renowned Israeli conductor Levi Meyer, the Peace Philharmonic Orchestra and Choir had been assembled in Jerusalem. The one hundred and forty piece orchestra boasted some of the best musicians, Jewish, Muslim and Christian, ever assembled in the history of music.

Marian was escorted to her seat beside the one reserved for Yossi on the official podium. The Peace Philharmonic, with the three hundred member choir behind, was seated 9 metres above her on a platform that had been constructed around the stone battlements of the Damascus Gate. Levi Meyer lifted his baton and the powerful light beams picked out the diminutive Israeli on his conductor's podium. On Petroni's television screen, the cameras panned in for a close-up of Levi, a light breeze ruffling his silver-grey hair, a look of concentration on his face. The cameras pulled back for a wide shot of the orchestra and choir. Like their conductor, the members of the orchestra were dressed in white dinner jackets and evening gowns, symbolic of peace. Behind them were the colours of the choir: on the left, a third of the choir were cassocked in the soft blue of the Israeli Star of David; on the right, brilliant green represented the universal colour of Islam; and between the two was the white of Christianity. The choir represented hope, peace and tolerance – the message of the great Prophets of history.

The sweeping strains of Beethoven's Choral Mass in C Major reached into the darkness of the night, across the Valley of Kidron to the Mount of Olives, echoing around the souks and alleys of the Old City, and across the parks and gardens of the New City. The music floated across Golgotha where Christ had spent his last hours, bounced against the Western Wall of Nehemiah's great second temple that had refused to succumb to the Romans, and splashed across the great Dome of the Rock where Muhammad had made his ascent to heaven.

Cardinal Donelli walked to his seat on the podium, his scarlet robes rustling in the breeze. He winked at Marian as he took his place beside her. She looked relaxed, calm and beautiful in the history of the moment.

Roma

'Petroni!' The irritation in the Cardinal Secretary of State's voice was strident as he answered the buzz from his secretary.

'I know you don't wish to be disturbed, Eminence, but Ashton Lewis from the State Department in Washington is on line one. He said it was urgent.' The long-suffering Father Thomas sounded nervous. Urgent messages from Knight Commanders of Malta were not to be ignored.

Cardinal Petroni snapped off the intercom without replying and composed himself.

'Ashton, good to hear your voice. How can I help?' Petroni asked, keeping his eye on the coverage of events in Jerusalem.

'I thought you ought to know, Lorenzo, that the Administration is treating the peace process in Jerusalem with some caution. Kaufmann has made far too many concessions to the Muslims, and the Jewish lobby here is outraged at the support for the removal of the settlers, especially from the West Bank. The next election is still a long way out, but a lot of the Republican senators are nervous.'

As Cardinal Petroni listened, his agile mind formulated a plan.

'I agree completely, Ashton, the Muslims can't be allowed to gain the upper hand and I'm much obliged. When are you coming to Rome? We must have dinner.'

Cardinal Petroni put the phone down and got up from behind his desk, deep in thought. Ever since that impostor Muhammad had tried to usurp the role of Christ in the world and proclaimed himself the messenger of God, the evil followers of Islam had tried to extinguish the one true Faith. Now they were trying it again and the peace process in Jerusalem was a clear danger. In reality it was an accommodation with Islam that must never be allowed to gather strength. His mind made up, Petroni punched the pre-programmed number for the Knight Commander of Malta in the CCN studios in New York.

'Daniel, it's Lorenzo. How are you?'

'I'm fine, Lorenzo, although we are all praying for Il Papa. It sounds very serious?'

'I'm afraid so, Daniel. He has been a wonderful leader and he will be very hard to replace. The good fight must go on though, which is the real purpose for this call. This peace process in Jerusalem has us all very worried here.'

'I couldn't agree more, Lorenzo. We seem to be making a lot of concessions to the evil of Islam.'

Ten minutes later Petroni was confident the story would get a run. Anything that kept the Muslims and the Jews at each other's throats could only be to the benefit of the one true path. Satisfied, he sat back to watch the progress of his intervention in the ceremony. Petroni was back in control, or so he thought.

Jerusalem

Marian looked at her watch, less relaxed now. 'I wonder what's keeping David and Allegra,' she whispered to Giovanni.

'They'll be here,' he whispered back. 'Patrick told me they had some very urgent business to attend to, but they'd be back as soon as they could. The music is telling you not to worry,' he added reassuringly.

'Isn't it magnificent.'

Giovanni smiled. 'God knew what He was doing when He gave Levi Meyer a baton,' he said, as the voice of one of the world's truly great sopranos, Michelle Ortega, carried clearly over the Damascus Gate. As the orchestra and the choir reached their finale, and to a growing applause from those seated, as well as from the thousands crowded into Nablus Road, Prime Minister Yossi Kaufmann and President Ahmed Sartawi came in from the Old City side of the Damascus Gate. They walked side by side towards their seats on the podium.

'In the one hundred and fifty thousand years or so that we have inhabited this planet,' Giovanni began when the applause had died down, 'we have fought and killed each other, only to have one war finish and another one begin. Sometimes it seems that we have not taken the slightest notice of the lessons of history, but I am here tonight to tell you that there are two great leaders behind me who understand the futility of killing your brother or sister.'

Yusef shivered as he fingered the small transmitter hidden in his pocket. From the shadows of the control marquee next to the podium that was located to one side of the Damascus Gate, he stared at the brother he no longer knew. The two had not spoken since that fateful day they had buried their family.

'Too often these wars have been fought in the name of religion and culture,' Giovanni said. 'As a Christian I can tell you that is not what Christ had in mind. He didn't believe that one man's faith and culture is better than another's and that we should all fight to the death to prove it. The Prophet Muhammad was also a man of great tolerance and justice,' Giovanni continued. 'He is credited with saying "if you wish for others what you wish for yourself, you become a Muslim", which has given rise to the Golden Rule. Sadly though, the Muslim is often portrayed in the media as a terrorist or a fanatic. I have come to know the true Muslim as a man and woman of peace and prayer. I have also had the privilege of meeting many marvellous men and women of the Jewish faith, a faith that alongside Islam and Christianity shares the one father, Abraham. So often we seem to behave like a bad family, arguing over his will, over what we think belongs to us. There are some within the Jewish religion who claim Abraham for their own, maintaining that God's blessings and the land are only for the Jewish people. There are some Muslims who claim Abraham as the model for Islam alone; and there are some of my own faith who would claim that the promises given to Abraham have only ever been fulfilled by Christ.' Giovanni smiled. 'Abraham is entitled to be a little confused.' Laughter reverberated off the ancient walls. 'Like all good fathers, Abraham has been all of those things to all his children. It would be a very strange God who, having created a Muslim child in Baghdad, or a Christian child in Bogotá, or a Jewish child in Berlin, would then turn around and close the gates of the Kingdom to two thirds of those children because they were not born into the correct culture.' Giovanni was being characteristically bold in his quest for greater peace and tolerance. This comment, he knew, would be greeted with quiet fury in the Vatican, but it was a stunning public admission from a cardinal that there was more than one path to the Omega, to eternity.

Yusef Sartawi listened. He was sceptical, but he was also touched by this man. Yusef felt the safety catch for the hundredth time, instinctively trusting this Christian priest, which made it more puzzling as to why the infidel would want him assassinated.

'I know,' Giovanni concluded, 'that Abraham, Muhammad and Christ would all applaud this peace agreement as a turning point in the history of civilisation. A turning away from the killing and the bloodshed, a turning towards tolerance and recognition of the values of different cultures and religions. A move towards justice and peace.' As the lights shone on the smiling Italian cardinal, the crowd rose to their feet in a standing ovation.

The tension in the CCN news room in New York was rising.

'We can't run that, Daniel! It will derail the peace process before it even gets off the ground,' Geraldine argued passionately. She glared at the Head of News and wondered how such a detestable little man managed to be so well informed.

'It may have escaped your notice, Ms Rushmore, but you do not decide what goes to air at this station. I do,' he said icily, his eyes more piercing than usual. 'The public has a right to know and we will run it. Now. Does Schweiker have the copy?' he asked, turning to his secretary. She nodded, alarmed at the ferocity of the meeting. In Jerusalem President Ahmed Sartawi was beginning his address.

'I am indebted to the vision and wisdom of His Eminence Cardinal Giovanni Donelli and to that of my friend, Prime Minister Kaufmann,' Ahmed began.

Yusef watched as his brother endorsed the sentiment of peaceful co-existence as the only alternative to the killing. His brother urged the West to get behind Yossi Kaufmann's broad-sweeping vision and to provide the support and investment for a Middle Eastern Economic Union. This and Giovanni's words on the futility of killing your brother brought back a long-forgotten memory, a memory of picking olives and of dreams for the future. Torn and confused, Yusef took his hand out of his pocket.

'For Palestine and Palestinians,' Ahmed concluded, 'it will mean equality and justice. Palestine will be a country that is characterised by neither a godless secularism, or a fanatical adherence to religion, but one that is based on justice and freedom of choice. I would remind those who might seek to impose their will to the exclusion of any other,' he said, in a clear warning to those at the militant end of the spectrum, 'that in countries where extremists have sought to impose their will, the results for Islam have been catastrophic. I am reminded of what the Great Prophet Muhammed, peace be upon Him, had to say about violence. For those of you who might not be familiar with it, let me quote from the Qu'ran:

> Do not argue with the followers of earlier revelation otherwise than in a most kindly manner – unless it be such of them as are bent on evildoing – and say: 'We believe in that which has been bestowed on high upon us, as well as that which has been bestowed upon you; for our God and your God is one and the same, and it is unto Him that we all surrender ourselves.

As the applause died down, Prime Minister Yossi Kaufmann rose to speak.

'I have shared a great friendship with Cardinal Donelli, over many years, and I am indebted to him for his leadership, his insight and his wisdom. I am also indebted to my friend and neighbour, President Ahmed Sartawi, for his leadership and patience during these past few weeks. It reminds me of a day some years ago when the three of us went fishing, and Cardinal Donelli, who was then a priest in the little village of Mar'Oth, remarked that there was a Christian, a Jew and a Muslim on a small boat and the only ones in danger were the fish.'

As Yossi's speech gathered pace, the crowd caught the mood and the message that finally there might be a real opportunity for peace. 'I am also reminded of the words of another Israeli, Prime Minister Golda Meir,' Yossi continued. 'Some fifty years ago, on the night the United Nations approved the new State of Israel, she was a minister in David Ben Gurion's first Cabinet. Not very far from here she addressed a crowd not dissimilar to the one we have tonight and she said, "It is not all that you wanted. And it is not all that we wanted, but let us go forward in a spirit of compromise and peace." Back then, as we do tonight, Israelis and Palestinians faced a stark choice. The choice of recognising the strengths and achievements of both cultures and the right to exist peacefully as good neighbours, or a decision to continue killing our children and our families. Sadly, back then, we all went to war and we have been killing each other ever since. Tonight we choose peace.'

Yusef Sartawi listened to the tall, distinguished Israeli and he was struck by the integrity of this prime minister. He wondered whether this time the Israelis and their US backers might mean what they said; perhaps this time there might be a chance for Palestinians to lead normal lives. Maybe after all these years of hating the Israelis, he could begin to let go and forgive. Maybe Ahmed had been right after all to adopt a peaceful path. He turned, and saw that the coverage on the Arab Channel on the banks of televisions in the control room was being interrupted by a live telecast from CCN.

'Even before the peace agreement has been signed in Jerusalem tonight, and as the ceremony behind me continues, pressure is mounting on the White House to step back from the commitment to support the removal of the Jewish settlers from what, at least in name, is now the country of Palestine.'

Yusef watched, his anger rising as Tom Schweiker's authoritative delivery was dubbed in Arabic and subtitles rolled across the bottom of the screen.

'The Jewish lobby,' Tom continued, 'has objected to any American tax payers' dollars being used for Arab development and has called for the United States to continue to provide the billions of dollars Israel is seeking to spend on American arms and military equipment to fight Palestinian militants in the West Bank and the Gaza Strip. A spokesman for the White House has said the US Government is committed to a just peace in the Middle East, but has refused to comment on the provision of the large amount of military aid requested by Israel.'

'What about the Jewish settlers, Tom?' Geraldine asked, reading from the script Daniel had given her.

'There are reports, Geraldine,' Tom replied, quoting his News Director's sources, 'that the White House is under fire from the strong Jewish lobby and the Christian right in the United States to pressure the Israeli Government into allowing the settlers to continue living on Palestinian land, especially those in the West Bank.'

'Wouldn't that derail the peace agreement, Tom?'

'In all likelihood, yes. It would mean a Palestinian State in name only. In reality, the country of Palestine would consist of a series of isolated Palestinian towns and cantonments overlaid with dozens of Jewish settlements and roads.'

'And the investment for the region?'

'Despite the support from European countries, the United States has yet to indicate it will provide any funding, but analysts here are suggesting that unless the United States provides strong support for the Kaufmann/Sartawi Peace Plan, resentment against the West will simply resurface.'

'Tom, thanks for joining us. We now return to our live coverage of the peace ceremony.'

Yusef Sartawi looked at the Israeli Prime Minister who was coming to the end of his speech and his hatred for the infidels and his brother's treachery reignited.

'This is a new beginning,' Yossi said, 'but it is only the beginning. Neither I nor President Sartawi underestimate the difficulties of the road ahead. There will be disagreements. When we negotiated the terms of this agreement there were some on our side who maintained that we'd given up too much. There were others on President Sartawi's side who believed Israel had not given up enough. The choice is clear. For there to be an equitable peace there has to be compromise on both sides.'

Deafened by his rage, Yusef didn't hear any of it. He didn't see his brother sitting between Marian and Giovanni. All he saw was a president who had sold out to the infidels who had demonstrated their treachery yet again. For once Yusef's calculating calm was overcome with emotion. He forgot to dial the encryption on Tom Schweiker's mobile and he didn't wait for the three targets to gather at the table. He raised his fist defiantly.

'Allah be praised,' he shouted, pushing the button on the transmitter. Yusef Sartawi died convinced of his place in heaven.

The production crew in CCN watched in shock and disbelief as an apocalyptic blast engulfed the official dais. Body parts and chairs were thrown into the air. The colours of the orchestra and choir were scattered across the back of the dais as metal and glass rained down on what was left of the audience. After the massive boom of the explosion the eerie silence of death fell over the gathering, and only the sound of spot fires and sparking electrical equipment could be heard. Then the crying and calls for help started – children sobbed, people called on their God for mercy. People horrifically burnt and injured dragged themselves upright

and were starting to run, panicking, trying to escape the scene of
devastation. Bodies were trodden underfoot as the chilling cry
of wounded humanity was pierced by the shrill wailing of sirens.
Convoys of ambulances were racing towards the carnage at the
Damascus Gate. The Semtex and the five thousand ball bearings
hidden in the panels of the lectern had created total devastation.

Cardinal Petroni watched dispassionately as the cameras took in
what looked like a battlefield. He was searching for evidence that
Donelli and Bassetti were dead. The cameras captured the fran-
tic ambulance crews working desperately around the official dais.
One of the crews raced a stretcher to the ambulance and Petroni
saw the blood-spattered form of Donelli. He smiled thinly until
there was a movement on the stretcher. Donelli was obviously not
dead yet and Petroni's smile was replaced by a seething snarl.

The news commentators were speechless as the grinding of
metal on cobblestones signalled the arrival of lumbering tanks.
The air was filled with the menacing sounds of combat helicopters. After so many years of practice the Israeli Command swung
immediately into gear.

'Good evening, Hafiz,' David had said earlier as the old security
guard got out of his car.

'Oh it's you, Dr Kaufmann. Evening Dr Bassetti,' he said,
tipping his cap.

'Evening Hafiz,' Allegra said, keeping her voice steady.

'Would you like to look in the briefcase?' David asked.

Allegra stifled a gasp. Had he gone mad?

'We could be taking those biros and paperclips back in you
know!' David grinned at Hafiz mischievously.

'No, that'll be all right, Dr Kaufmann. Sorry to bother you,
but we have to know who's here. I thought you would be at the
ceremony.'

'We're on our way, Hafiz. I just need to get something from the office,' David replied easily.

'A chance for peace at last. I can hardly believe it,' the old Palestinian said with a warm smile, returning to his car.

'I thought you'd taken leave of your senses back there,' Allegra said as they made their way to the vault.

'Fortune favours the brave,' David replied, draping the black cloth over the security camera. He got down from the ledge under the camera and made his way towards the vault doors.

Less than an hour later, the fragments of the Gospel of Thomas were safely back in the old olive wood box on top of some fragments of paper that David had added for bulk.

Mission accomplished, David and Allegra emerged from the depths of the museum but they knew immediately that something was dreadfully wrong. The sky was filled with helicopters, the blat blat blat of the rotors shattering the night. A pall of smoke hung over the Damascus Gate and a cacophony of sirens reverberated around the city.

'David, no!' Allegra held her hand to her mouth.

'Come on,' he said quietly.

The soldier at the checkpoint brandished his rifle and David brought Onslow to a halt.

'You can't . . .' The soldier recognised David and he pulled up short. 'I'm sorry, Sir, there's been a bomb explosion at the ceremony.'

'Any word on casualties?'

The soldier shook his head.

David swerved Onslow away from the roadblock and headed towards the Hadassah Hospital, getting behind a speeding ambulance.

As they pulled in to the hospital, the ambulance in front of them screeched to a halt. Two orderlies jumped out and two more ran to meet them. The young girl on the stretcher was not yet in her teens.

Her head was covered in a bloodied bandage but the blood was seeping onto her face that was now very pale as her life ebbed away. The overstretched doctors on duty would do what they could, but they would be too late to save many of those now arriving in a never-ending stream.

Through the chaos, David and Allegra were finally greeted by a duty sister.

'Oh, Dr Kaufmann, I didn't see you there. Sorry to keep you waiting.'

'That's all right,' David replied gently. 'Are my parents here? Is there any word?'

'One moment, Dr Kaufmann, I'll get the medical superintendent.'

Allegra took David's hand. They both knew that the old sister would only have summoned the superintendent at a time like this if the news was bad. The medical superintendent appeared and took David and Allegra down the corridor to a private waiting room.

Lorenzo Petroni was still glued to CCN's live coverage. Tom Schweiker appeared on-screen and Petroni moved forward in his seat. Giorgio Felici had obviously failed to eliminate the journalist, but for the moment he was more interested in the fate of Donelli and Bassetti.

'A shocking tragedy, Geraldine. Violence has once again taken the place of peace.'

'And the casualties?'

'All the government spokespeople will say is that Prime Minister Kaufmann and his wife Marian are in surgery, and that doctors are fighting to save them. The Palestinian President Ahmed Sartawi is believed to be in a serious but stable condition. He is also in the hospital here at Ein Karem, as is Cardinal Donelli.'

'Any word on Cardinal Donelli's condition, Tom?'

'Remarkably his injuries are reported to be not serious and he has been listed as satisfactory. He was furthest away when the bomb went off. The explosives are believed to have been hidden in a lectern which was replaced shortly before the ceremony began. The Israeli Prime Minister was at the lectern when the bomb was detonated.'

'No one has claimed responsibility?'

'None of the terrorist groups have yet claimed responsibility, although my contacts here tell me the Israelis are now focusing on the brother of the Palestinian President, Yusef Sartawi. He worked for Cohatek, the company responsible for providing the logistics and sound for the ceremony. He died in the blast so we may never know the extent of his involvement.'

Cardinal Petroni snapped off the television, his lips set in a hard, colourless line. Giorgio Felici had set the contract at twenty-five million dollars, payable in advance, which Petroni had disguised as a Vatican Bank South American Aid Budget, and there was still nothing to show for it. Giorgio Felici had a lot of explaining to do.

CHAPTER FIFTY

Roma

'*Avanti!*'

'The media release, Eminence.' Monsignor Servini, the Head of the Vatican Press Office, handed the momentous release to Cardinal Petroni. The world waited while Petroni checked every word:

> The Holy Father died at 9.37 this evening in his private apartment . . .
> A 8 p.m. the celebration of Mass for Divine Mercy Sunday began in the Holy Father's room, presided by . . .
> The Holy Father's final hours were marked by the uninterrupted prayer of all those who were assisting him in his pious death . . .

Lorenzo Petroni checked the release for accuracy and effect before he handed it back to the visibly distraught Monsignor Servini.

'Release it,' was all Petroni said, and he leaned back in his chair, contemplating the future with a degree of anticipation. Even after several meetings, some of the Curial Cardinals led by the elderly but immoveable Cardinal Castiglione were yet to be convinced of the need for the Pope to resign. Petroni had appealed to them on several grounds, including the obligation to put the good of the Holy Church above all else and the need to allow the Holy Father some peace in his declining health, but it had been to no avail. Even Petroni's none-too-subtle reminder of the immense harm that could be done to a rudderless Church if a Pontiff were to slip into a coma had not been enough to shift Castiglione. Petroni sniffed the air with satisfaction. The votes of Castiglione and the rest of his knitting group would not be necessary. The stubborn old Pope was dead at last.

Petroni buzzed Father Thomas as soon as Monsignor Servini had left.

'You may start the calls in the order of the list I gave you.'

'Certainly, Eminence.'

A short while later the red telephone on Petroni's desk buzzed quietly.

'Cardinal Fritsch in Berlin, Eminence.'

'Hans! *Wie gehts?*' Petroni asked, using the Cardinal Archbishop of Berlin's native tongue more out of flattery than courtesy. '*Zehr gut. Zehr gut!* The news here is not so good, Hans. Although not unexpected, this will still come as a shock, as it has to all of us here, but I wanted to call you personally before the news is released. The Holy Father passed away less than an hour ago at 9.37 our time . . .'

One by one Cardinal Petroni ticked off the names of the Church's 194 cardinals from the list on his desk. One by one they were personally informed of the Secretary of State's great sadness at the Pope's passing. The last call was to Daniel Kirkpatrick.

'Kirkpatrick.'

'Lorenzo.'

'It's a very sad day here, Daniel. Your coverage has had just the right touch and I wanted to thank you personally. As has your coverage of the bombing in Jerusalem,' Pentroni added, under-lining the real reason for his call.

'Thank you, Lorenzo, you're very kind to call at such a sad time. Il Papa will be greatly missed, which is more than I can say for some of those Arabs in Jerusalem. Never trust an Arab, especially a Muslim.'

'I agree entirely, Daniel, they run with the devil.'

'Although Cardinal Donelli seemed fully supportive,' Daniel Kirkpatrick responded, puzzled as to why such a senior member of the one true faith would side with the religion of terrorists.

'Another reason for my call, Daniel.'

A few minutes later Cardinal Petroni replaced the receiver. As he had been for the story on the peace ceremony, Petroni was confident the damaging story on Donelli would also get a run. Given Donelli's statements from Jerusalem, the story would seem quite plausible, even if it were subsequently found not to be true. Timing was everything and the information would be released just before all the cardinals were locked in the conclave to ensure any of those loyal to Donelli would not have time to offer anything by way of rebuttal. Petroni smiled. He could almost feel the Keys to Peter in his pocket.

Jerusalem

Geraldine headed back towards the news room and dialled the new mobile number she'd been given for Tom.

'New number, Tom?'

'The old one's playing up,' he said, not mentioning that the tech-nician who had examined his mobile had found it loaded with Semtex.

'We're going to kick off with the usual backgrounder,' she said, 'then we'll cross to you.' The pair ran through the standard bulletin preamble and five minutes later Geraldine was on air with Tom keeping ten million viewers up to date on the bomb blast.

'Welcome back to our live coverage of the latest bombing in Jerusalem,' Geraldine began. 'Shortly we'll be crossing to our correspondent Tom Schweiker for what we understand will be a major announcement.'

The four most senior members of the new Liberal Justice Party, including the Party's elder statesman and Deputy Prime Minister, Gideon Wiesel, filed in to the medical superintendent's office in a sombre mood and one by one they offered their condolences. Gideon looked first at his colleagues and then at David.

'I hope you don't mind, David, but we have had an informal meeting and we have a proposal to put to you.' His old eyes reflected a mixture of sadness at what had happened and hope for the future.

David nodded.

'It falls to me, for the moment, to take over the prime ministership. The opposition parties are prepared to support that and will not insist that the government resign, and for the time being that will provide some stability. I agreed with everything your father stood for, but I am an old man and more accustomed to working behind the scenes than in front of the lights and cameras. We have scheduled a meeting one month from now which will allow an appropriate period for memorials and reflection, but it is our intention to put one name forward for election to replace your father as Prime Minister of Israel. Judging from the responses from those we have had a chance to talk to, it will be unanimous.'

After the delegation had left them alone in the medical superintendent's office Allegra put her arms around David and held him for what seemed like a very long time. David quietly wept on her shoulder.

'I'm going to miss them so much,' he whispered.

Allegra wiped his eyes, and David smiled grimly. 'Thank you,' he said. 'You do realise that your life is never going to be the same again.'

'I'm with you all the way, David. I've never been more sure of anything in my life,' she said, her own eyes misty with tears.

'Well, the media awaits. Something that I'm afraid we'll both have to get used to.'

Dr David Kaufmann and Dr Allegra Bassetti took their place beside Gideon Wiesel in front of the huge media contingent outside the hospital's main entrance. It was David who spoke first, a significant moment not lost on the Israeli nation.

'It is with great sadness that I announce the death of my father, the Prime Minister of Israel, Professor Yossi Kaufmann, and my mother, Marian, his wife of forty-three years,' David said, pausing to regain his composure.

'I have lost a great father and a wonderful mother,' he said, 'and Israel has lost two of her most distinguished citizens. After an appropriate period the members of the Liberal Justice Party will meet to elect a new leader of this great nation. This is not the time for political statements, but it will be known soon enough, so I would rather you hear it from me. I have been asked to stand and I have indicated that I will. I am humbled and honoured by the faith, trust and sympathy that has been shown to me tonight and I hope that, in time, I can earn the trust of the greater Israeli people. In the meantime, a man of great integrity and wisdom, the Deputy Prime Minister Gideon Wiesel, will assume the day-to-day running of the government. He has our total loyalty and support. Finally,' David said, 'I would urge calm and cool deliberation before we reach any conclusions about tonight's atrocity. I am aware, as I'm sure many of you are, that the Palestinian President's brother has been implicated in this attack. An investigation will hopefully shed more light on that, but as far as the Palestinian President is concerned, I want you to know that I have met Ahmed Sartawi and I share my father's regard for him as both a leader and as a man of peace. My hope is that we can put this behind us and move forward to achieve my father's vision of peace and prosperity for two great peoples.'

David Kaufmann had more justification than any other Israeli in calling for a massive retaliatory response, yet he was urging peace. David was going to lead by example.

Allegra and David knocked on Giovanni's room on the seventh floor of the massive hospital.

'*Avanti! Avanti!*' Giovanni was propped up with pillows. His tired smile of welcome quickly faded. 'David, I am so sorry. Knowing your parents was a pleasure and a privilege.'

'Thank you, Giovanni.' David smiled grimly.

'Your father never ceased to amaze me. After all he went through in the Holocaust he was still able to apply that experience in a way that would reverse the treatment of the Palestinians. He was a real hope for peace here.'

'I hope I will be able to do the same,' David replied. 'He was a wonderful role model.'

'How are you?' Allegra asked gently, her eyes full of concern.

'I'm fine,' Giovanni replied sadly. 'Clearly my time has not yet come.'

'When they release you, you must come and stay with us,' David insisted. 'I promise the secret service will not be too visible. Allegra and I have something very important to show you.'

Before Giovanni could answer, the Vatican's spokesman appeared on the television that had been playing quietly in the background.

'The Holy Father died at 9.37 this evening in his private apartment . . .'

Giovanni, Allegra and David, together with millions around the world, watched with sadness as the Vatican confirmed the Pope's passing.

'The first General Congregation of Cardinals will be held at 10 a.m. on Monday, 4 April, in the Bologna Hall of the Apostolic Palace,' the spokesman concluded.

CHAPTER FIFTY-ONE

Roma

'Good luck, Eminence,' Vittorio said as he handed Giovanni the small suitcase from the back of the old Fiat.

Giovanni smiled. 'There is an old saying, my friend: "he who goes in a pope, comes out a cardinal". Besides, there are many far better qualified than I and it is not a job I seek. We will let the Holy Spirit decide, *non è vero?*'

Giovanni unlocked his suite in the new priests' accommodation that John Paul II had ordered built in the Santa Marta Hospice in the Vatican grounds and deposited his suitcase. He sat at his small desk to read his breviary and then took a stroll in the quiet of the evening. Soon enough there would be no such freedom. The cardinals would all be locked up from the outside world until a new Pontiff had been elected. As Giovanni walked in the centuries-old gardens, he fell into conversation with the Holy Spirit, asking for guidance – that he and his fellow cardinals might elect a Pope of the Spirit's choosing, perhaps someone like John XXIII, a man of the people, a man who could turn around the misfortunes and misconceptions of a Church Giovanni loved so dearly. Change would not come easily to a Church that for centuries had been rooted in dogma by those who put their own politics and power above the truth and the real message of Christ. Once released, the truth would be a beacon that civilisation so desperately needed. When all this was over, he thought, the revelations in the Omega Scroll might possibly achieve what John XXIII had not been able to.

As soon as the Vatican announced the death of Pope John Paul II, Tom applied to cover the proceedings from Rome. The day after the biggest funeral the world had ever witnessed, a weary Tom Schweiker prepared once again for another live cross.

'We cross live to Rome and to Tom Schweiker for his thoughts on the Papal conclave to elect a successor to the third longest reigning Pontiff in the history of the Papacy.'

'Good evening, Geraldine. It has been a long reign, although not without controversy. The media coverage of the Pope's death has been full of praise for this Pope and until now, very few journalists have been prepared to air any grievances.'

'A dark side, Tom?'

Tom nodded. 'I think so. During the nine days of mourning for this Pope, sixty thousand Africans will die of AIDS under a Papacy that has been promoting the absurd notion that condoms cause the disease. That's over six and a half thousand people dying every day, so you can imagine what some of the medical teams struggling with the disease think of that piece of dogma.'

'And celibacy has been another issue?'

'Very much so. Particularly when for the first thousand years of this Church, Catholic priests were happily married. And of course,' Tom added, struggling to keep the bitterness from his voice, 'this Pope did very little to strike at the cancer of paedophilia in the ranks of the priesthood. It was only when the media coverage of the abuse of children in Boston reached a crescendo that anything was done.

Even then, the cardinal who was forced to step down was given a senior appointment and a spacious apartment here in Rome, and was a celebrant at one of the Masses for the dead Pope, so it's hard to believe that the Vatican is very much bothered by paedophilia.'

'Is that likely to change with the next Pope, Tom?'

'Given that this Pope has appointed far more cardinals than any of his predecessors, there are many who are suggesting that the next Pope will be a cardinal in his likeness, perhaps even more conservative.'

'An Italian?'

'That's hard to predict, although certainly one of the front-runners is the present Cardinal Secretary of State, Lorenzo Petroni. A hard-line conservative and no great fan of Vatican II.'

'Does he have the numbers, Tom?'

'The doctrine maintains that it is the Holy Spirit rather than the College of Cardinals that makes the selection. There are 194 cardinals, of whom only 117 are under eighty and therefore eligible to vote. Of the 117 there are only twenty-three Italian cardinals. For an Italian to be elected he would have to carry a sizeable number of those and the rest of the European bloc, as well as two other blocs, such as Africa or Central or South America. During a conclave no cardinal is allowed to leave or have any communication with the outside world, and all telephones are disconnected except for one in the Camerlengo's room that can be used for emergencies. Even the windows are sealed.'

'Any "dark horses" in the field, Tom?'

'There are those who are saying it is time we had a Pope from one of the Third World countries and there are one or two outstanding candidates, although they will probably be blocked by the conservatives. There is another Italian whose name might surface, Giovanni Donelli, the present Patriarch of Venice. He is very progressive and would appeal to the liberals but the conservatives are likely to oppose him strongly.'

'And if they can't agree?'

'That's happened before, but before he died, Pope John Paul II introduced a new rule. If no candidate can achieve two-thirds of the votes, and if they can hold out until the thirtieth vote, then a candidate can be elected on a simple majority.'

'That was Tom Schweiker reporting on the Papal conclave in Rome. Now to the news at home . . .'

Lorenzo Petroni was hosting a lavish reception for the Italian and African blocs in his sumptuous apartment across the Tiber, the third such reception in as many nights. His plans were going well. With the final copy of the Omega Scroll locked safely in a special compartment of the Secret Archives, or so he thought, and Felici still confident that eventually both the woman and the journalist could be eliminated, Petroni was basking in the glow of his impending power. Even though Donelli had survived the bomb blast in Jerusalem, Petroni was confident that with the help of the Knight of Malta in New York, the Keys to Peter were his; and once he had them in his pocket, that would put an end to any investigation into the Vatican Bank. It would be the old cardinals' turn tomorrow night. Petroni would use the gathering to recognise the octogenarians' unique contribution to the Holy Church. Flattery was always so useful.

'Of course the Pope's new rules on voting give rise to some interesting possibilities, Agostino,' Petroni offered smoothly, addressing his remarks to Cardinal da Silva of Luanda.

'Do you have a candidate in mind, Lorenzo?'

'Someone strong, Agostino, and although there are many good African candidates, the time for that is probably next time around. But we do need a candidate who can promote the cause of the Church in Africa and he will need a good Secretary of State. Someone like you, Agostino. Champagne?' Lorenzo Petroni squeezed Cardinal da Silva's hand and moved on to his next guest, Cardinal Fiorelli from the Italian bloc.

'Vittorio, how good to see you again. *Come stai?*'

'*Molto bene, grazie.* Who do you favour, Lorenzo?' Vittorio asked, more comfortable with the politics of a conclave.

'We shouldn't speculate, and Il Papa has done a wonderful job, but it would be good to see another Italian looking after the Church. Someone who can reinforce the tried and tested values.'

Cardinal Fiorelli smiled. 'Who did you have in mind, Lorenzo?'

'No one in particular, but whoever is chosen should have someone like you as his Secretary of State, Vittorio. It is a difficult appointment and there are not many who have your skills. Champagne?'

As the sun set over the Tiber, and Giovanni strolled in the Vatican gardens, conversing with the Holy Spirit, Cardinal Petroni moved on to his next guest, the Cardinal Archbishop of Paris. 'Of course the Pope's new rules Jean-Pierre . . .'

New York

'One minute, Geraldine.'

The CCN anchor adjusted her posture and took a sip of water. To her surprise she looked up to find Daniel Kirkpatrick striding towards the news desk. The brief was headed 'Breaking news from Rome'.

'We can't run that, Daniel!' Geraldine hissed. 'The day before the conclave!'

'Twenty seconds, Geraldine.'

'We can, and we will,' Daniel Kirkpatrick said frostily. 'Those decisions are not yours to make, unless you would like me to find a replacement to read the next bulletin. And every subsequent bulletin after that?'

'Ten seconds . . . and live . . .'

At the end of the bulletin Geraldine turned to Camera Three and summoned every bit of professionalism she could muster.

'The Vatican has announced an investigation into the Patriarch of Venice, Cardinal Giovanni Donelli, over his remarks at the aborted peace ceremony in Jerusalem and an address he gave on religion and science in which he questioned the Catholic doctrine on creation. Cardinal Donelli has been seen by some as a possible contender for the Papacy, at this week's conclave in Rome. A spokesman for the Vatican said it would be inappropriate to comment on the investigation in any detail until after it has been completed. Cardinal Donelli's assertions that the promises given by Abraham might have been fulfilled by Muhammad as well as Christ were described by the Vatican spokesman as "unhelpful". It is understood that Donelli has also been widely criticised within the Church over his challenge to the Bible with the notion that life began as bacteria beneath the sea. There will be another news update in an hour.' Geraldine smiled, but only until the red light on Camera Three had gone off.

Jerusalem

'David! That's outrageous. It's got that arsehole Petroni written all over it!'

It was a side of Allegra that David did not see very often. She had even picked up some of David's more colourful expressions.

'Announcing that just before they go into the conclave is deliberate.'

'I think you're right,' David agreed, 'but I'm not sure there's much we can do about it.'

Allegra shook her head defiantly. Her eyes flashing angrily, she picked up the phone and dialled Patrick O'Hara's number. It was Sister Katherine who answered the phone.

'Thank you, Sister Katherine, I'll be there at half past eight,' she said, a look of frustration on her face.

'Patrick's in Bethlehem for the night, but I'll go round in the morning. It will be too late though,' she said resignedly. 'The conclave starts tomorrow. That bastard Petroni has timed this to the minute.'

Tom Schweiker roused himself from a deep sleep and reached for his mobile but it rang out before he had a chance to answer. It rang again. Whoever that is wants to speak to me now, he thought with a touch of irritation. Daniel Kirkpatrick probably. Tom had decided long ago that even if Ferret Face could have absorbed the detail he had more than likely been absent from the geography lesson that dealt with time zones.

'Schweiker,' he answered, without looking at the number on the screen.

'Sorry to bother you, Mr Schweiker, but I thought you should hear this as soon as possible.'

Tom sat up, trying to place the voice. 'Who is this?'

'My name is Hank Petersen, Mr Schweiker. Before he was killed my friend Mike McKinnon sent me an unusual parcel. The prints on the whisky glass were excellent, and I thought you might like to know they match those of a Father Rory Courtney. He did time in Montana for assault back in the late 1950s. His file is also flagged with a number of suspected paedophilia offences. No charges were ever laid, although the Catholic Church carried out an internal investigation that was handled by a Bishop Petroni in the Vatican. Courtney disappeared shortly afterwards. I'm not sure if that's any help, but if you were a friend of Mike's, it's the least I could do. If you're ever in Washington, look me up.'

'I'm much obliged, and I'll certainly do that.'

'Bastards!' Tom Schweiker swore angrily after he'd switched off his phone, his suspicions about the scar confirmed. Bishop Petroni was now Cardinal Petroni and Secretary of State, he thought bitterly. He looked at his watch – 2 a.m. Patrick O'Hara was probably the only person he could trust. He decided to ring him the next morning.

CHAPTER FIFTY-TWO

Roma

At the end of the Mass the lilting sopranos rose over the baritones in the choir as the haunting strains of Giovanni Pierluigi da Palestrina's 'Tu es Petrus – Thou art Peter' echoed around the vast Basilica of St Peter's and the 115 cardinals who had made it to Rome to elect the successor to John Paul II filed two by two into the Sistine Chapel that would soon be sealed off from the outside world. The special chimney was in place, as was the antiquated stove where the ballots would be burned, together with the chemical candles to colour the smoke. Black would indicate that no candidate had received the two-thirds plus one majority that was required for election. White would indicate that a candidate had reached the critical figure of seventy-eight votes.

Under Michelangelo's fresco of creation, six rows of desks and chairs stood in three rows on either side of the chapel. At one end near the altar, desks had been placed for the scrutineers and vote counters.

'*Extra omnes*,' the Camerlengo ordered in Latin. It was the order for all those who were assigned duties as assistants, including the two medical practitioners, to vacate the Sistine Chapel, although they would not be allowed to go any further than the Santa Marta Hospice. In accordance with protocol the Heads of Vatican departments, including Petroni, had all been suspended from their duties, except for five men: the Camerlengo, the Cardinal Vicar of Rome, the Major Penitentiary, the Cardinal Arch-priest of St Peter's and the Vicar General for the Vatican City State.

Giovanni took his seat in the second row on the right. He had been intrigued to find he was under investigation but not really surprised. It would not be the first time the Holy Church had reacted fiercely against anyone who questioned the fallibility of the doctrine. On each desk there was a copy of *Universi Dominici Gregis – The Whole Flock of the Lord*, Pope John Paul's revised rules for the election of his successor.

Giovanni looked around. Cardinal Thuku from Kenya flashed him a broad smile, as did Giovanni's preferred candidate, Cardinal Médici of Ecuador. Giovanni hoped for the sake of the Church that the election would be a short one, but if it went for two or three days, it would at least give him a chance to catch up with so many of his friends.

The Camerlengo, Cardinal Monetti, a short, bald, slightly built man, held up his hand for silence. 'Let us pray,' Cardinal Monetti began:

> Almighty God, we your servants ask for your guidance as we gather together in your name. Grant us wisdom as we deliberate on whom amongst us is to assume the awesome responsibilities as the successor to Peter, on whose rock your Holy Church has been founded, through Christ our Lord, Amen.

'Amen,' Giovanni joined the chorus of his colleagues.

'I will remind you again, Eminences,' the Camerlengo intoned, 'of the oath you have sworn to follow the rules of this election, to observe with the greatest fidelity the secrecy regarding everything that relates to the election of the Roman Pontiff and what occurs in this place of election, and if you are elected, to defend the rights of the Holy See.'

Six cardinals had been elected to assist the Camerlengo in the conduct of the election – three cardinal 'scrutineers' and three cardinal 'revisers' tasked with scrutineering the scrutineers – and the Camerlengo nodded to them as a sign for the ballot papers to be distributed.

Giovanni smiled his thanks as he took the small rectangular slip of paper inscribed with the Latin words, *'Eligo in summum pontificem'* – 'I elect as Supreme Pontiff'. Obeying the quaint instruction to disguise his handwriting, he inscribed his ballot with the name of Cardinal Rodriguez Médici and folded it. He took his turn to file up to the altar holding the ballot above his head.

Giovanni placed his ballot on the paten covering the chalice and knelt at the altar, praying silently for the Holy Spirit's presence, and as he rose he said, 'I call to witness Christ the Lord who will be my judge, that my vote is given to the one before God I consider should be elected,' and then using the paten he dropped his ballot into the chalice.

When all the votes had been cast the first scrutineer covered the chalice with the paten and shook it to mix the ballots, and when the scrutineers, checked by the revisers, had satisfied themselves that there were only 115 ballots in the chalice, the vote counting began.

The first cardinal scrutineer noted the name on the first ballot and passed it to the second scrutineer who did the same. The third cardinal scrutineer read the name out loud for the whole college to note.

'Cardinal Lorenzo Petroni,' the third cardinal scrutineer intoned, and he pierced the card through the word *'Eligo'* and placed it on a thread that would join the votes together to be burned or, if a Pope was elected, kept for his retention.

'Cardinal Giovanni Donelli.'

Giovanni shook his head but smiled. It didn't hurt to get one or two votes he supposed.

'Cardinal Rodriguez Médici.'

'Cardinal Lorenzo Petroni.'

'Cardinal Daniel Thuku.'

'Cardinal Giovanni Donelli.'

At the end of the first vote the Camerlengo read out the results: 'Cardinal Lorenzo Petroni, forty-two votes.'

Cardinal Petroni nodded imperceptibly.

'Cardinal Giovanni Donelli, thirty-two votes.'

Cardinal Petroni's eyes hardened. Donelli. Obviously the announcement of the investigation had had some effect but not enough and Petroni wondered who might be voting for him. Petroni decided to reinforce the dangers of heresy and of a long Papacy during the lunch break.

'Cardinal Daniel Thuku, twenty-four votes.'

Cardinal Petroni nodded to the Kenyan. It was around the number he had calculated. Again the counter to the Third World of 'not yet' would have to be reiterated, and he thought about how he might swing Thuku and his bloc of African votes over to his side. A twenty-four vote bloc, together with one or two more coming over, would give him at least seventy and put him comfortably in striking distance of the magical figure of seventy-eight. Once a candidate got close, Petroni knew that the next vote usually clinched it as the other cardinals all rushed to be on the winning team.

'Cardinal Rodriguez Médici, twenty-two votes.'

Again Cardinal Petroni nodded in acknowledgement. The Latin American bloc of Liberation cardinals would be harder to swing, but he had already listed those who might be vulnerable. The other votes were scattered in twos and threes and the Camerlengo gave orders for the ballots to be burned with a candle so that black smoke issued from the chimney.

Jerusalem

'There must be something we can do, Patrick,' Allegra said, her anger still flaming as Patrick O'Hara showed her in to his lounge room.

'I have to agree with you, Allegra, it's got Petroni's trademark all over it but the trouble is, once a conclave starts, the cardinals are sealed off from the outside world.'

'No doubt something Petroni was banking on with his timing,' Allegra said bitterly. 'Sow the seeds of doubt in the minds of those who are wavering on their candidate to ensure Petroni gets himself across the line, then he can claim it was all a misunderstanding.'

'Sorry to interrupt, Bishop O'Hara,' Sister Katherine said from the doorway. 'Tom Schweiker is calling from Rome, shall I ask him to call back?'

'No, no, we're in between a rock and a hard place here anyway, Sister Katherine. I'll take it in the study but you can serve the tea in here.'

It was nearly fifteen minutes before Patrick returned but he had a bounce in his step and his eyes were dancing with a mischievous anger.

'Tom phoned me on a personal matter, but I took the trouble to raise last night's broadcast with him and he is just as irate as we are,' Patrick said. 'He's got reason to believe that when Petroni was a bishop in the Vatican he was involved in covering up the Church's involvement in paedophilia.'

Patrick kept the allegations general. Tom Schweiker hadn't said as much, but Patrick had been around long enough to sense there was a deeper personal issue for the journalist, and he had told Tom his door was always open. There had been a sense of gratitude in Tom's response that heightened Patrick's suspicions.

'Tom tells me there was a heated argument in New York just before the item was aired. With only seconds to go before the bulletin opened, the CCN anchor was handed a brief headed "Breaking news from Rome". When she had a closer look at the date, she could see the information had come through from Petroni's office nearly a week before.'

'Then there's a link between Petroni and the CCN News Director,' Allegra said.

'Tom's certain there is.'

'So that would rule out any chance of Tom getting a story up that suggested the timing of the allegations is political.' Allegra was getting angrier.

'It doesn't stop *us* airing the allegations against Petroni,' Patrick said. 'I made a call to the one person in the conclave who is connected to the outside world, the Camerlengo. It's a long shot, but Tom's agreed to back us. The Camerlengo's absolutely furious, but I told him the media already had the story and it would not look good if it subsequently emerged that he refused to see us. To give us credibility I gave him Tom's number if he wanted to check. It took a fair bit of arm-twisting, but he's very reluctantly agreed to listen to us.'

The Italian in Allegra came to the fore. She put her cup down, leaned over and gave an astonished Patrick a hug.

'Patrick, you're a marvel!'

'Don't get your hopes up too much, Allegra,' Patrick cautioned. 'He's only agreed to see us. The Curia can be very stubborn. Will David come?'

'I don't see why not,' Allegra said firmly. 'The election's not due for another six weeks. Surely he can slip out of the country on personal business without the whole place falling apart. If Petroni gets elected Pope, it won't be just a backward step for the Catholic Church,' she said, her dark eyes smouldering. 'Given what's in the Omega Scroll it could mean the countdown for destruction will be accelerated.'

Roma

As they filed out of the Sistine Chapel for lunch, Cardinal Petroni managed to hide his irritation, but as lunch wore on his irritation increased. Petroni needed to speak separately with Cardinal Rodriguez Médici and Cardinal Daniel Thuku but both had been deep in conversation with each other for over twenty minutes. The lunch break was drawing to a close and Petroni waited for an opportunity, frustrated at being caught up in small talk with cardinals he didn't need to speak to.

If Petroni had known what Médici and Thuku were talking about his over-confidence would have been shaken by desperation and a sense that power was slowly slipping through his elegant fingers.

'I'm flattered by the support I've received, Daniel,' Rodriguez Médici said, 'but I'm going to have a word with one or two of my supporters to see if we can get behind the one candidate. One thing is very clear to me, it would be an unmitigated disaster if Petroni is elected. He has campaigned shamelessly this last week and as Pope he would set the Church back a hundred years. You might think getting the Curia to change their minds on condoms is a hard ask now. Under Petroni you'd be excommunicated for thinking about it.'

Daniel Thuku smiled grimly. 'Yes, and I think the chances of a third Vatican Council would be about zilch. What about this investigation into Giovanni?'

'That's got Petroni's mark all over it, Daniel, surely you can see that?'

'Yes, but can the others?'

Back in the chapel the Camerlengo read out the results of the voting for the second ballot.

'Cardinal Lorenzo Petroni, forty-eight votes.'

Cardinal Petroni disguised his cold fury. A paltry six vote gain on the second ballot. His vote had stalled. Something was not adding up.

'Cardinal Giovanni Donelli, forty-two votes.' Giovanni shook his head. Those around him heard him say softly, 'Please God. No. Please, no.'

Cardinal Salvatore Bruno, who was seated directly opposite, just smiled and nodded encouragement in Giovanni's direction. While Cardinal Petroni had been dispensing champagne and caviar, Giovanni's old mentor had not been idle in the lead up to the conclave either, quietly building Giovanni's candidature amongst others who also held the brilliant young cardinal in high esteem. Votes for both Cardinal Thuku and Cardinal Médici had fallen, largely at their own instigation, and both exchanged conspiratorial glances. Both were wondering if it was the kiss of death for Petroni, or if he might hold his position for another twenty-eight ballots to force a run-off on a simple majority. Cardinal Petroni's thoughts were running on similar lines.

Once more a cloud of black smoke issued from the Sistine Chapel chimney as Flight 401 from Tel-Aviv touched down at Rome's Leonardo da Vinci International Airport.

'I think I'm in the wrong business,' Patrick O'Hara whispered to Allegra as they followed David and the Shin Bet agents through a private doorway and the Italian customs agent waved them straight through.

'*Buongiorno, Signor, Signora. Benvenuti a Roma.*'

'It has its compensations,' Allegra agreed. 'Mind you, it would want to!'

There were two cars and despite David indicating that it was a private visit and a request for things to be done on a low key, they came with the inevitable *carabinieri* escort.

'At least the media aren't anywhere in sight,' David said to Allegra as they followed the police escort in the first car with Patrick following in the second.

'Give them time,' Allegra said cynically.

'Be fair,' David said. 'They haven't had someone quite so

photogenic as you in public life in years. Golda Meir might have
been a great stateswoman, but she was no oil painting.'

'David!' Allegra whispered, tilting her head towards the Shin
Bet driver and agent in the front seat. She needn't have worried,
the agents from the Personal Protection Unit had smiles wider
than David's.

'Do you think the media in Jerusalem will get wind of you being
away?'

'The most feared investigative journalist in Jerusalem is about to
join us at the Vatican. For the rest of them they'll be told it's urgent
family business.'

'I guess that much is true, Giovanni is certainly part of the family.
When do we raise the other issue?' she asked, raising her eyebrows
in the direction of the diplomatic briefcase that David had not let
out of his hands since they'd left Israel. Inside it was the priceless
Omega Scroll.

'After the conclave, if they can make up their minds quickly.
If not, you will have to stay on.'

'Let's hope they can decide,' Allegra said putting her hand on
David's knee and leaning over to kiss him. 'Thank you so much
for this.'

'There will be a price,' David said instantly.

'You are dreadful!'

Half an hour later the Swiss Guard on St Anne's Gate snapped
to attention.

Father Thomas showed them in to the Secretary of State's opulent waiting room. 'The Camerlengo sends his apologies,' he said
smoothly, 'but he has been delayed for a few minutes, can I get you
some coffee? Tea?'

'He might have agreed to see us,' Patrick warned when Father
Thomas had withdrawn, 'but he's no doubt furious at the thought
of interrupting the conclave. We'll just have to play it by ear.'

A short while later Patrick O'Hara's fears were realised.

'Absolutely out of the question, Bishop O'Hara!'

Cardinal Monetti's eyes blazed and his face suddenly matched the colour of the scarlet zucchetto that partly covered his bald head.

'Even if those allegations against Cardinal Petroni were true, which I very much doubt, the Holy Spirit decides this election and I will certainly not be an agent provocateur on yours or anyone else's behalf.' Cardinal Monetti turned to David. He reminded Allegra of a ferocious terrier.

'I regret that I cannot be of greater assistance, Dr Kaufmann, although I must confess to being somewhat confused as to why a possible future Prime Minister of Israel would allow himself to become so closely involved with such a tawdry allegation. If any word of this ever got out,' he said pointedly, 'it could cost you your election.'

'My decision to come over here today is guided by one thing and one thing only,' David replied evenly. 'The truth. To be blunt, Eminence, the Catholic Church has covered this sort of thing up for far too long and in many cases the truth has run a bad second to Church image and politics. That said, I respect your decision. I would ask that you respect mine.'

'Father Thomas will show you out,' Cardinal Monetti replied coolly. 'If you will excuse me, I have a conclave to attend to.'

'Where did they find him?' Tom asked as, to the consternation of their bodyguards, they decided to join the crowd that had gathered in St Peter's Square in the hope of seeing white smoke issue from the Sistine Chapel chimney.

Giovanni left the Sistine Chapel and retired to his room for a session of prayer in the break between votes. Initially he had been somewhat bemused, but as his name was read out an astonishing forty-two times he had become at first concerned, and then alarmed. He sank to his knees, his mind racing. What if they elected him? It was unthinkable. He consoled himself with the thought that Petroni had done as well as he was going to and the next ballot would see either of his friends Rodriguez Médici or Daniel Thuku come through. Either, he knew, would make an outstanding Pope.

Cardinal Thuku was chatting quietly with some of the cardinals from the African bloc. 'I know him well, my friend, he has a brilliant mind and a gentle heart. As to the other question, how much notice should we take of media releases that are timed to be issued the day before the conclave?'

On the other side of the room Rodriguez Médici was also in quiet conversation with some of his Asian colleagues. Some of the Italian bloc were listening quietly to Salvatore Bruno.

A short while later the crowd in St Peter's Square erupted as great clouds of white smoke poured out of the Sistine Chapel chimney.

'My God, David,' Allegra exclaimed, grabbing David's arm. 'They've reached a decision! Please God, don't let it be Petroni!' It was an entreaty to a God she had not spoken with for a long time.

Inside the Sistine Chapel the Camerlengo had announced the results of the third ballot.

'Cardinal Rodriguez Médici, one vote.'

Giovanni had stuck to his man to the last.

'Cardinal Lorenzo Petroni, twelve votes.'

'Cardinal Giovanni Donelli, one hundred and two votes.'

Giovanni felt utterly bewildered. Cardinal Salvatore Bruno was beaming at him from the other side of the chapel. As the Dean of the College of Cardinals approached down the centre aisle in the chapel, the words of Giovanni's old mentor flooded back to him: 'If they offer you the Keys to St Peter, accept. It will be for a reason.'

'Do you accept your canonical election as supreme Pontiff?' Giovanni heard the words in the distance and his reply caught in his throat.

'Yes, I do,' he said.

'And by what name do you wish to be known?'

Without hesitation Giovanni replied, 'John XXIV.'

The Master of Ceremonies joyfully threw in no fewer than six candles with the ballots and Rome's Il Capo di Fuoco Vigiliare could have been forgiven for thinking Michelangelo's priceless fresco was under threat as more white smoke belched out over the Piazza San Pietro. As the Cardinal Deacon came out onto the main balcony of St Peter's and intoned the words *Habemus papam*, the packed square of St Peter's erupted again.

'We have a Pope! Pope John XXIV!' At the mention of a successor to the much loved John XXIII of *'sono fa brutto'* fame, the roar of the crowd reached a crescendo. When Allegra saw Giovanni step onto the balcony of St Peter's her eyes filled with tears. Giovanni's secretary Vittorio also wiped away a tear. His beloved Church, he knew, was in good hands as the warmth of Giovanni's smile seemed to fill the square.

CHAPTER FIFTY-THREE

Roma

The next day Pope John XXIV knelt in prayer in his private chapel, asking for guidance and support. The task he had been given was awesome and Giovanni felt very alone.

The Spirit smiled.

Getting to his feet and crossing himself he walked back towards his study on the third floor of the Apostolic Palace to find Vittorio waiting for him. The two worked well together and despite opposition from Cardinal Petroni, immediately after his election, Giovanni had promoted Vittorio to Monsignor and asked him to stay on in Rome as his private secretary.

'Have the Israeli delegation confirmed for lunch?' Giovanni asked. The momentous events of the past few days had taken up most of his attention, and he had only been able to meet privately with Allegra, David, Patrick and Tom Schweiker for a few minutes. Apart from the joy of catching up, those few minutes had been vital. The contents of the Omega Scroll were never far from his thoughts.

'The Israeli delegation are confirmed for 12.30, Holiness, and the Papal Physician, Professor Martines, will be here to give you a medical at 11.30.'

Giovanni rolled his eyes and grinned. 'Medical check-ups come with the territory, I suppose. Any fitter and I'd be dangerous, but you can ask Professor Martines if he would like to join us for lunch and I'd like you to be there, too. The Omega Scroll will become public soon enough.'

'Thank you, Holiness.' It would be a hallmark of Giovanni's Papacy to include those closest to him as if they were family.

'When would you like to see Cardinal Petroni?'

'Let's get that out of the way first, Vittorio,' Giovanni said, his eyes clouding. 'Have you read my notes on the Vatican Bank?'

'I wasn't sure if I should, Holiness. They're in the safe.'

Giovanni smiled at the memory of Albino Luciani, a man who had taught him so much. 'Neither of us is used to Vatican politics, Vittorio, but we will need to apply the same rules here as we did in Venice. It is important that you be across everything in here, so when you have time, bring yourself up to speed,' Giovanni said gently. Almost to a word, Giovanni's advice had echoed that which he'd received from Pope John Paul I. 'Before you summon Cardinal Petroni, have the Commander of the Swiss Guard come to see me, please.'

'Of course, Holiness, and when you get a moment, the Curial Cardinals have prepared a speech for you, outlining the direction for your Papacy. It's on your desk.'

Giovanni smiled grimly. 'I'm going to have to get used to this I suppose, Vittorio.'

'You may wish to change it,' Vittorio said. Having read it, Vittorio knew that he would.

Giovanni sat at his desk and read through the address the Curial Cardinals had prepared for him. 'Important to continue the work of John Paul II . . . The Holy Church must resist the secularism and liberalism of modern society . . . To stick to the one true path . . . A beacon of light in the darkness of the modern age . . .'

Vittorio was right. A mish-mash of Curial clichés designed to keep the status quo. Giovannni suddenly felt the loneliness of leadership. At least Patrick was hanging around for a few days. He was a sounding board, a man in touch with the people and reality. Then Giovanni smiled as he had a sudden thought. Perhaps there were some small compensations that came with being elected Pontiff. The skills of the Patrick O'Haras of this world were invaluable. The College of Cardinals could do with those who would continue to stay in close touch with the faithful and now he had the power to do something about that.

Giovanni got up, went to the window and stared out over the piazza. It was still crowded with people but if the Curial Cardinals had their way he would be a prisoner, forever shut up in his apartments, with the cardinals controlling his every move. They were about to hear some bad news. If it was good enough for John XXIII to go wandering around with his people unannounced, it would be good enough for John XXIV. His thoughts were interrupted by Vittorio's knock on the door of his office.

'Cardinal Petroni is here, Holiness.'

'Ask him to come in, Vittorio,' Giovanni said quietly.

'*Certamente*, Holiness.' Vittorio could not remember when he had seen Giovanni so troubled.

'Holiness, our most heartiest congratulations. We are all delighted.' Petroni bowed, ever so slightly.

'I will come straight to the point, Cardinal Petroni. Sit down, please,' Giovanni said, indicating one of the armchairs around the low coffee table at one end of his office. Giovanni's tone was icy but controlled.

Petroni sat down, barely concealing his anger at having been ordered to sit down by someone who, until yesterday, had been his subordinate.

'When I had dinner with Pope John Paul I on his last night here he told me that he had sacked his Secretary of State and that you were going to be relieved of your duties the following morning. One of the reasons, as I'm sure you're more aware than most, was that for a very long time the Vatican Bank has been involved in criminal activities.'

'That's preposterous, Holiness. An utter fabrication.' There was a wariness in Petroni's snake-like eyes, as if he had been confronted by a mongoose.

'I don't believe so, Cardinal Petroni. Last night, despite the difficulties of getting through to the more remote parts of the Amazon, my secretary tracked down Monsignor Pasquale Garibaldi. I have ordered him back to Rome on promotion to Bishop to commence a thorough investigation into the bank's past activities. Depending on what his report has to say, I may have to refer the matter to the Italian authorities and La Guardia di Finanza.'

'That's entirely unnecessary, Holiness. I can carry out any investigation without the need for bringing Monsignor Garibaldi back from Peru.' There was an edge of desperation in Petroni's voice now.

'Before you posted him to Peru,' Giovanni continued meaningfully, 'Monsignor Garibaldi discovered some irregularities in the accounts, including an expenditure of ten million dollars on what Pope John Paul I and I knew to be a copy of the Omega Scroll.'

'That's an outrageous allegation!' Petroni hissed, the colour draining from his face. 'The pressures of office are already too much for you.'

Giovanni maintained his icy demeanour, determined that this time Petroni would be forced to confront his past.

'Monsignor Garibaldi also told me that before he left, he took the precaution of photocopying some key documents which he will bring back from Peru.'

Petroni's mouth opened but no sound came out.

'Last night I also ordered the Swiss Guards to seal off the Secret

Archives. I have ordered a thorough search and I am confident that the little known areas will turn up at least one copy of the Omega Scroll. It may also turn up a copy of the great Isaiah Scroll that was taken from the Hebrew University in an envelope marked with an Omega symbol. If it does, the Israeli police and the CIA will no doubt want to question you about any involvement you may have had in a double murder in Tel-Aviv. If such requests are made we will cooperate fully and you will be made available.'

Giovanni had thought long and hard about confronting Petroni with the rape of Allegra, but that was deniable and unless Allegra wanted to pursue it, he had decided that the other matters provided more than enough evidence for serious criminal charges to be laid.

'I have also had a disturbing report from Bishop O'Hara. You are no doubt aware he is here in Rome?' Giovanni raised one eyebrow slightly but there was no response. The Cardinal Secretary of State's face was now ashen.

'Father Lonergan, who you would also have known as Father Courtney, is being recalled to Rome and I have asked Bishop O'Hara to oversee an investigation into what involvement the Vatican might have had in his new identity and we will be cooperating fully with the FBI. I am promoting Bishop O'Hara to Cardinal and he will take over as Cardinal Secretary of State, effective immediately. You are dismissed from all your duties.'

Pope John XXIV stood up, moved to his desk and buzzed for Vittorio.

'Until these investigations are complete, the Swiss Guard have been advised that you are under house arrest and you are not permitted to leave the Vatican. I suggest that for the good of the Holy Church you give serious consideration to resigning from the priesthood. If you don't, regardless of the outcome of the criminal charges that will undoubtedly be laid against you, I will take steps to have you dismissed. May God have mercy on you for what you have done.'

CHAPTER FIFTY-FOUR

Roma

Father Vittorio showed 'the Israeli delegation' in to Pope John XXIV's private dining room and a short while later Giovanni arrived with the Papal Physician, Professor Vincenzo Martines.

'Allegra!' Throwing Papal protocol to the four winds, Giovanni kissed Allegra enthusiastically on both cheeks. *'Benvenuta di nuovo.* Welcome again!'

'David! Patrick! Tom!' Giovanni gave each of his guests a very informal welcome before introducing them to Professor Martines. Vittorio smiled. If nothing else, this Papacy was going to be fun.

'And you've set up the Omega Scroll,' Giovanni said, moving over to where the document had been laid out on a long table to one side of the room. 'That explains why I passed so many Swiss Guards in the corridors,' he said, winking at Vittorio and accepting a glass of wine from one of the Sisters. 'Though I guess it's waited this long, it can wait until after lunch. To old times!' Giovanni said, his smile filled with warmth now that the distasteful business of the morning was out of the way. 'They spoil me here,' he added.

'From the little I've seen already, the wine is superb. And the food,' Giovanni said, rubbing his stomach ruefully.

'You've never put on an ounce of fat in all the years I've known you,' Allegra chided.

'Watch this space. This is a twenty kilo appointment!' he said, winking at Patrick.

Patrick raised his eyes to the ceiling and shrugged. His smile said it all.

After lunch, the small group moved their chairs to the long table.

'The Omega Scroll,' David began, 'was written by Mechalava, a Master from within the community of the Essenes at Qumran. He wrote it during the period 20 AD to 40 AD, and those dates are supported by Allegra's carbon dating. The dates are very significant.'

Giovanni smiled. He knew what was coming. 'Encompassing the years during which Jesus would have formed his own philosophy,' he said, 'as well as the period of his ministry and crucifixion?'

'Correct, and as I think you're already aware, Holiness, the Omega Scroll is in three parts: the Magdalene Numbers; the origin of DNA; and a dire warning for civilisation,' David continued. 'As we will see, all three contain connected messages. The Magdalene Numbers come from a literary device known as gematria. Because numbers in languages like Greek and Hebrew are represented by letters rather than figures, the authors of many ancient texts were able to embed hidden meanings that can be obtained only by adding the values of the letters to arrive at the sacred numbers.

'The number that the Vatican fears most is 153, which has been encoded in the Omega Scroll. Although,' David said, looking at Giovanni, 'perhaps it would be more correct to say it is a number that used to be feared by the Vatican.'

'So you found it,' Giovanni said, smiling at Allegra. They both remembered Rosselli's assignment and a little beach near Maratea.

'The Omega Scroll records an odd phrase that is repeated in the Book of Revelation,' David continued. 'The passage translates as, "And I saw the Holy City, the New Jerusalem, coming down out of heaven from God, prepared as a bride adorned for her husband".'

Giovanni nodded in response. 'The New Jerusalem. Otherwise known as the Bride of Christ, a symbol of the new heaven and the new earth.'

'The gematria for this phrase totals 1224,' David said. 'The gematria for Jesus is 8. When we divide 1224 by 8 we get 153. In other words, this strange phrase incorporating "Christ" and "the Bride of Christ" is represented by the numbers 8 and 153. When we examine the gematria for η $M\alpha\gamma\delta\alpha\lambda\eta\nu\eta$, "the Magdalene", we find that the sum of the letters is 153.'

Tom whistled softly. 'So Mary Magdalene really was the Bride of Christ.'

'Yes,' David agreed. 'The clue was elegantly embedded in the Bible and the Book of Revelation.'

'And just as elegantly in the Gospel of Luke,' Giovanni added calmly. 'When the disciples are having no luck fishing on the Sea of Tiberias, Christ tells them where to cast their net and Luke, in what seems an odd statement, records that when the net is hauled in, there are exactly 153 fish.'

'The fish representing the harvest of humanity which, in the broader sense, is also the Bride of Christ,' Allegra observed, recalling Professor Rosselli's impish sense of humour and his remark that 153 was the number the Vatican feared most and that 'it may have something to do with fishes and cities falling from the sky'. 'Although this will be difficult for the Church,' she added, wondering how Giovanni would handle the Omega Scroll, not as Giovanni but as Pope John XXIV.

Giovanni smiled at her, and as if reading her thoughts, picked up the discussion. 'I am reminded of John XXIII's remark when he instigated Vatican II and likened his *aggiornamento* – his renewal of the Church – to the opening of a window of St Peter's. The Omega Scroll is like a great shaft of light, shining through the cupola and illuminating the darker areas of the Basilica. Regenerating the beauty of the Faith with the balance of the feminine,' he added, his face energised with the possibilities. 'I am not surprised to hear you say the three messages in the Omega Scroll are connected. We are at a critical time in history and I suspect the Omega Scroll is telling us to change course.'

'For a lot of people, confirmation of the union of Christ and Mary Magdalene will not be earth shattering,' Patrick observed shrewdly. 'A lot of well-respected scholars have already reached that conclusion, but for hundreds of millions of Christians it will call into question everything they have been taught to believe and a lot of them simply won't accept it.'

'We shall have to bring them along gently,' Giovanni said, looking meaningfully at Tom, 'by focusing on what this means. The New Jerusalem – Christ and Mary Magdalene – represents a balance of the male and the female in Christianity that, when we look for it, is also reflected in other religions like the yin and yang of Taoism and the Shekinah, the feminine aspect of God in Judaism.'

Tom and Vincenzo were looking slightly bemused so Allegra took Giovanni's point further. 'What this means is that the feminine is a very important part of spirituality and religion, and contributes equally to the notion of a sacred partnership which is the original birthright of humanity. The balancing of male and female in the teachings of religion creates a power of harmony, restores the Earth to its natural balance, and fulfils the divine yearning within all of us towards a complete union, to be made whole.'

'I suspect,' Giovanni reflected, 'that the feminine balance is emerging at this time in our history when the world is teetering on a precipice, hence the connection to the warning. At the extreme, we are facing annihilation from a clash of male-dominated interpretations of religion, but the other imbalances of the planet will also overwhelm us. The ills of the modern world are rising to catastrophic levels as the focus is skewed to one side of the equation, the masculine. The imbalance is showing up in ecological disasters, the persecution of minorities, a drastic increase in poverty and a universal unease. Put simply, the early Church Fathers were threatened by the feminine and our acceptance of their dogma has done untold damage. Ignoring the feminine side of the equation for so long has set the wheels in motion for human and ecological disaster.'

'The suppression of the feminine,' Allegra added, 'and the lack of acknowledgement of the union of male and female, or Christ and Mary Magdalene, also reflects the exclusion of sexuality from religious life.' Fleetingly she recalled the drive back from Maratea with Giovanni. 'That exclusion is a distortion, a denial, and a profound wounding of our basic nature.'

'The consequences of which are highlighted in the tragic imbalance of the clergy sex scandals that are tearing the Church apart,' David added.

Tom shifted uncomfortably. Patrick caught David's eye and shook his head.

David changed tack. 'Basically, addressing this imbalance will restore tolerance to humanity.'

Allegra nodded in agreement. 'And there is a link between the dangers of accepting dogma that is taught by rote, like the dogma of the creation story, and the second message in the Omega Scroll on DNA which is the real origin of life.'

As he had done so many times over the years, but now for the last time, Lorenzo Petroni stared out over the Piazza San Pietro and across the Tiber towards his apartment. The Keys to Peter should have been his. He had given the Church his soul, hiding people like Derek Lonergan and protecting the doctrine. What a powerful team he and P3 could have made with him on the throne of Peter. Vatican II could have been turned back and the power returned to the priesthood. The Vatican Bank would have risen to be a financial powerhouse to be reckoned with. Had Felici been halfway competent, the real Omega Scroll would now have been safe in the Secret Archives, instead of the Isaiah Scroll.

'How could you not know the difference?' he seethed, his bloodless lips parted in a snarl. Little flecks of saliva were forming at the edges of his mouth.

'Bastards!' Petroni frothed with anger.

The fog of despair consuming him, Lorenzo Petroni unlocked the top drawer of his working desk and took out the small black Beretta Cheetah from its leather case beside his black leather book.

'One day,' he mused bitterly, 'they will realise that there is only one true path to the Omega.'

'The second part of the Omega Scroll deals with the origin of DNA,' Allegra continued.

'If I recall, DNA wasn't even heard of until the middle of the last century?' Tom looked puzzled.

'A little before that on our planet,' Allegra said. 'It was actually discovered in 1869, ten years after the publication of the *Origin of the Species*. Friedrich Miescher, a Swiss biologist discovered it in pus cells on discarded bandages, although to be fair, he didn't recognise its significance. That came later, or earlier, depending on your planet in the universe.'

Giovanni smiled. He knew Allegra had one of the finest minds he had ever encountered and he was elated at just how far this brilliant Italian scientist had come since he had first met her at Milano's Stazione Centrale.

'Sir Francis Crick, the winner of the Nobel Prize for the discovery of the molecular structure of DNA, published a book on the origin of life for which he was roundly criticised. In it he postulated that the molecular structure of DNA was of such intricacy that there had been insufficient time for it to develop from a standing start,' she said.

'Crick proposed that it must have come from a more advanced civilisation, from one of the billions of galaxies like our own that make up the universe, and that it had been delivered by rocket vehicle or spacecraft.' Allegra placed a diagram of the hydrogen and phosphodiester bonding of the DNA helix on the table.

'Crick's view was fiercely opposed by many, particularly in the Church, as it directly contradicted the story of creation in the Bible. In the 1990s Michael Drosnin published *The Bible Code* which outlined the work of the Israeli mathematician Eliyahu Rips. Rips discovered hidden codes in the Torah which Yossi Kaufmann found replicated in the Dead Sea Scrolls. In a three-thousand-year-old document, Rips found the words "DNA spiral" and "DNA was brought in a vehicle". Drosnin concluded that the vehicle was yet to be found, but was somewhere near the Dead Sea.'

'Yossi wasn't so sure,' David said. 'For starters, he thought there was more than one vehicle.'

'Even if just one was delivered to the ancient seas of Earth, it would explain DNA combining with the amino acids in the primordial soup that made up the world's oceans four billion years ago,' Giovanni said, thinking back to his sermon in San Marco.

'Precisely,' Allegra agreed, 'and as David will translate, the Omega Scroll makes that very clear.'

David walked over to the second section of the Omega Scroll and read from the Koiné. 'And they came like stars from the sky, and were buried in the great sands of the desert, steel chariots bringing the seeds of life.'

'So the Essenes found the vehicle?' Professor Martines asked.

David nodded. 'The Omega Scroll records the discovery and, as the translation suggests, it confirms there was more than one vehicle. As well as DNA, each contained a diagram of the structure of the acid and a map of its destination, which explains the Essene models, including the tenth planet which we have only just discovered. It might also mean that ours is not the only galaxy that has been targeted.'

'A message we will ignore at our peril,' Giovanni observed. 'I think it is highly possible that another civilisation is trying to tell us that life on this planet is in our hands, but if we continue on our present course and annihilate the planet, in the scheme of the cosmos, that mistake will not be of great consequence. Other civilisations with greater wisdom will continue and take our place.'

'There is still time to heed these warnings,' Allegra emphasised, 'and reverse the damage that has been done. I suspect there is a connection between the DNA element of the Omega Scroll and the balance of the feminine element. There are roughly three billion base pairs in human DNA organised into twenty-three pairs of chromosomes. We all have twenty-two pairs, but the critical twenty-third pair has always been different, two X chromosomes for females and an X and a Y chromosome for males. That delicate balance has been a deliberate part of the design of the cosmos from the very beginning and the Omega Scroll's illumination of the origin of DNA contains a subtle message – any alteration of that balance will ultimately lead to our destruction.'

'A lot of people are going to find this a little out there,' Tom observed. His sceptical questioning was second nature to him.

'And a lot of people have closed minds to anything that is beyond their experience, Tom,' Allegra said firmly. 'Crick pointed out that the universe is so vast, it is beyond the imagination of many of us. Our galaxy alone has perhaps a hundred billion stars. Billions of suns like our own energising the planets that are circling around them. Just in our galaxy,' Allegra emphasised, 'and there are at least ten billion more galaxies, which allows for trillions of planets. Are we seriously suggesting that among all of these, our planet is the only one to have life, or that we are the most advanced?' Allegra spoke forcefully, then she continued more gently, 'Less than four hundred years ago, one of the most brilliant scientists our world has ever seen dared to suggest that the Earth was not, as the Church stated, at the centre of God's universe. He suggested that it revolved around the sun. That so enraged the Vatican that Pope Urban VIII had the scientist thrown into prison.' Allegra was smiling but the challenge was in her eyes if Tom wanted to take it up.

Giovanni grinned. 'Galileo Galilei, 1633. I'm sorry to say it took the Vatican more than three hundred and fifty years to apologise to Galileo. On 28 December 1991 we finally issued a press release admitting he had been right, although you both have a point,' Giovanni added diplomatically. 'Many people will close their minds to this, and nowhere more so than in the Church. When we close our minds, we close off many avenues of learning.'

'That is especially dangerous when I tell you why the Essenes recorded their warning for our civilisation,' David added ominously, but he got no further. The sound of a single gunshot from the floor below was deafening.

It took Professor Martines little more than a minute to reach the office of the Cardinal Secretary of State where he was met by a dazed Father Thomas.

'His Eminence . . . he's just committed . . .' Father Thomas ran to an adjoining door.

Even for a seasoned psychiatrist Professor Martines was brought up short with what he found. Lorenzo Petroni's brains, or what was left of them, were dripping down the wall opposite the window that overlooked the Piazza San Pietro. The autopsy would find a single shot through the roof of his mouth. Petroni's body lay beside his desk on the royal blue carpet, the black .38 Beretta Cheetah on the floor nearby. The back of his head was missing. Vincenzo Martines could hear Father Thomas being sick in the Secretary of State's bathroom.

Professor Martines shut the double doors to the Secretary of State's office and waited for Father Thomas. Several nuns and one or two priests, consternation marking their faces, were gathering outside.

'Do you feel you can stay?' Professor Martines asked Father Thomas when he emerged from the bathroom. 'For the time being we need to make sure no one comes in here.'

Father Thomas could only nod in reply.

CHAPTER FIFTY-FIVE

The Hindu Kush

The wind was light but at high altitude there was no warmth in the late afternoon sun that caught the granite and snow of the north-west frontier and Tirich Mir. Inside the cave complex Dr Hussein Tretyakov had handed over yet another of the deadly suitcase bombs to Abdul Basheer, who was now poring over a travel map of Sydney.

'There has been a slight change in our plans,' Basheer said quietly. 'I have decided to hit the infidel in a way he will least expect. Sydney will be attacked first, followed by Manchester and Chicago. While he is distracted by those attacks, in the ensuing panic we will hit New York and London.

'Sydney is especially vulnerable. We will deliver the bomb from the air and we have an excellent choice of surrounding airfields that are not subject to checks. The flight plan will be a standard vector into the nearby suburban Bankstown airfield. Our plane will not have to deviate from its flight path until the last minutes before final approach.'

'That deviation will be picked up by air traffic control?' Tretyakov ventured.

'Of course, but by then it will be too late. In a few short minutes our aircraft will be over the central business district. Unlike the Americans, the Australian infidels do not employ fighter aircraft on patrols over their cities so they will not be able to stop us. What will be the effect of an air-burst over that city?' Abdul Basheer asked.

'It will be similar to New York and London,' Hussein replied, 'although the air-burst will cause greater damage to the buildings and infrastructure. I have calculated that if the bomb is exploded above the city, perhaps two hundred thousand people will be killed by the blast, and hundreds of thousands more will die of burns and radiation. The Sydney Harbour Bridge will be twisted and buckled, and buildings and people around ground zero will be vaporised.'

'The loss of life is unfortunate,' Basheer said finally, 'but it will send a warning to the rest of the world that we will not stand by while our women and children are arrogantly slaughtered in Iraq, Palestine and Kashmir, and countless other countries where the infidel has set up his military machines.'

Hussein nodded, the memory of his wife and daughters still tearing at his heart.

'The attack on Hiroshima and Nagasaki brought WWII to an end,' Basheer observed. 'It is time for us to do the same. God willing, Muhammad, peace be upon him, and Islam will prevail.'

CHAPTER FIFTY-SIX

Roma

On his way back to the Papal apartments, Professor Martines reflected on his earlier diagnosis and suspicions. Back in the dining room, he quietly expressed his fears.

'Sometimes it is difficult to determine if someone falls into the category of a psychopath, Holiness, unless the patient is willing to undergo psychological testing and have relevant medical experts observe their behaviour. The symptoms include an inability to connect with others, a charismatic and charming manner and a lack of remorse or responsibility for their actions. Those who are incapable of love often substitute it with a desperate pursuit of power. I have suspected this for many years and done nothing,' Professor Martines concluded sadly.

'You can't blame yourself, Vincenzo,' Giovanni said gently. 'Lorenzo Petroni was a very troubled soul. However, he was not your patient nor was he willing to seek help. May he rest in peace. Do we know what causes this condition?'

'Not exactly, although it is often associated with trauma in childhood. A lot of research is being conducted into genetic influence, and the questions of nature versus nurture come up – whether these types of people are born or made. It is a very difficult question.' Professor Martines excused himself to attend to the removal of Cardinal Petroni's body and to start organising forensic investigations and inquiries.

'Should we handle this in-house, Holiness?' Vittorio asked, mindful of the intense media interest that Petroni's suicide would cause.

'No, Vittorio, we will not cover this up. Make a simple announcement to the media that his death will be subject to an autopsy and a police report, independent of the Vatican.'

'Could I suggest,' Tom offered, 'that you include something along the lines that you have sent your condolences to Cardinal Petroni's family, and that until the independent investigation has been concluded, it would not be helpful to speculate on the reasons behind the death of the Cardinal Secretary of State. It won't hold them off for long, but it will give you some breathing space.'

'Thank you,' Giovanni said gratefully. 'I'm obviously going to need some media training.'

'We can fix that,' Tom said, allowing himself a wry smile.

Giovanni turned to David, his face reflecting the gravity of what he suspected he was about to be told. 'You were going to explain the last part of the Omega Scroll,' he said.

'In the Omega Scroll the Essenes have recorded a cryptic message from the civilisation that dispatched the DNA which reads, "in order that life might continue beyond nuclear attack",' David said.

'I have an open mind on this,' Allegra added, 'although it's interesting that there have been a number of unexplained explosions recorded hundreds of thousands of light years into space. Several leading scientists are convinced they are not supernovas but more closely resemble nuclear blasts.'

'In another galaxy?' Tom asked.

Allegra nodded. 'It's certainly possible. They may have been trying to warn us, as well as sending DNA into distant galaxies, including ours, in the hope that life might continue.'

'The Omega Scroll goes further,' David said, 'with a terrible warning for us, regardless of whether another civilisation is involved. The threat to us from a nuclear attack is now very real.' He moved across to the last of the three sections of the Omega Scroll and began to read: 'And two Revelations will ridicule a third, though the Revelations be from Abraham, all of them. The third will have its Alpha in Mount Hira but its Omega in Tirich Mir, and in the beginning, the third will triumph over the first and second, but in the end, civilisation will be annihilated.'

'Muhammad and al-Qaeda,' Tom said quietly. 'The Alpha and Omega of Islam.'

'And two Revelations will ridicule a third?' Father Vittorio looked puzzled.

'Before Muhammad received his revelations from God at the hands of the Angel Gabriel, from which he wrote the Qur'an,' Allegra explained, 'the Jews and the Christians used to ridicule the Arabs. *Al-Lah*, which in Arabic means "God", had sent a multitude of prophets to the Jews and Christians, but none to the Arabs, and as the Arabs had received no revelations in their own language, the Jews and Christians claimed God had not included them in his plan.'

Tom nodded. 'And two Revelations will ridicule a third. We are still doing that now,' he added grimly. 'Many Westerners, especially Americans, have no idea how the Islamic mind operates.'

'And Mount Hira and Tirich Mir?' Father Vittorio asked.

'Mount Hira is a few miles from Mecca,' David said. 'In the month of Ramadan, starting from the time Muhammad was in his early forties, he would climb Mount Hira and it is there he received the first of his Revelations from God, through the Angel Gabriel, in his native tongue. To get to the cave, he had to climb to the top of Mount Hira and then climb over the summit.'

'I've been to Mount Hira,' Tom said. 'Muhammad's cave is on the vertical side of the mountain and quite secluded. The roof of the cave slopes towards a small opening at the back, and if you look through it you can see the Kabah in the distance.'

'You've been to Tirich Mir as well?' David asked.

Tom nodded. 'Tirich Mir is the highest peak in the Hindu Kush on Pakistan's north-west frontier with Afghanistan, up there with Everest. It's also a notoriously difficult area to police. Many areas are outside the jurisdiction of the central or provincial governments, which explains why the United States has had so much difficulty capturing bin Laden. Even if they do, there are a hundred more who will take his place.'

'It's a very clear warning,' Giovanni said, his face very serious. 'Unless we stop this madness that somehow one religion is favoured by God over the others, a madness that my own calling has been guilty of for centuries, we will destroy ourselves in the process.'

'I agree,' Tom said. 'From what Mike McKinnon told me about al-Qaeda, they are intent on unleashing a nuclear attack that will totally destroy major Western cities as soon as they are ready.'

Patrick had been very quiet, taking it all in. Finally he spoke. 'And having George Bush strutting around as if he's on a mission from God doesn't help.' He paused and looked at Giovanni, his mischievous look returning. 'Although now that I'm in charge of foreign policy, I'll be keeping those thoughts to myself, Holiness.'

'Patrick's right though,' David said more seriously. 'One of the keys to this is an engagement of the moderates for a recognition of all religions. I spoke to Ahmed last night. He thanked me for Israel's restraint after the Damascus Gate bombing, and we're both confident we can turn this peace agreement into a reality. That will be a big first step.'

'The problem is, Holiness, how do we handle this in the short term?' Patrick continued, looking at the Omega Scroll. 'The media will be having a field day,' he added, winking at Tom.

'In the end that's up to Allegra and David,' Giovanni said. 'I agreed to be part of any release, and I intend to honour that.' He turned to Tom. 'As well as the media conference, where the messages will probably be distorted, how would you feel about interviewing me for my views, one on one?'

'It's called an "exclusive" in the trade, Holiness, and I think the time-honoured response would be "is the Pope a Catholic!" The questions will still be difficult though,' he added. 'What will you say if I ask you whether or not you believe Jesus was married to Mary Magdalene?'

Giovanni smiled. 'I will give that some thought, although my initial response would be that many scholars are coming to that conclusion, and that our faith must always be based on truth rather than dogma, and it is therefore a subject that is worthy of debate.'

Tom raised an eyebrow and inclined his head in a silent gesture of respect for Giovanni's answer. 'And if I were to ask you about DNA being delivered from a higher civilisation?'

'I can see we're playing first grade here,' Giovanni replied. 'As a scientist I have delved into the extraordinary intricacies of biochemistry, but I have always felt that behind the exquisite design of nature lies an awesome and mystical Creative Spirit. Many people will rule this out until it has been proven. I have an open mind, preferring not to rule it out until it has been disproven.'

Tom looked pleased. The interview had the potential to be electric. 'And the warning?'

'The warning, like those contained in Isaiah and Daniel, is terrible and the threat is real. Unless the powerful Christian nations change course, accept the validity of other religions, and actively work towards an understanding and acceptance of them, I fear the threat will become reality. It is within our power to change the direction of annihilation in which we're now headed. It is something that I will touch on at the end of my inauguration ceremony in two days' time, which I hope you will all be able to stay for.'

'Yes, and it will be a great privilege to interview you, although I think any training that might be required in the art of the fourth estate will be minimal,' Tom said with a grin.

Two nights later, back in their hotel suite, Allegra and David watched the re-run of Giovanni's inauguration on CCN. At the end of the broadcast Pope John XXIV appeared on the balcony above the Piazza San Pietro.

Giovanni stretched out his arms and the warmth of his smile was felt by everyone in the square below.

'A philosophy of the great faiths of the world is needed now,' Giovanni said. 'More than at any other time in the history of humanity. The true messages of Christ, Muhammad, Abraham, the Buddha and others have a remarkable resonance and similarity. Love and tolerance for your neighbour, regardless of faith, gender or race.'

The Spirit smiled.

'The fanatics and fundamentalists on all sides, including Christianity, have to be persuaded that to insist on one path and an ownership of truth to the exclusion of all others, in a world as brilliantly diverse as ours, is to insist on a path that can only lead to the annihilation of civilisation. The truth will set us free. Let us follow our various paths in peace instead of war. For there is,' Giovanni concluded, 'more than one path to the Omega.'

Author's Note

*T*he *Omega Scroll* has been set in a framework of history that has
  necessarily involved a considerable amount of research. I am
grateful to many people who have given their time and their views.
A number of authors have provided inspiration and the following
list of sources is by no means exhaustive.

I am indebted to the work of Michael Baigent and Richard
Leigh in *The Dead Sea Scrolls Deception*. Whilst the boozy Derek
Lonergan and Jean-Pierre La Franci are fictitious characters, and
access to the Dead Sea Scrolls has improved considerably in recent
years, for nearly three decades the scrolls were kept from public
view, raising many questions as to why. David Yallop's *In God's
Name* provided a compelling case for the murder of John Paul II's
predecessor, John Paul I, who despite reportedly enjoying excellent
health was found dead after only thirty-three days in office after he
had intimated that there would be an investigation into the activities of the Vatican Bank.

The 1960's lifestyle of the inhabitants of Tricarico with their 'Men Only' westerns was beautifully captured by Ann Cornelisen when she disguised the little town as *Torregreca*. Armed with just her book, the photographs within it and the knowledge that 'Torregreca' (not its real name) was a town 'somewhere' between Potenza and Matera (of *The Passion* fame), I made several forays into the snow-covered Basilicatan mountains and was about to give up when I came across a signpost to Grassano and Tricarico. When the photographs of Tricarico matched those of 'Torregreca', Ann Cornelisen's secret was uncovered and the townsfolk of Tricarico were everything Ms Cornelisen said they would be, even when I got my Peugeot 206 stuck between buildings in one of their impossibly narrow streets. *Mi dispiace, sono Australiano!*

Many authors provided insightful studies on the Middle East and Islam, among them Mark Tessler's *A History of the Israeli-Palestinian Conflict*, Robert Donovan's *Six Days in June* and Karen Armstrong's *Islam: A Short History*. Paul L. Williams has written perceptively on al-Qaeda and the nuclear threat, and on the Vatican in *Osama's Revenge* and *The Vatican Exposed*. I am grateful to Elaine Pagels for *The Gnostic Gospels* and to Michael Drosnin for his detailed discussion of Eliyahu Rips' discovery of codes in the Torah in *The Bible Code*.

The greatest danger in the nuclear threat posed by al-Qaeda and other terrorist organisations would be for us to adopt an attitude of 'that can't happen'. Helen Caldicott's *The New Nuclear Danger* and Frank Barnaby's *How to Build a Nuclear Bomb* caused me to go back to my early days as a science student, and right now I think it is more a case of 'when' rather than 'if'.

In *Magdalene's Lost Legacy*, Margaret Starbird (as always) has produced some excellent work on the codes of the New Testament and 153, the number I suspect the Vatican fears most. There are no models of the tenth planet or the DNA helix amongst the depictions of the Dead Sea Scrolls and Qumran in the entrance to Israel's

Shrine of the Book Museum, but Dolores Cannon, who has travelled back through time using regressive hypnosis in *Jesus and the Essenes*, and Sir Francis Crick's *Life Itself: Its Origin and Nature* have shown what they might look like.

Amongst the books on my shelves are several by one of my favourite philosophers and theologians, Pierre Teilhard de Chardin, including *The Phenomenon of Man*. Daring to speak out, he prompted the Vatican's usual response of threat of excommunication, but with brilliant scholars like Hans Küng and Edward Schillebeeckx also speaking out, it is the dogma that is under threat.

Space does not allow acknowledgement of all the works I consulted in my research, and as much as some lawyers might see the need to footnote a novel, that day is still hopefully some way off. There are, however, several people who most certainly require my thanks and acknowledgement, although like the authors consulted in my research, the list is inevitably incomplete. Firstly, thanks go to the great team at Penguin and in particular to Clare Forster, who believed in *The Omega Scroll* from the start. Thanks also to Kerry Martin, who always encouraged me to write, and to Jody Lee and Janet Austin, my long-suffering and tireless editors. I'd also like to thank my literary agent, Jane Adams.

Sandy McCutcheon, the highly regarded author and ABC journalist, read (the much bulkier) early drafts and provided some much-needed advice. Thanks to Chris May for her encouragement, and Olivia Isherwood and Sophie; to Rob Eniver, my insightful Italian coach – any errors are mine alone; and to Antoinette and friends. I also send my appreciation to the wonderful people of Falerna and Tricarico in southern Italy – God knew what she was doing when she made the Italians – and in particular, Tatiana Mario, Nonna and Michaela, Ida and Willy.

And finally to Robyn, who was always there when the going was at its roughest.

Adrian d'Hagé

Adrian d'Hagé was born in Sydney and educated at North Sydney Boys High and the Royal Military College Duntroon (Applied Science). He graduated into the Intelligence Corps in 1967, and was later transferred to Infantry and served in Vietnam as a platoon commander, where he was awarded the Military Cross. His service in the Australian Army included command of an infantry battalion and Director of Joint Operations for Defence. In 1990 he was promoted to Brigadier as Head of Defence Public Relations.

In 1994 Adrian was made a Member of the Order of Australia for services to communications. His last appointment was Head of Defence Planning for security of the Sydney 2000 Olympics, including defence against chemical, biological and nuclear threats.

In October 2000 Adrian left the Army to pursue a writing career, moving to Italy to complete *The Omega Scroll*. He holds an honours degree in Theology, entering his studies as a committed Christian and graduating 'of no fixed religion'. Adrian is currently a research scholar at the Centre for Arab and Islamic Studies (Middle East and Central Asia) at the Australian National University, and is also completing a further degree in Wine Science.

GUARANTEED GREAT READ
or your money back

If you are not completely satisfied with this book, please complete this coupon
and return with the book and original proof of purchase to:

Marketing Department
Penguin Group (Australia)
PO Box 701
Hawthorn VIC 3122

Please allow up to 8 weeks for your refund. Refunds are only payable if the
book and original proof of purchase are provided.

Name: _____

Address: _____

_____

Daytime phone number: _____

Offer expires 31st January 2006